Unlawful Temptations

Star Crossed Series (Book 1)

Alexandria Lee

Contents

A Note

This series deals with potentially triggering topics such as parental neglect, drug abuse, and attempted SA.

For a list of full triggers, please visit my Linktree: https://linktr.ee/AuthorAlexandriaLee

Dedication

All of my writing, all of my love, all of my passion is dedicated to Judi Rowden forever and always.

Foreword

"Soulmates aren't the ones who make you happiest, no. They're instead the ones who make you feel the most. Burning edges and scars and stars. They hurl you into the abyss. They taste like hope."

—— **Victoria Erickson**

ONE

"**Y**ou're fired."

My eyes narrowed on the prematurely balding man sitting across from me.

"You're shitting me, right?"

Martie scoffed, pushing himself back from his desk and folding his arms over his ever-growing stomach. His wife, Gretta, did *not* know how to cook for less than six people, and it showed in each pants size good ol' Mart went up.

"Kat, *language.*"

The familiar annoyance in his hiss tensed the muscles in my neck. That hadn't been the first time he'd scolded me about my mouth, and we both knew it wouldn't be the last. I could have said my parents raised me better, but my parents barely raised me at all, so that excuse flew right out the broken window.

"Okay, *sorry*. No need to fire your best gal over a few 'fucks' here and there." I plastered a smile so shit-eating on my face, my cheeks actually hurt from the effort.

Martie looked between my cheeks at the straining grin and ran a hand over his plump face, trying and failing to smooth out his stress wrinkles.

"It's not that, Kat. It's everything else." Then he cut me a sharp stare. "And you're not my best girl. Not by a long shot."

I perked back in my seat, hand over my heart. "Now you're just trying to hurt me."

A flicker of humor eased along Martie's face, proving that, while I may not be his best employee, he *did* have a soft spot for me. During our morning meetings, I always got a laugh out of him with some dumb shit I'd say. Not to mention, he willfully turned a blind eye whenever he caught me or my best friend, Layla, pocketing a handful of tampons from the back.

The first time he caught us in inventory, he stopped and stared at the fistful of tampons in both our hands. I waved at him brightly with my free hand, and he groaned. Then, we both moved on with our day without saying a word about it.

Martie had been my manager ever since I got hired at the store three years ago, and while he may not totally *love* me, he definitely liked me enough not to fire me; of that I was positive.

Like, 89% positive.

"*Kat.*" My name was a grumble in Martie's throat unlike one I'd heard from him before. It set my positivity back a few degrees and my nerves on edge. I shifted in my seat. "You know I like you—"

"So if you like me, don't fire me. It's that easy."

"Except it's not that easy this time," Martie shot back, upset brightening his eyes under the fluorescent lighting in his office. "You were late for the third time this month alone, and that's not even considering all the other crap you do that I let slide."

I blanched at him, pushing myself back in my chair using the armrests. "Like what?"

"Like the extra long lunch breaks, you racing children up and down the aisles on scooters we haven't sold yet, stealing feminine hygiene products—"

"That shit should be free for all women, and you know it!" Defiance shot me up out of my chair to stand over Martie's desk, defending my vagina and all vaginas with a wagging finger. "And the scooter races? Kids *love* it! I've helped sell like fifty scooters that way!"

"Your job is not to sell scooters, Kat. You're a cashier! Now sit *down*."

Fire rolled through my veins at his authoritative tone, cleverly disguising the fear bubbling just beneath the surface. I could feel it winding through me and trying to reign me back in, but denial was a powerful friend of mine at the moment.

I'd been called back to Martie's office plenty of times for a talk like this.

It was all part of the show he'd put on to make it look good for the higher ups, but it never went past a talk. I'd smile and charm him, Martie would roll his lips together and sigh, and then send me on my way.

Wash, rinse, and repeat for three years straight.

Today, there was just the faintest itch in my chest saying *something* was off this time. It was irritating my confidence that this time was like all the rest, and so I sat down like he said, swallowing back anymore out of place remarks.

Just breathe and play nice.

"I'm sorry. I'll do better, okay?" Martie remained tight-lipped, and so I kept on. "You know my situation, so you *know* why I'm late some days, but I can try to see if Mrs. Sharon can take Charlotte a little earlier each day. Plus, she starts kindergarten next year, so that will help out a ton with my schedule."

Still, Martie didn't utter one word, reassuring or otherwise, and that slight itch in my chest started to worsen. I straightened in my chair, struggling not to let my confusion twitch on my face. This time did *not* feel like the others, and that scratching became a burning dead center between my ribs as Martie's unkempt, salt and peppered eyebrows dipped in sincere regret.

"I do know your situation, Kat, and it's why I'm truly sorry."

And that's when the panic set in. Fiery hot, blazing panic.

I steadied my stare on his in the silence, challenging, begging, *pleading* the finality sitting in his tired stare. He had to change his mind like he had before. He *had* to. There was literally no other option.

"Mart, you're not serious." I breathed a stiff laugh, trying to break through the unfamiliar tension in the room. Martie didn't share my laughter though. He didn't even blink.

He just shook his head, and said, "I'm sorry."

Pounding. My heart was pounding with the weight of those two words, and my faint smile slipped. I couldn't lose this job. It was barely keeping food on the table at home as-is.

"No—" I stuttered, catching the guilt sink Martie's expression even deeper. "You can't. Y-you *can't.*"

Martie turned to the side in his chair, looking painfully uncomfortable as I denied him again. But I wouldn't stop. I'd deny him over and over again until he caved and gave me one more shot. Just one more chance unlike the hundred I'd taken for granted before like a goddamn idiot. One more chance and I would do it right. One more chance and I *swore* I wouldn't fuck it up.

"Come on, Martie. I know I've gotten a bit lax on the job, but I'll fix it. You *have* to let me fix it." An unfamiliar lump of wording stuck in my throat, stealing my voice to a whisper that hurt every last bit of my pride. "*Please?* For Charlotte."

My younger sister's name dropped Martie's shoulders low, a frown deepening the lines of his sorry face. I didn't beg for anything and he knew that, but I would beg for Charlotte.

I'd do just about anything for her.

"Kat..." he croaked, his aged face an open display of guilt.

Guilt, but not surrender. Pity, but not empathy.

Holy shit.

This was really happening.

Shock dropped my lips apart, and all I felt was the *thump, thump, thump* of my heart that beat in the hollow of my throat. The air in the room stuck to my skin like a guilty sweat, drenching me in the cold and swift realization that this was real.

I was being fired.

Anxious tears pricked the backs of my eyes, each needled sensation a stab of horror, a stab of embarrassment, a motherfucking stab to the beating heart of my world.

As the source of my income hemorrhaged, I sat there feeling it flush my body hot, blood pumping loudly in my ears. Each thud of it got stronger, drowning out the voice of reason in my head until it was swallowed up whole by the furious blood without so much as a last gasp.

Tension piled through my jaw, and it clicked in fearsome anger. My panic took a violent shove to the backseat at the hands of my personal brand of hot-headed rage. It blasted into every inch of my body, my toes tingling, and fingertips feeling like they could shoot actual lightning.

I didn't need his pity. I needed a goddamn job.

"Fine." I shot up out of the chair, thrusting the piece of furniture back into the wall with the force of my movement. My hand fisted around my bag on the floor, snatching it up and tossing it over my shoulder.

"Kat, please don't be angry—"

"You just fucking fired me," I snapped back at him, not caring one bit that this wasn't really his fault. "Of *course* I'm angry. I'm really *fucking* angry." I spat the curse at him, watching his eyes round as my temper stretched its legs. "How much do you care about my *fucking* language now, Martie?"

Before he could respond, I tore his office door open and stormed out.

Fury coursed in my legs as I ripped through the store, anger so white-hot it blinded my vision in searing flashes. I couldn't see where I was going, didn't give a flying *fuck* where I was going so long as it was out of this godforsaken store.

"Three years," I hissed to no one as I rampaged. "Three *fucking* years."

Tunnel vision consumed me as I torpedoed ahead, multicolor children's books and toys gaining my narrowing focus with a bright target painted smack dab on their faces. The teddy bears smiles turned to frowns, the whimsical creatures on the book covers gasped—

And I kicked the fucking shit out of all of them.

Unrhythmic clatter dispelled through the air. Barbies were airborne. Books slid across the tile floor in every which direction. A Barney hit the ground and started singing *'I love you.'* With a snarl in my chest, I reared back for another kick.

"Kat, stop!" A hand locked over my wrist and jerked me around. Cautious brown eyes became the new centerpiece of my rage and jumped wide as they saw me. "What the hell are you doing?!"

My best friend, Layla, came into my tight focus. Her worried face caught my fire-breathing lungs in a pause long enough for me to find air to speak with rather than scream with.

"Martie just *fired* me." God, the words stung to say. The humiliation of them might have stung worse.

Her already big eyes doubled in size. "*What?*"

"Yup, and now I'm one-hundred-percent shit out of luck," I seethed, flashing my hands back through my professional ponytail and tearing the thing loose. Dark brown hair danced in front of my vision as I ruffled my fingers through my scalp in furious scratches. "I mean, who's going to hire a girl without a high school diploma who got *fired* from her last job? What am I gonna do about Charlotte or fucking rent for that matter!"

I tongued the inside of my cheek, casting a glance at the wreckage I'd caused around me. *Shit*, someone was going to have to clean that up.

"Are you sure he fired you for real, for real?" I dropped a fast look back to her, jaw cementing in place as I nodded.

Her heart-shaped face fell, thickly shaped eyebrows dipping in. Layla reached a comforting arm out, settling for a squeeze on my shoulder because she knew I wouldn't want anything else.

"We can try to talk to him together? He's awful at saying no to the both of us."

I heard her selfless suggestion. I really did. I just didn't have the patience at the moment to appreciate it past a grateful glance. "No. I don't need you getting canned too trying to help me."

She looked like she wanted to fight, but just sighed instead, her jet-black bangs fluttering over her forehead. "Man, that sucks."

Rolling my lips together, I nodded because it was obvious. It sucked. It really freaking sucked. "What the hell am I gonna do for a job, Layla? I've only ever worked here. I don't know how to do anything other than work a register." *God, how sad is that?*

"You could always bartend!" Layla beamed brighter as her idea struck. "You make killer drinks at parties."

Deadpanned, I said, "It shocks me how many times you forget I'm not twenty-one yet. Few more months, babe."

Her full mouth parted in an 'o', and then she quietly cursed herself. I hated being so young. Everyone looked down on you, and no one took you seriously, especially when you had a five-year-old attached to your hip nearly everywhere you went. Society just turned their noses up at you, assumed you were a screw up, and moved on with their perfect little lives.

Goddamn pretentious *assholes*.

"Oh!" Layla damn near startled me as she gasped, slapping the back of my arm in excitement. "I almost forgot!"

"How strong you are?" I asked, rubbing my arm with a pained sneer pulling back my lips.

"No, dumbass. I almost forgot my dad showed me this job opening the other day when he was trying to get me to quit working here!"

"Jesus Christ, is that guy ever going to stop trying to squeeze me out of your life?"

"Probably not. He's been iffy ever since the chocolate syrup incident."

"Ah." I nodded, remembering the drunken ice cream party I threw at her house when she graduated community college that ended in a chocolate syrup fight. Needless to say, their white couch was destroyed, and I was banned from ever coming over again. Worth it, though.

"What's the job?"

"It's this nanny gig he found online. Said the pay is good and hours are flexible for the most part. You know I think kids are midget spawns from Satan so it would never work out for me, but you, you love kids! You should call for an interview."

I paused, blinking at my best friend as the idea worked around the cogs in my brain.

A faint stirring of hope bristled in the back of my mind, and Layla and I shared a hesitant smile. Basically the same job I did with Charlotte on my days off and nights, but paid?

"You have that number?"

"Oh, Mother Dearest! I'm home!"

I closed the front door behind me, careful not to slam it and knock the knob off again. It wasn't cheap to bring someone out last time to fix the lock, and despite my best efforts, I was a shitty replica of my own Tim the Tool Man.

Tossing my bag on the countertop, I breathed hard through the stress of today as I slunk down to my elbows on the counter. The ever-present sting of sickly sweet cigar smoke tickled the back of my throat as I drew back air till I felt a pinch in my chest. That was the only thing my father left behind when he hopped town a few years ago—the stench of his fucking Blackstone's and us.

My eyelids were heavy and my fingers were mindless as I fingered through the mail and bills splashed across the counter. Anxiety crawled up the back of my spine as I took in the double and triple digit numbers printed on the pages I had to pay to keep this shithole up and running. Truth be told, this house was one strong wind gust away from collapsing in on itself, but it was the only home Charlotte knew, and the only one I could afford.

The kitchen was too small, the living room carpet had a nasty stain from when Charlotte was two and threw up spaghetti everywhere, and where it wasn't stained, it was burnt from either of my parents. No matter how many fake crystal ashtrays we had lying around, both of them preferred to put their shit out on the carpet.

Not having my own room at nearly twenty-one wasn't ideal, but our place only had two bedrooms and Mom never left hers, so Charlotte and I had bunked together since she was born. It was an all right sized house when I was growing up and it was just me, Mom and Dad, but when you're a kid, everything and everyone feels *huge*.

Now as an adult, the corners of this place grew tighter every day, and I couldn't believe how much it cost in bills to keep this tiny shack on shitty Memory Lane standing.

The piece of paper sitting in my back pocket with the interview number burned through my jeans, and I let the handful of mail tumble back to the counter with a sigh. I needed to call before my only chance at a job shriveled up.

Just then, a muffled groan sounded behind me.

The noise sank my shoulders and my already touch-and-go mood simultaneously. A unique cocktail of contempt and guilty responsibility sizzled in my chest, and I shut my eyes against the unwelcome feeling. *Over and over and fucking over again we go.*

Fists shaking, I jerked towards my mother's room and her cracked door. I pushed my way in, hardly registering the foul smell or haze of morbid sunlight trying to brighten this horror scene of a bedroom.

"Hey, *Mom.*" I walked over to her sleeping figure, sprawled out carelessly on her bed on top of the covers. "How was *your* day? Good? You shoot some shit in your veins and pass out again?" I asked with fraudulent enthusiasm vibrating my tone.

I paused and waited, kidding myself that she might wake up and respond because my sense of humor was just that goddamn masochistic.

She didn't—of course—and I rolled my eyes and muttered, "Good to see you're changing up the routine."

Huffing out a breath, I pushed her tangled hair that was the same color as mine from her forehead and slipped the back of my fingers over her skin. She was clammy and pale, a sickly version of the mother I grew up with on the outside. On the inside, she was nothing but rotting lungs and a hollow heart.

"My day was dandy too, ya know. I got fired, which was *super* fun, and now I've got one hope for a job or we're out on our asses."

I held my fingers underneath her nose and waited until I felt the gentle push and pull of air coming through her nostrils.

Not dead. Yet.

Pulling away from her, I gave her limp figure one last eye roll. "Glad to hear we both had *splendid* days."

Some things just never changed.

Lugging my tired legs back out to the living room, I gave a sweeping glance over the walls of our home, walls embedded with pitiful memories and shitty art my mom picked out before Dad left. Booming rap music vibrated those same thin walls as a car passed by outside. I gritted my teeth against the noise, watching the place carefully as it shook and the music pulsated the foundation beneath my feet.

Eventually, the car moved down the street, and their music dulled. All I could hear now was the proverbial sob in my sad story that cried out of the rundown house around me.

A timely knock choked the sobs to a silence.

5pm right on the dot.

"Come on in!" I called.

The front door pushed open, and a flash of blonde curls came barreling through. "Katty! Katty, I'm home!"

My favorite little voice rang through the house using my absolute *least* favorite nickname. I hated the name, but I loved her more, so unfortunately, the nickname wasn't going anywhere anytime soon.

"Hey, Bugs!" Charlotte ran at me full speed, and I dropped to my knees as she threw herself in my arms. The force of her hug pushed me back, and I fell on my ass. Pain twinged up my tailbone, but my sister's melodic giggling overshadowed the soft curse that slipped my lips. Despite the ache, a smile held solid on my face.

"Katty, look what I did with Mrs. Sharon today!"

Just as quickly as she took me down, Charlotte popped back up, tiny hands diving in her bag and pulling out a necklace made of uncooked macaroni.

"She helped me tie the knot, but I did the rest myself." A proud smile pulled up on her red-tinted cheeks.

"It's beautiful! I think they might wanna start selling this in stores."

"Yeah, I think so too," she said thoughtfully, nodding her head fast so her pigtails bounced.

"I was gonna keep this one for myself, but then I thought you would look really pretty in it so... here." Charlotte held the macaroni laced necklace out to me, sweet brown eyes the same shade as our moms shining with such a selfless love, it made my chest ache.

I was the only one stuck with our father's eyes. Springtime green, and I hated them.

"Aw, Bugs. Are you sure?" I hesitantly took the delicately made necklace between my fingers.

"Yup! I want you to have it!" She smiled brightly up at me, her joy and innocence piercing my heart the way only she could.

Twisting a piece of hard macaroni around my finger, I said, "How did you get to be so sweet? Did Mrs. Sharon feed you sugar cubes for lunch?"

"No!" She squealed at my joke, laughing and smiling and stealing my absolute breath away. In a world of gray and dreary, Charlotte was the brightest crayon there was, streaking her brilliant color all over my life to keep me focused and smiling. Her thoughts were big and dazzling, she dreamed without limit, and was a hell of a lot cooler than I ever was at her age, or even now.

Without her, I'd have checked out of this piss-poor town long ago and never looked back.

"No, your sister's just being silly." Mrs. Sharon drew my eye as she spoke, a wily smile on her beautiful, round face as she nodded to my sister. "Tell Kat what we had for lunch, little miss."

"Grilled cheese and hot dogs!" Charlotte beamed.

"That sounds *delicious*. Where's mine?"

My sister shook her head in dismissal as she turned her focus back to her bag. "You weren't there, Katty!"

"I know that. Doesn't mean I'm not hungry."

Mrs. Sharon gave a pity chuckle as my sister completely ignored my pull for a laugh, still rooting around in her My Little Pony bag.

"Do you like your necklace?" she asked.

Her small voice swelled my heart with warmth, and I looped the macaroni over my head and shifted it into place against my chest, right above my heart. "I'll never take it off."

"Good! I made one for Mom too." Finally, she yanked the second necklace she'd been searching for out with a clumsy tug. "Do you think she'll want it now?"

Immediately, the warmth in my heart turned prickly cold.

Goddamnit, her eyes were so vivid and hopeful. Ugly words warred in my lungs, slamming around to claw their way up and warn Charlotte that our mother didn't deserve her love, her kindness, or her macaroni necklace. Our mother was dirt and Charlotte was the moon, and her big, bright perfection would not be slathered in worthless grime.

Prepping the lighthearted lie on my tongue, I said, "Mom's sleeping right now, but we'll give it to her later when she wakes up, okay? I know she'll love it."

Charlotte's tiny lips dropped to a pout, her infectious energy dimming. "Okay."

Routine hatred jammed my teeth together in a furious grinding, and my nostrils flared. Every time our mother took a chunk of Charlotte's happiness away, my contempt for her leveled up. Nowadays, I wasn't sure if there was anything left inside of me *but* hate for the woman who was supposed to love me unconditionally.

"Kat, I've gotta go. Dinner's on the stove, but I'll see you tomorrow morning, okay?"

I spun to Charlotte's sitter who stood in the doorway, readying herself to leave. Mrs. Sharon had been a godsend these last few years, watching Charlotte during the days I worked, and all but for free. She was a stay at home mom with her son that was only a year younger than Charlotte, and all she asked in return was that I watched her son whenever she and her husband had date night.

The deal was sweet—too sweet for someone as sour as me—but I wasn't dumb enough to question a good thing.

"We'll see you then."

With that, Mrs. Sharon waved her goodbyes before taking off, her pregnant belly following her out the door. Was she five or six months now? I couldn't remember.

"Katty, can we go to my room and color?"

Bowing my head to Charlotte, I smiled. "Yeah, let's go."

"Okay! I call the blue marker first!" And with that, she took off down the hallway and beelined it into our room, leaving me chuckling in her dust. As I walked back to the bedroom, my hand traveled up, and my fingers clasped around the macaroni necklace tightly.

Determination set in my bones.

I *had* to get this new job.

Two

"**D**o you know what these people do for a living?"

Struggling to hold my phone between my shoulder and ear as I drove, I replied, "I know the wife said she was into real estate during the phone interview, but she didn't say what her husband did."

"Must be something rich if they can afford a full-time nanny."

"And to pay me under the table," I tagged on.

Layla huffed in agreement on the other end of the phone. "How old's the kid?"

"Uh, I think her mom said she was four. Apparently, their last nanny just stopped showing up to work last week. Been with the kid for almost a year and then just ghosted them."

"Rude, but good for you."

"*Very* good for me."

The more I thought about this job as I drove to the interview, the more I wanted it. Not only was it a chill gig, but it paid a few pocketfuls more than the store did. I'd be able to save up that extra money and put it towards school supplies for Charlotte next year and maybe even a trip to the dentist. She'd never been before, and I hadn't been since I got my braces off when I was twelve.

"By the way, I should have listened to you about wearing your clothes for this. Next time I don't listen to you, feel free to slap me."

"I won't forget you said that I hope you know."

Sighing into the phone, I tried not to focus on the outfit I went with and what these rich-ass people might think of me when they see it. I knew the saying was to never judge a book by its cover, but I also knew that people with money were judgemental as fuck.

I ended up going with jeans and a half buttoned down shirt. Turns out, I didn't have any dresses that fit anymore since they were all bought before I was 16. That was a fun find as I rampaged through my closet at 1am this morning to prepare for today.

The jeans I chose were my only pair without any rips, and the seafoam green shirt was fitted around my waist but not skin-clinging. I just hoped no one noticed the two missing buttons at the top.

Layla rambled on in my ear about Martie's and how much it sucked without me there to distract her from work. I laughed as she went on, but my attention faded in and out of the conversation as I turned into the neighborhood my GPS told me my potential next job resided in.

My eyes rounded as I drove past the neatly stacked houses on both sides of the road, all designed to look exactly the same. Cookie-cutter perfection and the unmistakable markings of wealth.

Lots and lots of wealth.

It was kind of horrifying how similar they all were, and I felt my lips curling back into a grimace as I drove by. They were all so monotonous and uniform, and the air filtering into my car from the outside stunk it up with arrogance. I could practically hear the houses sneering at my tiny blue Honda that clearly didn't belong among the sports cars and fancy BMW's that sat in every driveway.

But hey, I lived in a disheveled shack that lost heat at least once every winter, so who was I to talk?

Layla rattled on about wanting to spit on a customer yesterday for reasons I tuned out as I turned down the street, squinting my eyes out the driver side window as my foot slowed the brake.

224, 226, 228...

And then I pressed the brake to a stop, and my jaw slacked open as my car jolted to a halt.

"Holy *shit*."

"What happened?" Layla panicked on the phone. "Did you run over another cat?"

"What? No!" Her question shocked me out of my daze as I snapped my attention back to my phone. "You're not supposed to mention that incident, remember? It was fucking *traumatizing*."

"I was just checking!"

Soothing down my pitter-pattering heartbeat, I set my car in park and shut it off. With a little added force, I popped my car door open and stepped into the South Carolina summer breeze.

"Is the place nice?"

I parted my lips to say yes but fell into a breath of stunned laughter instead. *'Nice'* was putting it mildly. These were the kind of people that either had huge dicks, or at least wanted everyone in the neighborhood to think they did. The house was two stories, maybe three. Definitely taller than the houses that book-ended theirs.

The entranceway was fucking majestic if anything had ever justified the word before. Huge, stark white columns sat guarding the looming black doors that led into the house, and that was just the beginning. Their front yard had a winding brick-paved pathway that went from their driveway, looped around a goddamn fountain at the center, and right up to the intimidating front door.

The fountain was ridiculous. Plainly laughable, and I did laugh as I described it to Layla in all of its gaudy glory. Around it and under the several windows lining the first story of the house were flowerbeds of red, pink, and white.

The structure of the house was so... stiff.

Every angle was hard, every cut was rigid, and nothing about this house spelled out home sweet home. What it did spell out, however, were money signs between every stone-faced line that created the outside of this massive house.

The aroma of money wafted through the breeze and right under my nose, and with a pointed grin, I said my goodbyes to Layla and let the smell of money lure me up to the home.

Somehow, the structure grew more imposing the nearer I got, and I fought down the rumblings of nerves in my stomach. Remembering back to the phone interview I had with the wife—Heather—my gut pulled harder as I hoped first impressions didn't stick.

Please *Lord*, let's pray they don't stick.

Over the phone, Heather was a harsh-toned tight-ass, and even that was being nice. The first interview—if you could even call it that—lasted less than two minutes. All she asked for over the phone was my name, age, and a photo and resume. Didn't even bother asking about my experience with kids. She didn't seem to even *like* me by the end of the interview when I told her my WiFi was out, and I couldn't email a resume or photo, but she gave me a slot for today anyhow.

The husband must have been a special kind of pushover to put up with a wife like that, and fingers crossed I could sway him to my side during this thing. I had the experience, I could do the job well, and I *just* needed the chance to prove it.

As I reached the heavy looking, black front doors, the tips of my fingers tingled in anticipation, and I shook my hands out and tried to control my breathing. I ran my prickling fingers back through my thick hair, and the ring on my right hand snagged on a tangled strand and fucked up my loose curls that I'd spent the morning taming.

With a growl, I unstuck my ring and fluffed my hair up again, passing my tongue over the front of my straight teeth. Thank you, braces.

"Well, here goes... everything. Like, *literally* everything." I breathed a sharp sigh. "Fuck, I suck at pep talks."

Without letting another anxious beat pass by, I lifted my hand and rapped my knuckles against the solid wood door. Not but seconds later, the unmistakable sound of a door being unlocked startled my jostling nerves, and I took position.

Shoulders back, eyes bright, smile wide.

Showtime.

I polished my plastic grin and prepped a brown nosing comment about how lovely the house was as the front door swung wide open, and I awaited greeting Heather for the first time.

Except this wasn't Heather.

My smile stumbled as shock and an immediate swell of desire pulsed through my chest.

Holy fuck me.

I watched as his perfectly thick eyebrows jumped just so in what seemed like surprise of his own. A pair of exacting, smoke-gray eyes flashed up to meet mine, and for the faintest of seconds, we were both silent.

Not even the uncomfortable kind of silence that I hated, but the type that melted into your bones and engraved everything about the memory into your brain.

Like the soft nip of breeze at my exposed arms, and the way blood rushed to my cheeks to warm my goosebumped skin. The prickling at the back of my neck as this stranger's eyes swept over me just once, a quick up and down, and how I wanted to tug at the bottom of my shirt to fix any imperfection about my appearance for him. In the marrow of my bones, I *felt* his severe stare, and it was as explicit as a slap and flushed my whole body red-hot just the same.

Finally, the slight tick of his prominent jaw that was dusted in a 5 o'clock shadow shattered our pin-drop silence and kicked reality into high gear again.

"Hi!" I smiled wide, and the man in front of me knitted his dark eyebrows together.

"Are you here for an interview?"

"I am." I nodded and kept on smiling even past the second-guessing his obvious confusion inspired in my gut. "This is for the nannying job, right?"

The handsome stranger nodded slowly, running a large hand over his mouth and down his strong jawline as he stared at me. "It is."

He cleared his throat and readjusted his stance to something straighter; more confident. "Sorry, I'm just surprised to see my wife let someone so... young interview for the job."

"Oh." Simmering offense tickled the back of my throat, and I forced myself to swallow it down. "Well, we spoke on the phone, and she knows my age. The only thing I couldn't get over to her was a digital resume and photo. My internet has been busted for a bit."

And I haven't paid the bill in months.

Tomato. Potato.

Something clicked in place behind his eyes of melted steel, and strange amusement consumed his expression. A grin pulled up half of his pink mouth, turning his lips into a weapon of visual taunting.

"That makes sense."

My brows struggled not to sky rocket to my hairline just the same as my tongue fought not to lash out and skewer him until he told me what the fuck he meant by that. The man set his hands loosely on his hips, bringing my focus to his black slacks and tidied, pale-blue dress shirt with the sleeves rolled up. His forearms looked strong and his hands were huge, but I didn't miss the glint of a wedding band that made itself known around his ring finger.

Hello, Heather's other half.

Figures the man that had the balls enough to marry a woman as barbed as Heather would be a little off-putting too. Family dinners at this house must be a *blast.*

Heather's husband let out a stiff laugh while staring at nothing. The sound was knifing, and it wasn't even aimed at me. I shifted from foot to foot in front of him.

"Well, this should be fun." The man stole a glance at me, one that intensified the restless feeling in the pit of my stomach before he stepped aside and gestured with his head. "Come on in."

I swallowed the ball of nerves in my throat. "Thanks."

I followed behind the man on timid feet, prepped and ready to run in case my gut instinct that was already whispering that this might be a bad idea started to scream it. This house was massive, and I was only treading deeper into it with a man that was at least a foot taller than me and had a real American Psycho vibe about him.

And a flawless ass, but that was beside the point.

"Heather's in the living room," her husband threw over his shoulder at me. If I wasn't mistaken, there was an added pep in his step as he led me back. The floors we walked were a stunning white tile so squeaky clean, I could see my uneasy reflection in them. The ceilings were vaulted and daunting, the furniture reds and blacks that felt as cold as the temperature this place was kept at. We passed a dining room and what I assumed was a sitting room for... cocktail parties? Orgies? Fuck if I knew.

All I knew was how it all felt to me, and that was staged. This place was a house, not a home.

I felt stupidly out of place with my flip flops and purse where the faux leather binding around the handle had been fraying for the better part of a year, but I refused to let it show. In fact, I gripped the disintegrating handle of my purse even harder as we rounded a corner, and my eyes fell on a brunette haired woman sitting with her petite nose pushed into her laptop.

Her posture was perfect and her styled attire even more perfect, but her face was set in what looked like a permanent frown, and I pegged her right away.

Heather.

Her husband stopped walking so suddenly, I almost smashed into him. "Your next interview is here."

Heather's head snapped up from her computer, her short, sleek bob not daring to move an inch. Cold, pale blue eyes locked onto mine and immediately narrowed into unkind slits.

"Who are you?"

"Kat Sanders? We spoke on the phone."

"Did you not send the required photo?" Heather's voice was as accusing as her gaze, and I wanted to crawl inside myself and implode. *Why* couldn't she have been nice like I hoped? Stupid good for nothing hope.

Plastering a smile on my cheeks, I moved around her husband. "I didn't, but we actually talked about that on the phone, and you were kind enough to give me an interview anyway."

Shit-eating grin and remark, check.

Heather's nostrils flared, and the blue of her eyes got so hot, they could be flames. "I see."

Muffled laughter sounded from behind me, and it took every bit of strength to keep from whipping around and asking him what the hell was so goddamn funny. What was *with* this couple?

"How about we get started?" her husband suggested, casually walking around me to sink down in the blood-red chair next to his wife. Heather dug her stare into the side of his face, trying to blister his skin using just her fire-blue eyes.

With them seated, I hesitantly made my way over to the long couch arranged in front of their chairs. I winced as soon as I sat, the piece of furniture more like a sheet of rock under my ass than a couch. Shouldn't expensive furniture at least be comfortable?

"What did you say your name was?" Heather asked, her tone clipped and her eyes calculating.

"Kat."

She blinked at me, quiet for a beat. "Is that your real name?"

About a hundred different insults swelled in my lungs as I breathed deep, but I smartly swallowed them all down with a polite smile. "My full name is Katerina."

"That's an odd name," she replied dryly.

Bobbing my head, I said, "Yeah, my mom thought she was being unique and that it sounded elegant. I just think it sounds like an 18th century prostitute."

A brief chuckle—so soft it was barely audible—got caught in the tension in the room; and it came from her husband. His lips were tilted into a ghost of a smile as he played with the back of his thick, nearly black hair, eyes off to the side as he listened in.

"Very well. Ms. Sanders, you're 20, correct?" Heather waited with her fingers hovering over her laptop keyboard for me to fill in the blank.

"Yes."

"Where do you attend University?"

"I don't, actually. I worked full time until last week."

Heather stopped typing away on her keyboard to raise her superior stare to mine. "And what happened with that job?"

"I worked there for three years, but unfortunately the hours were sometimes difficult to meet with my schedule at home. That shouldn't be a problem here since you mentioned this job doesn't start until 9am."

Smooth.

I couldn't even pretend I didn't feel the pride swirling around my chest like a warm hug, telling me I'd aced my explanation. That was, until that warm hug turned into more of a suffocating death grip as I caught the flicker of cruel joy pass across Heather's pretty face.

"So, would I be correct in saying you were fired from your last job?"

Bitch.

My mouth rolled together as I hung in the silence of her comment. Against their couch, I curled my fingers into the rich material until I thought I might rip the thing open and tear out its stuffing just for fun. Every instinct inside of me was blaring to give this wife a verbal lashing and stomp out of here.

I needed this job though. Charlotte needed me to behave. She needed me to not so much be *me* right now, but a well-mannered, pushover version of myself. Be a 'yes girl' with a charming smile and the right words on my robotic tongue. For Charlotte, I would let this woman politely berate me with her carefully chosen words as much as she pleased.

"Yes. You would be correct in saying that."

Victory plagued Heather's perfectly symmetrical face, and she became ugly for that second. Truly hideous. She sat back in her chair just so, crossing her noticeably well-toned arms over one another.

"That's a shame." And then she fucking smirked. "Now, back to the fact that you only have your High School diploma. That's not ideal as we'd prefer someone with a higher level of education to be around our daughter eight hours a day. You have no idea how *susceptible* children's minds are to the people they're around."

Poor people like me.

She didn't say it. She didn't have to.

Well. There was no use lying. "Actually, I had to drop out of high school my senior year. Personal reasons."

Thanks Dad.

Heather's sapphire eyes rounded, and I'll be damned if a tiny sliver of glee didn't slice through her gaze. Piercing. Obvious. A clear stab right through any chance I had here today.

"Okay, so just to be perfectly clear—" Heather shifted her computer from her lap and slid forward in her seat, excited energy coming off of her petite body in waves that tried to drown every last hope I had. "You were fired from your last job, *and* you're a high school dropout?"

She was practically vibrating, and the man next to her hadn't said a damn word since we sat down. He wasn't even giving either of us his focused attention. Nope, apparently the goddamn floor was more interesting than a perfect stranger being verbally stripped down by his wife right in front of him.

Staring at them both in tight silence, I realized I'd actually stopped breathing to keep from producing any of the nasty words I wanted. I *felt* the words trying to brew as Heather challenged me with her stare, and I wanted to fucking scream. I wanted to rage. I wanted to know why the hell she'd decided before I even sat down today that she wouldn't give me this job.

No matter how right I was for it, it was becoming crystal clear that I never had a shot.

Maybe that's why her husband was laughing when I got here. Because he knew. He knew my time was about to be wasted, and my pride was about to be stomped all over by his bitch of a wife, and he was going to sit there and enjoy watching it happen.

God, I *hated* rich people.

On a quick conclusion, I sucked air back into my lungs. If I wasn't getting this job with these god awful people, then there was no need to keep up with the niceties, now was there?

"Yup. That's me." I slouched back into the stiff sofa, throwing my arm over the back. "An unemployed high school *dropout*. I tried pot once at a party if you wanna add that to the list."

Heather chuckled, a very genuine chuckle that curled up my spine with razored teeth. She was clearly more than amused by my failures and didn't even bother to hide it. Her enjoyment was palpable, and my fists were already clenched.

"Well, I think that's more than enough for us—"

"What about kids?"

Both Heather and I snapped our attention over to her husband, who was giving me all of his. Charcoal eyes were expectant on mine, and every bit of my runaway rebellion screeched to a dying halt. Confusion tugged at my eyebrows and held my tongue still.

"Dom, don't." His wife dismissed him with exhaustion in her haughty voice, not even bothering proper eye contact as she folded her laptop closed. He shifted in his chair towards her, relieving me of his acute focus.

"You haven't asked her a single question about child care. She deserves a full interview."

Heather sat straighter, gifting him a cursory glance. "I happen to disagree, and I think this is over. Ms. Sanders, you're free to go—"

"Ms. Sanders—" Her husband cut her off, chewing up my name and spitting it at his gobsmacked wife. "*Don't* leave."

Every muscle in my body twisted tight and froze at the severity of his throaty voice. The authority in it was a loaded gun, the open end aimed at Heather as he held his wife's furious stare.

What the fuuuuck.

Dom, I took it, woke up from his open-eyed slumber ready for war, going from zero to a hundred fast. My eyes were so wide with shock, I could feel them enlarging in my head as I regarded the married couple with caution. Okay, so maybe my initial assumption was wrong, and they were *not* on the same side. Maybe they were on opposite sides. In which case, I was totally being used as a pawn by them both in whatever fucked up game they were playing with each other.

Swell.

"I... is this like a trick answer kinda situation or...?" I drifted off, my fingers slowly tapping absent-mindedly in front of me as a distraction. It was like I was in a minefield, and any step I took was directly on top of a waiting bomb.

The husband, Dom, turned his heavy stare to me. "Do you want this job?"

Honestly? I don't know now. Still, I said, "Yes."

"Then you'll stay and finish the interview."

It wasn't a question either. I got the feeling that if I argued with him, those warring eyes of his would roll over white, and I'd be running for the door.

"You're being *ridiculous*. You know perfectly well that we are not going to hire a high school dropout," Heather spat.

Before I could think not to, I quipped, "Don't forget about the pot."

Heather flashed a bright blue warning my way, her mouth pinched and small. The urge to laugh clamored up my throat, and I just barely kept it down. Both the glare she was giving me and this entire interview were so fucking laughable, though.

This was *such* a shitshow.

There was nothing else I could do but laugh my way all the way to the unemployment office.

Choosing to ignore his wife and the transparent reality that this interview had gone to total shit, the husband went on. "Do you have any previous experience when it comes to caring for a child?"

This time, I allowed my lips to part and a soft laugh to fall out. This was insane, but I'd play along if not for the sheer satisfaction of *just* how much experience I had and to watch the realization dawn on the husband.

"I have a lot of experience, actually. I have a five-year-old sister, and I've been her primary caregiver for the last three years."

Heather scoffed. "What about your parents?"

"My dad's not in the picture anymore."

"And your mom?" That question came from the husband.

My eyes locked onto him and his oddly curious gaze, and I readied myself for the lie.

"She does her best."

His head angled just barely, the slight gesture intensifying his steel-cut stare. The simmering at the back of my neck from when we first saw each other started again, sizzling and prickling, and I wanted to squirm beneath his locked focus. I decided I didn't like the way he stared at me. It was dissecting and... almost intimate? As if his eyes were a cold sweat dripping down my spine, pulling me to attention and trying to seep beneath my layers of skin and baggage.

"Daddy, can I come in and watch T.V. yet?"

All three of our heads turned as a small voice rang through the living room. Standing with her front hunched into the wall that led into the living room was a little girl with brown ringlet curls and the sweetest big blue eyes set on her father. She appeared nervous as she carried a pout on her lips and refused to look at anyone but her dad.

"Maya, go to your room. We're not done yet," Heather snapped.

The little girl's eyes dimmed, and a flash of Charlotte blazed in my mind. Sad, scared, dismissed by her mother. My heart frowned for the little girl hiding against the wall.

"I'll come up and get you in a moment when we're done, okay, Munchkin? Then we can watch the movie together."

A small smile tried to dent into my cheeks at her father's sweet tone and eventually succeeded as his daughter beamed. This might have been one of the most twisted interviews, and this couple clearly needed heaps of therapy, but the husband got points over Heather in that moment. Dads who loved their daughters fucking ruled.

Getting comfortable in my new position staring over the back of the couch, I casually asked, "What movie are you gonna watch?"

Maya regarded me for the first time, timid eyes finding mine.

"Anastasia…" Her voice was so tiny, and she immediately jumped her focus back down to her colorful socks.

"Oh, I *love* that movie! Anastasia is absolutely the best princess. Hands down."

Maya's head flew up, her eyes almost comically large with newfound excitement. "Yeah… I love her, but Mommy doesn't like the movie."

To that, I scrunched my nose and shrugged my shoulders. "Yeah well, some people don't have very good taste."

At the same time, there was a sharp, feminine gasp and a riotous bark of deep laughter, but I didn't bother turning my attention to the couple's reactions. I was too busy winning over this little girl and shoving it in her mom's face.

"I love the song where she dances in the yellow dress!" Maya squealed, ecstatic energy bubbling beneath her skin. "And I want to get a puppy so I can name it Pooka!"

"Oh, you've gotta love Pooka." The little girl nodded vigorously and ran up to meet me at the edge of the couch. "You know, I actually dressed like Anastasia for Halloween when I was around your age."

This time, I got a full-blown smile. "Really? I want to be her so much!"

"Just gotta get yourself a puppy named Pooka, and you're set!"

"What about a Demetri?" Then she shot her wide eyes back to her dad. "Daddy, you could be him!"

Quickly, I waved her off and leaned in close. "You don't need a Demetri. Remember what Anastasia says about men?"

She thought it over for a moment, pulling her bottom lip between her teeth. Then, her cute little face burst with recognition, and we recited the line at the same time.

"All men are babies!"

Maya exploded in a fit of precious giggles, and I even heard an offended "*Hey*" come from her father behind us. Now if *this* had been the crux of today's interview, I'd be walking out of here feeling pretty damn good about my chances at getting the job.

Unfortunately, Heather had to jump in and ruin the fun.

"Maya, go to your room. *Now.*"

Maya's joy zapped out of her face in seconds as her mother's frigid voice hit the air, and she scurried off into her room without question.

Without even having to turn around, the anger in the husband's voice was enough to paint a furious picture in my head of his attractive face.

"Why did you have to do that?"

"What? She would have talked for hours about that movie and you know it. I've already got a headache, Dom. Don't start with me," she spat back.

Just before things got back on the toxic tracks, I was thankfully dismissed and somehow left with my head still intact despite Heather's best efforts. The husband wished me well and said they would be in contact within the next day or two if I got the position.

I knew he was only saying it to be polite.

A literal miracle would have to fall out of the sky for me to get that job after that interview, and I wasn't stupid enough to believe in miracles.

I was a realist.

I was a young, poor, jobless *realist*.

Fuck me.

THREE

So far, it'd been three days since the interview, and I hadn't heard a thing.

Three days of nothing but waiting by the phone, cutting out newspaper ads, and ignoring my shithead of a mother as best I could.

I filled one of the empty days babysitting for Mrs. Sharon so she and her husband could go shopping for baby supplies. Their son, Davion, Charlotte, and I played hide and seek, colored until our fingers hurt, and ate ourselves sick with all sorts of junk food Mrs. Sharon had stashed at their house.

By the morning of the fourth day, I'd begun to side-eye the section of the newspaper that advertised a strip club a town over. Charlotte never had to know, and from what I heard, strippers made pretty good money, right?

Then, on that fourth morning, in the middle of a perfectly executed pancake flip, my phone rang.

Shuffling the pan around on the burner, I answered. "Hello?"

Before anyone spoke, a ruckus clattered on the other end, and a masculine voice cursed. "Is this Katerina Sanders?"

Confused, I switched off the stove's burner. "It is. Who's asking?"

"Dominic Reed."

Dominic? "Doesn't sound familiar."

An annoyed sigh pushed into the phone. "From the interview a few days ago to be Maya's nanny."

Shock parted my lips and slowed my motions to a stop. The onetime familiar, low register of his voice cast me into a statue in the middle of my kitchen, phone in one hand and a paper plate in the other. The muted thump of my pulse acted as background music to the singular thought in my brain that stood out loud and clear.

The husband with the smokey eyes.

"Oh shit. I mean—Hi!" *Fuck.*

Mr. Reed bypassed my slip of the tongue and got straight to business. "Listen, I need a huge favor."

"Uh, yeah?" Quickly, I recovered from my internal glitch and gripped the phone harder to my ear. Charlotte playing on the living room floor peeked up at me as I placed her breakfast on the counter.

"We actually hired another nanny—" *Figured.* "But she fell through this morning, and now my wife refuses to come home and is planning on staying overnight in another town for work, and I'm late to work myself." My fingernails tapped an anxious beat on the countertop as I listened to him.

Mr. Reed breathed hard into his phone, the sound resonating his stress in my ear. "Honestly, you were my first pick for the position, and since Heather's not here to have a say, how does a trial run sound? Today?"

"Um..." Bugs gave me a pinch-faced expression, asking me what was going on with her little brows and pouting mouth. I responded with a flick of my finger to finish her pancakes before turning away so it was just me, the phone, and this *huge* potential opportunity to save our asses.

I'd question later on how in the *world* I was his first choice, and for now, blindly accept the bone that had been thrown our way.

"Sure, I can swing that. When?"

"Now. Right now."

Oh fuck. "Uh, now?"

"Yes. How fast could you be here? I'd need you to stay until around 10 tonight if you could."

Tension wound up my neck as I twisted back towards Charlotte, who was eating happily, syrup globbed on her chin. My heartbeat thunked inside my chest as toppling thoughts ambushed one another as I tried to work out a solution.

Think. Think. Think.

Our mother wasn't awake, and she wouldn't be for hours, nor would I trust her to watch Charlotte by herself. I'd already told Mrs. Sharon she could have these few days off, and I'd feel like such a shit for bothering her after that.

"Ms. Sanders, I don't mean to rush you, but I need an answer." Mr. Reed's voice came through my ear, controlled and rumbling. There was no waiver to his voice. No notes of consideration. Just business and demands. One singular demand he shoved at my feet.

"Yeah..." Pinching my eyes shut, I fisted my free hand together in front of me like if I clenched it hard enough, I'd open it back up and the answer would be in my palm.

Aw, hell, I need this job.

"I'll make it work," I spit out before I could take it back. "I'll be there in twenty."

A momentary lapse in breathing cued his relief.

"Perfect. Twenty minutes, Ms. Sanders."

The phone went dead, and my mind went completely berserk. The next several minutes consisted of throwing proper clothes on myself and Charlotte and pleading with Mrs. Sharon to watch Charlotte for the day until she took pity on me and said yes.

Promising Mrs. Sharon a lifetime of free babysitting, I was in my car and racing towards the house I never thought I'd step foot in again, stop signs and red lights be damned. The first time I drove there, it took me eighteen minutes. This time, I was parked on the street in front of the stone-faced house and sprinting up to the front doors in twelve.

I didn't get but two knocks in before the menacing doors swung wide open with Mr. Dominic Reed on the other side—

Clad in full police officer uniform.

"Ms. Sanders. Thank you for coming on such short notice."

He spoke, and I knew he spoke because sound came out of him, but whatever he said didn't have a chance in hell at being registered. Not when he looked like *that*. My brain misfired. My senses surged. I was a mindless defect on sensory overload who felt her desire like a towel snap across my whole body. Stinging, hot, and wet. So fucking wet.

The sting of just how attractive his six foot something, uniformed body was parched my throat, and I went to swallow down some relief. Except, like a misfortuned dumbass, I choked on my spit and coughed as I eye-fucked my new boss with zero ability to stop. Was he here to arrest me for the twenty plus stop signs I blew through to get here?

If so, I wasn't mad about it.

The dark blue material stretched across his wide chest and struggled to not burst back to single threads around his curled biceps as he held the door open. Casually, he kicked his booted foot out to prop the door open and took his hand back to shift his utility belt around his waist. Dominic Reed arched a thick eyebrow at me as I tried to maintain my coughing.

"I didn't know you were a... a cop," I managed to force out.

Words. Good. Words are good.

"Detective. I'm helping with patrol this week." When I didn't stop staring, he cocked his head to the side in an assertive way that brought my eyes back to his. "Is that a problem?"

My brain sputtering back to life, I shook my head frantically. "No, not at all. Just caught me off guard. I didn't know if I was walking in to babysit or be arrested." I gave a light chuckle. Mr. Reed only raised the side of his mouth just barely.

"Maya's inside in the living room watching T.V. I can show you in if you need—"

"Oh, that's fine." I waved him off, trying to salvage my shitty second impression by not looking at him too much. My tongue worked far better without the glint of his handcuffs shackled around it. "I think I can manage to find my way through this maze again without getting too lost."

In my fluttering eye's attempt to not stare directly at temptation, I did manage to catch a resounding sneer pull his full lips apart. "This house is ridiculous, I know."

Mr. Reed breathed a sharp breath as he patted his hands over his pockets and padded chest, doing a final check of items.

"Alright, my cell number is on the counter. She's already had breakfast, and there's a twenty on the counter so you can order a pizza for you two for dinner. If you have any questions about where things are, Maya should be able to answer most of them."

His dark eyebrows flattened to a straight line. "Do you have any questions you can think of now?"

"No, no, I'm good. Keep the kid alive. Eat the pizza. Don't burn down the house. I'm a pro."

A twitch of a smirk lifted the corner of his mouth as he side-eyed me. "Risky humor for a trial run."

I shrugged. "I enjoy toeing the line of recklessness and financial stability."

Mr. Reed hesitated for just a second, steel gray eyes framed by faint amusement. Then it was gone, and he and I were switching places, putting him outside and me standing in the frame of the door.

"If you need anything, just call. I have my cell on me at all times."

"Got it. Now, go! Catch some bad guys or eat a donut or something else stereotypical."

That joke clearly didn't play as well; he admonished me with a cutting glance that pulled my stomach inside out and then stalked off without another word. I stood there watching him go, trying so very hard to keep my eyes from drifting down as he moved with purpose to a silver Explorer in the driveway. With a strangled sigh, I closed the door between me and his perfect ass and locked it in place.

I sighed, talking to the door. "That man needs a stiff drink and an orgasm."

"What's an orgasm?"

The small voice erupted through the air, and I sucked back a gasp as I whipped around. I slammed my back against the door, my hand slapping across my chest to grab onto my next breath and hold it still as my stare fell to the little girl in front of me.

Maya stood there in princess pink pajamas, eyes wide and curious as she looked up at me for an answer to a question that never should have come out of her four-year-old mouth.

Fuck me and my flippant, twenty-year-old mouth.

"Uh..." My heartbeat danced erratically as I tried to think. "Just something your mommy needs to give your daddy."

"Oh..." Her large blue eyes blinked just once, and she pulled her bottom lip into her mouth as she nodded. "Okay."

My chest caved in as I let out a thankful breath. That was *not* something I wanted to come back and bite me in the ass if I managed to secure this job.

Both Maya and I stood in a familiarizing silence as we adjusted to each other and the time we'd be spending together tonight. I looked all around the pristine, forcefully put together house and grimaced at all the breakable shit around us. Rough housing was clearly out of the picture, but this poor kid needed some fun in her white picket life.

If we can't play inside...

Jerking my head down to Maya, I smirked.

"Where do your parents keep the fireworks?"

FOUR

Begrudgingly shuffling under her Anastasia themed bed cover, Maya gave me one of her best pouts. "But I don't wanna go to sleep now. We can play one more game of Hide and Seek! I'll let you win this time!"

"First off—" I helped yank her covers over top of her. "I don't need you to *let* me win. This house is just ginormous, and I thought I legitimately lost you twice. Second, we've gotta get you to bed so that when your dad comes home, he's happy and might let me come back to play with you again."

A puff of air ruffled some flyaways of her mocha brown hair as Maya conceded, slumping beneath her sheets and getting comfortable. Her bed was a tiny twin size that felt completely dwarfed by her room that was easily double the square footage of mine and Charlotte's. Hell, it was probably bigger than my kitchen and living room combined.

Maya rolled over in her bed to bring those big blue eyes to face me. She played with the edge of her comforter where Anastasia's face was. "I hope you come back..."

Melancholy swaddled my heart, and an ache bloomed from inside of it just after. *Damn*, she was good. A sad smile tacked on my cheeks. "Me too, kiddo."

"Shelly didn't come back," she murmured softly; heartbreakingly.

My chest squeezed. "Was Shelly your old nanny?"

Maya nodded.

Children should never look as forlorn as Maya did, and I immediately hated this Shelly bitch. Against my better judgment that screamed at me to not get attached to this little girl, I sat down on her bed and swept my fingers over her forehead to push back her curls.

"Anyone would have to be *crazy* to not want to come here and hang out with you. I'm sure Shelly didn't mean to leave like that. You two had a lot of fun together, right?"

Her small voice was a tight whisper. "Yeah."

"Then I'm sure she's missing you as much as you're missing her right now."

Maya lowered her stare to her fingers as she pulled her covers closer to her chin. "Daddy said that, too."

"Well, your daddy is a smart man." *And a stupidly hot cop.*

Slowly, she nodded and blinked her sweet stare back up to me. I smiled at her and she smiled at me, and that ignorant, radiating ache coming from my heart surged. *Dammit.*

I left her room a minute later, thinking about how much I was going to miss her if I never saw her again after tonight. She was like Charlotte in a lot of ways, and then completely opposite in others.

Both had shitty moms, and both were blindly happy despite them. At least Maya seemed to have a good father. I wasn't even sure if mine and Charlotte's sperm source lived on this continent anymore.

Making my way back down the rounding staircase, I padded into the kitchen and over to the giant, white-marbled island at the center of it where I left the box of half-eaten pineapple pizza.

Yes, I liked pineapple on my pizza.

Actually, scratch that.

I fucking *loved* pineapple on my pizza.

Most everyone who said they hated it only hated it because, at some point, society agreed that it was awful. Pineapple pizza was like the band Nickelback. No one knew *why* they hated it. They just did.

Flipping open the box, I scooped out a lukewarm slice and brought it to my lips.

"You like pineapple on your pizza?"

"Shit!"

It all happened within a matter of seconds.

I cursed. The pizza flew. Mr. Reed's face was there to catch it.

Both my hands slapped over my gaping mouth to hold back a gasp of horror as I snapped around to see him. If my eyes could have left my sockets, I was sure they would have, and I would have been so jealous. Then they wouldn't have to witness the hellstorm that was about to rain down on me as my potential boss stood there, pizza sauce sliding down his cheeks and giving him a clown nose in red sauce.

Two specks of yellow fruit were caught in his dark hair too.

Oh god.

"I didn't know you were there—"

"I know."

"You scared me—"

"I know."

"I'm so sorry—"

"I know."

His words were clipped, his voice and jawline tense. Mr. Reed's eyes were shut, and for the best, as red splatters were caught along his lashes and one of his eyelids. I swooped down to grab the culpable pizza from the floor, setting it back in the box with lightning speed.

Staring at him with the helpless beat of my heart pounding away, I floundered. "Can I... do anything or...?"

That hard-lined jaw of his ticked to the side and shut me up fast. He grumbled low in his throat. "A towel would be nice."

"Right! Sorry," I huffed, jumping into action and snagging a dish towel from the sink. As I laid the towel over his outstretched hand, a daring bite of laughter tried to break through as I took another look at his pizza splattered face. Mr. Reed fisted the rag, strangling the poor thing as he brought it to his face.

The silence as he mopped his marinara-painted face was suffocating. I wasn't a fidgeting kind of person, but this taut silence had me wringing my fingers together like a child in trouble. He let it sit for so long, and by the time he'd rid most of the sauce from his cheeks and forehead, I was dying beneath it. The silence killed my laughter, killed my appetite, and apparently most of my brain cells.

Mr. Reed missed a patch of red over his right eyebrow, and I moved. "Oh—"

Without thinking—*clearly*—I pulled the towel out of his hand just as he fluttered his eyes open experimentally. He jerked his head back as I came close, folding the stolen rag between my fingers. Those gunmetal eyes narrowed on me in suspicion.

"What are you doing?"

Pausing beneath his steely stare, I looked to the sauce on his head. "You missed a spot."

A steady beat hung between us.

I didn't wait for him to say anything more. Just got to work swiping the spot clean and doing my best not to acknowledge the body heat emitting off of him or how he felt like summer heat with eyes like a winter's snap. Cold. Biting. Serious.

Way too fucking serious for a man with pizza sauce on his chin.

I got rid of that too, riding the edge of the towel along the defined cut of his stubbled jaw.

"Also..." A smile did its best to wiggle onto my lips as I flicked pineapple from his mass of hair. Poorly, I rolled the smile between my lips and took a satisfactory step back from him. "There. All pretty again."

That dark gaze fell to my mouth as it twitched yet again.

"Are you laughing at me, Ms. Sanders?"

His tone was unreadable, but my willpower was failing.

"Desperately trying not to."

One of his thick brows arched. "Do you think this is funny?"

"No."

"Are you lying?"

A pause. "Definitely."

Slowly, so slow I couldn't even be sure it was happening, unmistakable humor reached up to his stare, brightening the whole thing. At the sight of it, muffled giggles started in my throat. My hysterics were choking me, and I had to let them out. Mr. Reed pulled his bottom lip between his teeth as he cast his eyes to the side, subtle shaking moving his broad shoulders.

Relief swept in fast and hard as he let a few rumbles of laughter roll around in his chest, and I let loose. Belly-aching joy threw my head back, spurred on by the low chuckles still trickling out of Mr. Reed. His laughter was soft and eloquent, deep and rich. Like velvet wrapped boulders echoing as they slammed together.

"You *have* to admit, that was funny shit," I managed through laughs and gasping breaths.

A lazy grin still denting his cheeks, Mr. Reed ran a hand back through his hair. "One of the weirder ways I've been welcomed home, that's for sure."

"Well, I *was* always told to make a memorable impression on the person looking to hire you."

He gave me an incredulous glance as he moved towards the box of pizza. "I'm not sure they meant to assault your boss with Italian food."

"Assault? Wow, first day on the job and you already have reason to arrest me."

That comment went ignored as he singled out a slice of pizza and began picking off the pineapples on top of it.

Rude.

"How'd it go with Maya?"

"Really great." Slowly, I started gathering my things so I could get going. "We watched a movie, played some games. She even showed me where you guys keep the fireworks."

Mr. Reed paused his hand bringing the pizza to his lips. "You two shot off *fireworks?*"

"Just sparklers and those popper things," I said to calm that severe look in his eyes. "Kid's got really good aim with those."

He let out a breath of a laugh that sounded more exhausted than anything.

"I bet she loved that."

"Yeah, she had a lot of fun with it. Made me pretend the sparklers were magic wands, and that we were casting spells on all the houses around us." He nodded in amusement as he folded his pizza in half and shoved the triangle end in his mouth. "She's got a wild imagination like my little sister."

He chewed slowly, lips moving and jaw working up and down. Each time he dropped his jaw to chew, it outlined the high cut of his cheekbones, and I realized I was staring.

"I bet the two would get along well," he tagged on after he swallowed.

He took another massive bite, nearly devouring the slice in two mouthfuls. I couldn't seem to stop watching him. Thankfully, Mr. Reed was too into his pizza to notice my concentration on his mouth, and I quickly slung my purse over my shoulder to force myself out of it.

"Yeah, they would. Speaking of my sister, I probably need to head out and get home to her."

"Of course." Mr. Reed dropped the crust of the pizza into the box, covering his mouth with the back of his hand as he finished swallowing. "Let me walk you out."

He went to stride towards me, but I put a hand out to stop him.

"That's okay. I remember where the door is." A reassuring smile tugged up on my lips at the same time that a yawn stretched Mr. Reed's wide. I gave a short chortle. "Plus, I think you'd fall asleep before you made it to the door."

He rubbed his tired eyes, pressing his fingers into their closed sockets and shook his head.

"You'd think, but sleep hasn't been the easiest thing to come by lately."

Curiosity pinched the back of my mind. "How long have you been having trouble sleeping?"

A deep breath filled his chest out, and he dropped his hand, allowing his red-rimmed eyes to find mine. "I don't remember."

His voice was just as beat as he was, sloggy with gravel embedded in each full-bodied note. As I stood there, an idea struck. Just be an extra bonus in my corner in case he wasn't sold on hiring me after I went ahead and slapped him with pizza.

"Do you drink?"

Mr. Reed slanted his head. "Occasionally."

"There's this drink I used to make my dad whenever he wanted it after a hard day. Or any day really. He claimed it helped him fall asleep, and my grandpa said the same thing. You have a pretty full wet bar, so... if you wanted me to make it for you really quick, I could."

His fatigued stare mixed with intrigue. "Don't you have to get home though?"

"It will take five minutes. Tops."

When he didn't immediately say no, I let my purse fall from my shoulder to the ground and told him to go sit and get comfortable. Just on the other side of the kitchen sat their wet bar, another white marbled slat with double sinks, a dark cherry, overhanging glass holder, and a mini fridge that wasn't exactly so mini.

"Whiskey or Bourbon?" I called over.

"Bourbon."

I hummed, plucking a bottle of bourbon I'd never heard of before that had a metal horse on the top. "My dad was a whiskey guy."

A few beats of quiet passed between us where all you could hear was the clinking of glass and sloshing of alcohol. In this giant house, the silence felt even more prominent, like its own living, breathing thing, and it set my nerves on edge.

"So, what's in this drink that makes it so special?" Mr. Reed's deep voice floated in from the living room.

Bustling back into the kitchen for a moment to boil some water in the microwave, I tipped a glance over to him. "I'm not telling."

"That's disconcerting."

"What? Secrets are secrets for a reason, sir."

As the microwave hummed behind me, a peculiar expression shadowed his chiseled face. "You don't have to call me sir, Ms. Sanders."

Leaning back against the counter, I asked, "What would you rather I call you?"

"Dominic or Mr. Reed. Whichever you prefer."

"What if I prefer *sir*?" The pointed look he gave me from across the room peeled a stupid grin up my face. "Kidding," I quipped. *Kind of.*

I'd get a hell of a kick out of calling him 'sir' and watching those melted metal eyes turn punishing. I wouldn't do it though, obviously. Probably...

I liked his name. Dominic. It was strong and masculine and sounded like royalty on his tongue. Part of me wondered how the syllables of his name would feel rolling around my mouth.

"So, are you going to tell me what's in this drink?"

Dominic stole my focus back to him, and I turned away from him to face the counter.

"What's the fun in that?"

"What if I'm allergic to this secret ingredient?"

I rustled through the cabinets for some honey. "Well, what are you allergic to?"

A long beat resonated between us.

"Cats."

The prolonged beep from the microwave punctuated Dominic's revelation, and a smile slid up my lips. Yanking the microwave open, I said, "Well, lucky for you, this drink is free of all things feline." I craned my head back to him. "Where do you guys keep tea bags?"

He pointed to a tall pantry on the other end of the kitchen I'd yet to make my way over to. I nabbed a lavender chamomile tea packet and sunk it in the boiling water, taking that and the honey back with me to the bar. My dad always preferred ginger tea while my grandpa liked chamomile in this particular drink.

Me? I fucking hated tea altogether.

As the drink was steeping, I fished lemon juice out of the not-so-mini fridge. These people really had *everything*. Throwing all the ingredients together in the piping hot glass, I made my way around to Dominic who sat in his crimson lounge chair, arms resting on both sides and a tall lamp hovering over him.

It cast this dark shadow over the top of his face, drowning the gray of his eyes to a near black as he watched me approach. I held the glass out to him, and he reached to take it, but stopped mid-motion and put his eyes on me.

"There aren't drugs in here, are there?"

My head reared back as offense punched through my body. "Yeah, because I'm *really* going to drug my potential boss on my first day."

"I don't put anything past anyone these days," he replied casually. So casually in fact, my nostrils flared at the accusation of it, and I had to bite back my rising temper. Through clenched teeth, I rolled my eyes back and brought the glass to my lips, letting the warm, honeyed liquid wash across my tongue.

God *damn*, I made good drinks.

The pleasant burn slid down my throat, and a delighted shiver wracked my spine as the alcohol touched my blood. Dominic never let his dark-eyed focus on me waiver, and I held the drink out to him once more.

"Trust me now?"

Slowly shifting forward in his seat, the angles of his face grew sharp in the new lighting. "That's a loaded question, Ms. Sanders."

He took the glass between his long fingers and raised it to his lips. I watched him, and he never took his eyes off of me either as he took a considering sip. The intensity of his prolonged eye contact burned as he tasted the drink I made for him. I felt the need to shift from foot to foot in front of him, but held my ground even as the dark liquid washed over his top lip. His tongue slipped out to clear the residue, and my mouth drew parched.

The heat that had poured through my body thanks to my one sip found its way to my stomach, pooling there as I watched a surprised gleam appear in his shaded stare.

"Do you like it?" I asked, quickly clearing my throat that had dropped to a murmur.

"Very much." He gave the drink a whiff before testing another sip. A curiosity plagued his stare as he flashed his focus back to me. "You said you were only twenty, right?"

Of legal age for all sexual acts? Why, yes. Yes, I am.

"Yeah, I'll be twenty-one in a few months."

What appeared to be amused suspicion narrowed the sides of his eyes as he leaned back in his chair. "So you're not allowed to drink yet."

The arousal I was feeling smothered itself at his question, and my hip popped out in rebellion, an uneasy fire brewing in me.

"Are you going to arrest me for taking a sip of alcohol in front of you?"

Dominic raised an eyebrow and held a scrutinizing beat between us.

"No. Just thinking about how you said you made this drink for your father, and you're not legally allowed to even drink yet, so I'm wondering how that worked."

"Because he was a shitty father?" I chuckled like it was obvious. "I knew how to make about fifteen different drinks by the time I was thirteen. It was our way of bonding."

"You said he's not in the picture anymore, right?"

"Yup," I replied, voice clipped.

Sincerity creased his brow line, dipping into his stare. "I'm sorry to hear that."

"I'm not. All he did was make me into a walking cliché of daddy issues."

Dominic nodded, tipping back another gulp of the drink. "I try my best, but I have no idea how to not pass any 'issues' onto Maya from me."

"Just don't be a piece of shit, and you should be golden," I said with a cheeky grin.

For the second time tonight, a rumble of soft laughter that sounded so unpracticed, so unfamiliar to his own vocal cords, drummed in his chest, and he tilted a humored look up to me. A *sleepy* humored look, and my pride jumped. He relaxed back into his chair, running one of his hands thoughtfully over his trimmed scruff as he stared at me with a lazy smile.

"You're funny," he said.

"And you're sleepy."

"I *am*." Surprise linked his words together as his eyelids dropped heavier, and he stretched his long legs out in front of him as he got comfortable in the chair. In the back of my head, I wondered if he'd be going up to his and Heather's bedroom or if he slept down here sometimes. He certainly seemed at home in the big red chair.

"All right. I'm gonna get going before you pass out." Locking my grip around the handle of my purse again, I pulled it up to take my leave when a thought stalled my feet out. The words rolled around in my head for all of three seconds before I said fuck it and snapped around to a nearly sleeping Dominic.

"Do I have the job, by the way?"

Part shock, part mirth lifted his eyebrows about an inch. As the seconds passed, the amusement pushed the surprise out of the way until this gaze was nothing more than fatigued enjoyment.

"See you Monday morning, Ms. Sanders."

FIVE

"Didn't Mrs. Sharon give you one of Davion's Dr. Seuss books to read?"

"Mhm. Go, Dog, Go."

"And have you started it?"

Charlotte paused, her hand clutching her bright orange crayon harder.

"*Bugs*, come on." My head snapped back as I dropped it with a sigh, swinging my legs over my bed. "You know you gotta read it. We've already read every book I grew up with a hundred times. Mrs. Sharon is really nice to let you take these home for a bit."

Charlotte turned her pleading eyes up to me, paired with that annoyingly adorable protruding bottom lip. "Can I just finish coloring this one picture first? Please, Katty?"

Oh hell, why did she have to be so freaking cute?

"Fine, last picture, then you go read, okay?" I ordered with a cocked eyebrow.

"Okay!"

She sunk back down to her elbows, coloring away furiously as she turned an elephant at the circus orange.

Flopping back down onto my bed, I picked my phone back up and resumed my mind-numbing round of Candy Crush. Level 1800. Yes, I was one of those weirdos that still played Candy Crush, and I would be until I could beat these fucking Jelly levels. I'd invested far more hours than I would comfortably admit playing this game, but it was free and didn't require WiFi, so it was an ace in the hole for me.

It was also perfectly distracting from thoughts and shit I didn't want to deal with. Like how nervous I was for tomorrow, my first *official* day of work for the Reeds. Maya was cool and all, and we'd have a blast together. She wasn't what I was worried about.

It was her mom. I clearly wasn't Heather's first choice for the gig, and if I ran into her tomorrow, I was sure she'd have a few choice words to say about my being there. Maybe take another jab at my education or lack thereof.

A curt knock on my bedroom door tore me from my irritating thoughts, and I propped myself up on my elbows in confusion.

"Kathy? It's like 11:30 am. What are you doing up?"

The door creaked open. "Sorry, but last time I checked, I was pretty sure I was your boyfriend, not your mom."

The voice that was clearly not my mom's brought a crooked grin up my lips and a snort through my nose as he walked in. "I'd use that term loosely."

Daren pretended to be offended as he strolled in, hand on his muscular chest and mossy green eyes pushing into mine. "Why do you wanna hurt me, babe?"

"Such a drama queen," I said, rolling my eyes as I sat up on my bed.

Daren and I had been seeing each other for a few months now. He came into Marties one day looking for beer pong balls and wouldn't leave until I said yes to a date. While his approach was annoying, he was charming in a boyish way and easy on the eyes. Daren was tall, lean, and knew his way around the female body well enough that I didn't have to waste money on batteries for my vibrator anymore.

We weren't serious since I wouldn't touch a serious relationship with a twenty foot pole, but he was fun. Fun and safe. Daren was someone I could spend time with, fuck around with, and all without having to worry about losing myself to him.

The thought of ever losing myself to someone was a fist in my gut, holding it tight and refusing to let me breathe or forget it was there at all. Giving my heart, my soul, my whatever to someone wasn't an option for me, and I wasn't even a little interested in the willing thievery. I couldn't afford the loss. *Charlotte* couldn't afford it, either.

Our mother fell into that dangerous love trap with our dad, and when he left, he ripped her essence out completely and left us with a husk of a woman. A woman whose heart was her compass, and she'd gone mad searching for it with no sense of direction left.

That's what falling into that delirious kind of love drunk state did to her, and I had zero interest in that kind of intoxication. Daren kept me sober.

My neck craned back as he came closer, bypassing a greeting to Charlotte. "How'd you get in, by the way? Did you break into my house?"

"I think the lock is busted."

Instant stress filtered through my lungs as I dropped my head back with another sigh. "Great."

There went more money I didn't have towards this shit pile.

"Don't think about that right now." Daren cupped the underneath of my chin, raising my head so he could reach my lips. "I missed you," he murmured against them.

Unable to help another eye roll, I smiled against his mouth. "I highly doubt that."

"What? A guy can't miss his girlfriend?" And then he kissed me, sliding his soft lips between mine in a kiss that would seem sweet if it weren't for his hand that was on my chin sliding down to rest on the rise of my breasts.

Pulling back some, I muttered between us, "Did you miss me or my tits?"

"Same thing, right?"

Daren yelped as I smacked the back of his head playfully, both of us chuckling as we parted our kiss.

"Katty got a new job!" Charlotte interrupted, beaming up at me proudly and only sparing Daren a quick glance to see his reaction.

Much like me, she liked Daren but didn't love him.

"Oh yeah? That babysitting thing?" Daren laid himself back on my bed next to me, fishing his phone out of his pocket.

"Yeah. The pay's great, the kid is easy, and the schedule works so much better for me and Charlotte."

"That's good, babe." Daren's focus was glued to his phone as he texted away. I fought not to loudly exhale my annoyance. I never liked when he did that or when *anyone* did that. "Maybe you'll finally have time to go out and hang like a normal twenty-year-old," he added.

Not so convinced, I just shimmied down to get comfortable next to him. "We'll see."

Daren made a whining noise in the back of his throat, rolling to his side to face me. "Come on, babe. You're always so busy with work and shit."

"*Language.*" I shot a cursory glance over to Charlotte, who was thankfully absorbed back into the world of circus folk and animals that needed coloring.

Daren groaned a lackluster apology that was laced with irritation, his hands finding the curve of my waist and holding on. "Babe, I wanna show you off. *Please?*"

"Like I'm a show pony?" I replied dryly.

"A sexy show pony."

"You're not cute."

"Eh, I think we both know you don't mean that." He winked, reminding me of that cheeky charm of his, and I rolled my eyes again at him. I realized I did that a lot around him.

"Come on, my buddy from work is having a party on Friday at his place. Come with me."

I arched an eyebrow. "So you can parade me around?"

"So we can hang out like a real couple, and I can prove to my friends that you're real and not just a *cat* like they keep messing with me."

Stiff laughter barked from between my lips. "Maybe I won't show up now because that's pretty freaking funny."

His hands around my waist squeezed, and his hazel eyes brightened. "That almost sounds like a cruel way of saying yes."

"*Maybe...*"

Now that I didn't have to work on weekends, I really didn't see why I couldn't go out for at least a *few* hours and let loose. Just a little. A couple drinks. A few dances. Maybe one game of beer pong. Charlotte was already going over to Mrs. Sharon's house for a movie night with Davion anyway, so I wouldn't have to worry about that.

"That maybe sounds like a yes," Daren mumbled against my neck as he drew himself close, lips skimming beneath my ear.

A grimace he couldn't see pulled back my lips. "What a creepy thing to say."

He ignored me, pushing a hand beneath my shirt to grab my bare stomach with a squeeze, and I fought not to gasp. His mouth that pressed a smooth kiss against the hollow of my neck right after didn't help matters.

"My sister's right there, Daren," I whispered, shifting beneath him.

"Charlotte, go to your room," Daren tossed towards Charlotte, not bothering to spare her a look.

"Hey—" I pushed his shoulders back without pause, pinning my stare to him. "Don't tell her what to do. Also, this *is* her room." *Dumbass.*

A frustrated breath of air blew across my face as Daren hung his head low. "I'm sorry. I would just really like to spend some time with my girlfriend. Alone?"

He snapped his focus back to me, lust still brimming behind his pointed look. That look was a reminder that it had been over a week since we'd last had sex, and my resolve took a quick beating. I rolled my fingers around his shoulders, fisting the material in my palms as familiar heat sprouted between my legs.

Like he could smell my growing arousal, Daren lowered himself back over me gently, mouth hovering just above my ear. "Let me show you how much I missed you, Kat."

The wet surprise of his tongue flicked my earlobe, and that was that.

"Hey, Bugs." Propping myself up on my elbow to give Charlotte my full attention, I pushed Daren off behind me. My sister batted those big brown eyes up at me. "It looks like you're about done with your coloring. Think you could go start that reading now?"

She heaved a gloomy sigh, her face falling into a pout. "Okay..."

Charlotte made sure to pick up her crayons and coloring book with as little purpose as she could muster, making her exit as dramatic and time consuming as possible.

No one could say that we weren't related.

Once she was out of the room, Daren's lips were on mine. His kisses were always smooth and quick, tongue sliding with mine and gone before I could ever really taste him properly.

Kissing Daren was like kissing anyone, really. It was nice to be kissing someone and have them kissing you back, but there were no sparks. No wild fire shooting through your veins and turning your every other thought that didn't orbit around this one person to ash. No famed stars. No nothing but lips and spit and tongues.

Those sort of star-seeing, firework-exploding kisses were rare and dangerous and nothing I wanted any part of. Hollywood could keep their happily-ever-after kisses to themselves. I was fine with this, with Daren and our kisses that were just fine.

Safe.

Daren worked down my neck in hurried paces, proving he wasn't a man who liked to wait for the prize at the bottom of the cereal box. His hands cupped both my breasts, squeezing them with a faint moan. My nipples ached for attention under his grip, but his hands disappeared seconds later, and I heard him messing with his belt buckle.

Whatever.

A content sigh blew past my lips as I brushed my hands over the thin graze of Daren's buzz cut as he trailed his tongue down my navel, teasing the band of my pants with his fingers. I closed my eyes to enjoy the sensations, feeling myself growing wet in anticipation as his fingers made quick work of removing my shorts.

Before I could catch up, Daren was over me, between my legs, sliding into me, and I rolled my bottom lip between my teeth to not gasp. My mouth dropped open in a silent moan as my back bowed, the feeling of his cock hitting where I needed him sending tingles down to my toes.

Daren's breathing in my ear was already turning ragged, and I huffed out loud, sinking my nails into his back as punishment for being so fucking close to coming already.

"*Ow*," he hissed, jerking slightly. "Watch the claws, babe."

Frustration and disappointment bubbled in my chest, but I pushed it aside and just closed my eyes. I focused on Daren's body, the muscles moving in his back, the low moans he was trying to muffle in my neck.

Sensations in my lower stomach were knotting together as he rocked his hips into mine, and I squeezed my eyes harder to hold on to those electric knots forming, growing bigger and tighter.

Just before those bindings snapped and came completely unraveled, just before I reached that peak and nosedived into the upcoming orgasm, an unexpected image glitched behind my eyes.

Gray.

All I saw was gray. Piercing, hypnotic, smokey gray.

The tempestuous wave of the unexpected color swept me up high and crashed over my body in an orgasm that had me turning my head to bite the pillow. Tears leaked through the corners of my eyes that were still squeezed shut as pleasure cracked and popped inside of me, the assault seeming never-ending.

Daren couldn't take it and came undone inside the condom seconds later, shuddering above me as I tried to catch my breath. I was heaving and stunned and sensitive to the touch laying there beneath him as he collapsed on top of me.

Each breath that wracked my lungs helped flood thinkable air back to my brain, connecting the dots in a gut-twisting revelation of why *exactly* that specific, menacing color of gray looked so familiar. Of where I'd seen that *exact* shade before in a pair of striking eyes.

Well, shit.

SIX

You know when you just have one of those days?

The kind of day that started off totally normal and then progressively got so mind-bogglingly terrible that by the end of it, you're expecting to wake up in your bed thankful that it was all a dream?

That would be today for me.

Today was Friday and the end of my first official week working for the Reeds. The week had actually gone well, much to my relief and even greater shock. I'd gotten lucky this week. Heather was gone before I got there each morning, and Dominic made it home before his wife each day to relieve me. Apparently, it wouldn't always be that way.

Dominic's schedule was the most consistent except when he had to pull a double and work patrol at night, so he said. As far as Heather's work schedule, he warned me it was chaotic and that she could pop up at any time she wasn't in the office or showing a house.

Lucky me.

Tonight was also Daren's friend's party. Mrs. Sharon ended up making the kids' movie night a sleepover so I could stay out later, and I wouldn't lie that I was a *little* excited to have one night of no obligations. Just drinking my face off, making reckless choices, and no guilt over it. I hadn't been *out* out in... God, I couldn't even remember how long. Plus, I hadn't seen Layla since I got canned, and within thirty seconds of me texting her about tonight, she was sending me photos of dresses.

I was *really* looking forward to tonight. I just had to get through the rest of the work day. Currently, I was lying on the ground, Maya on the couch with our board game sprawled in front of her on the cushions, the news on the T.V. in the background.

"But why do I have to move onto the red square? I didn't pull a red card."

"Because those are the rules, Ms. Kat!" Maya ran her hand back across her face to rid her forehead of stray hairs that had escaped her ponytail. "Pay attention."

"This is my first time playing. Give a girl a break. *Jeez.*"

I held my hands up in mock surrender, careful not to show off my cards and lose even more than I already was. This game either made no sense, or I was actually as dumb as Heather assumed I was.

Just then, the sound of the front door opening and closing echoed through the house, and both our heads snapped that way.

"Daddy!"

Maya scrambled off of the couch and flung herself at her father as he walked through the threshold of the living room; he barely had time to brace himself for his daughter's full on attack. Dominic let out half a groan as he caught his daughter in his arms, lifting her up to sit on his hip.

"Hey Munchkin." He pecked a kiss on her forehead.

"I missed you." Maya snuggled her head into her father's neck. She picked up his detective badge that was hanging around his neck like a necklace and fiddled with it.

"You saw me yesterday," he chuckled.

In a small voice, she replied, "I still missed you."

Dominic's face softened, and his grip on his daughter tightened a bit more. An uncomfortable pang went off in my chest at the display.

Eyes like the sky after a thunderstorm found me on the floor, and that pang turned into a full-blown gut punch. I sucked back a quick, sharp breath and steered my gaze back down to the game.

There were two reasons I couldn't look at Dominic Reed right now. One—and this reasoning had persisted all week long—was because of that stupid fucking, dumb as shit, mind-blowing orgasm he helped usher in last week when I was with Daren. It had come so far out of left field, I still felt a rush of guilt when I thought about it.

And horny. So. Fucking. Horny.

It was no secret that Dominic Reed was extraordinarily handsome, but he was also married *and* my boss, so you'd think my fuck-o-meter would turn off for him, but nope. In fact, he broke the damn thing, making me so hot whenever he looked at me now that I felt like I was shattering in a fit of boiling flames and guilty sweat.

The second reason was something new, but equally as combustible.

The peculiar sympathy in his eyes as he hugged his daughter and she hugged him back was infuriating. It was *insulting*. I didn't want or need his unasked for pity. I didn't need him dissecting what made me tick like a bomb whose fuse was always lit.

So my father was a fuck up? I didn't see any reason why that should intrigue him.

In the middle of trying to distract myself from the odd cocktail of insult and desire, Maya let an excited gasp rip across the room.

"Come play with us! You can be on Ms. Kat's team since she needs help."

Not looking at him, the pause he gave his daughter before answering read loud and clear. "Sweetie, Daddy's really tired. I have to go back to work tonight, so I'm about to go lay down for a nap."

"Please, Daddy? One game!" I cocked a keen eye over to Maya just as she clipped a glance to me and then back to her father. She leaned in close to whisper, but was loud enough for the entire neighborhood to hear. "Ms. Kat doesn't get how to play, and I know it's mean to say, but she's not very good and-and it's hard to play with her."

My jaw slacked in open offense. Dominic's now noticeably tired eyes slid over to mine, a spark of humor dotting them both. The corner of his full mouth tipped up.

"Just *one* game, Daddy?"

Dominic's face was weary, but I saw the cave coming from a mile away. There was no resisting Maya's pleading little stare. "All right, but just one game. Then it's nap time for both of us."

With an enthusiastic squeal, Maya jumped out of her father's arms and came soaring back to the couch with Dominic towing behind in labored steps.

"Sit next to Ms. Kat so you can see her cards," she ordered.

Shiny black shoes came my way, and I sat up, tucking my feet under my legs to get comfortable. Getting *completely* comfortable wasn't going to be possible given how Dominic looked today and how close he came as he sat down next to me. He was wearing a white button down shirt that pulled over his broad shoulders in a way I'd never seen material do before. It was like I could hear the material gasping for breath against his strong body when he moved a certain way.

The tan slacks he wore were softer than I anticipated as he lowered himself to the floor, and his thigh brushed my bare knee. The sensation was a flawless combination of soft and fire-hot.

Like he'd caressed me with a feather made of flames.

Dear lord. I had to get my shit together.

Next to me, Dominic barely looked awake as he spotted the T.V. from across the room. A vile reaction gripped his expression, and he grabbed the remote and clicked the news story of some nurse who'd been missing for a few weeks off the screen.

Sitting next to him, I got to see the back of his jaw tense and shift just before he shut his eyes. Then he rested his head back against the couch.

"Hey." I nudged his arm with my elbow. "You're supposed to be on my team. Perk up."

"I'm up," he spoke, eyes fully shut.

"You are *not*. How do you expect this team to win if you snooze your way through the game?"

With what looked like a lot of effort, Dominic twisted his head to lock eyes on me. "I think you might be taking this a little too seriously, Ms. Sanders," he replied with eyes half-hooded beneath heavy eyelids. "Besides, no one else wins at this game besides Maya."

"Well, yeah, because she's the only one who understands these ludicrous rules."

"That's because she made them up."

I paused.

"*What?*"

All he did was give a casual shrug. "We lost the rules for the game about two years ago. One day, she made up her own rules, and I let her. No one else understands what's going on in the game, but she always wins, so she's happy."

So I just wasted a solid forty minutes trying to understand a game with rules made up by a four-year-old? I blinked at Dominic, astounded and maybe just a little pissed that there was literally no way I could win this game. At all.

"You know if she always wins these games, she's gonna become a *really* sore loser later on."

Dominic watched me, his eyes doing that thing again. That analyzing, intimate, goosebump-inciting thing, but this time with a wry curve to his mouth. "Speaking from experience, are we?"

God, his mouth. I'd never seen such a beautiful mouth that I wanted to slap so freaking badly.

"Be quiet and help me lose this game."

About twenty minutes later, the game was over. Maya won, I sulked, and Dominic went up for a nap.

Maya went down for her hour-long nap shortly after, and I got busy with the household chores Heather found for me to do, so I wasn't 'just sitting around, making money.'

It wasn't much. They had a housekeeper that came by every week to do the real, deep cleaning. All I had to do was make the beds, clear out the dishwasher if it was full, and do their laundry. I'd already started a load of Maya's clothes in the wash when I walked by the upstairs home office, the door ajar.

The door to Dominic's office was almost always closed unless he was in it, and a quick survey of the inside said it was vacant. Curiosity boiled inside of me, and my fingers danced along the lip of the laundry basket I had clutched beneath my arm. I didn't *need* to go in there. I couldn't imagine there were many clothes lying around on the floor in there that needed washing.

But then again...

I had that stupid saying to uphold, didn't I? Curiosity killed Kat.

I pushed the door the rest of the way open, sliding inside the room with unusual grace and wandering eyes. One thing was clear right off the bat. Whoever decorated the rest of this house hadn't set foot in this room. There was none of the tacky furniture or an overabundance of red, white, and black.

There was just a wooden desk pushed up against the wall that curved around to a right angle. That, and a chair. A simple chair, and a simple, light wood desk.

My feet brought me over to the desk, brought my fingers to slide across the curved edge of its sides. Papers were scattered across it, as were manila files with even more papers spilling out. Most of what was on the pages were printed letters and numbers that all blurred into nonsense. Case numbers and police jargon and a whole lot of other shit that I couldn't make heads or tails out of even if I tried.

I walked further around the desk, squinting at something that caught my eye. Something blue.

His name. *Dominic Reed.* Hand-written in deep blue ink.

My fingertips were on the D of his name before I could even think about what I was doing or why. Was this his handwriting? It was at the bottom of some paper, like signing off on whatever it was that was contained on that page, so it had to be his writing, right?

The indent of the pen was hard against the paper as if he was furious at it when he was signing it. As if he wanted to stab through the paper with the pen like it would tear through the truth of whatever was on the page and make it not true anymore. It was also elegant. Cursive. Refined. Beautiful handwriting.

A beautiful man should have beautiful penmanship, I supposed.

I wondered what my name would look like in his handwriting. My full name. All curvaceous and swooping and rich, unlike me. A lie in permanent ink.

I picked up the page with his name written on it and read it over, wanting to know what it was that made him so angry as he was signing it. There were locations I didn't know and names that didn't sound familiar... until one did.

Becky Johanson.

"The nurse?" I whispered, unable to contain my confusion. That had to be the same Becky Johanson they were just talking about downstairs on the news, right? The nurse that had been missing for weeks now, and police said the trail ran cold.

"Snooping is generally frowned upon."

The unexpected deep voice zapped shock through my entire body. My head ripped up in a short gasp while my hands dropped the laundry basket and the paper, letting it float back down to the desk.

Dominic Reed was standing in the doorway, hands hidden away in his pants pockets and indiscernible gaze set on me. One look at his neatly styled hair, despite its thickness, told me he hadn't laid down for the nap he said he'd be taking yet. So here he was instead, catching me red-handed doing something I was definitely *not* supposed to do.

The way he was staring at me held my tongue in place and fritzed my brain down to basic mechanics. All it left was the faintly spoken lie I heard myself say next.

"I was cleaning the desk."

One of those thickly shaped brows of his cocked sharply. "Do you have anything better than that?"

Another fighting breath pulled down through my lungs as I parted my lips, and then his words registered. His mocking words. My voice stalled out, and I blinked back at him, my browline drawing in tight on my forehead.

Dominic didn't move an inch. Simply waited.

He knew I was lying to him, knew I was somewhere I wasn't supposed to be in his house, poking around through his things. He caught me in the lie *and* in the act, but he didn't seem angry so much as... interested in what I'd say next.

So I searched my brain for a fresh lie. "A breeze rolled in and blew the papers down, so I came in to pick them up."

He nodded to something behind me. "The window's closed."

Turning over my shoulder to see that the window was, in fact, closed, was more for show rather than consideration that he might be wrong. I knew he was right. He knew he was right.

"Uh, so then scratch that." Snapping back around, I dug into my veins for the theatrics I knew were in there. "I actually fell into the room, rolled my ankle, knocked the paper off the desk and was picking it up just as you walked in."

The slight curve that formed on his mouth was almost cocky. "Awfully clumsy of you, Ms. Sanders."

"Yeah, I'm a total klutz."

"Finally something that's believable."

My lips twitched in what wanted to be offense but folded into a smile instead that I rolled between my teeth. I didn't *want* to smile because of him, but here I was, biting a grin down so hard, the metallic taste of blood overwhelmed my tastebuds.

Trying to ignore him and the bitter flavor in my mouth, I dropped my focus back down to the desk. To one blue-signed paper in particular. "You're working the missing nurse's case?"

The pause that followed killed the teasing atmosphere between us. When I drew my gaze back to him, that strange playfulness had slid off his face. It was back to being something close to frostbite. "One of many."

I didn't want to stop myself before I asked, "Is that the reason you have trouble sleeping?"

The chill in his stare grew to gray ice. "One of many."

Silence held between us, and I felt the heaviness of it sitting on my chest. An awkward, cement brick pushing down on my chest, trying to force out words to end the quiet. I *hated* the silence.

Noise. I needed noise around me at all times. It's why I was so thankful when Dominic eventually spoke again. "That's why I came to find you, actually. Do you think you could make me another one of those drinks?"

Surprised, I nodded brightly. "Sure."

Collecting the laundry basket from the ground, I went to leave, approaching Dominic in the doorway where his shoulders nearly touched the sides. He was standing so tall and straight, appearing larger than I'd seen him yet. Ducking my head as I got close, the interruption of his deep voice forced my head back up.

"Oh, and Ms. Sanders?"

"Hmm?"

Staring down the bridge of his nose at me, authority burned his charcoal irises. "This door stays closed for a reason."

Rebellion flared hot in my lungs, and a quick memory jumped forward on my tongue.

"Yes *sir*."

His reaction was slight, but worth it. A little shocked. A little angry. A little impressed.

Kat: one
Dominic: zero

SEVEN

I t didn't take long to make Dominic his drink. Five minutes tops, adding on an extra few for when I went to the bathroom before I made it.

Still, not a lot of time at all. Except, apparently, it was too long for him.

When I made it to the Master bedroom, the door was open and the King size bed was occupied. Dominic was lying on top of the cream-colored covers, legs straight and arms folded over his chest as he slept. He was still in his work clothes down to the black wingtip shoes around his feet.

The stiff way he'd fallen asleep said he was waiting for me to bring him his drink and sleep swooped him up before I got there. I walked in anyway, warmth feeding into my palms through the drink I held for him. The drink that was now totally moot.

At least he was sleeping.

Strange tingles clustered in my chest as I scanned his sleeping face. The lines of stress I thought were chiseled into his face permanently had melted away. His skin was smooth, almost golden, and I wondered how much sun he got on the job. That taut browline of his was relaxed, and the furrowed crease between them vanished. Dominic looked nothing like the man I saw every day this last week. He was softer. Younger, even.

How old was he, anyway? I'd never really given much thought to it up until this moment. Somewhere in his thirties, if I had to guess.

Placing his cup on the mahogany nightstand next to the bed, I started gathering up discarded clothes scattered on the floor for laundry. It was mostly Heather's clothes or the occasional sock from Dominic, and the former annoyed the hell out of me.

Heather was a neat person. *Too* neat to leave clothes on the floor, which meant she was doing it on purpose just to leave me a subtle 'fuck you' every day.

I'd have to thank her some day by accidentally dying all of her pants a nice puke green.

Just before I left the room, a peak of crumpled royal blue stood out against the bed cover. A heavy sigh sunk my shoulders, and I dropped the pile of clothes I'd collected in the corner before trudging over to the bed.

The discarded shirt was stuck underneath a sleeping Dominic, because why wouldn't it be? I felt like the entire bedroom was giving me a giant middle finger, the maroon curtains over the double windows going as far as to sneer at me using its pleats.

It was saying *'get out, you don't belong here'* and I was trying my damnedest to listen. I didn't like being in their marital bedroom, especially while Dominic was sleeping in it. I didn't like thinking about what they did in here. The conversations they had. The knockout fights. It gave me the chills, like if the walls could talk, it would be a creeping whisper down my neck, sharing dirty little secrets I didn't wanna know.

Just get the shirt and go.

Jitters curling up my body, I set my eyes on the blue shirt wedged underneath Dominic's torso. I'd always prided myself on being strong and independent, and I mean *literally* strong and someone who didn't need help from anyone to do anything; not open any jars, reach anything at abnormally tall heights—nothing.

I didn't need a man for anything.

But I needed this fucking man to get off of this fucking shirt *right now.*

No matter how carefully I reached over him and tugged, the material had no give. Dominic was simply too large. Too masculine. Too weighed down by the heavy muscle his body was made up of. He was pure man, and I was turning into a woman at the end of my rope.

In determination, I lugged a knee up on the mattress, sinking into it for better leverage as I pulled. An inch finally gave, and success roared through my veins. I tugged again, awarded with another inch and had to stifle a victorious chuckle.

I would make this shirt my bitch if it was the last thing I did today.

In each of my pulls, I was *so* careful not to touch Dominic. Not a graze of his strong thighs or a brush of my stomach against his as I leaned over him. Could you imagine what a fucking predicament that would be if he woke up with the new nanny perched over him like she was trying to ride him?

God, I'd be fired. More than fired.

I'd die and *then* be fired postmortem.

And then, because I was *just* that unlucky, *just* that much of a dipshit for tempting the universe, my world flipped, and I saw the writing on my gravestone spinning with me.

My sharp gasp hit the air just as my back hit the mattress.

My eyes shot wide in my head with the sudden movement, and my heart exploded in panic. Wildfire stormed my blood, setting it ablaze with fight or flight as firm hands locked around my shoulders and pinned me down. It wasn't just the hands holding me down either. A pair of legs shackled mine on either side, nailing them tight together till I couldn't fucking move, couldn't squirm, couldn't escape.

All I could do was scream.

And I heaved back a breath to do just that when I saw storm clouds above me. Swirling. Dangerous. Swollen with wrath instead of soothing raindrops.

The menacing gray clouds sucked up all my air I was going to scream with and left me with only puffs to shake my chest. The shivers in my body vibrated the bed, my surprise and terror now a physical thing that the body overtop of mine *must* have felt.

Dominic blinked at me, and a sliver of recognition broke through the clouds.

"Kat," he breathed, shock in my name.

Not Ms. Sanders. My *name*.

And it sounded like dark chocolate tasted. Sweet, rich, and a little raw. My name was an unprocessed, unique flavor on his tongue that he was tasting for the first time.

Quick breaths worked my lungs as I stared up at him, at his sharp eyes that were staring right back at me as he caught up to the moment. Him on top of me, pinning me down to his bed like I was the prey to his predator.

"You were laying on the shirt," I huffed. "I needed it for laundry."

Dominic's eyes jumped to my fist that clutched the criminal shirt, his understanding slow-forming. A strand of hair dangled across his creased forehead in a totally uncharacteristic way, and for a moment, I was glad my arms were trapped. Or else I might have reached up and tucked the piece back in with the rest.

Or mussed the rest of it up to match. I kinda liked the wild look on him.

And God was he wild right now. Wild and alert... and threatening.

Eyes flared, dark brows slanted, mouth parted and giving me small tastes of him. He filled me up without realizing it, smelling like all of the elements combined, completely earthy and musky and addicting.

It was confusing me, making my body pliant beneath his, my muscles loose and my mind unhinged.

Unhinged enough to say dumb shit like, "In hindsight, I probably could have left the shirt for later."

Dominic watched the words form and fall from my lips, still so dazed by his own actions. His attention on my mouth dried it right out, and I licked my lips as an afterthought. Dominic's stare followed the small action, and the defined cut of his jawline ticked dangerously.

The severity of the storm clouds hovering just above me came roaring back, a different shade of darkness than before. A daunting darkness. One that dominated any and everything it wanted to.

"You shouldn't be in here," he rumbled, voice low and throaty.

Heart crashing around inside my chest, I swallowed hard. "I was bringing you the drink you asked for."

Slow awareness filled his eyes, widening them a touch. The darkness was doused just like that. His vice grip around my shoulders loosened, and he pinched his eyes shut tight.

"Right." Remorse sliced an open wound across his face. "Did I hurt you?"

The care in his thick voice made my lip twitch, and I shook my head against his pillow. "I'm not so easy to break."

Something caught along Dominic's expression, pulling his face in concentration as he gazed at me. "Good…" The word came out of him languid and low, like he was still half asleep.

He hadn't moved yet, still holding himself over me as I watched his face sail from thought to thought. Maybe if I wasn't such utter shit at reading people, I'd be able to tell what he was thinking.

But Dominic Reed was fucking hieroglyphic.

Below him, I shimmied my shoulders just barely as a tight breath wracked my lungs. The moment was starting to get weird and… hot. He was still closer than he ever should have been, and I needed him to move right now before my already-horny-for-him subconscious made too much out of this accidental moment.

Like he could read my thoughts or what the heat in my body meant, Dominic finally leaned back to his knees and passed a rough hand through his imperfectly perfect hair. "I didn't even realize I fell asleep. I'm sorry."

The space he created between us allowed me to finally take a deep breath and scooch back on the bed. My heartbeat was still pounding, and I wasn't sure it would ever stop, but I gave him a lighthearted chuckle regardless to ease the tension in the air.

"It's really okay."

He didn't look convinced, gaze still trapped by shame. "You would tell me if I hurt you, right?"

"*Jeez*, you really are a dad." That comment finally cut the apology in his eyes in half, disapproval wielding the sword. Thank fuck. "I'm *fine*, I promise."

It took him a while, but he eventually nodded with a sigh. I felt sorry looking at him, seeing every worry line back where it started. Dammit. *I* did that to him. Not his job or his wife, but me.

Should have just left the goddamn shirt alone.

Awkwardly, Dominic cleared his throat as he shifted off the bed to stand. "I apologize if I made you uncomfortable."

Following his lead, I threw my legs over the edge of the bed. "You didn't. Just took a few years off my life."

I huffed a tension-relieving laugh as I went to stand, stare focused on Dominic. It was because I was staring directly at him that I saw *and* felt the moment my foot clipped the edge of the bed, and I stumbled. His eyes rounded. My breath hitched. My stomach catapulted through to the floor I felt myself nearing.

And then he caught me, righting me back on two feet with lightning speed.

"*Woah,*" I breathed, steadying myself on his arms. *Head rush.* I blinked rapidly, fixing my focus back on Dominic who stared at me. "I swear your bed just tried to trip me."

The corner of his mouth trembled, and his shoulders relaxed some beneath my hands. "Or you weren't lying when you said you were clumsy."

"*Or* I'm just off balance from when you *manhandled* me moments ago," I jabbed back at him.

Breathy laughter pushed between my lips because I thought we were having fun. Then the ropes of muscles beneath my palms went tight, and his eyes lowered to the floor. He took his hands around my back with them.

"Again, I apologize," he replied flatly. Clipped.

His sudden change from teasing to tense felt like whiplash. I didn't like it and wanted the easy air back between us. "Where'd you learn a move like that anyway?"

I tried to ignore it as the backs of his jaw cemented down. "Self-defense training. It's a simple move to apprehend a threat."

"Does that mean you think I'm a threat?" I joked.

My eyebrows were arched in mockery, but I felt it stumble as his stare flashed to mine. Heavy. Probing. Un-fucking-readable. My lips parted with the look, and I didn't know whether I was confused or startled or both. Probably both. For a quick moment, Dominic dropped his weighted stare to my unlinked lips, and ice contoured his eyes to frozen daggers.

"No, Ms. Sanders. I don't."

Then he ducked away from me, long legs taking him several paces away. Behind his back, I openly blanched at him, dumbstruck as to what the fuck just happened. Was he mad? At me?

Shit, if he was, I had to fix things fast. I'd only been here a week, and I was not losing this job because of some accidental physical contact. It was an *accident*, but he clearly felt rattled by it.

Compliment him. Yeah, that's good. Men *loved* having their stupid egos stroked.

"Do you think you could show me how you did it?" I hurried to catch up to him before he left the room. "The move, I mean. It was so *fast*."

As I jogged up behind him, I saw Dominic's back go rigid. My steps slowed as I came around in front of him just in time to watch his Adam's apple bob like he was having trouble swallowing. "That wouldn't be appropriate for me to teach you," he spoke carefully. Deeply.

"What? Why not?"

His nostrils flared as his sharp stare snapped to mine. "Because you're my employee, and that should be enough of a reason."

Insult slapped my chest in a heat wave. I stood there, having no other choice but to sit in the stew of gross humiliation he'd just brewed. Why the *fuck* would he say something like that? And not just the words, but the way he said it. Like I was a moron for even asking.

"Uh... *okay*?"

Uh oh. I heard it in my tone before I realized it was already in motion. My temper. She was reaching out and twisting around my insides, screwing up my body so tight, I just *had* to snap.

"Well, that was super fucking awkward, so I'm gonna go."

Dominic reacted harshly—*stunned*—like he didn't expect me to say exactly what I wanted to.

"Ms. Sanders—"

"Save it." I held up a dismissive hand as I walked out, my feet picking up speed. "I've got chores to do like a good little employee."

This time, his tone was disciplining. "Ms. *Sanders*."

But I kept moving, and he didn't stop me.

Fuck that guy and *fuck* this day.

Tonight couldn't come soon enough.

EIGHT

The party house for tonight was straight out of a wannabe angsty-teen movie. Dub-step blared from the house, shaking the ground beneath my feet as I walked up the front steps with Layla. The lawn was littered with empty bottles and empty-headed drunkards who half slurred, half howled obscenities at us as we walked by.

Tonight, I would be one of those mindless drunkards.

I was so fucking pumped.

Inside, sweat-glistened bodies were everywhere, writhing to the bass of the music that vibrated the walls all around us. I didn't recognize a single face, and I smiled a toothy grin. *Good.* I wanted to get shit-faced without having to worry about what any old co-workers or idiots from high school would think about *why* I wanted to get sloppy drunk.

I just *could*, and that was the impetus for tonight.

Layla wrapped her fingers around my arm and yanked me close. "Where's Daren?"

"Fuck if I know," I yelled back over the music. "I texted him that we were here."

She nodded, giving a sweep of the mosh pit of bodies, then snapped her smokey-eyed focus back to me. "Shots?"

I scoffed back in insult. "Obviously."

Layla dragged me alongside her, our arms looped so we wouldn't get separated. I kept an eye out for a familiar buzz cut head in the sea of screaming, dancing, blitzed out of their mind people, and still didn't see Daren.

Daren's whereabouts slunk to the back of my mind as Layla and I finally made it to the kitchen, and excitement spiked in my blood as I laid my eyes on the counter. All the bad decisions I planned on making tonight cheered as I looked over the line of liquor bottles set out, mouth salivating for which one to start with.

A neon pink shot glass being handed to me interrupted my sightline.

"What is it?" I asked, taking it from Layla.

"Vodka, I think."

"Fuck, I *hate* vodka."

"It's free. You'll love it."

Groaning, Layla and I clinked our plastic glasses together and kicked back the shots.

Immediately, my head jerked back with the foul taste incinerating my taste-buds. I bared my teeth as I swallowed and dropped my tongue out of my mouth like the air could dry the awful taste off my tongue.

"Nope. Nope, not better if it's free."

A none too pleased frown sat on Layla's lips, and she nodded. "There's gotta be Jack or José somewhere in this house."

"Yeah, I'm in a tequila kind of mood anyway."

"You know—" Her doe-like brown eyes cast a glance down my front. "Tequila makes your clothes fall off, and you're not wearing much to begin with."

She had a point. Since I never really got to go out, I splurged on my look tonight a *tad* bit. I deserved to, though. I deserved one night of getting dolled up and wearing those high-waisted, black shorts I rarely ever touched and curling my hair. I deserved lace tights. I deserved this little red crop top that Layla lent me last year and to dye my lips the same sinful red.

I *deserved* to feel fucking good about myself, right?

"Is it too much?" I asked with a wrinkled nose.

Layla jerked her head back, eyes wide. "Hell no. You look fucking hot."

"I'd have to agree," a voice purred in my ear, hands sliding around my bare waist. I'd have jumped out of my skin and slapped wherever the voice came from if I hadn't recognized it.

"You finally found us." I craned around to see Daren and his stare that was plastered down my shirt. He hummed, sliding his hands down to my ass.

"I did." Then his face was gone as he called to someone behind him. "I told you she was here, dickhead."

My stare flew to find a shaggy, blonde-haired man with his hand gripping onto Daren's shoulder and his eyes on me. *All* of me. His mouth was agape like a goddamn fish, and an immediate wave of hatred went off beneath my skin. *Daren*, however, had the stupidest grin on his face as he let this dude eye-fuck me to his dick's content.

"*Hey.*"

Pervy snapped his liquored up gaze to me, squeezing Daren's shoulder. "Who the fuck are you?" I demanded.

"I'm who the fuck's house this is," he laughed, lust weighing his hazy eyes back down my body. "There's *no* way you're with Daren."

Out of the corner of my eye, I caught Layla giving both Daren and Pervy the stink eye.

"She is, man!" Just to prove it, Daren grabbed a handful of my ass, and I yelped, punching him in the shoulder. "Tell him, babe."

Side-eyeing him with daggers, I brushed his hand from my ass. "Yeah. I'm dating this dipshit. Happy?" I turned my head up to Daren, and his lips slanted into a cocky grin.

"I could have gone without the dipshit part but yeah, I'm happy."

"Good. Now, let's go so Layla and I can kick your ass at beer pong."

Pervy let out a riotous noise, egging on the challenge I'd laid at Daren's feet. Layla cheered too, calling out that she was running to grab us another shot before we started the game. Daren hovered over me, hands finding the dips of my waist as a smirk found his lips.

"I see my kitty kat came out to play tonight, didn't she?"

Tilting my head back with a soft laugh, I leaned into his chest until my lips met his ear. There, I grazed his lobe until I felt a shiver run the length of his body, and then I whispered. "No. She came out to *win*."

Three games later, and Daren was being a little bitch in the corner of the room.

He was fine after he lost the first game. He was a little less fine after the second loss, but still kept his cool. After the third loss, however, he knocked over the last remaining cup of theirs and splashed beer all over the place, including on Layla and I.

Fire erupted up my throat as I spewed a few choice words at him before Layla ushered me away and to the bathroom to clean ourselves up. Fucking Daren. You know what? Anastasia was right. All men *were* babies. That and sore losers.

So what if I was a sore winner and danced every time they lost and we won? That wasn't the point.

The point was that Daren sucked, and I needed more alcohol. Since we didn't lose a single game, Layla and I were *far* too sober by the end of it. After we cleaned the stench of beer off of us in the bathroom and fixed our makeup, we went on the hunt for that tequila we wanted earlier.

And *boy*, did we find it.

We found twelve shots of it divided unevenly between the two of us.

It landed us on the front porch that was mostly deserted by now, passing the emptying bottle of Jose back and forth, spilling our drunken guts out to each other.

"I missed you *so* fucking much, Kit Kat." Layla plopped her head in my lap, staring up at the stars as I stared down at her and her three eyes. Fuck, four? They were moving too fast for me to count. "I wished you worked at the store still. I'd suck everyone in management off if it got you your job back."

Laughter peppered up my throat and drifted off into the night air. "What about Scott?"

"I'd do it."

"Tony?"

"There is not a dick there I will not suck for you."

"Patrick?"

She paused.

"You don't even have to bribe me to do that one."

Running my fingers through her soft hair, I curled a piece around my pointer finger, the onyx black of her hair contrasting against my skin. "I appreciate the offer, Lay. You're the MVP ride or die."

"That's right. I'd fucking die for you."

"Then I would just have to die with you, because I can't imagine life without you."

"Oh my god!" Layla shot up off my lap, locking her hazy excitement on me. "Then we could be ghosts together and haunt people and shit!"

"Oh fuck, I would draw so many dicks on bathroom mirrors when people were showering."

Layla cackled in return, throwing her head back. "That's like, the dumbest thing you could do as a ghost."

"Hey! Don't judge my style of haunting. I'd draw *really* small dicks. Like four inchers. Now that's fucking terrifying."

Layla blinked at me, a seriousness drawn into her face. "I have chills."

"Told ya."

After a few seconds, a groan came from Layla, and she clutched her stomach. Worry piqued in my head as I watched her and wondered if she'd hit her limit for the night. Thankfully, she seemed attuned to the same thing as she struggled to stand up and find her footing.

"I'm gonna go get some chips to soak some of this tequila up. You want anything?"

Shaking my head, I snatched the bottle from her hand.

"Nah, I'm set with this for now."

"Suit yourself," she mumbled, staggering into the house in search of food.

The front door closed behind her, the pulsing music turning to a muffle again. Sighing, I laid my head back against the hand railing of the porch stairs and tightened my grip around the neck of the tequila. A breeze nipped past, icing my blood, and I tipped back another swig until the burn of alcohol warmed my chest.

It wasn't cold outside. Not even a little, but night time always made me cold. No matter if it was 100 degrees out, the lack of sun always left me shivering.

Plus, I kind of liked the numbness being drunk brought to my veins.

I liked to imagine the alcohol swirling like ribbons through my body and cutting off circulation to everywhere but my heart. I didn't feel my fingers or my toes. I didn't feel the goosebumps riding my skin. I didn't feel my problems or internal aches like the constant sting they were.

I was just numb and happy and floating.

Even if just for a few hours.

In a roundabout way, I knew I was lucky that I couldn't drink often. I liked the numbness way too much to ignore the addiction genes that ran through my veins. Every now and again was doable. Sustainable.

Safe.

Down the street, a movement caught my lazing stare. I squinted, but no amount of narrowing my vision helped to focus it. My eyes were half-full of tequila, and anything that wasn't right in front of my face was drowned out to a blur in it.

All I could make out were swipes of dimly lit houses down the road and the street lamps that lit them. Tall globes of light. They each looked like their own moon, glowing sharply against the stretch of black earth. At that thought, I reached my head back all the way to the sky, rooting out the real moon with my half drunk eyes.

"Moooon," I cooed, sing-songy and soft. "Where the fuck are you?"

Laughter sputtered out of my mouth at myself. *Fucking weirdo.*

Then I remembered the movement down the street like it was a shiny object that nabbed my attention again. I cast my gaze back down to it, and it was closer than before, and it was *actually* shiny. Big and shiny and white and black and—

"Oh fuck," I breathed. Sharp dread stabbed my stomach, and I shot up off the porch steps. My hand slapped on the handle of the front door, and I threw it open with a devastating holler.

"Cops! Cops are here!"

The blasting music swallowed my screams to the masses, but a few party goers heard my cries and looked right at me, terror holding their muscles still.

"Go! Fucking move!" I yelled, pushing my way into the throng of bodies.

The further I got and the more I screamed, the more I started to see people jump into action, spreading the news like wildfire. I could see it flurrying through the crowd and scorching everyone's fun. Some brushed it off with an eye roll, but others like me, who knew they were way more fucked up than they were legally allowed to be, panicked, and that's when hell broke loose.

People were running, jumping, hiding in the bathroom. Those above the legal drinking age were trying to calm those of us that weren't and were about to be busted. The music came to a screeching halt and all it left were loud voices toppling one over another, crying, and lots of panic.

"Layla! *Daren*!"

My eyes flew in every which direction searching for the two of them. People were scattering, tripping over one another like cattle trying to not be the one caught by the wolf that invaded their land.

I stumbled into the living room, heart slamming in my eardrums as I pulled back another breath to scream for Layla and Daren one last time. That air choked in my throat as I finally landed sights on one of them, and a fury set off in my blood so vicious, it overruled the alcohol.

"Are you fucking kidding me?!"

Daren didn't hear me—couldn't hear me, in fact. He was too busy getting his ass through a window and stranding me here *even though* he was twenty-two and wouldn't be in trouble.

Unlike me.

"*Asshole*," I cursed under my breath.

Clamour went off towards the front of the house, followed by a booming voice. "Everyone stay put!"

Fuck no.

This would not be how tonight ended. Not for me. I was not about to be arrested on the first night I let loose and acted my age in Lord knows how long. No, I was getting out of here, and I was getting out of here now.

"Layla, you sneaky bitch, I'm leaving you in five seconds if you don't come out!"

Nothing but dwindling chaos met my call, and I waited until I couldn't wait anymore.

A mixture of determination and guilt trampled my chest, but Layla was a big girl and twenty-one already. Plus, she didn't live too far away and could run there if she really wanted. She was fine, and I had to focus on myself.

On getting the fuck outta there. *Now.*

I bolted around corners and flashed past the kitchen, thanking the heavens that I chose only slightly heeled combat boots for this outfit. They were perfect for running, perfect for escaping a cozy night in jail.

My mind was pumping fast, intertwining actions and thoughts together surprisingly well as I diverted around furniture and headed for the back of the house where the authoritative voice was *not*.

Adrenaline rushed my lungs as I spotted a door against the furthest wall of the house that had to lead outside. I raced for it, tearing the thing open and was smacked in the face with fresh air. Fresh air and freedom.

"Yes!" I took the steps down the backstairs so fast, my feet were a blur of persistence. I hadn't been in the backyard yet, but it was an open space with stringing lights all over the place, knocked over lawn chairs, and shadows of retreating partygoers.

Breaking into a sprint, I dodged the fallen chairs on the lawn and even jumped over one for the hell of it. Pride cinched up my cheeks as I laughed.

"I'm one *skilled* drunk motherfucker."

There were houses on either side of the one I'd just come out of, and I swooped right to make a final break for it. Heart pounding, wind breaking across my face, alcohol pumping my blood faster and faster, my legs carried me around the corner of the house to where I could finally see the empty street. Finally see freedom.

And then, out of the shadows at the end of the narrowed pathway appeared an even bigger shadow. One with a glint of a badge settled across his chest.

My feet skidded in the grass, heart striking a loud bang between my ears.

My grin slipped and crashed. Fear gripped my entire body in a searing burn, and I spun without looking back, tearing into the grass with my heel and took off in the other direction.

Only to be pulled back by a jarring gasp as I saw that the huge shadow had a friend, one that was waiting with his arms out on either side, ready to catch me if I made a break for it. Clammy horror poured through every cell, every nerve, every inch of me until I was heaving terror-filled breaths.

No. No. No. No.

"Ma'am, stay where you are."

That came from the shadow's friend in front of me, his face illuminated by an overhead motion sensor light that came on as soon as he stepped beneath it. The spotlight was unflattering on the rounded edges of his face, revealing a man pudgier than he originally appeared.

I could probably out run him.

My heel tipped upwards with the thought, and the police officer in front of me watched me do it. "That would be a really stupid thing to do, Ma'am."

More stupid than getting caught and arrested for underage drinking when I was solely responsible for my younger sister? Not even close.

I *had* to run. There was no other choice *but* to run. I felt trapped—cornered. No, I was in fact both trapped *and* cornered with no foreseeable way out that didn't involve a magical carpet appearing out of thin air.

Stupid fucking fairytales and their false expectations.

"Ma'am, hands behind your back." The cop in front of me trudged closer. I jumped back, feet feeling like they were lit with sparklers just dying to shoot off.

"I'm 18!" I cried.

"Don't you mean 21?"

Fuck! I was too drunk for this. "Yes! Sorry. Slip of the tongue."

"Where's your I.D?"

"It's, uh... in my car."

The overweight cop rolled his eyes at my lie and shook his head, reaching into his belt to pull out his handcuffs.

This can't be happening.

Dread pushed up and down on my chest, and my fingers twitched as he got closer. The flash of handcuffs blinded any logic I had left at the moment, and all I could see was Charlotte. Her round face. Her sweet eyes. Her crushing disappointment in me when I didn't pick her up from Mrs. Sharon's tomorrow because I was stuck in jail.

No. I refused. I fucking *refused* to put the same sorrow in her eyes that our mother put there daily. I had to try. I had to run. I had to run for Charlotte.

A feral cry tore through my throat as I dug my toes into the dirt and twisted around, ducking to dodge the huge shadow behind me.

A flash of the empty black road was as far as I got.

Two large hands caught my shoulders and shoved me back, holding me in place with a stiff grip. A ferocious cry split between my lips as I thrashed in the shadow's tight grasp, baring my teeth as he clamped down harder around my bare arms.

From above came the shadow's voice, ominous and dark like a shadow's should be. "I suggest you stop trying that."

"Get your hands *off* of me," I growled, shaking myself back and forth in his grip.

Breath tickled the top of my head as the shadow spoke again. "Put yours behind your back first."

Electrified rage shook my bones until they felt like they could rupture and slice through this man with its splinters. How dare he sound so arrogant, so smug, while he ruined my life *just* because I wasn't twenty-one yet.

The tequila running through my blood tangoed in a poisonous concoction with my temper, and I reared my head back to spit the vile result at him. "Suck my dick, you—"

Every single insult I had locked and loaded tumbled back down my throat. Bafflement dropped my lips apart as I scanned the shadow's familiar face and realized I knew his deep voice too. And those eyes.

There was no mistaking those eyes.

"Kat?"

All of me trembled as he said my name again, vibrating in shock just as it had hours ago. Dominic's eyes worked across my face in slow lines, taking me in as I did the same to him.

"You know her, Reed?" the other officer asked.

"Sort of." Dominic's answer was a low, even mumble. He was still studying me, looking down at me as if he had a million questions and he could crack me open and suck out the answers. The intensity of his stare crept an unhealthy dose of anxiety into the fiber of my bones, and I squirmed beneath his gaze.

"I've got a couple in my squad car already. You wanna bring her in?"

Horror flared inside of me, and I knew it made it up to my face because of how Dominic reacted. That razored jaw clicked. Those eyes smoldered. The hold he had around me grew punishing.

"Yeah. This one's mine."

NINE

"So, does this mean I'm fired?"

Dominic sighed but didn't answer.

We'd been driving for less than a couple minutes, but the silence made it feel like hours. Hours trapped inside my boss's police vehicle after he caught me committing the dumbest crime. A few more months, and this wouldn't have been a big deal.

Had I said that I hated being young, yet?

Bored, agitated, and drunk, I pulled my legs up in the front seat and ran my fingers over the soft lace of my tights to distract myself from the brooding man next to me. I'd never been in a police car before, and I wasn't so sure the 'criminals' were supposed to sit up in the front, but that's where Dominic sat me. Tossed me, actually.

He threw me in the front seat, slammed the door, and locked me inside with him and his downright glowering energy.

The inner workings of the car were actually sort of fascinating. All sorts of buttons and knobs glowed like neon candies, and I wanted to touch them all and see what they did. There was a laptop-looking thing in the center console area, and I cocked my head at it.

Without thinking, I lunged forward in my seat.

"What does this do?"

"Wait—"

"Oh shit!" I gasped in shock. Red and blue flashing lights strobed around us, the signature police siren singing along to the beat. "This is so cool!"

Just as quickly as it started, the fun was over.

"Don't touch anything in here." Dominic's scold was biting, and I twisted my neck at his tone.

Then I flipped the siren on again.

Thunder clapped in his eyes as he flashed them over to me.

"Ms. Sanders, watch yourself," he warned, grinding my name through his teeth.

He reached out and flicked the switch back. God, and I should have stopped. His patience was tested, and my luck was shot for the night. Yet, shoulda, woulda, coulda... the tequila riding in my blood carried my hand back over to where it was ordered not to be.

"No." Siren on.

"Yes." Siren off.

"Stop doing that!" Siren on.

"It's my car!" Siren off.

"Mr. Reed!" Huffing, I reached out once more to play my turn, except it appeared Dominic had had enough of our little game. In an instant, the car came to a jerking halt, and a warm hand caught my wrist.

In the time it took me to gasp back a flurry of curse words, an unmistakable clicking echoed through the car.

My words paused. My head snapped back. My jaw fell through the floor.

"Did you just handcuff me to your car?"

I yanked at my wrist that was now thrust back and locked to the metal barricade that separated the front and the backseat.

"You didn't give me much of a choice."

A groan pulling through my mouth, I leaned back and pinched my fingers as tiny as they could to try and slip out of the metal cuffs. I pushed at it with my free hand and grit my teeth as I struggled, alcohol dulling the pain of my crushing bones and peeling skin.

Eventually, I fell back into my seat with an exhausted exhale, chest rising and falling like I'd run a marathon in here.

"I was just having fun," I grumbled into the passenger window.

Stupid rules. Stupid cops. Stupid Dominic Reed.

"Ms. Sanders, don't pout," he clipped.

His short order dove my eyebrows together and my gaze down. Sure enough, my bottom lip had jutted out on its own accord, and I curled it back with a snarl.

"Why not?"

"Because you're not a child."

I shifted towards him, facing his profile head on. "Isn't that why you arrested me though? Because I'm a *child* who can't drink alcohol yet?"

His hands fisted around the wheel, knuckles breaking white and fingers twisting.

"I didn't arrest you." He quickly tagged on, "Even though I should."

"Are you going to?"

A strong beat.

"No."

Relief deflated the balloon of worry holding my breath still in my lungs. Tonight was a huge, huge fuck up, but at least there was that. Releasing a steady sigh through my nose, I rested my head back on the window while keeping an eye on Dominic's profile.

Did he have to be *so* good looking? Honestly, it was offensive how exquisite he was.

His nose was strong and straight, and I could see long lashes silhouetted in each street lamp we passed as he drove. I already knew his lips were perfect, but this angle solidified it. Supple and full and totally fucking kissable. Every few seconds, there was a painful-looking clench to his jawline that I was pretty certain had been carved from marble. The tension knotted together his high cheekbones in a periodic pulsing as he was swallowed up by thoughts in his head.

He spent a lot of time there—in his head.

"Were you there by yourself?" he questioned.

Keeping my eyes on him, I shook my head. "No. I went with my best friend."

"Did she make it out okay?"

His fishing for information with a simple question almost made me smile. Dominic Reed was clever. I didn't say my best friend was a female, but he wanted to know, and now he would.

"Hope so. She..." Confusion hollowed out my voice, the background of where we were catching my attention behind Dominic's head. I perked up in my seat. "Wait, where are we going?"

"You need food," he said simply, turning the wheel with one hand. The car rocked as we peeled off the road and into a Burger King parking lot.

A flummoxing array of emotions slapped my chest at once, and I felt dizzy. My head swirled, and I held my breath until a familiar weed stuck out of the field of disarray, and I plucked at it and ran my mouth with it.

"I don't need you to get me food. I'm not destitute," I snapped at him.

Irritation burned along his sculpted cheeks. "No, but you are intoxicated."

"I don't need *food*."

"Fine, then *I* need food." His hands around the wheel flexed, knuckles bleeding of color. "If I get extra and you happen to want it, have at it."

Dumbfounded, I stared at him with such a heavy wariness in my gaze, my eyes felt tired from the effort.

He was... strange. Yeah. Dominic Reed was strange. An enigma of peculiar kindness hidden behind frostbitten eyes. He yelled at me earlier in his bedroom, then busted me for underage drinking, and now wants to buy me food to sober me up?

Pick a lane, *Dom*.

He pulled around through the drive-thru and up to the order box.

"Hi. I'll get two number one's, just the burgers for both. No combo."

A squeak cracked between my lips before I could stop it. Dominic slid a heavily unamused glance my way, arching an eyebrow at me.

Holding eye contact, he tagged on in a dry tone, "Actually, can I get fries with one of them?"

I beamed despite my sour mood ten seconds ago, and he closed his eyes with a soft exhale.

"What to drink, sir?"

"Dr. Pepper!" I called to the woman in the box, leaning over Dominic.

"*Water*," Dominic cut in. My mouth popped open to fight and ask him why the hell I couldn't have Dr. Pepper when he snipped my vocal cords with a bullish glare.

"You need *water*."

Mockery pulled my eyebrow to an arch. "I thought I needed food?"

As close to him as I was, the flutter of his eyelashes as he processed my banter was subtle, but read so vividly. He liked it. In fact, he was holding back how much he enjoyed it. Pride swelled my chest as I scanned him up close, wondering what else I could read about him from this angle.

"You need both." And then he tacked on yet another order with a gesture of his steel eyes. "And to get back in your seat."

"So bossy," I muttered, lowering myself back.

I watched him closer this time, not missing the quick dance of his eyelashes as he held down the corner of his mouth. Though my mind was foggy, a new and spontaneous goal for tonight formed as I eyed him.

Make. Dominic. Laugh.

One *genuine*, belly-aching laugh as loud as the thundering clouds his eyes were made of.

After we got our food, we pulled off into a spot in the parking lot so we could both eat. Turned out the worker had gotten confused with our bickering and gave us both a water bottle and a giant Dr. Pepper—

Which Dominic took for himself. Apparently I had to 'hydrate' or some shit.

"God, I would fuck this burger so hard," I groaned, mouth full of beef and lettuce. Dominic slid me a suspicious glance, resting an elbow back on the ledge of his window while he held his burger in his other hand. He'd just barely angled himself towards me, and I scoffed at his judgemental gaze.

"What? Don't pretend like you wouldn't." I tore into another bite of the beef.

Trying to stifle a smile, he said, "Just eat, Ms. Sanders."

He opened his mouth and settled a huge bite between his teeth, eyes on the trees looming in front of the car. The way he ate, his hard jaw working in slow, paced motions, was sort of mesmerizing. His dusted cheeks hollowing out with every oversized chew, pillowy lips pursed just so.

What *was* it about this man and the way he ate that was such a turn on?

I shifted in my seat, heat slicking between my thighs and the leather seat. The heat *he* made me feel specifically. His heat was different from others I'd felt. Somehow it was more... feverish. Sticky and sweltering.

And I guess it was because I was still partially inebriated that I said exactly what was on the forefront of my mind.

"Your mouth is so... *nice.*"

Dominic blinked a startled look over to me. "Excuse me?"

"Yeah. When you eat it's just, like, such a *manly* mouth. It's big and strong and—"

"I think you should stop talking," he interrupted sharply.

"Why?"

He struck a big hand over the Dr. Pepper and brought it to his lips. "Because you have a habit of saying inappropriate things, Ms. Sanders."

Dominic wound those perfect lips around the straw and sucked back the dark drink. Watching him, I knew it was only because my blood was polluted by bad decisions, but all I could think about was stealing the soda and putting my mouth where his had been to see if he tasted sweeter than liquid candy.

I bet he tasted like Winter, actually. Fresh and minty, and so cold, he'd turn my desire into something visible. A crisp fog of hot and cold that would muffle the line between us.

"I'm pretty sure we obliterated the line of appropriate and not for today, *sir,*" I rasped.

Dominic turned stiff. "And I apologized. It won't happen again."

"Good." In my seat, I crossed my thighs to put pressure at my core as I remembered him over me, pressing into me, staring at me like he could devour me. "I don't like being manhandled unless it's going somewhere good."

As I readjusted my position, the metal shackle around my wrist tugged at my skin. The bite stung, and a hot breath stole between my lips as I peeked up at the cuffs. I couldn't tell anymore what I was drunk on between the tequila and lust, but either way, my mouth was unhinged from my brain in every sensible way.

"Like these handcuffs. I've always wanted someone to cuff me." Impulse tugged my lips up as I batted a heady glance back to him. "I just never thought that someone would be my boss or in front of a Burger King."

"Ms. Sanders. Stop talking." Dominic was barely holding onto his breath; the strain he was exuding showed in the tense cords in his thick neck. He wouldn't look me in the eye either.

God, I wanted to laugh. He was so easy to rile up.

"Why? Is it bothering you?"

His jaw tensed at the same time the corner of his mouth twitched.

"Very much."

"Hm. Couldn't tell by the little smirk on your mouth."

"Stop looking at my mouth."

"Stop telling me what to do."

A fit of giggles stuck in my chest as Dominic groaned aloud and changed the subject.

"Do you know the people that threw the party tonight?"

Slouching back against my seat, I stuck a fry in my mouth. "No, but my dipshit of a boyfriend does."

Dominic was in the middle of crushing the leftover paper from around the burger into a ball when his fists stalled for only a second. Just one faint moment. He picked up like normal so fast, I forgot it even happened.

"Was he there, too?"

"Yeah, he left me behind." Rolling my eyes, I brought the bottle of water to my lips. "Caught him hauling ass out a window when I went looking for him after you guys got there."

Dominic grunted—a truly self-satisfied sound. "Sounds like a real catch."

"Oh, and Heather's a fucking walk in the park," I barked in laughter.

There always came a point in my intoxication where I said something I shouldn't. Again, why I was lucky I didn't get to drink like this much. I had a nasty habit of sticking my foot right through my mouth, and I was crap at dislodging it.

Like right about now.

I paused. He paused. The world around us stopped moving. Regret sunk my eyes closed with a sigh.

Fuck.

If I wasn't getting fired before, I sure as shit was now.

"I shouldn't have said that." I shook my head, the burger in my stomach rolling uncomfortably. "I'm sorry. I think the alcohol is still talking and... that wasn't cool to say. I didn't mean it."

The silence that lingered in the car was so suffocating, I almost bolted and made a run for it just to escape it. I couldn't look at him. The muscles in my neck literally wouldn't budge to turn my head in his direction.

Dominic's heavy voice vibrated the air between us. "You're a terrible liar, Ms. Sanders."

This time, it was *my* jaw that clenched like a fist. Dammit. How did he always know when I was lying? Was I really that bad at it?

"Okay, so I did mean it, but I shouldn't have said it." I dared a quick glance at him. He was staring straight ahead, stiff as stone. "That was—that's not my place to say."

"You're right. It's not." Fuck, his voice was leaden, his tone punishing. Silence followed. Loaded, ugly, stomach churning silence that made me want to scream and—

"Doesn't mean you're wrong though."

My head snapped toward his guilty voice. There was a knitted frown between his eyebrows and on his mouth, making him seem angrier than ever before. Well, in the week I'd known him.

I had the urge to get closer to him again just to see if it was really anger stringing up his expression, or if maybe the rage was just the front man. The one that was easiest to recognize and name, but was just for looks and easy to sell. Maybe there was another emotion to it that didn't want credit, quietly composing his reactions or humming new melodies for his soul to sing to.

I highly doubted that Dominic Reed was a man as simple as anger, but it was all he allowed to play on his face as he flashed those storming eyes over to me.

"Don't look so shocked. I know how my wife can be."

In the cocktail of moonlight and street lights, Dominic's eyes looked almost silver.

Fucking stunning.

"Was she always like this?" I heard myself asking. A seriousness that wasn't there before settled inside the car, and neither of us moved or made any unnecessary noise.

"No." Certainty bloated that one word from his mouth, but fell away as he shut his heavy stare. "Or maybe she was and I just didn't notice. I don't really know."

"How'd you two meet?"

I didn't care about Heather. I didn't even fucking *like* Heather, but I liked Dominic I decided. Yup. In that split second, I decided we were friends even just for tonight, and friends listened to each other's problems and made each other feel better.

That's what I wanted to do with the rest of tonight and the tail end of my alcohol confidence.

Bring the thunder clouds a ray of sunshine.

"Senior year of high school," Dominic started recalling. "She'd just moved to town and was immediately the most popular girl in school. I was the head of the baseball team and followed her around for weeks before she agreed to go out with me. We got married a few years later."

"Sounds like you were young when you got married."

His silvery eyes slid to mine. "Right around your age."

The idea of marriage *at all* turned my stomach inside out and made me sweat. The idea of it now at my age was lunacy.

"Where'd you guys go to school?" I asked.

"Nowhere near here. I'm from Georgia originally, near Atlanta. We moved here about a year ago for my work."

Dominic lowered his gaze to his hands right after that, probably looking at his wedding band and wondering where it went wrong. How he ended up talking to his nanny in the middle of the night in his police car about his marital woes.

That was the unlawful thing about love though. It didn't have rules to follow to your happily ever after. It was just mayhem. Pure madness with life-lasting consequences.

Heartbreak was inevitable—unescapable—when you checked the box that said, *'yes, I want to fall into insanity'* and gave yourself over to love. You were asking for it. Dominic asked for it when he fell in love with Heather at a stupid age, and now he was getting the full treatment that romantic love had to offer.

Disappointment. Defeat. Being forced to watch the person you love turn into some hideous version of themselves like some horror film you couldn't wake up from. People can fuck your heart a thousand times over again and then walk away like they never knew you or loved you, and *that* was romantic love.

Poor Dominic didn't want to hear that though. He wanted to hear some crock of shit pep talk, and tonight as his friend, that's exactly what I was going to give him.

"Look, you guys have been together for how long?"

"I've known her almost thirteen years. Married for nine."

"*Okay*, so that's no chump change, right?" *Even though my parents were together on and off for eighteen years and that still went in the shitter.* "If you wanna make it work, make it work. Things will get better."

Damn. I sounded a hell of a lot more convincing than I felt. Suck on that lie, Dom.

Dominic inhaled deeply, as if he was sucking down my words to process. Steadily, he blew out a doubtful, "Maybe."

"I hate maybes," I mumbled, popping a lukewarm fry in my mouth.

"Yeah?" Intrigued eyes latched onto me, and I got the feeling that he was happy to have the spotlight off of him. "Why?"

Chewing, I got comfortable against the backrest, tucking a leg up beneath the other. "I don't like anything that's not certain. I want to know if something is sure-fire or impossible so I don't waste my time."

A short breathy laugh pushed out of Dominic, bitter sounding and musing. "You're too young to consider any of your time wasted yet."

"I don't feel young."

Dominic languidly traced the backs of his knuckles over the sculpted edge of his jaw, watching me in that analytical way he often did. "Is that what tonight was about? The party?"

I opened my mouth to spill out a lie, but one look from him, and it fell flat on my tongue.

"Actually, yeah, that's dead on." I laughed. Dominic joined in with a soft chuckle.

"Speaking of age, how old *are* you?"

He tweaked up a dark eyebrow in an attempt to admonish me for my question, but I rolled my eyes and he eventually answered.

"I turned 31 in July."

"July was like two weeks ago."

"Very perceptive of you."

I scoffed. "Don't be a dick."

He laughed, but not enough.

"Do you have such fond names for all of your employers?"

"Oh yeah. You're not special."

Sitting straighter somehow, Dominic cocked a peculiar look at me. "You have no respect for authority, do you?"

"Is it that obvious?"

Reaching for the Dr. Pepper again, he shook his head. "You're many things, Ms. Sanders, and subtle is not one of them."

Oh, this was dangerous. I knew the question I was about to ask could open up a whole can of worms, but the tequila in my blood was telling me to get a little messy.

"What else am I?"

Somehow, his stare focused even tighter on me. He hummed in consideration, the sound resonating down his body, into his seat and leaching into mine. Tingles sprinkled up my legs, dancing into my lower stomach, and I fought not to fidget.

Dominic Reed overshadowed any other man I'd ever seen, and if there were Gods among us, he was definitely one of them with his unique eyes and carved features. He pursed his perfect lips, giving me every bit of his focus. "Nosy."

Then he narrowed his gaze in review, mouth tilted into a humored smirk.

"And a very bratty drunk."

I gasped as if offended, but fell into a hyper state instead. "Oh yeah? Well, you are..." I wracked my fumbling brain for the right words to describe him. "Brooding. And-and mysterious and *tall*. Why are you so tall?"

Okay, maybe I was still a little drunk.

"I'll work on it," he chuckled softly, watching me closely.

"Good." I sat back, satisfied with myself.

We kept eyes on each other, fully facing each other now with our backs against the doors. A sudden burst of impulse shot through me, and I reached for the Dr. Pepper sitting between us and took it. He didn't stop me. He let me put my lips where his had been, let me taste his candy-coated flavor, and kept his fixed focus on me while I did it.

After a moment, he added, "You're also very good with Maya."

Mouth around the straw, I raised an eyebrow. "Are we doing compliments now?"

"Just that one."

Licking my lips, I leaned forward. "I've got one."

Dominic probably didn't realize it himself, but his gaze tracked my tongue as it swiped across my mouth.

"Yeah?"

I nodded, teasing the straw against the plumpest part of my bottom lip. "I wasn't surprised when you said you were a baseball player."

Pride warmed my chest as he warred with his better self, losing each time his eyes dropped to my mouth. His jaw cemented in place and his voice came out thicker.

"How come?"

I cracked a wily grin. "Because you've got the proper ass of one."

A belly-deep, slap of laughter exploded from his chest, blanketing the entire inside of his patrol car. Excitement sliced up my throat as I gasped and beamed so hard at him, it felt like my teeth were actually shining. Lines crinkled adorably next to his eyes as the richest sound I'd ever heard tumbled out of him.

Now *this* was the full-blown smile I'd been searching for.

And he had fucking dimples too.

Damn him. Damn him and his adorable dimples.

"Those words never should have come out of your mouth." He smoothed a hand down his chest, as if trying to stabilize his laughter. It was infectious. *He* was infectious and poisoned my inebriated heart with fluttering electricity to see him smile, and I mean *really* smile.

Once his shoulders stopped shaking, Dominic tipped me a charming glance beneath thick brows. "Has anyone ever told you that you have a way with words?"

Breathing out the jittering energy he inspired, I lent my attention to my trapped wrist. "See, if that were true, I would have been able to talk myself out of these handcuffs by now. Speaking of which, I think I've learned my lesson." I yanked twice at my restraints, stretching my fingers out to keep circulation moving.

Dominic shifted with a labored sigh, fishing keys out of his back pocket. They flashed a glint in the palm of his hands as he raised them towards my locked wrist. He stopped just short of releasing me.

"Do you promise that you'll be good and not touch anything?"

Using my free hand, I signed a dramatic X across my chest. "Cross my heart and hope to die."

A smug grin I'd been holding down wrestled partially free as he swept a surveying glance over my face, spending just a hair longer on my mouth. He shook his head at me.

"Smartass," he mumbled.

"*Cursing*, Mr. Reed? How unprofessional."

Barely sparing me a look, he made quick work of the handcuffs. "I think you'll survive."

"But my innocent ears."

I stole back my wrist, rubbing the red-ringed skin with my fingers as I kept attention on Dominic. On the way his face grew stern and how his moonlight eyes eclipsed, darkening in seconds as his husky voice did the same.

"There's nothing innocent about you, Ms. Sanders."

The intensity of his staring stuttered my fingers' movements, and I might have stopped breathing too. He looked so *pissed* again, but pissed in a different kind of way. Like he was mad at me for being there, sitting there, taking up his air with my lungs.

Instead of feeling bad about it or threatened, I wanted to soak it up more. I wanted to get in his face and steal every bit of oxygen from him until it was all mine and he had to ask me for permission to breathe. I wanted to test his limits and see how far I could push him before he pushed back, and that wasn't even the alcohol talking.

That was just me.

"I don't know if I should be offended or turned on by that," I spoke truthfully, feeling both reactions sitting in my stomach like a time bomb.

Dominic paused, exhaling a stiff breath. Gray eyes jumped to mine. "*Line.*"

"What?"

He leaned back in his seat, putting obvious distance between us. "Every time you say something that's over the line of what's acceptable to say in our working relationship, I'm going to start saying *line*."

Hm. Fair. He wasn't wrong about my habit to say shit I shouldn't, but he was wrong about my ability to care about it. I was bad with people, but I was worse with men.

"Trying to keep me in my place, huh?"

The wind must have been blowing outside because shadows danced across Dominic's face at that exact moment, highlighting the sharpness of his cheekbones and casting those eyes of his pitch black.

"Something like that."

TEN

"Where am I dropping you off tonight?"

"Just right here is fine."

We left the Burger King parking lot about five minutes ago and had been driving aimlessly in silence ever since. The quiet wasn't completely quiet since the sky was talking in occasional rumbles of thunder and whistling winds.

Night rain was my favorite type of rain.

Dominic shot me a look. "This is the side of the road."

"Your detective skills are *sharp*."

I was ready for our night to end though. The carbs from the burger and fries soaked up every last drop of alcohol, leaving me tired and weak instead. I still had a long night ahead of me walking all the way back to Layla's house, and I needed as much of a head start as I could get before the rain hit.

"Just pull over here." I placed my hand on the passenger door handle and waited for the car to slow to a stop.

It didn't.

"I'm not letting you off on the side of the road."

"Why not? I've walked by myself at night tons of times."

"*What?*" Dominic hissed. The sudden change over from adamant to livid made me do a double take in his direction. His dark eyebrows had slanted in and his mouth turned grim. "Don't do that anymore. If you need a ride, call someone."

"There's not always someone to call. Plus that was last year when I didn't have a car for a couple months."

Dominic nearly slammed on the breaks. "You walked by yourself at night for a couple *months?*"

"Kinda had to, yeah."

"Do you know how dangerous that is? How stupid?"

Offense hit hard and fast, twisting any enjoyment I'd found with him tonight into a tight ball of electric fury. "Okay, I don't need Dad Lecture 101. I still had to go to work and make money. That's not stupid. That's being responsible." *Dick.*

His hands on the wheel flexed outwards, like he was radiating too much rage to possibly contain.

"Promise me you won't do that again." His voice was at least two octaves lower than usual.

My head snapped to him, defiance breathing life into my lungs. "What? *No.*"

Thundering eyes flashed to me, lightning striking a fire in his pupils. "You have no idea what or who is out there or how quickly you could be gone and never seen again. Is that what you want?"

The match was in his debasing tone and lit my temper ablaze. In no time at all, I was roaring.

"I *want* to get out of this fucking car," I seethed, latching onto the passenger door handle—

Only to feel it lock milliseconds before opening.

"I'm not letting you walk home, Kat."

"It's after work hours. You don't get to *let* me do anything." I plucked the lock back up, winding my fingers around the handle when I felt *and* heard him set the trap again. Snarling, I went to tug the lock out of place again, but this time, it didn't move. Not a goddamn inch.

"Did you just use fucking child locks on me?"

Insult vibrated my voice, vibrated my entire body as I fisted the door handle and yanked. I pulled and jammed it, shoving my shoulder against the window again and again. The car was rocking with my efforts and the feeling of being trapped spidered over every inch of my skin. Stinging, pinching, searing desperation like an open knife wound across my chest, spilling out my screams.

"Unlock the fucking car!"

Dominic didn't respond. Didn't move a fucking muscle.

"Isn't this considered kidnapping on some level?" I lashed out, sinking low in my seat, arms folded.

"I'm not kidnapping you. I'm keeping you safe."

"Sounds an awful lot like something a kidnapper would say."

Even though I wasn't looking at him, I could imagine he was clenching his jaw, acting all exasperated and broody.

"Just tell me an address to drop you off at, and I'll happily take you there."

Frustration crawled up my throat, shaking my vocal cords as I sank my cheek against the window. Cold seeped through my skin, pulling goosebumps to break the surface as I looked outside at the passing night. Silhouettes of overhanging trees and horizontal billboards slid by as we drove. Living here my whole life, I recognized exactly where we were, and it was about ten minutes from Layla's.

Fishing my phone out of my back pocket, the battery read at 18%, and I used the last bit of juice to send an emergency text to Layla, begging her to come get me.

"Are you texting your boyfriend?"

My shoulders caved in annoyance. And he said *I* was nosy. "No. It's my best friend who's probably not even awake still."

"What's her name so I can look up the address? I'll take you there."

Was there a chance he was just trying to do something nice? Sure. Did the thought cross my mind? Maybe. But did I want his help or trust him even slightly? Nope. I'd gotten by just fine these last few years without leaning on anyone outside of my very *small* circle, a circle that happened to consist of only two women.

Layla and Mrs. Sharon. Outside of those two women, my trust was non-exis-tent and my ability to ask for help was too. So Dominic Reed might've *seemed* like a nice guy with nice intentions, but I'd also met the devil before and he was dressed in men's clothing.

"If she's not awake, then I'm not getting in unless you wanna help me break and enter?"

Dominic let out a sigh and slapped on his blinker, turning off the road and into a random neighborhood. The car slowed as we passed residential houses all sleeping and still for the night.

"Kat, just let me take you home."

"I don't want to go home."

"Why not?"

Funny story. Telling my police officer boss that I didn't want to go home and deal with my heroin addict, shit show of a mother wasn't exactly on the top of my 'to-do' list.

The nights tended to be her prime time of the day. On one hand, I was grateful because Charlotte was always asleep when it happened, but on the other hand, I fucking loathed the tired routine.

Sometime between midnight and one in the morning, she'd start moving around, scraping something together to eat. Sometimes, she liked to chat if she was still soaring in the peak of the high, but that never lasted long. A few moments of drug induced affection and then came the letdown, and that's when things got ugly.

She would always cry. Every. Damn. Time.

About how sorry she was, about her addiction, about how she raised me and treated Charlotte. She'd cry big crocodile tears that were bloated with lies and false promises. I'd seen and heard it all so many times, and each time, those waterworks always ended up in a pool dedicated to one person, and it wasn't me or Charlotte.

It was our fucking father.

She'd cry. She'd moan. She'd yell, and then she'd fall asleep. This happened a few times a week, and the only part I took in anymore was making sure Charlotte slept through it and rolling my mother on her side as she slept.

I was living a goddamn fairy-tale life, I tell ya.

"It's none of your business why I don't want to go home."

My entire body jerked forward, and I choked down a gulp of air as the car slammed into park. There was a *thunk* in my chest as my heart walloped against it with the sudden stop, and I snapped my head towards the man responsible.

"What the hell?"

Dominic faced me, giving me all of his attention. Every ounce of his concentrated, penetrating, skin-prickling focus. "Either you tell me why I shouldn't take you to your house, or I take you back to the station to sleep in the holding cell for the night."

His words pulled my posture straighter, filed my temper sharper. I narrowed my fine-tipped daggers at him.

"Did you really just try to bribe me for personal information by threatening jail time?" There was the slightest stumble in his rigid browline. *Good.* "Real fucking sweet of you, Dominic."

That was the first time I used his first name, and I saw it splash across his face. Every syllable stuck to his sharp features like egg on his face and I wished it felt good. Instead, disappointment boiled in my chest and for the dumbest of reasons. Whenever I said his name in my head, it sounded so *special* rolling around up there, and I always thought saying it out loud would sound the same. Instead, it was bitter and the resonance of it was soured.

"Kat." My name was a husky plea in the deepest part of his throat. "Please just tell me where to take you if not home."

The word 'please' drew my gaze over in shock.

He was waiting for me with eyes as begging as the word he used, and it stunned my temper to a pause. The lack of anger left me cold, chills blanketing my bare arms and shaking my whole body. Dominic observed the shiver, worry knitting between his brows.

Worry that I might be cold. Confusion settled in my gut as I stared at him, a heavy fist sitting in between my heart and stomach. Any way I moved, I couldn't escape the uncomfortable feeling of his concern.

"Why won't you let me walk by myself?" I asked, sincere wonder softening my voice.

"Because I'm a cop, and I see the worst of the worst, and the worst is out there waiting for pretty girls like you to pick up off the street, and we'd never see you again."

Ignoring the fact that he just called me pretty, I let my eyes fall from his to my lap. He had a point. A good point. His good point sunk between my ribs, stabbing all the way to my back and lodging there. It was now a part of me, fusing to bones and splitting cells to make room for itself and what it meant.

What it meant *hurt*. It hurt so much, it ripped my voice down to a pathetic whisper.

"I don't need you to watch out for me."

Quietly, he spoke. "I happen to disagree."

"Can't we agree to disagree?"

"Not when it's about your safety."

Fuck. The nicer he was, the sharper the pain in my sternum became. That kind of pain was crippling to the mind *and* body. I needed to pull it out. I needed to rip out his kindness, shredding flesh and spewing blood until the gaping hole in my chest was back where it belonged. Empty and scabbed over, protected against any foreign compassion from any concerned bosses.

Tilting my head up towards the window, I leaned my face until I could see the sky above. We filled the seconds with our breathing, and I could feel him watching me while I watched the sky. Casually, I laid my finger on the button for the window, lowering it smoothly and closing my eyes as the night breeze hit.

You could smell the rain in the air tonight. Fresh and dewy, and I breathed in deep until my lungs were soaked with it.

"Looks like it's about to rain," I spoke gently.

Next to me, Dominic grunted in agreement and we left it there. I placed both hands on the opening where the window was, pushing my face out further to really suck down the flavor of the night.

That, and get a good starting grip.

Moisture was already in the air, dusting my face in a frosty mist. Again, a shiver wracked my shoulders visibly, shaking out a vulnerable exhale, and I wondered if Mr. Reed was staring at me with that same frowning worry as before.

It was with that painful thought that I tore his thorn of kindness straight out of my chest.

With a burst of energy, I hoisted myself up and out of the window, arms flailing towards the ground.

"Kat!" Dominic boomed. Adrenaline shot through my veins like explosive firecrackers as hands wound around my ankles, trying to pull me back inside the car. Growling, I kicked and thrashed and fought for freedom until my palms hit rough asphalt.

Holy fuck. I made it!

Excitement thrived through every inch of me until I felt like I was floating. Rather, I was toppling head first out of a car window, but I didn't feel the pain of falling. Didn't register the scrapes to my elbow or knees or the pebbles from the road embed in my wrist.

All I felt was free.

That was, until the slam of a car door snatched it away. Panic shot me up off the road to my feet, heavy breaths caving my chest in and out as a dark head of hair dipped out of the car, standing tall and menacing on the other side of it.

"Get back inside the car," Dominic barked, eyes hot.

I shook my head, my stare flickering up and down both sides of the street. My thoughts were flying too fast to consider which one was the better route to take, and my feet were bouncing, ready to fly on command.

"*Katerina.*"

Both my breath and head hitched up at the domineering call of my full name. A rush of something indescribable shuddered my heart as I saw Dominic at that moment, and I pulled a full, enlivened grin. Nowhere was the concern or kindness on his face anymore. Both stupid emotions had been chased away by the chill of winter that had sharpened every angle of his handsome face.

He was the physical manifestation of danger, and I was his victim of choice.

"You don't want to run from me."

"Pretty sure I do, old man," I breathed, confidence riding my tone. My entire body was soaring with it, electrified by the arrogance that I could outrun him. I was ten years younger, sprier, and bubbling with determination. He'd be winded by the end of the street.

A crack of thunder echoed above us, stealing both our gazes up to the angry sky. It was coming. I could feel it like I could feel my own skin.

"It's about to pour!" Dominic shouted. "Do you really want to get stuck in the rain?"

Leveling my stare back down to him, I smiled through the darkness. "No. I wanna dance in it."

And I took off.

The quick breeze hit my face as I ran fast as my feet would take me, slapping against pavement and zooming past rows of slumbering houses. A feral groan timed perfectly with my starting sprint, and a second later, echoes of shoes stomping against the ground trailed behind me.

The noise propelled my legs to push quicker, slicing through the black night like a flash of lightning. The thunder was right on my tail though and eating up the space between us fast. I didn't need to spare a look behind me to see where he was. I could *feel* his presence pressing against my back as if it had its own gravitational energy.

My determination snarled, pumping faster and faster, now trying to outrun not only Dominic, but the dread that was closing in as he defied my logic. According to my quick conclusion, he was older than me and hence, I would be able to outrun him, right?

Except, I didn't consider how tall he was, a fact that led to the conclusion of long legs. Long legs that were easily catching up to me. Also, the dude was *jacked*.

He clearly worked out, which meant he more than had the stamina necessary to run the distance it took to meet me.

I just didn't consider any of this until it was too late.

Burly arms swooped in front of me, clamping down over my waist and both arms. Panic engulfed my mind, submerged my blood and turned my entire body into a vessel of hysteria.

"*No*—Stop!" I cried, thrashing in his tight grip. Abruptly, my feet and the earth were no longer touching and the absence of stabilization slipped me even further off the edge "Let me go!"

"Kat, *stop*," he ground out next to my ear. But I didn't stop, *wouldn't* stop until I was either running to freedom again or shackled up in jail. Nothing and no one would make me go back to the house tonight.

"Get *off* of me!" I struggled harder as my heartbeat skyrocketed, thumping a quick tune for my mind to dance itself off a cliff to. Fingers around my shoulder caught my eye's attention, and the arm they were attached to caught my mouth's.

"Ow! Did you just *bite* me?" More shock than pain was painted through Dominic's voice, and his hold on me intensified.

Squirming against his front, I snapped back at him. "It wasn't hard. Calm down, princess."

"Oh my God—" Annoyance lathered his words. "That's *it*."

"Woah!" The world flipped along with my stomach as Dominic shifted his hold on me, and I went flying over his shoulder. My face landed at the small of his back at the same time his vice locking arms strapped around my hanging legs.

"Hey!" I pushed my hands against his back so I could see, ropes of muscles flexing beneath my palms. "What the fuck did I *just* say about manhandling?"

"Certain requests go ignored when you lose your goddamn mind on me."

"Well, excuse me for not enjoying being chased or trapped in your car!" I shouted, slamming my fists into his back over and over again as he walked with me. "I'd rather *fight* you tonight than go *home* tonight, and that's *my* choice."

"I'm not fighting you, Kat."

His words were lacerated by the clenched teeth he spoke through. Then the world was spinning again, dizziness sloshing in my head as Dominic heaved me off of his shoulder, my ass hitting a cold surface.

A sharp intake struck my lungs when a powerful hand flattened over my chest and pressed my back against the same freezing surface. Hands lashed to catch both of mine, pinning them above my head with Dominic holding them and all of me down.

"I'm detaining you," he growled over me.

Shock and dewy air punctuated my next gasp. He was so close, I couldn't fathom it. Couldn't concentrate long enough on any part of it to form a single thought about it. Not the rogue strand of nearly black hair hanging across his forehead. Not the heady hit of sugary-sweet breath that pulled and pushed from between his lips. And certainly not the lips themselves or the crazy urge I had to lean up and sink my teeth into the bottom one.

My eyes jumped back and forth between his as he loomed over me, heavy breathing rising my chest and his as one.

He had dominated every single inch of me in seconds flat, and I realized in that moment his name suited him *very* well.

A slyness rising on my lips, I breathed, "How'd you know I like it rough?"

Dominic's stare flickered with irritation. "Why are you *so* determined to make bad choices?"

Though I couldn't physically rear my head back being pinned how I was on the hood of his patrol car, I still tried.

"What the fuck is that supposed to mean?"

"Running away from a police officer, trying to walk home at night, drinking underage."

"Oh, you're right. I basically killed someone. Fucking crucify me already."

"Just because there are worse things you could have done doesn't mean any of what you've done tonight is right or even remotely smart."

"*God*," I groaned in frustration, arching my back against the hood. "Why do you even care? Why are you going through *so* much effort tonight to keep me safe and make me go home? Who says home is even safe?"

Dominic pulled back a serious look. "Is it not?"

"That's not your business!" I exploded, overwhelmed.

"As a police officer, it is."

"And as my *boss*, it's not."

A brusque sigh pushed through his nose, tickling my cheek as he observed me closely. The backs of his jaw were working hard tonight, pulsing in concentrated fractures of restraint. Slowly, he unwound his thick fingers from my wrists one by one. I laid there like a good little criminal as he peeled himself from me bit by bit, gray eyes watching me with warning.

Don't run or else.

Above us, another warning clapped loudly, and I flicked my stare from Dominic to the sky. It was completely pitch dark. The upcoming storm was a secret assassin cloaked in all black. It was blind to the naked eye, but it would get us nonetheless and drench Dominic and I from head to toe if we didn't get back inside his car.

Neither of us made the move right away.

A heated hand appeared beneath my elbow, cupping it gently. His fingers pressed against my skin in a silent sign to sit up. I did, and he helped me, sliding his hand up the length of my arm until I was sitting properly. Dominic was still close—not as close as before—but close enough that I was having trouble remembering why I was so angry at him.

Then, he reminded me so perfectly.

"You need to make better choices than you did tonight," he began, voice feather soft. "If I hadn't been helping out on patrol, you could have easily ended up spending the night in jail."

Dominic Reed really was such a *dad* in every stereotypical sense of the name. If these lectures about my behavior were any indicator, Maya was going to get *very* good at backtalk in her teenage years.

With that thought, curiosities whispered in my head about what Dominic might have been like as a teenager. Was he as straight-laced and strict as he was now, or was he a *normal* teenager who made normal teenager mistakes?

"Are you trying to tell me that you never did anything bad? Not once?"

There went his jaw again. Ticking, tensing. The thing was going to crack in half by the time he was forty. His gaze fell from mine, sitting on the hollow of my neck as his eyes clouded over to match the storm brewing above us.

"Ah, so you have," I hummed. "See? You're not so perfect."

Piercing eyes sliced back up to me. "I don't pretend to be."

Oh, but you do. You and all men.

I knew better though. I knew the knight in shining armor was fabled to fool women. I knew everyday men were weak and selfish, driven by one thing and one *hot* thing only. Dominic Reed was an everyday man, and I'd wage millions he'd bend to the will of lust like the rest of them.

"Whatcha do that was so bad, huh? Was it something that made your blood race?" I murmured, watching his pupils dilate.

Stubborn desire hitched my breath as Dominic allowed me to lean into him just enough to blur lines and brush chests. For just a second, his breath and my breath were the same thing, both tasting of Dr. Pepper and regret. I inhaled all of him, dizzy on our sweetened shame as an ache tickled up my chest that urged me to get closer. Test him. Push him.

See just how stereotypical and disappointing he was.

Surprisingly, I only made it an inch closer before two rough hands grabbed my knees and pushed us apart.

"Stop trying to divert," he hissed, mouth screwing up into a sneer. "God, in some ways you're so *textbook* and in others you're a goddamn paradox."

Puffing my chest out, I bit back. "Why are you trying to figure me out?"

"I'm not," he denied quickly.

"You *are*. Every time you look at me, I can see it. You're dissecting me, trying to work me out in your head." This time I pushed at his chest, and he didn't budge an inch. The clouds grumbled. "You're always in your head, Dominic. *Stuck* up there, and I wanna know what you've figured out about me."

His attractive face pinched together, that brooding ferocity about him radiating out and twisting my insides together as I waited for his answer. His hands on my knees were a nice distraction from the waiting. For a man who could rival the iceberg that sank the Titanic, his touch was fire. Hot, calloused flames that engulfed my knees and made everything under them look small in comparison.

Those inferno hands squeezed both my knees suddenly, ripping my focus back up to Dominic. The look waiting for me in his sculpted face was pointed, poking a hole through my bloated temper.

"I've figured out that you're a better person than getting wasted at some frat party."

As if the depleting anger was something physical, my chest deflated with a sigh. Suddenly, I was completely and utterly exhausted. I was tired of fighting, of running, of being depended on to do the right thing every second of every day.

My eyes rolled shut, and I just sat there, feeling his hands resting on my knees and nothing else. They were heavy but strong. Rooting me down to the moment.

"I just wanted one night of stupid fun," I murmured aloud but sort of hoped he didn't hear. It was a shitty thing to say. Selfish and shitty.

"To spend with a boyfriend who abandoned you the moment the party got interrupted?"

That assumption was so shallow and had me shaking my head and bunching my eyebrows together. "I don't care about him enough to let that bother me."

"Then why are you with him?" he pressed, cocking an almost peevish look at me.

I shrugged. "He's cheaper than batteries."

Dominic's lips parted and then flattened together immediately. His expression drew grim.

"Line."

Ah, but I knew better now. I *knew* his tells and watched with a ghosting smile as his eyelashes fluttered three or four times as he ducked his focus from me to the hollow of my neck again. The tremble in the corner of his mouth seemed so obvious now, too.

"Then why are you laughing?" I asked.

A sharp exhale punctuated the air, a poorly masked attempt to disguise his laughter. His hands over my knees tightened yet again.

"Because, despite all of your other infuriating qualities, you're funny." Silver eyes flashed to mine. "You're hilarious, in fact."

And he seemed upset that I was. Not *really* upset, but bothered enough to make me wanna push his buttons a little. Or a lot.

"And nosy."

His eyelids dropped a hair, hooding his moonlit stare just slightly. "And nosy."

"And bratty."

A rumble groaned in Dominic's chest as he agreed. "So goddamn bratty."

"And pretty."

The man in front of me was filling his chest with night air audibly when I spoke, so I heard the exact moment when he stopped breathing. He stole his silvery focus away from me for a moment, dropping it to his new favorite spot on my neck where the backs of his jaw stressed.

"You said it," I spoke to break the silence. "That people were out there waiting to pick up pretty girls like me."

A bolt of thunder crackled above us at the exact second Dominic put his storming eyes back on me. "I remember."

He shifted his stance in front of me, standing taller and wider somehow. I righted my posture with him, feeling an intensity enshroud him as if he was his own rainstorm. His hands on my knees began to burn too as Dominic pinned me with a look so devastating, I felt the consequence of it instantly.

"I'm very aware of how you look, Ms. Sanders."

Heat lightning struck between my legs as if Dominic controlled the elements swarming above us. I sucked back a tiny gasp, feeling so suddenly small sitting beneath him like this. Like I was a raindrop and he was all the clouds, absorbing and ruling over me.

So he'd noticed me. My body. My face. Was he noticing me right now and how my top had pulled down in the struggle and the swell of my tits were visible? What about the peeking red lace bra I had on underneath?

Would he touch me right now like he enjoyed what he saw if he wasn't married?

Ease my thighs apart and nip that dip of my neck he'd been eyeing all night. Kiss me until my lips were as full as his and then do it some more. Kiss me until he drowned me, consumed me, shredded holes through my lace tights like a proper caveman for better access to what he wanted most.

Fuck. My runaway fantasies weren't helping the simmering ache between my legs and neither was the way Dominic was watching me. Like he knew exactly what I was picturing and was *so* pissed about it.

I didn't help the situation either.

"Back to Ms. Sanders?" Feeling brave, I tagged on, "I liked it when you called me by my first name."

Dominic lowered the tilt of his face, turning his blackened gaze severe. "Is that so?"

I nodded, angling my chin up in contrast. "Say it."

The cords of his neck pulled tight against his skin, and I knew I'd gone too far. His eye contact was dangerous now, smoldering and smoking and creating a burn so ice cold on my cheeks, it was actually hot. Flaming.

God, the way he was staring at me was like he was going to eat me. As if he hated me so much for such an obviously flirtatious request, he wanted to throw me over his knee and make me take it back until my ass was red and my cheeks and pussy were drenched.

The very thought made me press my legs together on the hood of his car.

Dominic's fingers tightened their grip around my knees, catching my breath in my throat as if he knew what I was doing, knew the itch I was trying to scratch.

That's why I was so surprised when he parted those supple lips of his.

"Katerina," he spoke thickly, my name a rock lodged in his throat where it didn't belong.

But *fuck* did it sound like it did.

A shiver tracked up my spine as I heard him say it, each letter so *purposeful* and knowing and fucking erotic. He shouldn't have said it, but he did, and every inch of me was hot with the fact of it. My eyes were on the perfect mouth that spoke my name in such an extraordinary way, wondering how much I'd hate myself in the morning if I reached up and kissed him right now.

"Stop looking at my mouth." His repeat from earlier lifted a smile to my lips, and I ignored him.

"You gonna bring out the handcuffs again if I don't?"

I watched his mouth flatten and then part.

"Line," I said with him.

Flicking my stare back to him, I rolled my lips between my teeth to hold back any snickering as he gave me such a scolding glare. With the teasing reminder of our *line* though, the tension in the air dissipated back to something normal and breathable.

Probably for the best, too.

Then, as if the clouds were waiting in tight tension with us, the first raindrop of the evening finally released. It hit my shoulder, drawing my focus as the water slid a thin line down my bare arm.

"You need to get back in the car."

"I'm not going home."

His wide shoulders fell a sliver. "Will you tell me why?"

I shook my head, pulling my bottom lip into my mouth.

This time, Dominic kept his stare right ahead and nowhere near the lip I had tucked between my teeth. A drop of rain splashed on the rise of his cheek, and he brushed it away before I could.

He cast his gaze off to the side, over to one of the houses watching our stolen moment. He held the moment as his own, taking a gamble that I'd allow him the silence to think. Surprisingly, I did, finding that tracing his strong profile with my eyes was a lovely distraction.

"You were right," he spoke suddenly. "Partially. I have tried to analyze you. Like you said, I spend a lot of time in my head breaking cases and people down so I can understand them better. I've tried to do the same to you."

"Any luck?"

He shook his head of dark hair as pitter patters of rain began to drum on the asphalt and top of the car. "Not as much as I'd like. I know that you hate silence. You use humor as a crutch, and you're very good at it."

"Thank you, thank you."

His shaped-to-perfection profile disappeared as he faced me, expression stiff. "And even though your father is the one who left, your mother is the one you never talk about."

I froze.

I was very aware that I hadn't blinked because my eyes were starting to burn, but I couldn't move. My lip twitched, and that was about all. I couldn't even look away from him and his eyes that were taking in and analyzing every single ticking second of this, of my reaction to what he had the fucking balls to say to me.

Finally, my teeth clanked together as my muscles unstuck, my lip pulling back just barely.

"*Line,*" I bit out.

A weighted breath heaved out of Dominic, like he knew he'd just hit an explosive nerve. "Before we hired you, we did a background check and—"

"You did *what*?"

My head shot up, furious flames scorching through my blood. Every single drop of rain that dared to fall on top of me thereafter could have passed right to steam my body was so boiling hot with rage.

Dominic had the audacity to look justified as he was pelted with water. "That's standard before hiring anyone, Ms. Sanders."

"You didn't *tell* me you were doing that though. I wouldn't have agreed!"

He swiped his palm over his forehead, smearing away the fallen rain. "You were going to be in our home five days a week with our child. Of course we were going to do a background check."

"But you didn't find anything on *me*, did you?" I seethed, knowing goddamn well what his answer would be.

The guilty answer was there, mucking up his stunning eyes before he even answered.

"No. I didn't."

Too many powerful emotions collided head on inside of me to control anything I did next. Wrath, humiliation, violation, shame. God, the fucking *shame*. The crash was brutal, and the monster it unleashed inside was completely and dangerously untethered.

"You fucking *snoop*," I roared, shoving back against his chest.

"Kat—"

"Well, now you know about my fucked up family." His eyes jumped wide as I shot up, feet steadying on the lip of the car. His hands jumped to my waist to stabilize me, and that was a big fucking mistake that I was so blessed for.

"Hope you're *happy*!"

A pain-filled grunt wheezed out of my boss as I took one of my knees he'd been holding onto and shoved it right in his groin. I didn't bother to stay and watch him wallow in well-deserved agony. The monster inside didn't care if he was in pain or how delightful the show might be. All it wanted to do was stretch its legs, and that's exactly what I did.

I bolted around Dominic and took off through the rain, speeding down empty streets, not knowing or caring where I was going. Just that it was away from him.

I could have run until my feet bled, so long as I didn't have to face him again. Not now. Not now that he *knew* and violated my privacy. No wonder he was kind to me tonight. No wonder he probably felt pitied into not taking me to jail.

It wasn't because he was a nice guy or cared or any of the tricks his kind liked to play on women to get them to trust them.

It was because he knew my family already had one jailbird, and that our cage wasn't big enough for two.

ELEVEN

It was another two weeks before I saw Dominic again.

I hadn't seen him since the night of the party where I flirted with him and then straight up assaulted him. I woke up the next morning with three missed calls from him after having pounded on Layla's bedroom window until she woke up and let me in. He even left a voicemail demanding I call to let him know I made it somewhere safe, and I just threw my phone down and went back to sleep.

Part of me never called back because I was afraid he'd fire me if he got on the phone with me. The other part of me never wanted to see him again, and at the end of the two weeks, I was beginning to think I might get my wish.

Maybe he was just busy at work or maybe he was avoiding me, but I was happy about his prolonged absence. *Thrilled*, in fact. Aside from having to interact with Heather for the last two weeks at the end of every work day, not seeing Dominic helped bring a couple things into focus for me.

I was dumb around him. Like, really fucking dumb.

I could blame some of what I did that night on the booze, but that excuse only went so far. There was a very conscious, sober part of me that night that actually enjoyed his company. The banter and jokes, the stories and blurry lines, his reactions to me and mine to him.

There was this... energy between us. Chemistry, I guess normal people would label it.

And chemistry was fucking toxic.

Chemistry was like my mother's heroin. It was addictive and made you do stupid shit just to get that extra high, like flirt with your married boss because you liked the way his winter gaze on you made your whole body tingle.

Having this time away from him helped me realize how goddamn dumb I was that night. It was an honest miracle I still had this job, and I didn't say that lightly. Miracles were a child's game and so fucking fickle.

As was proven in the next few seconds as my glorious streak of not having to confront my problems was ruined by two gentle knocks on Maya's bedroom door.

I was lying on Maya's floor when it happened, deep in character at a high society tea party with her and her dolls. Maya stood up in a flash of brown curls and high-pitched squeals.

"Daddy!"

Surprise and dread cranked my head up off the floor, sitting up on my elbows just in time to see Maya jump into her father's arms. Dominic hauled his daughter up to sit at his waist, a tired smile stretched across his mouth.

"Hey, Munchkin."

"Ms. Kat and me are having a tea party! You're just in time for dessert! Stay here, and I'll go get the ingredients from the store to make the cake."

Dominic arched a thick brow up at her. "The store?"

With an adorable roll of her eyes, Maya huffed out a sigh. "The pretend store, Dad."

Understanding flooded her father's stare and he nodded, setting her down. I sprung up as Maya went to leave, sitting criss-cross-applesauce.

"Do you need any help? I've got two hands prepped and ready to carry any extra ingredients."

Please. Please. Please.

My swelled hope deflated as Maya shook her head, and I tried my damnedest to not let my disappointment show. "No, you stay here with Daddy and drink some more tea!"

"Is it spiked?" I mumbled to myself.

"What, Ms. Kat?"

"Nothing."

Maya brushed me off like I'd never spoken and urged her father to go sit next to me. I groaned aloud, pushing my hands up over my face and fell backwards to lie down. Immediately, I regretted how loud and obvious I was in my frustration, but I *hated* awkward situations.

Almost as much as I hated silence.

Almost as much as I hated that he *knew* I hated silence.

Which meant he knew how much I was festering internally over the quiet that consumed the room since Maya left. Hopefully she'd be back soon. How long could the pretend store take, anyway?

Footsteps creaked the floor beside me. My mind jumped to full-alert. A few seconds later, a manly groan and the rustling of clothing. Curiosity bubbling up in my chest, I risked a quick peek between my fingers.

Dominic's back was to me, big and broad, his shoulders sunk in exhaustion. He sat just next to me, knees up and elbows resting on them, head in his hands. A deep breath lifted his back, outlining the slabs of muscle in his upper body. How he had his arms bent stretched the material of his shirt over his curled biceps too, and—

Aw fuck. I was already perving on him, and we hadn't been alone ten seconds.

I snapped my fingers closed, shutting out temptation. Except, that meant I had no distraction. Nothing to fill my focus on anything but the silence stretching between us.

Then a notion occurred, and I simply couldn't hold it in.

"Are you purposefully not talking because you know I can't stand it?"

A heavy beat slung between us, my heart pounding.

"It crossed my mind."

Don't call him a dick. Don't call him a dick. Don't call him a dick.

"You're a dick."

Dammit.

And double dammit for how exquisite the smile I pictured on his face was while he said, "Another lovely endearment, Ms. Sanders."

Exasperated energy centered in my chest, and I inhaled deeply to try and reach it, poke at it, and get it to stop before I burst. The energy was for him—for us—and I didn't want it. I didn't want the chemistry or fucking tingles or the perfect flirting quip trying to wrestle itself free so I could keep this banter going.

I just wanted it to all stop.

My hands slacked from around my face so I could push myself up off of the ground. "I'm gonna go see if Maya needs help."

"Wait."

His voice stopped me as if it had hands pressing down on my body. I waited like he said to, easing the muscles that were rearing and ready to bolt. At the last second, I propped myself up to my elbows so that I hadn't *completely* fallen under his command with one word.

The movement caught Dominic's eye, and he twisted his head back to me, staring at me from over his shoulder. Apprehension took over the jitters in my chest as those gunmetal eyes found me, loaded up with guilt.

My stomach flipped right before he spoke.

"I shouldn't have brought it up."

And then it crashed. *Hard.*

Ice cold dread splashed up with the impact, drenching all of me in a paralyzing freeze. My lips parted to tell him I didn't want to talk about this, to scream it if need be, but nothing came out. My voice was frozen. Everything about me was frozen besides my heart that slammed against my ribcage, trying to break out and run away to anywhere that wasn't right here.

"I apologize," Dominic spoke since I didn't. "Not for doing the background check but for bringing it up like I did."

An ambush attack. That's what it had felt like that night. As if he'd cracked open my head, pulled out the dirtiest of memories, and slapped me across the face with it.

I nodded, digesting his apology and trying to decide if the shine to his eyes was sincerity or pity. I mean, who wouldn't pity the girl whose mother had been arrested for solicitation last year just so she could get her fix? I'd pity me if I wasn't me.

"I don't wanna talk about it if you think we're about to have some heart to heart."

Gray eyes searched my face for a moment before he agreed with a nod. Tension hovered between us, but not the usual kind. This kind was nauseating and made me want to hurl the longer we sat in it.

He knew the worst thing about me. The thing I hated most about myself, and he learned it as easily as a few clicks of his fingers. He probably knew about the thirty days my mother spent in jail after being arrested and the fine *I* had to pay with our bill money.

Funny thing was, I was actually stupid enough to think it would wake her up. I thought her being forced to get clean on the inside and being arrested for offering sex in exchange for drugs to an undercover cop would have smacked some sense into her.

Within a week of being back home, the needle was back in her arm.

She just couldn't fucking deal, and her weakness made me sick.

"Now that it's out there, I do have to ask—"

"You don't have to ask me anything because it's none of your business," I cut him off, feeling like my stare was as sharp as knives. From this view, the cementing of his jawline felt more severe, the angles of his face harsher and refined.

His nostrils flared. "Are you and your sister safe at home?"

And there he went right ahead and asked anyway. Put the string of words together with a pretty little question mark at the end that I wanted to hang myself with. Fearsome anger clicked in my bones, fingers cracking in the silence as I bared my teeth at him.

"I don't need some hero cop coming in and trying to save me, okay? I've been keeping Charlotte away from it all. She hasn't seen any of it *once*. She's safe, and she's happy."

Dominic didn't react to my biting comment. He didn't react at all, in fact. He just kept that intrusive stare on me, concentrated and dazzling.

"What about you?"

Three words, and my anger stumbled.

Me?

I blinked at him because I didn't know what else to do. No one asked about me. No one worried about me. Anyone who knew me just assumed I was always fine because... I always *acted* like I was fine. I didn't stop moving long enough to ever sit down and think about if I was anything other than fine with how things had worked out because of my mom. I knew I hated her as much as you could hate someone who used to be your entire world, but that hate was what kept me fueled.

My gasoline was equal parts hatred for my mother and love for my sister.

Being happy was never really on my radar. *Surviving.* That was my constant. Just keep surviving, and any happy blips that came along the way were extra.

"What did I say about a heart to heart?" I asked, voice smoothed of all angry wrinkles.

A softness eased over Dominic's eyes. "Right."

It was strange how fast he'd taken the peak of my temper and quieted it with one question. I felt like a lighter he'd flicked on and off in the same second, igniting my flame and snuffing it out in a whiplash motion.

"Either way," Dominic continued. "I'm sorry it happened, and I'm sorry I brought it up."

Something moved inside of me. Rotating to life, shaking off dust, and stretching wide with a yawn. That something breathed its first breath of life in years, expanding my chest and filling it to the brim with fireflies, bumping around, and attempting to brighten my view on what was being resurrected.

I twisted with the movement, unable to get comfortable with the new feeling. It was warm and tingly and familiar, but I didn't recognize it until the swarm of anxiety rushed along to follow. Then the realization hit hard enough to shock my lips apart.

I wanted to believe him. I wanted to *trust* his apologetic words. I actually wanted to trust that he was sorry and that he cared enough to *be* sorry.

Dumb. Holy fuck. This man made me *so* dumb.

Lowering myself from my elbows to lie flat on the floor, I closed my eyes and pushed the dumbass feeling to the back of my mind to deal with... never.

"I'm not sorry I kneed you in the balls," I mentioned casually.

A stiff laugh sliced the air. "I can accept that."

"Good."

After a second, Dominic released another weary sigh, and I snuck a peek to see him lying down. The small sliver I'd left to see through cranked wide open and my heartbeat skyrocketed. Like it was totally normal, he put his back flush to the carpet the same as I was, like an arms length away from me. Close, but not close. Laying together, but not.

I laid there quietly while he shut his eyes and picked up conversation like nothing was out of the ordinary.

"So, how's it been with Heather the last two weeks?"

I sucked back a quick breath. "Peachy."

"Could you try a little harder to hide your sarcasm next time?" he mused, voice thick with sleep.

"I can't. It's my favorite language."

Eyes closed shut, a ghost of a smile curved up his mouth. "Charming."

"I still don't know why she hated me before she even knew I was an uneducated hillbilly," I said, staring up at the fluffy white clouds painted into Maya's bedroom ceiling.

"You're not—" Dominic cut himself off with a serrated breath. I peeked a side-eye at him, catching him working his jaw back and forth. It struck me how quickly he jumped to defend me from myself, but he thankfully dropped it.

"It would only take a small amount of deductive reasoning to figure out why she didn't prefer you."

Now *that* piqued my intrigue. Rolling over onto my side to face him, I gestured a challenge with a small head nod. "All right. I'm game. Help me out, Detective."

Watching me out of the corner of his eye, Dominic rolled his silver stare shut and breathed deep. That faint grin still teased his lips though, so I knew he would play along.

"Did she seem to like you when you had your phone interview?" he began.

"I would use 'like' loosely."

Both of his dark brows shrugged as if to say *'that's fair.'* He pinched the bridge of his nose, massaging his fingers along the sides. "And what about when you showed up for your in person interview?"

"You were there. She hated me before I even said a word."

Dominic dropped his head towards me, giving me a brazen look.

Oh God, was I stupid? He seemed to think the reasoning was so obvious. She tolerated me on the phone—barely. Then, when I got here, she took one look at me and decided she—

Wait.

"Because I'm hot?" I blustered. "She hates me because I'm not ugly?"

"Or old. Most of our candidates were in their 50's and 60's."

Rolling onto my back again, I shook my head up at the ceiling. "Jesus, that's dumb. Hate me for something with substance at least, like my personality."

"Oh, I don't think she's too fond of that either."

Soft laughter breathed through my nose. "See now, that makes sense to me. Rich bitch and poor bitch don't really mesh."

"*Line.*"

I shrugged. "That's fair."

We laid there for a few moments without sharing words. My head was full of them though, sifting through letters and trying to decide what words I wanted to form next while also trying to not pay attention to how close and not close Dominic was to me.

Deciding on the first memory I had of him, I asked, "Is that why you were so weird the first time we met?"

"I was weird?"

"Oh yeah. You gave off a real 'I'm about to murder someone, and I'm stoked about it' vibe."

Even though I wasn't staring at him, I could feel him going back to that moment in his head where we first met. When he first opened the door. What I first said. What he first said. Over-analyzing it. Replaying it.

"I suppose," he spoke quietly. "You weren't at all what I was expecting."

I curved my sightline to him. "In a good way?"

His hard gaze stayed trained on the ceiling. "I haven't decided yet."

A moan stretched my vocal cords, and I slumped my chin towards my chest. "You know how I feel about if's, and maybe's, and uncertainties."

"You don't prefer them."

"No, I *hate* them."

Finally, steel-cut eyes grabbed onto mine as he turned his head. "You use that word a lot. Hate."

"Yeah, because I hate a lot of things."

The unhurried scan his eyes performed over my face did funny things to my stomach. Like, first day of school, first crush, first kiss kind of funny feelings.

"Seems like that would be exhausting."

His lips moved slower than usual, or maybe it was just the ungodly low register he spoke in that made everything about the sentence feel like time had slowed around it.

He didn't tell me to stop staring at his mouth this time, but I eventually did once his words floated to my ears, and I had to laugh at them.

"It's very easy actually."

Hate and love were like swimming, except one happened in a pool and one happened in the ocean. One, you could swim around without worry, open your eyes under the water, and touch the bottom if you got tired. The water was calm and non-threatening, and that was hate.

Love was the ocean. It was unpredictable, creating waves to roll you up in, only to crash you back down in a tumble of salt watery eyes and burning lungs. It was infested with vicious animals, lurking and waiting to attack if you didn't drown in the riptides first. One way or another, the ocean would destroy you, and love was marked with that same promise.

I'd rather take my chances in the pool, thank you very much.

A vibration went off in the room, and Dominic reached in his pocket for his phone. As soon as he scanned the screen, his eyelids crashed shut and a wave of fatigue poured out of him.

"Work been kicking your ass lately?"

"You could say that," he replied with a sigh.

"Is it the nurse's case?"

Dominic wound his fingers around his phone, squeezing it. "I can't talk about any of it with you."

I paused, counting the seconds in my head until I got to ten. "Do you wanna be a rebel and talk about it anyway?"

A smile touched my cheeks, infected by his first. Dominic lulled his head to face me, any traces of stress from whatever was on his phone chased away by the mirth dancing in his stare.

"No, I'll save all the rule-breaking for you."

"I'll have you know, I decided to turn over a new leaf." I shifted my shoulders on the floor, giving him as much of my attention as I could without rolling over to him and throwing myself on top of him.

He arched a disbelieving eyebrow. "Is that so?"

"Mhm. No more parties or drinking for me until Charlotte is outta the house and on her own."

"You really think you could last thirteen plus years without doing anything remotely reckless?"

"I'm a woman. Lasting long enough isn't an area *I* fail in."

The quip was out before I realized it, and I was sure it would go one of two ways. Either he'd laugh begrudgingly, or he'd call 'line', and we'd pretend I never said it.

What I didn't anticipate was a secret option number three—an option where Dominic Reed blew my mind and expectations wide open and set my veins on fire.

Because for once, it wasn't me who couldn't stop staring at his mouth.

It was *him*, and those thunderous eyes that were zeroed in on my lips.

"That smart mouth of yours is going to get you in trouble one day."

The mouth he was so focused on went dry at his throaty voice that was so promising, so fucking erotic, I knew it couldn't have been intentional. Dominic Reed was a weapon of seduction, and he didn't even know it. I swallowed, noticing how his eyes followed the movement down and then right the fuck back up to my lips.

Goddamnit, he wasn't making this easy, but I'd let him off with a quick joke.

"Oh yeah?" I teased. "You gonna cuff me again?"

A humored twitch jumped the corner of my mouth, because I thought we were joking. My small smirk fell when Dominic didn't return it. My pulse thumped when he fixed his exacting eyes on mine. My entire world caught on fucking fire when I realized we weren't joking anymore.

"Keep talking, Ms. Sanders." *And we'll see.*

The unspoken subtext of his words flared my eyes wide, thick eyelashes fluttering fast and distorting the incredible sight of him. Temptation carved the angles of his face into pure poetry, each line a dedication of unearthly beauty and sin. He was angelic and devilish all the same, ruling my heaven and my hell.

Good and bad were one in his eyes. Hot and Cold. Fire and Ice. Dominic was all of it, and all I was was a hypocrite, falling victim to lust with a few easy words from a man I couldn't have.

A man I shouldn't even *want* to have.

Desire licked between my thighs as Dominic watched me in that way only he could, absorbing and collecting every single tiny reaction I gave him.

The parting of my lips was his. The way I slid my wet tongue over them was his. The ragged breath that inflated my lungs as I imagined the cold metal digging into my hot skin was his. All of it—all of *me*—was his in those sinful seconds.

It happened so fast. Just a few words and burning eye contact, and our heroin chemistry was in my blood. Intoxicating, boiling, terrifying.

And then, just as quickly as it started, a cold needle of adrenaline straight to the heart shocked me back to sobriety.

"I'm here!"

Maya's cheery voice ripped the next breath straight from my chest. Heavy horror filled it instead as I snapped my head up, finding her bounding into the room, completely unaware of the tension she just exploded right through. She had no idea. She was just smiling and happy and holding—

"Oh my god," I sputtered in laughter, sitting up. My heart was throbbing, but Maya was presenting me with an excellent distraction, her arms full of bags of sugar, flour, a carton of eggs, chocolate chips, jelly beans, and pink and purple sprinkles clutched in each hand.

No *wonder* it took her so long.

Dominic stifled a quiet chuckle next to me as he sat up too. "Baby, I thought you said the pretend store. Not our kitchen pantry."

"I got everything for our cake!"

God, she was so freaking cute standing there, beaming with pride. You couldn't even be mad. In fact, I could have hugged her for the free excuse to pretend like nothing was just happening between her father and I.

Nothing inappropriate whatsoever.

I had to put my fist over my mouth to keep from laughing too much, turning my head to the side to mumble to Dominic. "I'll help her put it all away."

He lent me an amused side glance. "Thank you."

I nodded once and went to twist my neck back to Maya, but his gaze lingered. It was just for a moment. A fraction in time where I couldn't look away. It was a quiet acknowledgement through shared eye contact of what happened. A few words from him. A telling reaction from me. None of it professional.

And we both knew that.

Dominic's face was, as always, unreadable. I could assume he was thinking the same thing I was though. That he'd crossed that line he always warned me about, and took me over it with him, and it could never happen again.

One of the very many good reasons *why* it could never happen again entered the room at that exact moment.

"I didn't know you were home yet."

Heather's icy voice sliced through the room, slashing all three of our heads over to where she stood in the doorway, thin arms crossed and mouth screwed up.

We weren't doing anything, I wanted to cry. It was true. We hadn't been doing anything when she walked in just now aside from staring at each other. Had she entered the room about sixty seconds ago however...

I'd be trying to explain away why I was flirting with her husband in her own home.

It was like I was *trying* to get fired.

Guilty sweat sprouted and stuck to every single inch of my skin as I dared a glance up at Heather. She wasn't looking at me, and for that I would count myself lucky because the glare she was giving her husband was nothing short of viperous. Narrowed and suspicious.

Though, Dominic didn't seem to care. He wasn't even giving her his full attention as his eyes fell shut and pinched tightly.

"I just got home," he replied, his tone worn down to the bones.

"Mommy." Maya tilted her head up, almost losing her grip on the jelly beans. "Do you want to make a cake with us?"

"*No.*" Heather didn't even have the heart to look at her daughter as she denied her. She was zeroed in on her husband, her eyes like the hottest part of a flame. "Dom, may I speak with you?"

It wasn't a question, and every adult in the room knew it. I'd gotten good about being able to tell when a couple was about to have a really big fight. Growing up, my parents had these knock down, drag-out fights where the walls of my bedroom would shake they'd yell so loudly. There were always a few key tells or word choices people tended to use before a blowout fight.

And Dominic and Heather were about to have it out.

With a labored sigh, Dominic heaved himself up off of the ground without a word. I tried not to watch him go, not wanting to give Heather any other implications to latch onto and beat Dominic over the head with during this upcoming fight.

Right before she left, Heather pinned me with her daggered stare. "It'd be really nice if you could get up off the floor and help our daughter put all of this away."

"I was—" *planning on it.* But I was smart enough to bite my tongue on this one. "Okay."

Victory plagued Heather's expression, haughty and demeaning. Dominic trudged out of Maya's bedroom, shoulders rigid and spine stiff with Heather hot on his feet.

As soon as they both left, I slunk forward like I'd been holding my breath the entire time, palms splaying out into the fibers of the carpet. I stayed there, breathing heavily for just a few moments before gathering myself together and ushering Maya back down to the kitchen to put everything for our cake away.

The entire time, I took a page from Dominic's book and was lost in my head about what happened upstairs. It was so insignificant—we hadn't even touched—but the thing was, it didn't *feel* insignificant. Those few words and few seconds felt volcanic, like he'd touched all of me with a sharp look and insinuating words.

Fucking *chemistry* was going to get me fired, and no dick was good enough for that.

TWELVE

When I saw Dominic again on Monday, everything was normal.

Same went for Tuesday and Wednesday. He'd relieve me at the end of each day, we'd share a few anecdotes about our days—surface details only—and then I'd be on my way with a wave and a smile.

Thursday, Heather was the one to relieve me come 5:30, and that went about as well as anyone would expect. A quick flick of her wrist and a 'You can go,' and I was out the door.

I made it all the way until Friday before my week of normal turned anything but.

And it started with a broken door lock.

The thing had been on its last legs for weeks, and this morning it finally bit the bullet.

I called up the lock repair service on my drive to work after I dropped Charlotte off at Mrs. Sharon's and crossed all my extremities that they'd lowered their prices.

Mrs. Sharon was at the tail end of six months in her pregnancy, and I knew I'd have to find a replacement sitter soon. She told me she'd go until she had the baby, but realistically, I knew that probably wasn't true.

Thankfully, with a bit of extra cash coming in, I could afford a few months of paid babysitting.

That was, if shit around this house would stop breaking.

"200 bucks for a *lock* repair? Are you serious?"

"Yes ma'am. That's standard for this kind of service."

This guy. This fucking customer service guy on the other end of the phone sounded so smug, and I'd bet anything he was a prick in real life. My fingers squeezed around my steering wheel, and I imagined it was his puny little neck.

"It's replacing a lock, not brain surgery. How can it be so expensive?"

A staticky pause hung over the line. Then he went on like he didn't even hear me.

"Would you like to book for today? We can come out to your residence around noon."

Even if I could get Kathy to wake up long enough to let the repair guy in, she didn't have the money to pay him. All of our money was my money, and I wasn't naïve enough to hand her a dime of it. It would be shoved in her arm or between her toes just like the money my grandparents left behind until that was all dried up.

I didn't know how or where she got the money for her habit now, and down to my blackened soul, I did *not* wanna know.

"I can't make it work today *or* for that price."

"That's the only price we have to offer, ma'am."

Frustration rumbled in my throat as I pulled into the Reed's expansive driveway, setting my car in park. I sounded untamed—animalistic—and I felt that way too. Jittering and ticking and furious at the world.

"You know what? I have tomorrow off. I'll fix it my own damn self."

"Sounds grand. Best of luck."

And the line cut dead.

I yanked my phone away from my ear, staring down at the screen. "Mother-*fucker*."

Guess I'm fixing a lock tomorrow.

Closing my eyes, I breathed deep and fisted the steering wheel, pressing all of my early-morning rage into it. Bits of dried up rubber flaked off in my palms, and

I rolled my eyes at it before dusting both hands together over the passenger seat carpet.

What a shitty start to the day.

Things could only go up from here, right?

Wrong.

Someone should have hit me over the head as soon as I thought the cliché phrase. Even *thinking* it practically ensured I just jinxed myself.

As I entered the Reed residence that day, that theory was proven right.

The door was open like usual—because this was that type of swanky neighborhood where you could do that—but I always flipped the lock once I was in for the day. My ears perked as soon as I stepped foot in the entryway, angry voices echoing down the stairs.

"She shouldn't have been in there in the first place!"

"She's a kid, Heather. Kids are messy by nature."

Okay, so *both* wife and husband were home this morning. Joy.

A short, fiery scream came from Heather. "That's so typical of you, Dominic. Take everyone's side but mine every time."

"She's my *daughter*," he bellowed back.

"And I am your *wife*. I am so sick and fucking tired of you never having my back. Not once!"

"Not when you're screaming at Maya and calling her an *idiot* over spilt milk. You're losing your goddamn mind over literal spilt milk, Heather."

"All over my work documents!"

"So reprint them," Dominic spoke pointedly.

An awkward shiver walked up my spine as I shut the front door behind me. I didn't want to listen to this. This fight was absolutely none of my business. I just needed to keep my head down, my mouth shut, and find Maya.

Tiptoeing to the living room first, I peered around every corner, searching out the head of brown ringlet curls. Maya was usually downstairs in the kitchen with either Dominic or Heather, but I didn't see her anywhere.

I walked in careful steps up the stairs, worry beginning to pulsate in my chest for where she was and exactly how much of this fight she was hearing. If she was in her bedroom, she was hearing all of it. Every single resentful word her parents threw at each other.

My heart thumped harder at the thought.

The further I made it up the stairs, the louder and clearer the booming voices became, and the sharper the ache in my chest felt. By the time I made it to Maya's bedroom, both the ache and voices were screaming.

"You're way too easy on her!" Heather peaked in her rage. "You have to *punish* her when she screws up like this. Not coddle her!"

"She spilled her morning milk, for god's sake. That's it."

"All over my work documents! The work that pays for our life, for this house—"

"Christ. Don't bring up the house *again*."

Maya's bedroom door was shut, and it was hard to hear over the sound of her parents biting each other's heads off, but as I pressed my ear against the wood, the noise on the inside and the crack in my heart were undeniable.

Sorrow dropped my breath into my stomach as I twisted her door open and pushed my way in. My heart wailed as the once muffled cries popped with clarity, soft sobs drenching the room.

Watery eyes leapt up as I entered, big teardrops welling and falling over even faster as Maya saw me. "Ms. Kat, I—" She hiccuped. "I didn't mean to."

Her lips trembled in guilt that was *not* hers to own, and my throbbing heart dropped me to my knees and gathered her up in my arms in seconds. "Oh, I know. I know. You didn't do anything wrong."

She pushed her head into the crook of my neck, pouring sobs and tears into it. A loud cry ripped out of her chest that was so anguished, my hold around her closed tighter as if I could squeeze out the pain.

"I was just play-playing," she cried, tiny body shaking.

"I know, kiddo. We've all knocked our fair share of drinks over. Trust me, I know I have."

She sucked back a quivering breath against my neck. "R-really?"

"Oh, for sure. I'm a *total* klutz. Always falling over, knocking things over. You name it, I've probably broken it."

I started rocking us back and forth on the floor, trying to soothe her cries and calm her breathing. After a few seconds of slowing sniffles, she whispered, "Why do they always have to fight?"

My head fell back against the wall, kicked back by the blow of sadness in her small voice.

Fury engulfed me as I held her, knowing she shouldn't even be *capable* of such a degree of despair as a child. That shouldn't be possible. That wasn't fucking right. I pulled my face back down to hug my cheek against the top of her head, rocking her still.

"I don't know, but I can promise you it's not your fault. Your mom and dad are just angry with each other right now. Not you."

Maya rubbed her hands over her eyes before tangling them in my shirt, holding herself closer. Wisps of her baby hairs tickled the tip of my nose, but I didn't move.

Not even as there was a creak by her bedroom door, and someone came into the room with us. I felt his guilty presence sitting like a shadow in the corner of the room, watching over us.

Maya shifted in my lap as Dominic's footsteps made the floorboards moan, lip quivering as her father came close. I didn't take my eyes off of Maya's face long enough to spare him any attention. Her tear-stained face broke as he knelt next to us, opening his arms wide for her to jump in.

She did, no questions asked.

"Daddy, I'm sorry!" she wailed, throwing herself into his chest. Dominic caught her and held her tight, remorse slanting his whole expression downward. "I didn't mean to make you or Mommy mad."

"Baby, you didn't." He shushed her, rubbing his hand over the back of her curls. "It was an accident and accidents happen. It's nothing to cry over."

Those last five words of his inflamed my temper, chest burning hot with fire I wanted to spit at him. She wasn't crying because of the goddamn milk, and the detective should have known that.

Maybe Maya would grow up with daddy issues after all.

He continued stroking Maya's hair lovingly. "Do you want me to read you a story?"

She sniffled, pulling back a stuttering breath. "No, I want Ms. Kat to."

"Oh." Dominic's voice was light with shock that read just as vividly on his face as Maya wiggled out of his arms and came back over to me. Feeling especially protective, I pulled her in and picked her up, sitting her on my waist as I stood. She hugged her arms around my neck, and Dominic's face fell.

"Okay."

Maybe on a different day I would have felt bad for him, would have suggested he stay and we read her a story together. I'd have done whatever I could to erase the rejection raining in his sky gray eyes. Today, all I cared about were the raindrops streaming down puffy red cheeks, and I couldn't find one ounce of sympathy for the man that helped put them there.

I wasn't hiding how pissed off I was at him very well either. Or at least, that's what the flinch in Dominic's composure told me as soon as he locked himself in my sightline.

Questions clouded his gaze, and his confusion jacked my temper up to a hundred and one. A brutal cocktail of a sneer and an eye roll were Dominic's exit music played by yours truly.

I did both and spun away from him, taking his still teary-eyed daughter with me in search of a cheerful story to read to distract her from the hardship of her own.

Maya fell asleep a little before her early afternoon nap time. Probably exhausted from all the crying. I didn't cry much, but whenever I did, it was a monsoon strong enough to knock me out cold for hours.

The last time I cried that hard was about two years ago.

Mom's first overdose.

My heart still felt heavy as I slumped down the stairs after putting Maya down. This morning brought up a slew of nasty memories I'd rather drink away than ever have to remember. Alas, it was only noon, and I was still at work.

Padding into the kitchen, I reapplied my strawberry chapstick that I'd chewed off during the heated morning and plucked the banana I'd brought with me from my purse. My eyes shut, and I munched off a bite, sighing as the sweetness rolled around my mouth.

"Ms. Sanders."

Jesus. Did he have to say my name like *that*? Like he'd struck the lowest key on a piano and resonated the note to the tune of my name.

I rolled my eyes open, finding him standing in front of me, hands stuffed into the pockets of his tan slacks. He was dressed for work, the detectiving kind, and his hard stare was waiting for mine.

"What're you still doing here?" I asked, snapping off another bite of banana.

Dominic moved his eyes to his wingtip shoes. "I worked the night patrol shift yesterday. Got in at 6am. I'm headed back out soon. I just wanted to see how Maya was."

"She's sleeping, so she's fine."

He gave a slow nod, peeking up at me beneath thick brows. "She go down easy?"

"Pretty much."

"That's good."

All I gave him was a short hum in response. A hum to say, '*It is. Now leave me the fuck alone so I don't snap at you*'. I wasn't used to holding my tongue when I had an opinion. Martie never had the balls to punish me for anything I did or said until the day he fired me. My parents breezed by the whole discipline lesson when I was growing up, and it showed fantastically.

My tongue was wild and my teeth were sharp, and if I had an opinion, I wanted you to know it. Though, this job was different. It *had* to be different if I wanted to keep it long enough to pay for the babysitting Charlotte was going to need soon.

I had to be good and bite my tongue instead of bite his head clean off.

Unfortunately for me, Dominic Reed made it *so* damn hard to be good.

"Are you mad at me?" he asked suddenly.

I nearly choked on my banana. My eyes bugged just a bit as I swallowed it down, smoothing my palm over my chest. Throat cleared, I lied. "No."

Not even three seconds passed before—

"You're lying."

An inaudible sigh pushed past my nose as I rolled the peel of my banana between my fist. How did he *always* know?

I stalked away from him, tossing the peel in the trash. "So I'm lying. What does it matter?"

Heavy footsteps tracked my path behind me, pushing my steps faster and my anger hotter. My feet carried me all the way around their kitchen, rounding the corner that led back into their living room. I was literally avoiding him, running away in an attempt to save myself from exploding, and it was like he was tailing me with a lit match, wanting to watch it happen.

"Ms. Sanders—" Dominic cut me off, swooping up from behind me and planting himself firmly in front of me. "I'd like to know why you're mad."

Not-so-simmering rage jazzed my body into a barely contained frenzy as I pulled my lips to the side and scoffed a humorless laugh.

"Boy, you must really love fighting."

"No, I like communicating," he replied explicitly.

I barked a real, disgusting laugh this time. "Loudly. Really, *really* loudly."

Dominic crossed his arms over his wide chest, staring me down over the straight bridge of his nose. "So this is about the fight."

"Of *course* it's about the fight."

The middle of his forehead turned to a frown, matching the one pulling at his mouth. He sent his gaze back to the stairs where his daughter slept and where I'd heard his wife's clacking heels not too long ago. "I didn't think Maya would hear it."

"Yeah, well she did."

Thundering eyes flashed with warning. "Clearly we weren't thinking about how loud we were."

The beast inside slammed forward, cracking my defense wall and allowing a line of poison to ooze out. "No, *clearly* you weren't thinking about your daughter in the other room."

"Ms. *Sanders*." My name was a punishment in strict syllables. "That's too far."

I stopped to exhale and save myself from saying anything else stupid. Deep breaths. Deep. Fucking. Breaths. Snapping my eyes back to him, I said, "You're the one who wanted to know why I was pissed at you."

"Yes, but—"

"And I won't fight about it in here." I pinned him with a hard stare. "If you want to continue this conversation, we go outside."

The backs of his jawline clicked as he loomed over me, stiff lines angling his features extra sharp. I stood my ground below him despite how menacing he looked, puffing my chest out to match his as much as possible. Our gazes battled, thunder vs. lightning; a storm worth sheltering from.

Though, it was Dominic who let out a buckling exhale seconds in. Glimpsing over my head, he sent a stiff nod towards the back of his house.

"Come on."

Dominic moved first, placing a heated hand on the small of my back to guide me. My brain registered the gesture and how nonchalant it was, and that was all I allowed it to acknowledge. Not how heavy a presence it was on my body, or how I had to literally fight off the urge to lean into it.

He led us to the back patio I'd only been to once when Maya was giving me a tour of her house. It sat against a sizable, and mostly empty backyard save for a lonely tree and a tool shed. The patio wasn't exactly an area designed for kids with its sharp, iron-made table and chairs, woodfire pizza oven, and the cobblestone-faced bar area loaded up with breakable—and probably expensive—glassware.

It was a place built for parties and wine nights and fancy get-togethers, but every surface was caked in layers of dust. The only place that looked like it got any use at all was the bar, and I imagined a lot of lonely drinks being had out here by the man in front of me.

He crossed those masculine arms over themselves and got right down to it.

"Okay, we're outside. Now talk."

During the walk back here, my temper had actually slipped into hibernation. I'd been distracted by his strong hand on my back and judging the patio that rarely saw any action.

His demand—his two word demand—brought it creeping back.

I narrowed my stare on him, and everything about Dominic tightened and hunched together from his face to his posture, as if to protect himself from whatever I would say next. As if his ropes of muscles and hardened expression were armor from my lacerating words.

I folded my arms to match his, filtering through my brain for the appropriate set of words.

"How often do you and Heather fight like that?" I asked evenly.

The strength in his stare lost its standing and dropped, like I'd cut him down to half his size with one question. With his arms crossed and his sleeves rolled to his elbows, I could see every perfect indent of his veins standing out beneath his forearms as he flexed his own temper.

He lowered his voice just as he lowered his gaze.

"Often."

Slowly, I nodded, taking a single step towards him. "And how many times has Maya been in the house during those fights?"

At that, his jaw set to the side like it always did when he was anything less than laughing. He ground his teeth together in a bone-tingling way and carved holes in the porch patio with his eyes of the same color.

"And where do you expect me and my wife to fight if not in our own home?"

My eyebrows shifted up in challenge, and I took another step closer to him. Another point to drill home. "Did your parents ever fight in front of you?"

Dominic's chest inflated with a sharp sigh. "Not that I heard."

"And I *assume* you lived in the same house as them?"

The rolling storm in his eyes grew darker. "I understand your point."

"Do you though? Do you understand what it's like to sit in your bedroom and listen to your parents scream and *scream* for hours, thinking it's because of you?" Dominic went to speak and I cut him off with malice. "Because I do, and you can see what a *peach* I turned out to be."

Swarthy eyebrows dove together, and his mouth pinched in disapproval as I took a swing at myself. Sarcastic self-deprivation was what all the cool kids were doing nowadays, right?

He didn't correct me or comment. Just stayed stiff as stone, slow-realization chipping dents in his exterior. I knew I had a hammer in my words too, in my less-than-ideal childhood that would help knock some brutal reality into him.

"Do you want me to tell you what Maya's feeling every time she hears her parents fight?"

Nothing in Dominic's face seemed like he wanted to know, but out of regret or responsibility, he solemnly nodded.

I steadied myself and my voice, eyes fixed on him. "Guilt. Like if she were a better daughter, you two wouldn't be fighting."

There went the first split in his composure. Agony cracked a clear line down his handsome face. Dominic watched me, eyes bright as my anger morphed into something fragile. Something I'd rather have stayed forgotten.

"She's thinking that maybe if she hadn't spilled that drink or played too loudly or cleaned up her toys like she was asked that Dad wouldn't be so mad and maybe Mom would stop crying."

Heather clearly wasn't crying, but both he and I knew I wasn't just talking about Maya anymore.

His entire face fell, and he shook his head. "That's not true."

"*You* know that. She doesn't. Kids are stellar at blaming themselves. Trust me," I mumbled.

I'd gotten good at it. I'd gotten *so* good at blaming myself, in fact, that as an adult, I had zero gauge for faults of my own. I was either completely to blame for everything going wrong, or you'd have to break all my teeth to get an apology to spill out.

There was nowhere in between. I was either stubborn or terminally apologetic.

Dominic shut his eyes, passing a hand over his long face. He stopped to press his fingers against his eye sockets, a soft groan humming in his throat.

"I guess I just always hoped the walls were thick enough."

"That's a shitty excuse."

His hand fell from his face, those unique eyes worn with shame. "Maybe I'm a shitty father."

I couldn't help it as my eyes turned with exasperation.

"Don't throw a pity party. You know you're a good dad. You just fucked up. You have time to fix it though."

Maya was young. If her parents stopped their public fighting now, who knows? Maybe her immature brain would repress all the bad shit and all she'd remember was the good shit from her childhood. That was the hope, at least.

Dominic cast me a heavy glance, arms hanging loose at his sides. "Whenever Heather and I argue, it's like I have tunnel vision. All I can think about is how *upset* I am."

Exhaustion mounted on top of Dominic's shoulders that was so palpable, I felt weak just staring at him. Every line on his face grew deeper, the bags under his eyes darker. A pang of loss hit my chest as I took him in and wished for the younger looking version of him I'd seen when he was sleeping.

Or his dimples. I wanted the dimples from when he laughed so hard, his cheeks literally winked in joy.

Dominic took his gaze out to the iron gate fence around their backyard. "I think that might be the difference with my parents," he said, adrift in his head again. "They were happy."

Oof.

This took an unexpected turn. I hadn't given it much thought since our night in his patrol car three weeks ago, but Dominic had mentioned his marriage then too. His worries and woes. Now looking at him, the man was practically drowning standing up on dry land.

Again, it wasn't my business, but—

"How long have you been unhappy?"

With his head angled to the side, I saw perfectly when that infamous tick of his jaw snapped into place. He chided me in a thick voice.

"This is probably a 'line' moment."

"Probably."

Silent seconds ticked past that I let slide by without calling attention to it or forcing some type of noise. The moment was his, and I did my very best to patiently wait and watch as the easy breeze rustled one pesky strand of hair at the peak of his hairline while he orchestrated his thoughts.

When he finally did speak, his voice was low. So low, I wasn't so sure it wasn't the wind's lonely whisper instead.

"I've tried for a long time to be happy. A *long* time..."

Damn. I wasn't a hugger type of person, save for Charlotte and sometimes Layla, but every muscle in my body fritzed with energy trying to make me go over and hug him. He was so impossibly sad. A man broken by love, and all I could think about was that someone should have warned him.

Love was not something you could win.

Love would chew you up and use your broken heart to pick its teeth.

"I guess that's the takeaway from this then," I said, hoping to change the subject and awful mood. "Even in your worst moments, it's still your responsibility to save Maya from them. As parents, it's your job to protect and love your kids *even...* if you stop loving each other."

Dominic's eyes heaved shut, a sullen sigh pushing through his nose.

Seemed like he already knew that last bit.

Just hadn't heard it anywhere but inside his head.

After a few tense seconds, Dominic swiveled his focus back to me, sealing his misery back up behind those eyes of stone. "Your sister is really lucky to have you."

"Eh. We'll see when she's fifteen and hates me."

Dominic released a puff of a laugh. "Teenage females terrify me."

"As they should. We're a wild bunch."

He cut me a quick side-eye. "You're twenty. You don't classify as a teenager anymore."

"Are you calling me *old*, old man?"

"No," he regaled, pointing his stare up at the sky. "I'm saying it for my own peace of mind."

Before I could respond, the police radio attached to his hip sputtered to life and cut me off.

"All units, we have a break in at address 1357 Oakwood Drive. Reported mother and child on scene. Units respond."

Any teasing humor held on my face dropped. *Shattered.* Ice rippled through my veins, freezing my blood, freezing my thoughts, freezing my heart to a dead stop.

Horror held my eyes wide open, locking on Dominic as acute caution drew in his features as he took me in. My lip trembled. My breath hitched. My heart fucking obliterated logic as it screamed so loudly, the freeze encasing it exploded in every direction, cutting my vocal cords free.

"That's my address," I whispered.

THIRTEEN

"Oh my god, could you *please* go faster?"

"Kat, I'm going as fast as I can. My partner's on his way there too."

Dominic's words did little to stunt the wild and painful beating of my heart as we sped down familiar roads, siren blaring, red and blue lights flashing. I was malfunctioning in every way a person could as we drove to my house. I couldn't breathe, but I also couldn't stop hyperventilating. Couldn't move a muscle, but couldn't stop fidgeting. I couldn't think, but couldn't stop the questions barrelling through my head that were pushing me to a quick insanity.

Who broke in and why? Was it random?

Why is Charlotte there and not with Mrs. Sharon?

Was anything taken?

Was anyone hurt?

"The lock," I muttered to myself, fingers beating against the car door. The motherfucking lock that I was too goddamn stubborn to pay to fix today was the reason this had happened. My fault. My fault. Always my fault. "The fucking *lock...*"

"What're you saying, Kat?" Dominic's voice was even and firm, like he was trying to keep me alert and talking and sane. *Sanity.* What a goddamn joke.

"The lock!" My stare knifed through his as I exploded, panicked energy zipping through my veins. "The fucking lock on our front door broke this morning, and I didn't fix it. I didn't fucking fix it yet."

"Kat, this isn't your fault—"

"You don't know that! This could be *directly* my fault all because I didn't want to pay to get it fixed. Because I-*God*, can't you go any faster?"

His lips parted like he was going to argue, but he tightened up his jaw instead. Gray eyes flashed back to the road, knuckles breaking white around the steering wheel as the speed of the car picked up.

"When we get there, you have to wait for me to go inside first," he stated.

He sounded so serious, but my attention on him was muffled. I ignored him, staring out the window at the cars pulling over to let us by. We were getting close, and the closer we got to my house, the more my thumping heartbeat deafened everything around me.

All I could hear was my blood pumping. All I could feel was the terror.

Dominic called my name again, but I barely heard him, barely registered him at all as we turned onto my street. My house. It was there. I could see it's dusty blue outside, the crooked mailbox, the weeds growing between the rocks of our makeshift driveway getting more focused.

My breathing escalated, drying out my lips as I shifted in my seat, hand resting on the door handle. We pulled up, and before Dominic could even set the car in park, I busted out.

"Kat!" Dominic's shout fell behind me as I raced up the uneven driveway, rocks of gravel digging beneath my shoes as I tore my way up to my front door. Dread slashed through my stomach, bile rising in my throat.

It was open. My front door was jammed open.

I crashed through it in one frantic motion.

"Charlotte!" I hollered, desperation tearing apart my voice. My eyes tore around the scene of the crime. My home. My home that had been absolutely ripped to shreds. Terror fisted my gut as I screamed for her. "*Charlotte!*"

"Katty!"

A wild shriek echoed from down the hall that led to our bedroom. My heart jammed forward as wild blonde pigtails came running around the corner, her red blotchy face stealing the breath right out from my lungs.

"Oh my god," I breathed, dropping to my knees. Charlotte slammed into me, and I scooped her up, holding her so close and so tight. I felt her warmth, her rapidly beating heart, her signs of life.

"Are you okay? Are you hurt?"

"I'm okay." Her mumbled voice, tears, and shaking breath all stuck to the crook of my neck. I squeezed her tighter, feeling faint from the rush of dizzying emotions.

I pulled her back a tiny bit, pushing my palm over her streaks of tears. "Why are you home and not over with Mrs. Sharon?"

She sniffled, dropping her swollen eyes to the collar of my shirt. "Mrs. Sharon went to the hospital. She said her tummy was hurting, and she was worried about the baby."

Cue another tailspin of overwhelming dread. Fuck, I bet she called me too. My phone was back at Dominic's house, still in my purse where I hadn't touched it all day since I arrived at work. I normally checked it around lunchtime, which was right about now.

Behind us, the floorboards whined as someone walked in, and I spun to see Dominic enter my home. He nearly had to duck to not hit his head on the doorframe as he came in, eyes alert and hand resting on the butt of a black gun I hadn't noticed before.

The sight of it made me recoil, tucking Charlotte's body into my chest more. I hated guns, hated being around them, never wanted to use one. Ever.

In my arms, Charlotte tugged at my shirt to get my attention, not-so-quietly asking me who the huge man in our home was.

"Don't worry. He's a friend."

Dominic swept an inspecting glance over my sister before bringing his tight focus back to me. "Is she okay?"

I nodded, smoothing my hand over the back of her head with a trembling breath. "She's okay."

"What about your mom?"

His question shook me, guilt sliding another splinter through my chest that I hadn't even thought about my mom once. She was here. She could be hurt.

"Bugs, where's Mom?"

It was as if I'd broken her heart with my question. Her innocent face broke with sobs, tears sliding faster down her cheeks than I could catch them.

"Sh-she left me, Katty."

My sister's sadness slipped and slipped down her face, and I simply froze. She sucked back a huge breath, her tiny chest shuddering with grief.

"I was out here drawing, and the man came in and started screaming at Mommy, and she started, um, crying and-and then he threw things! He threw my crayons and Davion's book! She ran into her bedroom and left me out here..."

I couldn't tell anyone exactly what I was feeling at that point.

It wasn't a feeling I'd ever felt before.

I pulled Charlotte's head down against my chest and held her there so she couldn't see my face and how blank I could feel it had gone. Whatever this new feeling was, it was bad. It was a negative *something*.

Numbing and overwhelming at once. Still and violent at once.

Dominic was staring at me. I could feel it *lasering* into the side of my face, branding his pity into my skin 'till I was scarred with it.

He might have known I was the girl with the junkie mom before, but now he *saw* it. He saw me with all my nasty little barriers torn down, shaking in exhaustion as I fought and failed to keep the walls of my world from collapsing.

My sister wept in my arms, crying out trauma she wouldn't understand until she was older. All she understood now was that her mom abandoned her when she was scared, but she didn't get why. *I* didn't get why either, but I sure as shit was going to get the answer.

"Hey, Bugs?" I spoke in hushed tones against her hair, bouncing my knees to rock her like I used to when she was smaller. "I'm gonna take you back to our room, check that it's safe, and then I'm gonna close the door, okay? Just for a bit to go find Mom."

Hidden against my neck, she nodded.

She pulled her face back, and I used the sleeve of my shirt to wipe a trail of snot that had started from her nose. We started back towards our bedroom, and I talked quietly to her the whole way. That *feeling* was getting bigger inside of me, turning my veins over to live wires and my blood to coursing electricity.

I didn't feel like myself. I didn't feel like a living, breathing thing at all.

I felt like lightning before it struck.

When we made it to the bedroom, I kissed her on the forehead, tucked her into my bed, and closed the door. On electric feet, I walked back to the living room.

Past the knocked over DVD stand with all of our movies spilled out, bills scattered over the floor, the broken drinking glasses that had been sitting on the counter when I left this morning.

I walked past it all and went straight for my mom's room.

In the background, I heard someone else enter my cluttered home. Probably Dominic's partner. I didn't slow down to check.

My steps stopped in front of her door, pausing to listen in on the other side. I didn't know what I'd find on the other side of this door, but I wasn't ashamed to admit that I hoped it was brutal.

And not in the sense some might think. I wanted to open the door and see my mother knocked out on the floor, blood dripping from her nose or the back of her head or *something* to give her a reason. Some incapacitating excuse for why she wasn't with Charlotte when I arrived.

Maybe if she could give me that, I could lie to myself and say that she was running back here to call the police to protect her child when the intruder got to her. She was *trying* to do the right thing, and she was just attacked in the process.

That was a scenario I could process.

Anything less and...

And I didn't know.

"Kat." Dominic caught my hand on the doorknob to my mother's bedroom, folding his fingers over mine. "Let me check the room first."

The muscles in my neck refused to loosen enough to look at him, so I just slipped my hand out from beneath his as a go ahead. Dominic slid his tall frame between me and the door so I couldn't see what was on the other side when I heard the knob turn and click open.

The door swung open, but Dominic didn't move.

His authoritative voice resonated in his back. "Ma'am, are you all right?"

For the first time in my entire life, I begged for silence.

I shut my eyes and prayed like I hadn't prayed since my grandma passed when I was sixteen. I prayed so much for her to get better, and she died anyway. Faster than her prognosis even. Prayer had gotten me jackshit and toyed too closely to magic for me to trust it.

But right then, I prayed.

And right then, prayer proved that I was right the first time.

"I'm here," her voice came, shaking and broken. "I-I'm here. This is my home."

Inside of me, that *something* feeling surged forward fast and screamed. Its cries vibrated my blood, electrifying it until my limbs shook, my vision shook, my entire fucking foundation shook like I was a self-contained earthquake. That feeling shot me forward, pushing past Dominic into my mother's bedroom.

And there she was.

Her brown eyes jumped to me, red-rimmed and sunken. Dark mahogany hair that matched mine in color hung in tangled strands on either side of her hollowed face, lips cracked and pale. Tears lined a clear path over her skin, giving her more color in her cheeks than I'd seen in months.

She was red with fear.

Crimson with boiling shame.

A sound creaked from her pale lips, something that sounded wounded and weak, and she stood from where she was huddled on the floor protecting herself. Protecting *only* herself.

It was at that moment that the feeling inside of me—that negative, numbing, overwhelming *something*—found its circuit... and the lightning finally hit.

For the next however moments, all I saw was blinding white.

There was screaming and sobbing, and on some level I was aware that some of the screaming was coming from me. I could feel it pouring out of me like lava, trying to incinerate the broken woman in front of me. My chest was hot, so fucking hot. It absolutely burned like hell, but there was nothing cold enough in all of existence to cool me down at the moment.

Suddenly, the sheet of white hot fury ripped out of focus as delicate fingers touched my arm. Reality came jolting back in a vision of sorry eyes and dark hair. Her touch filled my lungs with quick-acting fire, and I bucked at her hand immediately.

"Don't you fucking touch me," I spat and watched as my mother's face fall.

"Katerina, please—"

"Why did you leave her?"

"What do you—"

"Don't play *stupid*, Kathy."

She recoiled from me in a flinch, face squishing together as she heaved a breath. "Don't call me that. You know I hate it. Call me Mom."

The audacity she had drew me back, my voice low and vibrating. "Don't tell me what to call you. You *lost* that right. What kind of mother would leave her five-year-old daughter alone when a stranger breaks into the house?"

Her eyes rolled so hastily, I nearly missed the hurt that lingered in them. "You don't get to yell at me. You weren't here!"

"And if I was, the last thing I would have done was leave Charlotte alone. How could you *do* that?"

"It's not like he would've hurt her!"

Shock filled the silence and my mother's watery stare as she realized her mistake. I stepped into her—a threatening pace that stiffened the air.

"You *knew* him?"

My mother's gaze dropped, darting back and forth over my chest. She was so washed out and thin, I could almost see her heart pounding against her chest as panic got the better of her. The fast beating of her heart and goddamn *palpable* panic invited me in, stoking the lightning coursing in my veins.

"He was here because of you?" I hissed, watching as she picked and plucked at the dead skin on her lips. A nervous tick I knew well and unfortunately got from her.

"I didn't know he was coming..."

"Who was he?" Her eyes widened as I towered over her. God, she was small. All hunched over and pathetic.

"A-a friend. It was a misunderstanding."

"A misunderstanding that ended with our living room being ransacked? What was your *friend* looking for, Kathy?"

She shook her head so fast, I knew she was ready with a lie.

"Nothing."

"Did he take something?"

"Of course not!"

I relented despite her lies, my volume rising as my patience slipped. "Why was he here?"

The more I pressed, the more my mother began to lose it. She began rocking back and forth on her toes, fingers now in her mouth as she gnawed away at her nails. They'd surely start bleeding if she didn't stop. Incoherent mumbling started as she shook her head, mist hazing over her eyes as she looked to me.

"I owed him money, baby," she whispered, swollen teardrops spilling over. "I-I don't know how he found out where we live." Desperation streaked across her stare. "I swear I didn't tell him. I didn't. I *swear*. I didn't. I didn't..."

A heaviness sunk over my chest; an exhaustion I hadn't thought possible hit so suddenly and hard. My body swayed under the draining reality of what her words meant. The *horror* it brought.

"And now this man can come back *any* time he wants."

"He shouldn't!" Kathy was quick to jump on that, inching closer. "He shouldn't. He... should be good. He's-he's good for now."

My lungs stilled in the following seconds.

Disbelief held my whole body hostage aside from my lip that twitched and head that ticked.

No.

Painfully slow, life pulled through my lungs just enough to ask, "What do you mean he's *good*?"

My mother didn't respond. Instead, more tears, more fidgeting, more lip pulling. That half a step she dared to take went in reverse, and she slowly backed away from me. Each pace she furthered, the quicker oxygen pumped back through me and the harder I breathed. Each step, my chest heaved wider and filled hotter, nostrils flaring and teeth baring.

"He came here for money, Kathy. You don't *have* any money, so how is he good?" I asked, each syllable a pointed blade getting sharper and louder.

A tremble wracked my mother's body, whimpers breaking past her lips. Each one made me want to rage, made me want to shake her until her ruined porcelain skin shattered between my fingers and spilled the words right out.

"Your shoebox," she muttered, and I thought I misheard her.

I *had* to have misheard her, because she wasn't aware of my shoebox. Not the one I kept under the kitchen sink that had all of my emergency money I'd been saving up for almost three years. Any spare cash I made went in that shoebox strictly for medical emergencies. We didn't have insurance, and if Charlotte were to ever get really sick or injured, that's what I had the shoebox for.

And I'd never told Kathy about it ever before.

"What the fuck did you just say?"

Deadly. My tone was pure venom.

My mother was suddenly so serious, shaking her head at me like *I* was the one who should know better. "Katerina, I *needed* to give him it. I didn't have a choice."

A tiny gasp punctured the air, and it came from me.

"Kat."

That was Dominic somewhere in the background trying to get my attention, attempting to distract my temper for just long enough that my mental strings didn't snap. He was afraid I was about to lose my barely tethered mind on my mother right now due to her *spectacular* choice of words.

And he was goddamn right.

"Did you just say that you didn't have a choice?" I began, disdain scratching my vocal cords. "That you had no other choice than to *steal* my money? Money that is for Charlotte in case she gets sick or hurt?"

"Baby, I—"

"How did you even know about it? Is any of it even *left?*" I yelled, my hatred peaking.

Or so I thought.

I watched her scramble for an answer, her eyes turning beady and forehead shining with sweat. She shrugged a pointy shoulder, not making eye contact with anyone in the room. "I found it a while ago. I don't know—"

"That money is for *emergencies.*"

"This was an emergency!"

"You owing a drug dealer is not an emergency. It's fucking typical," I spat.

"Katerina!" My mother's eyes shot wide and right back to Dominic. "That's not what it was for. It was—"

"Don't lie to him," I snapped, cutting her off. "He knows. That's my boss, and he already knows because your addiction *haunts* me. It fucking haunts me everywhere I go, and now he's got a front row seat to the shit show that is my life."

She gasped like she was horrified or even offended, balling her hands together into fists. "That's not fair. You're not being fair." She shook her head, the water holding in her eyes turning bitter. "You have no idea what I go through *every day...* just trying to make it through."

I jerked back like she'd slapped me, teeth clenching. "I have no idea?"

Considering I was the only person to stand by her side when Dad left three years ago and got VIP seating to the emotional, mental, and physical downfall of my mother, I'd say I had *some* idea.

"Do you hear yourself or do you just not care how you sound? I guess the answer is obvious though considering you left your daughter out there by herself with a dangerous man while you hid like a fucking coward—"

"I wasn't hiding!"

Confusion bunched my face together as my mother and I stared each other down, and I tried to make sense of her words. Tried to make sense of her sobs that she muffled into her hands, and why her hysteria seemed to triple in the last seconds.

It poured through her fingers, seeping into her carpet tinged with mildew smell and crawled all the way up to me. Her hysteria knocked on my shins, clawed up my body until it found my brain and burrowed itself inside, realization dawning in a full body shutdown.

"Oh my god..." I breathed. "You ran to save your stash."

There was no question in my phrasing. It was the truth, and even she couldn't hide it. My entire body numbed. Thoughts dulled, hearing faded, taste soured, feeling flatlined.

All I could do was see, and what I saw was red. It edged in all around my vision, creating a ring of red—a ring of fire—around a woman who was barely even human anymore. She was all chemicals. Poison ran through her blood and altered her DNA to this thing in front of me that was no more living than weeds.

She was physically there, encased in flesh that was rotting from the inside, but she had no function other than stealing life from the sun and strangling the flowers around her.

Ringing. It had started small, a faint drilling between my ears, but got louder and piercing as the mindless weed dared to speak.

"He took it. All of it," she whispered. "It's been a couple days since I-I..." Her voice cracked, and then she did. "You know I'm not well without it, baby."

The red was getting tighter around her, closing in a shade closer to blood with every inch. And the ringing, the fucking *ringing* was frightening. It got so loud, I felt like glass beneath it. The pressure was too much, bending my bones and heating my pores.

It got louder and shriller, stabbing at my ears until it consumed me. Until I was made up of the ringing and nothing else. Until it expanded inside of me too much, and just like the glass, I shattered in a hundred deadly shards under its high-pitched pressure.

I was moving before I registered it, a cry following me as I ran forward at the woman with the mahogany hair. The cry bled down my throat and sounded like torment embodied.

As if heartbreak had its own sound.

Coffee-colored eyes shot open as I came at her and shoved as hard as I could, watching with a grin as she knocked back into the wall. She crumpled to the ground, and I loved it. I fucking loved seeing her terrified and hissing in pain.

I was the lightning, and I would strike her again and again until she was nothing but ashes and tears.

She shrieked beneath me, and my fingers flexed, wanting to hear the noise again. I was uncontained, chaotic, the fever coursing through me too volatile to control.

My blood sizzled, fingers tingling, smile widening—

And then I was gone. Airborne, legs kicking out beneath me as a strong arm around my waist carried me backwards, screams pouring through my lips.

"Let me go! She fucking deserves it!"

My back hit a wall, eyes blinking wildly as nothing and everything came into focus. The hate was too much, too powerful, and I struggled against the brick wall of muscle that had grabbed me.

"*Kat.*"

Thunder.

The lightning quieted for just a fleeting second to recognize the thunder booming above me and its hands around my arms, pinning me back against the wall. I bucked in his hold, his fingers pressing deeper into my skin to keep me in place.

In the middle of a cry, the thunder rumbled right next to my ear. "Remember what you told me about yelling in the house."

I sucked back a breath that stunted my next scream. The flashes across my vision quieted just barely, and the thunder used the lapse to talk deeper, sweeter. "I know it's not even close to the same thing, but try to calm yourself."

Thumbs ran over my arms, soothing strokes back and forth. Each stroke centered my haywire focus bit by measured bit. The lightning was still inside of me, pulsing and burning my blood, but the thunder absorbed just enough so I could see again.

And all I saw was gray.

Soft, cool gray that hovered above me like I was staring up at the moon, just as magnificent and otherworldly. My head lulled back against the wall, heavy breaths still working my chest.

"I can't," I whimpered to him. "I-I can't calm down."

"Yes, you can." All of his attention was fixed on me, like he could tell I was too hot and was trying to cool me down with his winter eyes. "Breathe."

I shook my head and stopped breathing all together instead. I couldn't do it, even if it made me a hypocrite in the flesh. I couldn't breathe and couldn't calm down and didn't even want to. What I really needed was edging in my throat, tiptoeing up and up with razor blades.

Eyes on him, my voice stole to a whisper one step away from breaking. "I need to scream."

Dominic took his gaze all across my face, doing his indiscernible dissection. He eventually brought it back to me, settled his eyes on mine and nodded.

"Okay," he spoke quietly.

A hand grazed up my arm to the back of my neck, fingers splitting into my hair. If I had the oxygen to, I would have asked him what he was doing as he anchored my body away from the wall and into him.

A tiny breath hitched in my squeezing throat as Dominic pressed my face against his chest, his other hand flattening on my back. His smell was everywhere around me, shoved down my nose that was smushed into his shirt and so potent I could taste him on my tongue.

He held me—and I mean he *really* held me—but I still didn't know why until his lips brushed the top of my head with a single instruction.

"Scream."

My heart jumped, startling me like I forgot I had one. I fisted my hands in the material of his shirt as soon as I understood him, as if I might have fallen over without him there. Something moved inside of me, and I couldn't be sure what it was because I didn't have time to think about it. There was no time because the scream was coming fast, shoving everything else out of its way.

Racing. Burning. Shredding me apart from the inside out.

My lungs filled with fire as I breathed back, the pain knifing up my throat, my fingers destroying the neatness of his pressed shirt.

And then it was out.

Dominic's hand on the back of my head pressed down harder, swallowing up my scream against his body as much as possible. The scream bled out of me, causing almost as much pain as it was releasing. It hurt and it healed, and by the long-winded end of it, water had formed in the corner of my eyes from the sheer effort of it.

Dominic didn't let go even as my scream faded, leaving me panting and raw on the inside. Only my heavy breathing filled the room, and for a moment, I wished I could disappear inside Dominic's arms where the only thing that existed was his elemental scent and warmth.

I wanted to fill myself with it and float through the darkness, drifting along the current of *him*.

Yet, the *weed* across the room still wasn't done sucking life and spewing lies.

"Baby, I'm so sorry," Kathy sputtered. My tired muscles jerked. "You know I love you and your sister."

Slowly, Dominic loosened his hold on the back of my neck so I could look up. His hand on my back disappeared but secured against the wall behind me, keeping a stiff barrier between me and my mother.

Over Dominic's arm, I found her on the other side of the room, shivering and tear-streaked.

"You don't love us," I rasped. "You haven't loved us since he left."

"I tried! I—"

"You didn't fucking try." She shut her mouth as I lost it. As my voice cracked. As the monopoly my temper had over my emotions exhausted itself, and everything poured out all at once.

"You left us at the *exact* same time Dad did. Charlotte may not have been old enough to remember any of that, and I am so fucking thankful for that, but you can't lie to me like I can lie to her. I was there. I remember *all* of it. I remember holding your hand through your heartbreak and then holding your hair when you puked it all up."

A violent sob broke past her cracked lips, tearing tremors through her whole body.

"I doubt you remember much of the first year after he left because you were drunk through all of it, but I remember it. *I* was the one who found you and drove you to the hospital the first time you had to have your stomach pumped. *I* was the one who had to clean you up and put you to bed almost every night. I was the one who thought you'd *died* the first time you overdosed."

I was the one to find her that time too, scared out of my mind because I didn't know she'd fallen to drugs yet. One day, I was splitting her vodka in half with tap water, and the next she was gone to heroin. It owned her so fast, I didn't even catch it happening.

She went from an abusive relationship with my father, to one with alcohol, to one with heroin. She was passed from one pair of noxious arms to another, and I watched it all happen until I couldn't anymore.

"I watched you poison yourself because of him, because of a man who *never* deserved you."

My mother shook her head, letting it drop into her hands as she wept.

"You let him take everything from you, and you never even tried to stop it because I *begged* you to, and you didn't. I cried for you to stop, signed you up for classes to get you help. I *loved* you through it all, and it wasn't enough."

Knots tied around my throat as I kept talking, but I couldn't stop it. The painful words were coming out whether I wanted them or not.

"Nothing I did was ever enough to make you want to be *here* with us instead of fucked up for him. You let me bleed myself to a husk for you, and then you *left* me that way," I cried, voice breaking as my eyes welled with tears she didn't deserve.

A shaking breath shuddered in my chest as my heart broke open. "You used to be so good. Even when times were shitty and Dad was being Dad, *you* were still trying to be decent. I used to think that if he left us, everything would get better."

A wet, humorless chuckle pushed up my throat. "But then he *did* leave and you couldn't handle it, so you threw every responsibility my way at eighteen, and I took it. I fucking took them on because you were my mom, and I *loved* you. I chose *you* over graduating high school. I chose *you* over going to college."

I paused, a hot tear sliding down my cheek.

"But you never chose me back. It was always him. He's always been your first choice."

Grief I thought was long gone ripped down my chest, a heavy sob tipping out. "Why don't you love us as much as you love him?"

The room was silent of everything but my choppy breathing. The look on my mother's face was awestruck and wrecked. I'd never told her any of that before. I'd never told *anyone* any of that before.

I didn't even remember I felt that way.

I spent much of the last three years since Dad left deflecting anything that hurt me because I didn't have time for it. Surviving was just so much easier when I could forget I even had these feelings.

These weak, crippling, lonely feelings.

I'd forgotten Dominic was holding the back of my head until his hand relaxed to rest on my shoulder, and I tipped my eyes up to him.

My first reaction was to feel embarrassed. I mean, I still had tears drying on my cheeks and my broken heart bleeding all over my sleeves. That wasn't me. I didn't cry.

But I was just too exhausted to feel embarrassed right now. All I wanted was one thing.

"Can you arrest her?" I asked.

A startled gasp came from Kathy's side of the bedroom, and my nostrils flared. Dominic looked so fucking sad as he shook his head. "We haven't found any drugs on the property yet. My partner did a full sweep of everywhere but in here."

"There's nothing," my mother practically choked out. "You won't find anything."

"But what about the break in? That happened because of her when a small child was home. Come on, that has to be *something*."

Disappointment crushed his eyebrows together, his chest sinking.

"Most we can do is run a drug test on her. If she was on something when the break in happened, then we can get her for Child Endangerment. She can also give us a description of who broke in and..."

He kept talking, but I stopped listening.

His voice became sonorous background music for me to drift away in my mind to. I was so fucking tired from today, from everything. If he wasn't going to arrest Kathy, then I didn't wanna be here anymore.

"Do you need me back at work today?"

Dominic stopped talking, eyebrows curving in as he trailed his eyes down the wet stains of evidence on my face. Quickly, I ran the back of my hand over my cheeks so he'd stop looking.

His mouth frowned, and he shook his head. "No. I'll text Heather and ask if she can stay home for the day and work from there."

I nodded barely. "Excuse me, then."

Dominic didn't move right away. His hand stayed where it was on my shoulder while his other boxed me in. The look on his face said he didn't want to let me go, said that he had more to say, but he never did.

After a second, he agreed with a nod and moved back, and I slid out.

I passed my mother, and I passed Dominic's partner as I left the room, not giving either of them a second look. The only person I wanted to see was at the end of the hallway, curled up under the sheets of my bed.

That's exactly where I found her when I opened the door. Her eyes were sleepy and red from crying, and I pulled the sheets back and snuggled up with her. Charlotte huddled into my chest and lapsed into a deep sleep in minutes while I pushed my fingers through her hair.

As worn out as I was, I never slept.

My heart was beating too fast for sleep. It hummed a tune too anxious to do anything but lay there and obsess over what happened, the possibility of it happening again, and the why of it all.

Everything that happened today stemmed from a broken heart.

A broken heart created a broken woman.

A broken woman created a broken family.

Love broke us.

Love obliterated my life before it ever really started.

FOURTEEN

Since everything that happened on Friday, I took Charlotte with me to stay at Layla's for the weekend. Her parents may not like me, but they adored Charlotte, and after Layla told them about the break in, they opened their door right up.

Saturday had been relatively chill. We watched movies all day in our pajamas, and Layla's parents cooked a huge dinner for us that night. Homemade tacos, empanadas, rice and beans, grilled corn, and tres leches cake for dessert.

Which I'd never had before, and holy fuck, I never thought I'd cream because of cake.

Today, we three decided to get afternoon ice cream by Lakeside park. The ice cream place was this outdoor only space that I went to a ton growing up. I was *obsessed* with it when I was little. Their roof was painted like an ice cream cone and everything. To this day, they served the best double chocolate ice cream in town and let Charlotte have as many samples as she wanted.

Daren texted on our way there and decided he'd tag along with one of his work buddies. I'd never met this one before—*Kyle*—but we were only twenty minutes into this strange fivesome, and I already wanted to put my foot in his ass.

"I don't know. I'm with Daren on that one." Kyle jabbed a chummy elbow into Daren's shoulder, a stupid grin on his face. "If I had the chance to run or be caught, you can betch'r sweet ass I'm runnin'."

I rolled my eyes, licking off a dollop of my chocolate swirl. "And they say chivalry is dead."

"What's chivalry?" Charlotte asked, mouth full of strawberry ice cream and sprinkles.

Layla swooped in to answer. "It's when you're at a party with your boyfriend and he *doesn't* jump out of a window to leave you behind."

Daren clicked his tongue at her. "Didn't you leave her too?"

"I was drunk. I can't be held accountable."

"Plus, you fell into a bush, and I spent the next morning picking leaves out of your hair," I quipped.

Kyle sputtered, leaning back against a railing and passing a hand over his backwards baseball cap. "You fell into a bush?"

Layla shrugged him off. "What can I say? It was a great party."

"Yeah," Daren scoffed, flicking his wadded up straw wrapper into the grass. "Until Kat's cop boss had to show up and whip out his badge."

Kyle's umber eyes bulged. "Your *boss* broke up the party?"

"Sure did." I cocked an indignant look his way as Daren answered for me. "From what I heard, everyone else under twenty-one who got caught were written up, 'cept my Kitty Kat over here."

Aggravation rolled my eyes back again, and I tried to ignore him and exactly what he was implying. I only filled him in on the basics of what happened that night after he called a few days later to 'see how I was.'

Daren wouldn't care about the specifics of the night or how enjoyable it actually was up 'till the end. All Daren cared about was that I wasn't arrested, and that I didn't care about him enough to be mad at him.

"So, whatcha do to get out of a write up, *Kitty Kat?*"

Gross.

I didn't even like it when Daren called me that lazy nickname, but coming from Kyle, it actually sounded like bolts grinding in a garbage disposal.

"Did ya ride his baton real good?" Daren snickered at his friend's lameass joke and then joined in.

"Oh, I bet you let him give you the *full* pat down, huh?"

I glared at them both, unamused. "Are you two done?"

Usually, I was a whore for sexual innuendos, but these two pissed me off. It set my stomach on edge them talking about Dominic like that. Especially Daren. Dominic did a hell of a lot more for me that night than he would have. He did a hell of a lot more than most people would on Friday too.

Go figure. A man in this world that wasn't a complete tool.

Miracles really do exist.

Just then, a force hit me from behind, shocking and scaring the shit out of me.

"What the—"

"Ms. Kat! Hi!"

The curse on my tongue evaporated, and I jerked my head down to see two tiny arms wrapped around my waist. An easy laugh fell from my lips as I made the connection, and I patted my hand that wasn't holding up my ice cream cone around one of those little arms.

"Kiddo, did you become a linebacker over the weekend? Because *jeez.*"

Maya's giggles bubbled through the air, her hold on me squeezing tighter. Somehow, I managed to twist around to face her, passing a hand over her ringlet curls as she beamed up at me.

"Ms. Kat, did you know we were here too?" Maya asked, hanging herself around my waist like I was a jungle gym.

"I didn't! Who is *we*?"

Cue one masculine answer.

Around the corner of the ice cream shop jogged Dominic, the sun backlighting his entrance as if the Gods who made him had planned it just to steal my breath away. A large silhouette of strong shoulders to a narrowed waist and long legs came near. I was only vaguely aware as I straightened my spine for him and forced a clip of air back in my lungs.

Silver eyes I hadn't seen since Friday flashed to me, a lopsided grin curving his mouth. A funny feeling somersaulted my stomach, but I smiled through the weird sensation as he stopped in front of me, looking sheepish.

"Sorry. I tried to grab her before she took off."

I waved him off with my ice cream hand, the other steadying on Maya's back. "Oh, it's okay. She's fine."

"I told you she would want to see me," Maya's little voice bragged, her head hanging backwards.

"I didn't think she wouldn't want to see you. I just also think it's her day off, and you'll see her tomorrow." Dominic was trying to be gentle with Maya, but the gentle approach bit him in the ass as she suctioned herself to me harder, squeezing wisps of laughter out of my stomach.

"It's really okay. We're just getting some ice cream."

"That's why we came too!" Maya exclaimed. "I got bubble gum flavor."

I hummed, head bobbing as I peered up at Dominic. "Make up ice cream?" *For Friday.*

He nodded, chest puffing wide as he breathed deep. "Yeah. You?"

I confirmed. "Make up ice cream." *For Friday.*

Fucking Friday.

Next to me, Charlotte popped up, shoulders back and pink ice cream smeared on her chin. Maya was solely focused on her father and I when Charlotte appeared and she flinched when she noticed my sister.

Charlotte tilted her head at Maya like she was something to inspect, and then abruptly stuck her hand out to her.

"I'm Charlotte, but Katty calls me Bugs."

A little bit of pride and a lot of amusement pulled at my lips as I stared at her. Maya, however, shrunk back into her father, reaching her arms back in search for his hands to hold onto. Dominic wrapped her tiny hands in his with a soft chuckle.

"Can you tell her your name is Maya and that Ms. Kat hangs out with you during the week?"

"Yeah." I bumped my hip against Bug's shoulder. "I think you two could be friends."

Maya remained tight-lipped and skeptical of Charlotte, keeping her back glued to Dominic's legs and hands roped around his. The difference in the two girls was glaring, but Charlotte didn't let Maya's shyness deter her. Not one bit.

She took her bold attention to Dominic, staring up at him like he wasn't a tower compared to her.

"You were at my house," she said matter-of-factly.

His browline inched up, a peculiar something streaking across his eyes. "I was. You're right."

Behind me, Layla broke back into the conversation. "Wait, wait. Are *you* her cop boss?"

Dominic arched a quizzical brow at me.

I nodded a shrug. "That's what they call you."

"Ah."

And I'll be damned if there wasn't a ghost of a smile riding his full mouth.

Suddenly, pain spiked in my shin, a sharp cry choking in my throat as I shot a glare to Layla on my left. Her eyes were bugging the fuck out, silently screaming the obvious at me about Dominic.

"Yeah, I know," I muttered, brushing her off. *Jeez.* Spinning back to Dominic, he was gifting me another questioning look, mouth pursed and brow cocked.

"Oh, you're hot, and she's just—ow!"

This time, she went for the toes, and she went for them hard. I hopped on one foot, holding my throbbing toes and gritting my teeth at Layla.

"*God*, you're lucky I can't curse right now."

In return, she fucking winked at me. A scoff tried to rise in my throat but got strangled by laughter. *Dammit.*

Testing my foot back on solid ground, I hobbled my focus back to Dominic. "This is Layla. Best friend."

Connections formed in his eyes, and I knew he was placing her at the party in his mind. He tilted her a stiff nod.

"Good to meet you."

Someone else cleared their throat and made me wanna punch him right in it. Swiveling to an expectant Daren with annoyance sitting heavy on my chest, I flicked a finger in his direction.

"And uh, this is Daren and..." My finger aimed at Kyle. "I barely know this dude."

Kyle blew a sharp exhale up through his shaggy bangs, slouching back against the railing. Next to him, Daren visibly puffed his chest out, jutting his chin up at Dominic.

"So, you're the one who busted her at the party, eh?"

Shock blew my eyes wide.

Instant fury coiled around my muscles, stringing them tight. I dared him, fucking *dared* him like I had telepathic powers to look at me. Look at me and let me boil him alive with my hellfire glare.

"And you'd be the one who abandoned her at the same party," Dominic countered with ease.

My eyebrows hit my hairline, and my jaw hit the fucking floor. I snapped back to him, flushing hot at his casual confidence and lasered focus that cut straight through Daren.

Free-falling laughter spilled from my lips, rolling through Layla as she joined me in laughing at Daren's expense. Charlotte tagged in too, even though she had no idea what she was giggling at, and she was by far the loudest.

Hand on my chest, I said, "Oh, now that was fun."

Daren rolled his eyes and sulked like a child, whipping out his phone as a distraction from the massive burn Dominic just scorched him with. Dominic appeared a little smug about it too, and I immediately hated how good a shade of arrogance looked on him.

"Ms. Kat?" All laughter faded as Maya commanded the group's attention. "Can you play with us? Just for a little?"

Dominic lowered to his knees, his big hands around her shoulders. "Baby, Ms. Kat is busy today."

"We can go on the swings!" Charlotte hollered out of nowhere, jumping in front of Maya. Her cup of ice cream was still clutched in her hands, but mostly empty.

Surprisingly, Maya began to nod. Slow at first, but got faster and her stare cranking brighter. "Okay!"

And there you have it. Instant friends.

"Can we, Ms. Kat? Five minutes!"

"Or ten!" Charlotte negotiated.

The two of them were so giddy and wide-eyed and a million times better company than Daren or Kyle. It was an easy yes, and the girls cheered and bolted for the swings not too far away.

Dominic had an eye on them as I spun back to Layla, whose stare was firmly on Dominic's ass. He was wearing jeans today. I'd never seen him in jeans before, and it had taken an exorbitant amount of strength to not find a reason for him to bend over in the last couple minutes.

"*Hey.*" She jumped as I snapped in front of her face. "You're okay if I go for a bit?"

She blinked a few times, and then nodded sharply. "Uh, *yeah.* Because if you don't, I will."

I knocked my shoulder into hers, a wily smirk stretching my lips. "Keep it in your pants."

Just as I turned to go, Daren stopped me.

"Uh, Kat?"

"What?"

His hazel gaze trained on me, he lifted his eyebrows like I was supposed to know what the fuck that meant. I did the same back to him to show him how annoying it was, and he scoffed.

"Can you come here?"

"Why?"

He did that entitled eyebrow raise again. "So I can kiss my girlfriend."

My mouth formed an 'O' and with Dominic still a staggering presence next to me, I realized *exactly* what Daren was doing.

"Are you sure it's not because you wanna put a chastity belt on me before I go? Maybe tattoo your name inside my vagina?"

Daren was actually dumb enough to act surprised that I called him on his territorial bullshit. Upset seeped in through the corners of his eyes, his top lip snagging on a sneer.

I cocked my head at him with a bright smile. "No? Okay then."

I spun on my heel to Dominic who was freely giving away how amused he was, and even a touch impressed if the sun wasn't playing tricks on me. His fucking dimples were even winking at me.

Jeans *and* dimples today.

He was killer looking, and even though I hated Daren's little display in front of him, I could at least understand where it was coming from.

Just before Dominic and I left, I tipped my head back to him. "You did bring the condoms, right?"

Those attractive dimples deepened as he shut his eyes. Layla was cackling and even Kyle too. My own laughter bubbled up as Dominic tipped his stare to the sky and shook his head, probably cursing whoever was up there that put me in his path.

"Not funny, Kat!" Daren called behind me as I walked away.

I shouted back, "Then why is everyone except you laughing?"

The high I got from telling him off rode me over to the playground on light feet. Charlotte and Maya were on the swings, trying to see who could make it higher. There wasn't too much to this park and never had been. A set of swings, a monkey bar jungle gym with swirly and straight slides attached—the metal kind that burned your skin at the hottest time of day—and a few animal teeter-totters. I'd put in some *miles* on the cheetah one growing up.

There was a sizable lake though, and a lot of times when I brought Charlotte here, we'd lay in the grass and pluck the blades, watching the sun dip behind the waterline. She usually fell asleep or made dirt pies, but I always watched until the sun was completely gone.

People who watched the sunrise did it because they loved the idea of starting fresh. A new day.

People like me who watched the sunset did it because they loved endings. A chance to rest.

Dominic came up next to me in a few long strides, still wearing that easy smile that was devastating on him. "You know you could have told him I'm married, right?"

"Eh. That's not as much fun for me. Plus, he could have just looked at your ring finger instead of being a possessive twat."

His gaze cut to me as I licked off another scoop of my ice cream. "You really don't seem to like him very much."

"Neither do you."

"Do you want me to like him?" Dominic asked, eyeing me down the bridge of his nose.

"No." I shook my head, curving my hand so my melting dessert didn't run all over it. "If you could hate him actually, it'll make me like him even *more*. Tell me you forbid me to see him ever again!"

We came to a stop in front of one of the blue benches lined up in front of the lake. I leaned the small of my waist against the back of it, Dominic planting himself in front of me with crossed arms.

"Do you want me to ground you if you see him?" he tried, playing along.

"Could ya?" I batted my eyelashes at him, an innocent twist to my lips. "I'll even call you Daddy, if you want."

Any playfulness I'd encouraged in him died immediately beneath the heavy frown that collapsed his mouth. I barked a stiff laugh; his mood change was like whiplash.

"Oh, Daddy's mad," I hummed, watching his veins flex in his forearms. One I'd never noticed before pulsed in his thick neck, and I chewed on my bottom lip to keep my stupid grin from breaking my face.

The gray of his eyes had turned punishing, as had the sharp tick of his jawline. Under thickly shaped eyebrows, he rolled those eyes away from me. "Shut up and eat your ice cream."

I did as he said, stuffing my mouth full of the dessert to push down more laughter. I passed a glance over to the girls who were still exactly where we left them. It was actually a really nice day out. The kind where the breeze was constantly rolling, the sun was on full blast, and the mixture of the two created the perfect weather for jean shorts and sun tops like I was wearing.

Dominic was dressed for the nice weather too, more casual than I'd ever seen him. A plain t-shirt, so light gray it was almost white, clung to his chest and around his sculpted arms, hanging a bit looser around his torso.

And then those jeans. Those fucking jeans that were going to make me come in my own.

His hair was the same as he wore it to work. Mostly in place but too thick to completely cooperate. *God*, I wanted to run my fingers through it and mess it all up. See what he looked like totally unkempt and undone.

Maybe I would if there wasn't that pesky little reminder that was noticeably absent.

Even though I didn't want to sour the mood, I still had to ask.

"So where's Heather?"

"Out of town for work."

"Again?"

He hummed and nodded. "She'll be back tomorrow."

I didn't know anything about being a realtor, so I had no idea it required so much work in other places. I guess it made sense since apparently Heather sold to a large market across several cities. Still, it seemed like a lot of time away from her husband and kid that, last I heard, were all on rocky ground with each other.

Chucking the last of my cone in a trash can next to us, I said, "You two ever kiss and make up?"

Dominic lowered his head to stare at his—holy shit, were those sneakers? And here I thought he only wore fancy-ass wingtips.

"We don't really make up. Just move onto the next fight."

The misery in his tone picked up my chin and turned it up to him.

Words. I didn't have them. Not the ones necessary to smooth over the harsh lines etched into his handsome face. Those kinds of lines were permanent. Heartbreak couldn't be erased.

There was no remedy I could sew with words that would cinch the cracks in his heart together. Pep talks were for cheerleading, not broken marriages. We all knew I was shit at them anyhow. What I *could* do was distract him from his unwanted emotions.

I was a pro at that.

"Have you ever had tres leches cake before?" I asked.

He slid a side glance over to me, perplexed but curious. "No?"

"Oh my God, you have to try it. We're staying with Layla for the weekend until I can fix our lock tonight, and her mom made it last night, and—" I blew a chef's kiss. "Better than an orgasm."

One of his dark brows curled up, a roguish curve to his pink mouth. He peered away from me as the wind flirted with his nearly perfect hair.

"Sounds like y—"

Then he stopped himself.

I waited, and nothing. Confusion cinched my eyebrows together. "What?"

Still, he didn't say a word. Just shook his head and kept his stare straight forward. Weird. Even the backs of his jaw were tight like whenever I said something to piss him off or—

I exploded with a high-pitched gasp. "Were you about to say something dirty?"

His Adam's apple curved up and down his throat, his strong chin tilting downward. For a man as impassive as him, he wasn't hiding his guilt well. He was *visibly* tense, practically having to unlock his jaw to talk.

"It was thoughtless and inappropriate."

"What was it?"

"I'm not going to say it."

"Can I guess?"

"No."

"Was it…" I tapped my pointer finger to my bottom lip, filtering his words through the gutter of my brain. *Sounds like, sounds like, sounds like…* "I said it was better than an orgasm so…" *Holy shit.* "Were you about to say it sounds like I need better orgasms?" I finished, astonished and aroused in one.

A victorious grin splashed across my cheeks as Dominic let out a forceful exhale through his nose. I was right, and he was a dirty, *dirty* cop boss. Fuck, I loved it. Knowing that somewhere in that austere, straight-laced, law-abiding mind of his was something just a little filthy.

Just a little wrong in the right kinda way.

Dominic eased his loaded stare back to me, peering down at me with an intimate awareness about him. As if I was a know-nothing little girl and he was an expert in the things I didn't know.

"No cake should be better than an orgasm, Ms. Sanders," he murmured deeply.

Holy fuck, could I get a recording of him saying the word 'orgasm' to take home, please? I'd listen to it on repeat and come undone in my bed for him each time he said it—like it was an order straight from him to me. The word was sin embodied on his tongue, rolling around and promising he could show me heaven and hell in one sitting if only it was allowed.

I breathed back a breath, trying to cool myself down from the inside out. "Well, this cake was. Better than any I've had anyway."

With unimpressed leisure, Dominic carried his acute focus to where Daren and the others were. "I'm not surprised with who you're dating."

My lips popped open, surprise holding them there. Someone forgot to turn on their filter this morning. Talking about my orgasms *and* throwing shade? Weekend Reed fucking ruled.

"Mr. Reed, are you telling me I need to date more experienced men?"

A pause lingered between us. Dominic still wasn't looking at me, but I was locked on him, trying to catch any small token of a reaction he forgot to hide. I watched and waited until it happened, until he gave me that slight shift in his expression followed by a shift in his stance.

For just a nanosecond, Dominic Reed was in *distinct* strain.

And then it was gone, and he was steering his steely gaze over to me with a strong arch in his brow. "I'm telling you that you could have any man you want, and *that* shouldn't be it."

Those words hit my stomach in a funny way. I took my stare from him, lending it back out to the girls now on the slides.

After a moment, Dominic spoke. "Did I say something wrong?"

I sucked back a breath, shaking my head quickly. "No, no."

"Then why did you get quiet?"

My ice cream suddenly wasn't sitting so well. It cramped up as the familiar flutter of anxiety tortured my chest. I pulled a squeezing breath through my lungs, forcing words out. "Most men who say something like that have a reason for saying it, so—" I shrugged, feeling suddenly defensive. "I'm just wondering what yours would be."

I ducked my stare down to my fingers, pinching the skin on the softest part of my wrist for a distraction. At least it wasn't my lips. I was making a conscious effort to not pick at my lips like my mother did. The less things we had in common, the better.

Beside me, Dominic angled himself to me, and I could feel him staring down at me. Probably calculating my fidgeting against what I'd just said.

A hand, big and warm, closed around mine and stopped my anxious fingers. The shock of his touch brought my gaze up.

Gray silk eyes waited for mine. "There's no reason. It's just true."

What a gorgeous liar.

"Yeah? You think any man would want me and all my fucked upness? You saw it firsthand. I'm kind of crazy."

"You're not crazy."

"I'm a little crazy."

His perfect mouth flattened some. "You love your sister a lot."

He had me there. I dreaded bringing her back to our house tonight. Even after I fixed the lock, I'd never feel safe with her there again. Not while the thing that used to be our mom was living there.

"I need to get her out of that house," I said, watching Charlotte as she played. "I just can't afford it yet."

Dominic turned his head but not his body. He watched the girls playing the same as I was, and the moment was quiet and still.

I didn't totally hate it.

"She's a lot like you," he spoke, voice deep and even. "Bold and confident."

I smiled at his words, despite the fact that I hoped she turned out nothing like me.

"Thanks. Maya's a lot like you, too." I nodded, bringing my gaze back to him. "Strapping muscles and perfect five o'clock shadow."

A breathtaking grin broke across his cheeks instantly, a sharp breath of laughter pushing through his nose. It was one of those smiles that made him look younger than he was, his eyes bright and shining for a change. I enjoyed making him look like this.

I probably enjoyed it too much.

So, I spun away from the man with the devastating lopsided grin and climbed up on the seat of the bench we'd been leaning on. I took a second to be with the lake, to feel the sun bouncing off of the water and heating my skin. Tingles sprinkled all over my body, and an easiness tugged at my lips with the feeling.

Then I turned my back to the sun and propped one foot up on the backrest of the bench. Arms out, I steadied my balance.

"Ms. Sanders, what are you doing?"

I pushed my other foot off the seat of the bench, standing tall and narrow on the backrest of it. "Pretending I'm on a tightrope."

"And what if you fall?"

"Then that'll be really embarrassing for me."

One foot in front of the other, I wobbled only slightly, tensing the arches in my feet to keep my balance. My heart thudded for only a second. Dominic walked alongside me as I righted myself and kept going.

His eyebrows were knotted, his thoughtful focus on the ground. "Why didn't you say that I'd catch you if you fell?"

"Why would I say that?"

"I think most people would. Most people would trust that whoever they were with would catch them."

"I'd probably say that if Layla was with me."

"What about Daren?"

"*Hell* no."

Dominic stopped as I stopped at the end of the backrest, carefully positioning my feet to turn back around and go the other way. "So, you hold me and your idiot boyfriend to the same standard?"

I chuckled, teetering a bit as I twisted my feet to face him. "I hold *all* men to the same standards."

Dominic laid his hand to his chest. "On behalf of all men, ouch."

"Oh, did I wound the impervious Detective Reed?" I taunted, hands on hips.

"Impervious?"

"Yeah, are you shocked I know a big SAT word?"

"No." He tilted a steamed look up at me. "I'm shocked that's the one word you'd use to describe me."

A wicked chuckle got stuck in my throat. "Well, the word I'm actually thinking would probably get me in trouble."

The gray of his eyes smoked, and a satisfied smirk turned up my lips. Messing with him was way too much fun. He didn't need to know that I was serious, and that the word flashing through my mind right now was completely and thoroughly *fuckable*.

Dominic upbraided me with a slow shake of his head. "Trouble. That's a *very* good word to describe you."

"Aw, I'm flattered."

This time, it was my turn to place my hand over my heart in a dramatic display. Except, when I did, I flexed my foot out without thinking, and the inevitable happened. Well, inevitable according to Dominic.

A gasp punctured my lungs and my heart jumped. Knees wobbled, arms flailed, and forward I fell.

It was almost stupid how fast Dominic's reflexes were. I was falling for less than two seconds before firm hands clamped around my waist, steadying my fall. My hands gripped onto his shoulders for support in a flash of instincts, fingers biting into the thick muscle beneath his shirt.

Feet still on the backrest of the bench, I was stuck at like a 70 degree angle, panic rounding my eyes. Dominic was right below me, smug as ever as he held me up.

"Lucky catch," I breathed.

His face drew with confidence that intensified his sex appeal immediately.

"Luck had nothing to do with it, Ms. Sanders."

My eyes were everywhere over his face, searching for signs of what he meant by that.

Was he trying to say that he was different from other men or that he was reliable or some shit? It was one catch. One catch didn't mean anything when life was full of constant stumbles.

Plus, it wasn't his job to catch me.

I was trapped between figuring out how I felt about his words and how the sun dazzled his eyes to make them look like actual silver. Almost like diamonds.

"I'm gonna jump," I said, staring him dead in his diamond eyes, seeing as they curved in confusion.

"What?"

I didn't give him time to realize I was serious.

"One. *Two!*" Muscles in my legs stretched as I jumped off of the bench, heart soaring and readying to obliterate into the ground in familiar disappointment. The let down was welcomed, because if anything in my life *was* reliable, it was that.

I was ready for the pain and to be proven right.

When I took off, his hands were still around my waist. In mid air, I waited to feel the fumble of fingers and then the disappearance of them all together.

Instead...

They squeezed tighter.

A gasp cut through my throat as my body stopped moving mid air and didn't come back down. Not thanks to the sturdy hands locked around my waist and the man holding me up, arms stretched above his head. My eyes fluttered about a million times staring down at him, heaving breaths working my chest for no other reason than shock.

Dominic's face tilted back to me, a peculiar light riding around his irises.

"You jumped on two."

Still reeling, I mumbled, "It was a test."

That I thought he would fail.

His expression was so relaxed and even pleased. "Did I pass?"

Dazed and staring all around at the sidewalk I should have been laying on right now, I nodded. "Seeing as I don't have a mouth full of cement right now, I'd say yes."

Slowly, he lowered me down like I weighed no more than a sack of feathers. I held my breath tight as our bodies brushed, the shirt I was wearing riding up my front as I slid down his. Hard muscles and warmth were all I knew until my toes met the ground with ease.

Then gray took over.

Sweet winter gray that numbed my mind blank. Actually, all of me had gone numb to the look Dominic was giving me from only inches away. He was close, like *very* close, and I still felt his hands heating the dips of my waist.

And my hands, they were... touching something soft. No, *fisting* something soft. His shirt. I was holding onto him just like he was holding onto me, and I wondered if he could feel how fast my heart was beating.

"See?" His pillowy lips moved, and my eyes followed their slow dance. "Some men will catch you."

"Yeah..." Slowly, I twined my fingers in his shirt, feeling his hard chest with a careless graze of my knuckles. That somersaulting sensation went off in my gut as Dominic's chest rose beneath my grip, but he didn't stop me.

Flicking my eyes up to his, I spoke like it was supposed to be a joke.

"Only the taken ones."

But it didn't feel like a joke. The breathy register I'd dropped to didn't sound like a joke. How Dominic was staring down at me didn't feel very joking either. We'd toyed this fine line of chemistry between us well enough so far because, of all the inappropriate things I'd said, none of it had been serious. We got away with it because I was teasing and flirting, but never serious.

Except this felt serious.

This felt like I seriously wanted to yank him down and kiss the ever-living fuck out of him. Turn his pink lips red and his gray eyes black. I wanted to tangle myself in him, limbs and tongues intertwined until neither of us knew where the other started or stopped.

Whether he was aware of it or not, Dominic's stare was turning that burning degree of ice. My neck was hurting with how far I craned it back to hold his stare, but I couldn't stop. He had that look about him that made me feel like he *hated* me, like he wanted to push me up against one of the trees around us and show me just how much he hated me.

My thighs quivered with the thought. I felt like I couldn't breathe, or that I was breathing too much while Dominic's chest was a steady rise of up and down against me. Neither of us were moving or speaking, and I wasn't sure I could even do either.

Having both functions inoperable was probably for the best considering how badly I wanted to kiss him or tell him to kiss me. I shouldn't want to feel his lips with mine, but I did. I wanted it so badly, the chemistry created by us that lived inside my blood ached with need.

My entire body literally *ached* to know what it felt like when lightning met thunder.

"Kat! Let's go!"

A shout from Daren shattered the moment, and I dropped my hands from Dominic's shirt. A quick-acting embarrassment squeezed around my throat as I shot a glance over to Daren to see him waving me over and looking pissed doing it.

He clearly saw what happened, which meant that there was something to see to begin with between Dominic and I. My boss and I. My *married* boss.

Oh, holy fuck.

"Sounds like you're wanted," Dominic said, chest rumbling. He took his hands from my waist, and I backed away with a forced laugh pushing through my body.

"Yeah, *ugh*." Another fake chortle. "Save me, please."

I passed a hand through my hair, ruffling it back as a distraction. A quick look at Dominic said he recognized my behavior, and that was about it. His expression said absolutely nothing else and was as stiff as I'd ever seen it.

It was with that stiff mouth that he said, "Just stop dating him." Like it was the obvious solution, and I should listen to him or else.

Make a joke. Make a typical me joke.

"Now call me 'young lady' and send me to my room," I quipped, giving him fleeting eye contact. He wasn't paying attention to me though. Rather the ground where it looked like he was trying to make his own cracks in the sidewalk using just his eyes.

Spinning on my heel, I began walking back to everyone with my heart thudding in each step. A second later, Dominic caught up to match my stride, hands stuffed in his pockets.

"Whatever you do, don't ask me to spank you."

Face pinching together, I shot him a glance. "Why not?"

Dominic shook his head, brows heavy and eyes hardened to charcoal.

"Because I just might do it."

FIFTEEN

Mondays are said to be the worst day of the week.

So far today, I'd have to agree.

I barely got any sleep last night because it took me so goddamn long to figure out how to fix the lock on our front door. Then, I got word from Dominic that, by some backwards miracle, my mother passed her drug test taken on Friday. To top it all off, I also started my period that morning.

Fuck you too, Mondays.

As I settled down Maya for her nap, I was already daydreaming about racing through the laundry and bed-making so I could lie down for a power nap of my own.

Then, Monday struck again.

The doorbell chimed obnoxiously right after I shut the door to Maya's bedroom. A deep groan strangled in my throat. Whoever that was better not have just woken her back up. That child was *not* a fan of nap time.

Padding down the stairs, whatever delivery person, solicitor, or Mormon boy that had chosen this house to interrupt mid-day was about to be seriously sorry.

Tearing open the front door, my perfectly prepped face of annoyance stumbled as I saw who was standing on the other side.

"Daren?"

"Hey, babe."

His endearment was sweet. His tone was not.

I cocked my hip out to rest on the doorframe, cutting his view into the house. "Uh, what the fuck are you doing here?"

He squished his mouth to the side, evidently not pleased. "I wanted to talk."

"About what? That's sort of the point of breaking up with someone. You don't have to talk to them anymore."

"*That*. That's what I want to talk about."

Joy.

After yesterday at the park, I actually did something Dominic told me to for once.

I broke up with Daren.

We were barely even a couple to begin with, just two people who hung out and fucked a couple times a week, so it wasn't a big deal to break it off. Or at least, I thought it wouldn't be a big deal, but Daren sure as shit tried to make it one.

He got all pissy and tried calling me a good ten times *after* I hung up on him during the initial call. Yeah, I did it over the phone. At least it wasn't over text.

Still didn't give him any reason to be here—*especially* here.

"How did you even find out where I worked?" I asked.

"Easy." He put an arm up on the doorframe, leaning in closer. "I had a buddy help me out."

"That's... creepy."

Daren's face fell slowly, upset pushing his gaze away from me. "I was hoping you'd think it was romantic."

I parted my lips, sucking back an awkward breath and shaking my head. "Nope."

An audible sigh lifted and dropped his shoulders, and I thought he was getting ready to turn around and leave. Wave that little white flag, shake hands, and call it quits.

That's why I was so fucking surprised when he pushed his way past me into the house instead.

"Hey!" I hissed, snapping around to grab him. "You can't be in here."

He shook me off, shaking my temper awake in the same move. He moved through the house like he was searching for something, pacing in determined steps with me running up behind him.

"This is a nice house, Kitty Kat."

He tilted his head to the vaulted ceiling as he spoke, terror clenching my gut as his voice echoed, drifting upstairs towards Maya's bedroom.

"I'll be sure to let the owners know." I rounded on him, feet planting right in front of his path. Daren stopped walking, peering down at me and my cocked hip. "Now *leave*."

He stood there for a bit, jaw hard-locked and suspicion edging around his eyes. "Are you fucking him?"

The shock of his words jerked my head back. "Excuse me?"

He folded his arms over his chest, setting a wide stance. "Your boss. The cop. Are you fucking him?"

This time, my jaw actually popped open before my entire face screwed up tight. "*What?* No. No, I'm not *fucking* my boss, Daren. Why would you—"

"Because you two looked close yesterday," he cut in. "I wanna know if that's why you ended things with me."

"There was barely anything to end," I argued, trying to keep my voice down.

A look of frustration passed across his face before he squared his shoulders back. He pinched his mouth to the side again, and it looked like he was chewing on the inside of his cheeks. He was going through an array of multi-colored emotions I'd never seen in him before. He was like a Rubik's cube that had always been perfectly color coordinated and was now twisted all out of whack.

Daren was always laid back and happy. Or horny. Sometimes mad when he was drunk, but that was the extent of it. He never seemed to really care about anything before today.

He sighed and put his hands on his waist, giving me a pointed look.

"Kat, I like you."

"No, you like having *sex* with me."

Agitation burned red across his cheeks, but then his brows rose a bit. His eyes widened a touch, and he started nodding. "I like more than that, but yeah, the sex is great. I'd like to keep doing that."

Annnd boom goes the dynamite.

"And I'm flattered, but the answer is no. Now, *get out.*"

"Why?" I flinched as he snapped, the whites of his eyes smearing red. "We were fine one second, and then you broke up with me out of the blue. What changed?"

"You got on my nerves like you are right now. You can't be here. I could lose my job if my boss walked in right now and saw you."

The lips that I'd kissed plenty of times pulled back over his teeth. "And you care so much about what he thinks."

"I care about my *job*, Daren."

And with every second he was still here, my stomach knotted tighter with the fear that someone was going to walk in. Dominic, Heather, Maya; it didn't matter. Any one of them could walk in right now, and I'd be royally fucked for letting a strange man into their house.

Daren wasn't planning on leaving from the looks of it, angry muscles flexing in his neck as he cut an inflamed glare my way. "I guess I just don't understand why, if all I ever was to you was someone to fuck, why we can't keep doing that *unless* you're already sleeping with someone else."

"Oh my god, this has literally nothing to do with sex." I dropped my face into my hands, rubbing my fingers over my eyes. Then a thought occurred, and I whipped my hands down and pinned him with a hard stare. "Also, you went into this with the same understanding that I did. We were casual. Nothing more."

Daren stood taller. Took a step closer. "Well, it became more to me."

"And that's not my fault," I shot back, dead serious.

Even if it was true and he wasn't lying just to get in my pants a few more times, I didn't ask him to like me. In fact, I told him flat out at the beginning of this that I wasn't very likable and to not try. He laughed. Maybe he thought I was joking.

Guess he knew now I wasn't.

His head was down, but I could see his mouth still thinned together. He was thinking, foot tapping, my pulse following along the anxious beat.

Finally, he pulled his stare back up. "Fine."

I let out a tiny exhale of relief.

"But if all it was was sex, why don't we at least give ourselves a proper goodbye?" Gone was the animosity as he sauntered my way, and my eyebrows about shot off my forehead.

"Are you asking for break up sex while I'm at work?"

"Oh, come on." He lingered nearer, hands slipping around my waist. "Where's your fun side?"

I put my palms to his chest, leaning away from his efforts with a breathy laugh. "Daren, no."

He made a whining noise, intensifying my snickering as he nuzzled into my neck. His fingers around my waist tightened. "I'll be quick, I promise."

A bark of laughter popped through my throat, and my head fell back.

"Oh boy, what every girl wants to hear."

Daren ran his hands up my back, locking me into his chest as he pushed out a vexed sigh. "You know what I mean."

"Yeah, and I said *no*."

I pushed my hands against his shoulders this time with more bite behind my words. He didn't budge, just kept walking backwards, making me trip over my own damn feet twice trying to keep up.

Hot blood filled my head, sloshing as I stumbled back into a wall. Daren quickly sealed his body over mine, every curve and dip of him pressing against me even as I struggled. The feel of him curled my skin into itself, my heart pounding faster.

The touch of fingers pushing my shirt up spiked my pulse like my heart gasped.

"Babe, please?"

"Don't *beg*. You're not a fucking dog," I snarled, tearing my shirt back down. Then, like he was trying to prove me wrong, he growled like a goddamn animal and wrestled the hem of my shirt back in his grip.

Rage breathed life inside of me, and I bucked my shoulders against him. He only advanced harder, trapping me like prey he was hunting and prepping for slaughter. I was that prey, eyes wide, claws out, struggling for life beneath his hands like razored snares.

A cry sliced my throat as a hand thrust my shoulder back into the wall, the blade connecting painfully. The ache throbbed, spotting my vision with blurry dots.

My voice slipped away, hiding inside of me as I blinked my vision back to normal. *What the fuck is he doing?* My blood was boiling with each second, a searing combination of dread and anger fighting for top spot.

Suddenly, the unmistakable sound of material shredding ripped through the air. My heavy head drooped forward, staring down at the god awful tear at the top of my shirt, exposing my blue bra.

My heart was on fire, setting the rest of me ablaze as I tore my head up. "What the fuck is wrong with you?" I yelled in a whisper.

He fucking shrugged with an audacious wink. "Easier access?"

Panic flared my eyes as I realized in that moment he thought this was okay. He thought we were playing and he was winning. With a horrified breath squeezing my throat, I picked my foot up and tried to bolt around him.

He grabbed me, shoving me against the wall with a vile smirk stretching across his lips when another cry knocked from me as my head hit the wall. Prickling white poked holes in my vision, my voice making a shaky appearance.

"Daren, *stop.*"

A hot breath fanned over my neck. "I thought you always liked it rough, babe?"

His words coiled around my body, a violent shiver struggling through. Dread had won out in the battle over anger, pumping fast through my veins as fingers fumbled with the button on my shorts. It struck a match inside me, firing up my fight or flight so fast, even I didn't register as I started hitting him.

"*Kat*—Kat stop!"

My fists were everywhere, pounding into his chest, his back, his stomach—anything I could reach. When he latched onto both hands and captured them back against the wall, I used my head and snapped it forward.

Pain erupted in bright flashes, groans following right after from both of us. The room spun in circles of red and black and hazel green, twisting my stomach in on itself. One of my hands slouched free as Daren dropped it to cover his reddening forehead.

Opportunity sparked, and before he could right his focus on me again, my knee was in his crotch.

A grunt writhing in agony split Daren's lips and down to the floor he went. Relief stabbed between my ribs, sharp and alarming. I sucked down a huge breath and dashed to the other side of the room, shielding myself behind the sofa.

"What the fuck is wrong with you?" Daren wheezed, rolling around on the floor.

Weighted breaths pushed and pulled my chest, terror still riding high in my head. "What the fuck's wrong with *me*? No, what the fuck's wrong with *you*, Daren? I said no!"

I couldn't catch my breath, couldn't stop the room teetering in and out of blurry focus.

"You're overreacting. You could have stopped me if you wanted to without kneeing me in the balls!"

"I *tried*, Daren. I said stop. I said no. I told you to get off, and you didn't *listen*."

Landing a hand on the red lounge chair, Daren wobbled as he pulled himself up. "But we've had sex tons of times, Kat."

"What the fuck does that matter?" My shriek bounced off the walls all the way back to me, slapping me in the face. I was loud—too loud—but I couldn't contain it. My veins were live wires again, fritzing and zapping my rationale to burnt crisps. "I said no *now*. Even if I said yes in the past, that doesn't give you a pass to fuck me whenever you feel like it. No means fucking *no*, Daren."

His long face was vacant of understanding. He stood there like a goddamn idiot, mouth open but no words or apology spilling out, because he didn't *get it*. Or maybe he just didn't want to get it.

He took one step towards me. I stopped him with a finger, hate holding every one of my muscles *so* tight.

"Get the fuck out of this house before I call my boss and he arrests you for trespassing in his home."

Daren went rigid, except his eyes that softened. "Babe, you don't mean that—"

"Yes. Yes, I do."

We had a standoff in the Reed's living room, the wreckage of anything good left between us souring in the air. I could taste his guilt like I could feel my nails lacerating into my palms. Even if he didn't know why he was guilty, his experience of it was tangible.

Daren left in slow, sorry steps, casting a hopeless glance back at me before he left. I didn't go near him as he walked to the door or when he walked out of it. As soon as it clicked shut, I sprinted and collapsed against it, jamming the lock in place.

I fell back against the wood, getting myself as close to it as possible to soak up the chill on my heated skin. I was still running hot. Too many emotions were zipping around in a relentless loop through every cell, atom, and molecule I had. They were going, spinning, and running so fast, my skin could have been humming with their ferocity.

Some of those emotions tried to worm their way up to my brain to help form intelligent thoughts over what had just happened, but I cut them off. I didn't want any thoughts about it at all, smart, dumb, or otherwise.

I just wanted to forget it happened.

My head knocked back into the door, and I winced as pain spidered up my skull. *Great.* After all that, a splitting headache was *just* what I needed. Holding my sore head in my hands, I shuffled off the door and went to check on Maya.

She was still sleeping—thank fuck—so I dragged myself into the bathroom down the hall to see what the damage was.

Now, I'd looked like shit before, but this was next level. My face was both flushed and pale at the same time, making me look patchy and gross. I had a bright red bump forming where I'd head-butted Daren, and my shirt—one of my *favorite* shirts—was toast.

Ripped straight down past my cleavage, and no amount of fashionable knots I tied made it look any better.

After a few minutes, I gave up trying and threw open the bathroom door, focus pointed down at the shitty knot holding the top of my shirt together. I only got a few steps out of the bathroom when a giant figure climbing up the stairs caught my eye.

"Ms. Sanders."

Dominic's greeting was a leveled rumble in his chest, and the sight of him shocked blood back into my cheeks. I froze, a playthrough of Daren in this home, groping me, hurting me, scaring me while Maya slept, flying behind my eyes.

If Dominic had walked in just five minutes earlier, he'd have seen it all, and I would be on my knees begging for my job right about now.

I made the decision to lie to him so fast, I left no time at all to prepare for it.

"Hey, boss man! Home already?"

Internally, I cringed at my overcompensated enthusiasm. It didn't play nearly as nonchalant as I hoped, and Dominic was immediately suspicious.

"I stopped by for lunch." Between his swarthy brows formed a wrinkled frown. "Are you all right?"

"*Yeah*. Definitely."

Sharp eyes slid lower and narrowed.

"What happened to your shirt?" *Dammit.*

"Oh, I ripped it when Maya and I were playing outside earlier."

That was believable, right? Totally. Dominic didn't verbally question it, but his inspection of me didn't stop at my shirt. He did a full sweep of me, pulling my gut inside out as he checked every inch for any further abnormalities in my appearance.

I sucked a breath through my teeth as his scrutinizing came to a pause on my forehead.

"Why is your head red?" *Double dammit.*

"Same thing. I just ate dirt and, ya know—" I gestured a hand over my face and body. "Fucked everything up."

A forceful chuckle pushed past my lips, hoping Dominic would start laughing with me and forget all about my wrecked face. Call me clumsy and move on. Like, *now*. Cue the laugh track and let me tap dance off stage.

He wasn't though, and my nerves were turning to jitterbugs the longer we stood there, me not speaking and him doing a full-on C.S.I of my appearance. How did he *always* know when I was lying? Was it a sixth sense he had as a detective or was it just me?

It was going on way too long. The dissecting. The suspicion. The silence during both.

"I actually have to pee, so—"

"You just came out of the bathroom."

I blinked at his reminder. My lips parted, and the first thing I could think of spilled out.

"I forgot to go."

The first *dumbest* thing I could think of.

Well, that settled it. He might have been the world's greatest detective, but it didn't matter because I was the world's shittiest liar. I made his job a friggin' picnic.

With Dominic still staring at me, I filled my lungs like there was more to say, another excuse ready to march off my tongue and fix this most glorious fuck up. Except, nothing came out, and my chest deflated with an awkward, "Excuse me."

I spun on my heel right back into the bathroom and shut the door.

Oh God. The cringe. The cringe was unbelievable. Every inch of me was tense with it as I shuffled across the tile. I held my middle fingers up to the ceiling, shaking them and silently cursing this day and all Mondays that would ever exist.

The saying was true after all.

Mondays could suck a dick.

SIXTEEN

hree days later, Dominic was home again for lunch and appeared in the archway of the kitchen where I was eating a granola bar while Maya napped.

"Ms. Sanders." I peeled my attention from my game of Candy Crush up to my boss. The muscles in my neck went rigid beneath the barbed stare waiting for me.

Something was wrong.

His words barely made it through his gritted teeth. "If you could follow me to my office."

That was not a request.

It was a command, and one he didn't wait for me to respond to. He showed me his strong back and expected me to follow him blindly, and, well, he was right. I scurried up behind him, blood pumping in my ears as I tailed him from a safe distance up the stairs.

What was this about? Did I do something wrong? I mean, probably. Like, a solid 98% chance that I definitely did something wrong today, but what?

Dominic stepped up to the landing of the second floor, me only a couple paces behind and totally not checking out his ass. Which looked *flawless* today.

Or so I'd assume.

I followed him into his office, which I hadn't been in since he caught me in there that first week. It looked pretty much the same, paper and files and more nonsense strewn about. The only thing out of turn that caught my eye was his computer desktop, which had been jerked around to face the door where we entered. The screen was black.

Dominic went up to it, hand hovering over the computer mouse.

He met my stare and held it. There was something about him that made me curl my toes into the floor, sweat sprouting on the back of my neck. I had every bit of his acute attention at that moment, and I wasn't sure I wanted it.

"Tell me what happened on Monday again, Ms. Sanders."

Panic splintered in my chest. The sweat collecting on my baby hairs dripped down. *Oh shit. Oh fuck. Oh fuck, fuck, fuck, fuck.* Did he know about Daren? Was that why he was asking? Was I giving my guilt away without even saying a word?

A mental check in with my face said yes; my expression was screaming with guilt. I could *feel* it, muscles shocked still and eyes blown wide.

Still, I tried to play it off.

"What do you mean?"

My voice was meek, a rarity. Another tell of guilt.

Dominic had an ace in his harsh pupils, targeted and holding out for me to give him reason to play it. "How you ripped your shirt and hurt your head. You told me it happened while playing with Maya, correct?"

Oh God, he knew. Somehow he knew about Daren and that I had lied to him. Heat flooded my ears, roiling with humiliation at being caught and being so stupid as to think I could get away with it. I should have told him. *Fuck*, I should have just told him.

"Sir—"

"*Correct*, Katerina?" he chided, eyes boiling.

The sound of my full name yanked my spine straight, mouth drying out. It had slipped out of him so naturally, like my name belonged to his teeth and scolding tongue, and anyone who'd ever said it before him was a thief.

I was in trouble, and there were no more flimsy lies I could tell to get myself out of it. My heart sank to my feet, my whole body heavy with dread as I whispered, "Yes."

Dominic had me and he knew it, settling his long fingers over the computer mouse. "Were you aware Heather put in nanny cams around the house about a month ago?"

And there was his ace. Cameras. I shouldn't even be surprised that Heather had them installed after I started working here. It was very on brand for her and very bad luck for me. I lowered my gaze, rolling my lips together.

"No."

He spoke deeper than I'd ever heard him before, the rich sound rolling my shoulders forward. "There's one in Maya's room. The entrance to the house. The kitchen. The upstairs loft. The *living room.*"

He punctuated those words with the intention of them to humiliate, and boy did they ever. Shame washed hot over every inch of me, desperation welling up beneath the heat and pouring out.

Time to beg.

"Sir, I didn't know he was coming over, I *swear.*" Thoughtless feet moved me into the room and closer to him. "I didn't even let him in. He *barged* in himself."

Dominic's jaw clicked dangerously. "I saw that."

"He was just pissed that I broke up with him, and he wouldn't leave and—" The more I worked myself up, the more hopeless I felt. My hopelessness blanketed me, suffocating my pride until I couldn't even feel it inside me anymore. "Look, please don't fire me. Please? I know you have every right to. He was in your house while your daughter was sleeping, and that's all sorts of fucked up, but *please.* It won't happen again, I swear."

Dominic observed me with sharp focus as I panted through the end of my pleading. It was exhausting to beg for anything, let alone your future financial stability. My muscles weren't used to it. I'd plucked my ego dry over the last thirty seconds so I was completely bare, letting Dominic see just how desperate I was, and that kind of debasement was a workout.

Finally, Dominic's hand over the mouse fell to his side, and the razors in his eyes dulled.

"I'm not firing you, Ms. Sanders."

Shock lifted my head. "You're not?"

"No." He tilted his chin down to the computer screen. "Even though I'm sure that was Heather's hope when she showed me the video this morning."

"She's the one who found it?"

"Yes. She goes through the footage every few days."

Talk about being kicked when you're already down. Dominic seeing that footage was one thing, but knowing Heather had seen it and brought it to her husband like she'd hit the fireable offences jackpot was something else entirely.

Dominic said he *wasn't* firing me though, which was some type of miracle if they'd ever existed.

"So, if you're not firing me, why am I here?"

It was like I'd turned a dimmer low in the room, the mood shifting dark and Dominic following suit. His entire being clenched up. Not just his jaw like normal. All of him turned to marble, chiseling him into a statue worthy of the Gods approval.

Without anymore said, he clicked the mouse.

The computer lit with life, dulled colors forming moving bodies across the screen. *My* body. Daren's too. Nerves clustered in my stomach as a movie of my life played out, one that I definitely didn't buy tickets to.

Daren had me against the wall, and my hands were already on his shoulders. I cocked my head at the screen. I never realized I looked so small next to him. He wasn't terribly big, and I wasn't terribly short. I was 5'3" and Daren couldn't have been over 6 feet, but he looked it there.

He was monstrous over me, or maybe it was just what he was doing that made it seem that way. A few more seconds of screen time showed my shirt being ripped and warmth slapped my cheeks with Dominic standing right here.

How many times had he watched this...?

The situation was sufficiently awkward now with my tits sort of out, and I weirdly scolded myself for not wearing a cuter bra that day. *So* not the point, but if I'd known I'd be watching a video of this a few days later with Dominic, I might have gone with the red lace that morning.

Next came the stuff that got a little fuzzy in my brain. When I watched Daren help knock my head back into the wall, I figured that might be where the specifics all went. My neck tensed as if it was about to happen again.

A flash of my face caught the camera, and I cringed. Saliva pooled in the sides of my mouth, my stomach twisting in a sickening sort of way. I swallowed both and cast my focus to the middle of Dominic's chest.

"Why are we watching this?"

Seconds passed, and he didn't answer me. I didn't know which I hated more. The silence or being ignored. Out of spite, I switched back to watching the screen and just in time too. I was hitting Daren, going absolutely apeshit on him until I snapped my head into his.

Next came my knee, and Daren finally dropped to the floor. Another quick snapshot of my face in the camera brought the unsettling sensations back, and I shifted on my feet.

I looked terrified.

A perfect screenshot of helpless.

The scuffle came to an end as three-days-ago Kat ran behind the sofa. Dominic pressed pause. Silence followed.

I moved my eyes back to the middle of his chest, watching the buttons down his shirt strain as he stretched his chest with a deep breath. Watching him breathe was sort of calming.

Everything that happened next, however, was not.

"I haven't been able to stop watching that. It's been burned behind my eyes all day." His weighty tone pushed my eyes closed. Movement shuffling in front of me fluttered them back open.

Dominic was there. Waiting. Anguished. Furious. "Why didn't you tell me? I was there *minutes* after it happened."

I pulled back a breath, swallowing the thick air. "I thought you'd be mad?"

His browline bunched together like I was stupid for saying it. Like he was pissed that I was so stupid. "Why would I be mad at you?"

I recoiled back, trying to make the same picture with my face that he was giving me. "I don't know, why are you mad at me now?"

"Because you didn't *tell* me. I could have helped you."

"It had already happened," I pushed back. Then, I felt the slap of his words resonate. "Plus, I helped myself just fine."

Dominic Reed came as close to rolling his eyes as I'd ever seen. "Barely."

I set my shoulders back, teeth edging in ready for a deadly bite.

"Excuse me?"

If he heard my brewing temper, he didn't adjust his reaction to it. In fact, the cut of his steel-gray gaze sharpened, needled straight at me. "I said barely. You *barely* escaped, Kat."

"But I *did*. I got out of it by myself."

"With a lucky shot."

I scoffed and lowered the pitch of my voice, provoking him. "A lucky shot that worked on you."

Memories of the night I cup checked him burned across his face, scorching the whole thing a threatening shade of red. "That's not the point. The point is that you couldn't defend yourself."

Oh my god, I was gonna throttle him into the next room. I felt the want to lash out bubbling beneath my skin, popping off like tiny firecrackers every second I was still instead.

Through bared teeth, I said, "I'm *fine*, Dominic."

"But you almost weren't."

He narrowed the space between us so fast, I nearly stumbled. In no time at all, he wasn't even an arms length away, shooting my pulse through the roof and blistering me with his frostbite severity. "Do you realize if you hadn't gotten that lucky shot in, that video might have been of your rape instead? Tell me you understand that."

"Yeah, I get that." I jerked my chin high, keeping his stare. "I was there."

Dominic was growing mountainous over me, his restraint visibly trembling. "Would you have told me then, or would I have found out by being blindsided with a video of it while having my morning coffee?"

His words rattled my head, making me take a step back and puff my chest out at the same time. "Is this about you? I'm really confused right now, because that just sounded like this was about *you* and how *you* feel about it."

"*No.*" He took another step in. "This is about you and asking for help when you need it."

"I didn't need it," I bit back.

He bit back harder and much, much louder.

"You did!"

In a quick breath, my index finger was over my mouth, and my other hand was over his chest. Gripping, fisting the material of his shirt to ground him back down from his peak of anger. His heart was thrashing beneath my hand, telling me with each frantic beat just how uncharacteristically shaken up he was.

Harsh eyes steadied on my finger over my lips, recollection that Maya was sleeping just a couple rooms down snowing over them both.

Heavy lids closed over the storm, pinching tightly. The space between his brows furrowed so he looked like he was in pain, and any of my temper left standing was shoved to the side to make room for surprising concern. I wanted to smooth out his frown lines and poke at his dimples that were hiding.

Actually, I wanted more than that, I realized. My hands wanted more than just that. They wanted to touch his whole face. His cheeks, forehead, nose, mouth, everything. They wanted to trace a map from his eyebrows down to his stubborn chin and then get lost everywhere in between.

I didn't know we'd made it so close to the wall behind me until Dominic set both hands on it, caging me in. He was tall enough that, even with his head hanging low as it was, I didn't feel like he was too close.

Too close for boss and employee, yes.

But not too close for us.

That inexplicable chemistry riding between us whispered that this was okay. It caressed down the raised hairs on my neck where Dominic's breath kissed and focused all my attention on him.

On the weight burdening his strong shoulders, trying to tear him down to my feet. I watched him closer than I'd ever watched anything as he dragged his eyelids up.

And then *pain*. It stabbed through my chest, and I tried not to gasp or wince or show any sign of it. It felt like someone had exchanged my heart out for a soda can and crushed it inside of me when I saw his eyes.

They were like someone had taken a hammer to river rocks and smashed them to bits. Agony radiated out of the breaks in his stare and only got worse as he looked to where the bump on my head was nearly healed.

He didn't touch me, but he didn't hide the fact that he wanted to either. There wasn't much at all hidden about him today. He was letting me see it all, and somehow having the full picture muddled my understanding of it even more.

"You need to learn how to defend yourself," he started, voice low. "He overpowered you too easily, and it could happen again."

I dropped my head back against the wall, shaking it. "He's gone. You don't have to worry about him anymore."

Even as I said it, I could see him ignoring me and going to the worst places in his mind. His breathing became choppy, the angles of his jaw crushing together.

"Do you want to press charges?"

"What?" A wash of cold exploded in my chest. "No. It's not that big of a deal."

A look passed over him that warred between a sadness that could sink him or a rage that promised to control him. His torrid eyes went everywhere over my face, touching every inch of it that was already flushed and making it burn just a little more.

"What happened was a very big deal," he said, voice like gravel.

"Well, I don't wanna do anything about it."

If we did anything about it, then it became something that *happened* to me, and I was so sick of being that girl. I'd already had enough *happen* to me in my life that was out of my control. Right now, I could brush this off as an ex-boyfriend who got too handsy if I didn't think about it too much.

Dominic's head sunk past his shoulders with a rasped sigh. "*Dammit*, Kat."

Frustration ebbed out of him. Out of the corner of my eye, I saw him trying to press as much of it as he could into the wall. Fingers bent, knuckles leached of all color, tendons and veins flexed beneath his skin.

My attention ripped back to his face as he jerked his head up, eyes the brightest shade of gray I'd seen them yet. "You have to let people help you sometimes. I can help you *now*."

"How?" I asked, on defense without thinking about it. It was just my go-to. Fists up, claws out. "How do you want to help me, Dominic?"

"Let me arrest him."

"No."

A growl—there was no other way to describe it—thrummed up his throat. "Then let me teach you how to defend yourself against men like him."

"I thought you said it would be inappropriate to teach me self-defense?" I threw back at him.

At that, he dropped his hands from the wall on either side of me and stood tall. The lines of his face carved deep. "That was before I watched you be sexually assaulted in my own home."

Sexually assaulted.

Sexually a—

I put a mental block up before the words could finish a second time. If I didn't think them, then they weren't true. If I didn't think them, then the twist in my stomach when I heard them meant nothing.

I was *fine*, and Dominic was *wrong*.

"I don't need you to help me or protect me or whatever it is you've convinced yourself you have to do for me."

His eyes darkened so fast, I actually thought I heard a boom of thunder outside.

"That video says otherwise."

"That video proves that I handled myself just fine, and I can do it again."

I held my head high and didn't *dare* look away. The not-so-friendly lightning in my veins kept me upright, vibrating my body with too much energy to back down from now. We were in a standoff, and I tried to remember that saying about thunder and lightning.

Something about whenever you see lightning, count the seconds until the thunder claps, and that's how many miles the lightning is away from you. That's how far you are away from danger.

If that were true, Dominic and I were screwed. There was no warning between us. No few seconds to run and find shelter. The lightning and thunder were simultaneous, here and now, and we were both about to get fried.

A flash of gray pierced my stare before he sealed himself off again. He became stone, his voice following the same flat path.

"You honestly believe you could fight off any man, whenever you want?"

I jutted my chin up. "If they've got balls, I can smash them."

A moment of silence passed between us.

Dominic skirted his gaze down, nodding slightly. Victory trembled the corner of my mouth, daring to inch up as Dominic seemed to back down.

I won.

Thunder: Zero

Lightning: One thousand, because it's my scoreboard.

It was in the middle of mentally fudging my own points that it happened.

And it happened in the time span of a sharp breath.

That was all I let out anyway as a hand lashed around my wrist, and the room went spinning. I didn't even yelp as I was shoved up against the wall I had my back to half a second ago, almost smacking the thing with my cheek.

The world was too dizzy, and I was too slow to realize what had happened until my arms were locked behind my back, and Dominic was the one holding me.

"What about now?"

I didn't answer, *couldn't* answer him right away. I was still reeling from the happenings of it and mentally checking in with every part of my body to feel out which ones were trapped and which ones were free to kick his ass.

Unfortunately, *most* of my body was ensnared by his, and I wiggled between the wall and him searching for a way out. When I didn't immediately get it, a flame lit inside of me, holding still under my heart and slowly catching the whole thing on fire.

"You can't move, can you?"

The flame got even hotter at how fucking certain he sounded.

"I could still kick your ass right now," I grit out, breathing already turning reckless.

"Then do it. Prove me wrong." He adjusted his fingers around my wrists to get a better grip. "I know you're dying to."

A snarl coiled up my throat, my chest heaving as much as it could pressed against the wall. I struggled harder, jerking my shoulders until they cried in pain. Dominic's firm hold didn't let up.

I bowed my back to ease the strain on my shoulders, breathing heavily. "You know you're just pissing me off, right?"

"Because you know you can't get out of it, and you're too stubborn to admit it."

The wailing in my shoulders and huge presence behind me told the rational part of my brain that he was right. Except the willful side of me was still in the game, and it always played to win.

"I can still move my legs and my head. I could easily—"

His hand not holding my wrists appeared on the back of my neck, fingers pinching the nape. The move pulled a gasp from me and straightened my spine all the way up.

Oh god. Every fighting muscle in my body loosened. The pressure he had on that exact spot was...

Absolute dominance.

Like when an animal bites the back of a smaller animal's neck, not to kill them, but to control them. Calm them down. That's exactly what Dominic's particular grip was in human form.

While he was busying my mind with that, he'd taken the expanse of his frame and sealed it up against me so I couldn't move *any* part of my body. The only part of me that was moving was my heart, and it was fucking flying.

"You were saying?" Confidence coated his tone while his soft breath brushed the shell of my ear.

Fuck, what was I saying? Something about winning or losing or...

"I don't know," I breathed honestly.

Literally, I couldn't think of anything that wasn't his confident grip on the back of my neck or how his entire body was touching mine. I could feel every curved muscle, where his belt buckle was digging into the small of my back, how warm he was, everything.

And it all felt so good.

The inspired feel of him was doing all sorts of haywire things to my brain. It was melting all the coherency away like snow, revealing the core of my makeup: a filthy desire to do just about everything I shouldn't.

I wanted to be a little bit bad and moan his name to see if I could feel his taut muscles tensing to the immoral sound of it rolling off my tongue.

Scratch that. I wanted to be *a lot* bad and wriggle my ass against him to feel the outline of his cock grow inside his pants. Just the idea that I could feel him so intimately rushed blood straight out of my head and between my legs. My tits got heavier, nipples tightening, lips parting as I began to pant.

"No man should be allowed to get this close to you without your permission," he murmured. His voice was unadulterated sin, and thank God he had me so tightly against the wall, or I would have fallen to my knees and asked for forgiveness later.

Hot breath eased along the curve of my neck, my pussy fluttering at the sensation and throaty voice that followed.

"I could do whatever I wanted to you right now."

Like he was proving his own point, he moved his fingers on my neck just so, a small massage that bowed my head back for him and slipped out a faint moan, both actions involuntary.

His deft fingers squeezed my wrists as I let the small sound go free, a punishment and warning in one. My head was swimming, too much humid air filling it to keep track of what I was doing or saying. I'd never been this pliant before, my body feeling more like water than anything solid.

Dominic had done that to me, and I was desperate to know if he did it on purpose. Was I putty in his hands because he wanted me to be or because this was part of the lesson?

"*Anyone* could get this close," he snarled in my ear, closer than ever and shooting electric tingles down my legs.

His anger was back, and I couldn't help but gasp at it and how biting his grasp was on my wrists. It was good though, *so* fucking good. I squirmed as much as I could between him and the wall, stifling whimpers.

Dominic must have mistaken my squirming as uncomfortable because he eased off, loosening the hold he had around my wrists. A cry of protest surged up my throat, but I caught it as his hand on my neck moved.

It was slow and thoughtful, a gentle ride of skin over skin. "There's so much bad out there. You need to learn to protect yourself from it."

I held my breath, not willing to risk even breathing if it could shatter this moment. Dominic was officially lost, forgotten to his words and surroundings, and I was shamelessly curious for what his wayward mouth might say.

An absent-minded touch traced across the baby hairs at my nape. "You have no idea how..."

He dropped off, and my heart squeezed.

I was hanging, dangling in mid-air for him to finish what he was going to say in the softest voice to ever touch my ears. It was like a cloud, wispy and gentle, floating in some limbo sky we'd created together.

A sky where thunder and lightning blended in harmony. An affair orchestrated of blinding lights rolling in dark clouds, pirouetting to an endless drumbeat.

Unfortunately, I never got to hear what else he had to say. In the next second, I was dropped out of our sky as a lonely wind rushed over my back. It was cold—freezing, in fact, and I clammed up all my muscles trying to hold on to the heat that was there seconds ago.

It all happened so quick. One second he was there, confusing and arousing the fuck out of me. Now, I turned to find him at the far end of his desk, huge shoulders hunched over it and staring at paperwork as if he could will it to catch on fire.

Breathing. I wasn't quite doing it yet, and my heart was smacking against my lungs trying to get them started again.

What the hell just happened?

My lips were locked open in shock as I dove off a cliff in my head, diving into all the questions and assumptions forming. Like, 95% of that was him proving his point about self-defense. It was the 5% left that had my brain glitching.

What was he about to say when his brain had untethered itself from his mouth?

Dominic was ignoring it all completely, standing over his desk and pretending like he hadn't been sandwiching me against the wall like ten seconds ago.

Even as he spoke to me.

"Heather's having dinner with her parents tomorrow night. Do you think you could get someone to watch Charlotte so you could stay late?"

Tomorrow. "How late?"

Words. Oh wow. That was a surprising success on my part.

Still, no eye contact. "Just a couple hours."

"What about Maya?"

This time, he flipped a paper over on his desk to give merit to how invested he was in it and why he couldn't be bothered to meet my eye.

"I'll set her upstairs with a movie."

I opened my mouth, the words coming out slow. "So you can teach me self-defense?"

Lord, it sounded even more asinine when I said it out loud.

Gunmetal eyes cut up to me so unexpectedly, my heart snapped back. He was all business now. "As we've established, you need to learn."

Yeah, but is that smart?

The heroin chemistry riding in my veins whispered yes. Everything else in my body screamed a big fat no.

It didn't seem as I had much of a choice, though. Still standing there like my wires had been short-circuited, Dominic clipped a disciplined glance down my frame.

"Bring workout clothes."

Dear lord, my thoughts were in a tailspin. So much was happening too fast. I tried to think if I even had anything that would qualify as workout clothing, but my mind couldn't even manage that. I was fried. Turned out I was right about Dominic and I, but the storm we created struck us both in different ways.

It shocked Dominic back to the basics. Rules and order and control.

Me? I was fritzed to the bone, hairs still standing on edge, and heart racing towards an attack.

Dominic didn't spare my malfunctioning self a second glance.

"That will be all, Ms. Sanders."

I blinked. Somehow, I got my feet to move and shuffled out of his office, head still full-on spinning.

Well, tomorrow'll be interesting.

SEVENTEEN

W as it just me or did big mirrors make your clothes shrink?

I turned to the side in the guest bathroom, smoothing my hands over my flat stomach with a wrinkled expression on my face. God, was this *really* all I had to grab for today? Black cotton shorts that hugged just under my ass and a tanktop Layla got me last year as a gag gift that said *'Let's Get Moist.'*

I hated that word about as much as I hated working out. Layla knew both, and so the gift was actually pretty funny. I doubt either of us thought I'd ever actually be wearing it, let alone in front of my boss. It was the only themed shirt I had for exercise though, so I *had* to wear it. Why I thought I had to be on theme for today was anyone's guess.

I was anxious as fuck when I chose my outfit for this, okay?

No amount of breathing exercises I did were helping either. My nerves were shot, my cheeks were flushed pink, and my mind had already thought up about fifteen different ways this could go wrong.

Only thirteen of them were perverted.

My work day had ended about twenty minutes ago, and I'd spent the majority of that time freaking out in the bathroom and wrestling the hem of my shorts down. My hair was unnaturally wavy today, rebelling against this idea as much as the rest of me. Best I could do was throw it up in a bun to get it out of the way and hope it stayed.

The green of my eyes looked like it had been cranked up in brightness, shining a violent shade of emerald that stung to stare at too long. Sighing, I shut my eyes and sunk down to my elbows on the bathroom countertop.

The granite was cold, a welcomed change from the heat swelling my pores.

Why I was so nervous for this wasn't totally clear, but my pulse hadn't stopped racing since the clock hit 5:30.

"Kat."

Dominic's full-bodied voice resonated through the wood of the bathroom door, tripping my heartbeat over itself.

"Come to the garage when you're ready."

My head snapped to the door as if I could see Dominic behind it. "Okay!"

I flinched back when my voice fucking *squeaked* like I was a goddamn school girl. I slapped my hand over my forehead and waited to see if I felt feverish or was just losing my freaking mind.

It had been like this since yesterday.

Our chemistry had created small moments before, but nothing quite like yesterday's. That one time in Maya's bedroom had been flustering, but it was only a comment. The incident in the park on Sunday had been unexpected, but my lust for Dominic had never been subtle, and it shouldn't have taken me by surprise that I wanted to kiss him.

Whatever it was between us was predatory and attacked whenever it saw an opportunity, but I had been its sole victim over the last month and a half. Dominic might have felt nips of it here and there, but he'd remained mostly unscathed up until now.

Until yesterday.

Something about what happened with Daren pushed him off his kilter of right and wrong. Our dynamic was upended when he had me against that wall. We had a strict set of unspoken rules that Dominic broke yesterday.

I teased him and flirted with him because I was reckless and young and I could. Dominic was the older rule-loving authoritarian who let me have my fun but kept me from crossing any lines.

Except the thing with Daren hurt him. It enraged the opportunistic thing between us so much that it finally took a chunk out of Dominic, and he lost his grip on us. He touched me like he *wanted* to touch me. Talked to me like he wanted to blur those lines.

He was slipping, and I didn't know how to react to it.

With a final mirror check, I smoothed my palm down my chest in a lame attempt to quiet my palpitating heart and exited the bathroom.

I'd never been inside the Reed's garage before, but one step inside told me it really wasn't much of a garage at all.

It had been made into a home gym for the most part. It was a three car garage, and the very end had a space where a car would go, but everything else was equipment and heavy weights.

No wonder Dominic is so jacked.

Speaking of, my boss hadn't noticed my entrance yet. He was turned from me, unfolding and laying out blue mats on the floor. He bent over, and...

Was it dramatic to say time stopped?

If it was, I didn't care. I was a dramatic person, and that was an ass worth being dramatic over. He was wearing *sweatpants*, for fuck's sake. Didn't every man know that sweatpants were like kryptonite on a perfect ass?

They were the color of gray his eyes got when he was lit by moon or sunlight. The shirt he was wearing wasn't helping my hormones either. It was a freaking muscle shirt. I already knew the muscles were there. I'd *felt* them, but did I really have to stare at the taunting outline of them for the next two hours?

Did he want me to learn *anything?*

"Kat?"

My lips parted with a faint smack as shock entered my lungs. I pulled my focus up, finding sterling eyes waiting on mine.

"Hi," I breathed, sounding like a dumbass.

Dominic ignored my equivalent of a vocal hard on and lowered his gaze about a foot.

"Nice shirt."

Nice ass.

"Yeah, I don't exactly have 'quote unquote' workout clothes, so…" I shrugged, sending a distracting scan around the garage. It was a nice size space and far enough away from the main rooms of the house that it felt secluded. A not-so-cozy nook of the house just for Dominic. The space and everything in it were stoical just like him.

There were a few messy exceptions. A couple half-drunk water bottles lying around, an empty glass tumbler that probably smelled like bourbon, a discarded pair of sneakers in the corner—a different pair than he wore to the park. His park sneakers were around his feet right now while I was rocking the barefoot look.

I even painted my toes with some red polish I'd dug out of my closet last night.

My red toes clashed with the blue mats as I stepped on one, the air squishing out beneath my heel. "So you'd rather be here with me than at some fancy family dinner with Heather and her parents?"

My stare cut across the room just in time to see Dominic's jaw lock tight.

"I wasn't invited."

If I was still standing in front of that giant bathroom mirror, I would have just watched my eyes bulge out. Heather didn't even *invite* him? Talk about next level shitty.

Rather than dwell on it, he put on his cop boss hat and got down to business. "Let's begin."

"So serious," I chuckled, trying to lighten his mood.

It had the polar opposite effect, and his eyes turned glacial.

"Self-defense is a serious thing, and I expect you to take this seriously."

I froze up beneath his gaze and had one of those moments where you carefully think out how you *need* to react over how you *want* to react. I *wanted* to sink my teeth into him and tear him a new asshole.

However, given that he was only here because his wife ousted him from dinner plans, I forced my tongue to draw all the colorful insults I had planned on the inside of my cheek instead.

Dominic watched me with anticipation, his muscles hard locked and braced for my reaction. Almost like he wanted me to lose it so he could lose it too.

Unfortunately or fortunately for him, all I did was nod. I'd be a good little student tonight to make up for what a bad little wife Heather was. A tiny smile pushed my cheeks in for him. Dominic looked at the gesture with distrust.

His browline was so sunken in, and the tips of my fingers tingled with that strange desire to rub the stress out of them. I curled them into my palm to stop myself.

Dominic still appeared wary, but shook himself out of it to go stand in the center of the mats. "Let's start with how I had you yesterday."

"Not up against the wall?"

A look of friction captured his expression. "We can skip that part."

Okay, so he *definitely* knew yesterday had been a big no-no. Somewhere up against that wall, we'd found our line and crossed it, and now he was trying to wheel us back.

Mentally high-fiving myself for being right, I traveled across the floor to him. How Dominic touched me today compared to yesterday was like a business transaction. There was no touch unwarranted. No body contact not necessary.

His hands locked my arms behind my back like he had yesterday, and that was the extent of it.

"So there are a few ways to get out of this. Your goal is either to surprise or hurt your attacker enough to distract them so you can get away." His fingers around my wrists tightened my focus on his next words. "You're not fighting anyone, okay?"

I bobbed my head from side to side. "I mean, I am."

"*No*, you're not. You do these moves and then you run away. You don't stay and fight." His next question was pointed. "Do you understand?"

Over my shoulder, I twisted my neck to zero in my disbelief on him. "If someone tries to *attack* me, you don't want me to fight back?"

"No. I want you to run."

"That's dumb."

"That's being safe."

Swiveling my head back forward, I rolled my eyes. "Whatever. Let's just keep going."

A sigh with audible irritation inflated his chest to brush my back. Then it was back to bare bones physical contact and Mr. Serious.

"In this position, it'll depend how they've grabbed you. How I have you now, your easiest way to hurt me would be to step on my foot as hard as you can, especially if you have heels on. That, or smash your head back into my nose."

"I head-butted Daren, but it hurt like a *bitch*."

"You went forehead to forehead in the video. You want to aim for their nose whether you're hitting them from front or behind."

I cocked my head just a bit. "Can I practice that?"

"I'd rather you not," he replied, deeply unamused.

An exhale of dramatic proportions slumped my entire body. "Then what's the point of this?"

"We're getting to that."

The low notes of his voice struck like slaps of wind, the chill digging goose-bumps out of my skin. I breathed through the reaction, trying to remember why I was here and move it along. The faster we went, the quicker I could get out of here and resume my denial that nothing out of the ordinary was happening between me and my boss.

Pressure released around my wrists as Dominic loosened his grip, moving up to my shoulders. "To continue, I'll have to wrap my arms around you. Is that all right?"

Heat thwacked my chest, bleeding up into my cheeks. He'd never asked to touch me before. He maybe should have on any one of the occasions that he'd touched me or held me or even picked me up off the ground, but he hadn't. The fact that he was now was inarguable, *humiliating* proof that yesterday, we'd gone too far, and Dominic was acutely aware of it.

"Yeah, that's fine."

Gently, he eased me back against him, burly arms circling my upper body and trapping my arms at my side. "A lot of times, men will grab you from behind like this so they can pick you up and carry you wherever they want."

I was hearing him, I really was, but it was difficult to focus on learning defense moves when all I could think about was how I wanted things to go back to normal between us. No awkwardness. No tension. No asking for permission to touch me like we were back in middle school.

Part of me wanted to scream and shake him and tell him to get over it and stop making it such a big deal. He was attracted to me. Big whoop. Though, putting it out into the open like that would probably only make him clam up more.

I just needed to unfreeze him. Make him laugh. Make him remember the easiness between us when we fell back into what worked for us.

"I'll be sure to eat a huge breakfast that day so I'm too heavy to lug around," I said. "Really carbo load that day."

It was a few seconds before he said anything. A few seconds before he released a short exhale that sounded both begrudging and amused. "Even if you were wearing a weighted vest, you'd still be easy to pick up."

"What?!" I snapped my head back around him as much as possible, showing him my outrage. "You're exaggerating."

His eyebrow cocked in confidence. "I'm not."

"What about when I'm dead weight?"

Without giving him warning, I dropped myself in his arms to a ragdoll of limp muscles and flimsy bones. His forearms stiffened around my chest, locking beneath my armpits. I was a noodle and he was the fork trying to hold me in place, and I hoped like fuck he thought this was funny.

"Ms. Sanders," Dominic grumbled.

"I can't hear you. I'm dead."

His hold around me shifted and reinforced. "You will be if someone comes after you and you don't know how to defend yourself because you were goofing off during these lessons."

"I'm not goofing off. I'm proving a point. *This* is my defense tactic."

Eyes closed, tension balled up my stomach into a knot of nerves. I was hanging in his arms, legs flopped out on either side and one-hundred percent committed to this bit now. It'd gone on too long to pretend otherwise.

It made sense in the moment when I went full noodle. I imagined him laughing, scolding me a little, and then we would move on like yesterday had never even happened. Except, in the reality of it, there was no laughing. Only scolding and now silence.

This was backfiring fast.

My heart was full on throttling itself, and I was sure Dominic could feel it, beating an apology out in morse code for how stupid this was.

Just before I threw in the towel and heaved myself back up standing, Dominic moved.

He bent at the knees, one of his arms loosening its grip keeping me up. An inaudible gasp caught in my throat. He was dropping me, and I couldn't blame him. At least my landing would be soft.

I braced for an impact that never came. Dominic scooped an arm beneath the bend of my knees instead, lifting me fast. My arms jumped with my heart and latched around his neck, holding on for dear life.

I was all shock and no words as he cradled me—fucking cradled me—into his chest. Hard muscles I'd felt from behind yesterday were now right there and accentuated by his tight shirt. Arrogance destroyed my next several breaths looking so damn good on him as he stared me down from so close.

"It's a lousy defense tactic. You're still too tiny for it to matter."

Focus. Focus. Focus.

"I am not tiny," I argued. "I'm 5'3."

"Fine. You're petite."

"That's just a fancy word for tiny."

The corner of his mouth crept up, and he moved his thoughtful gaze out before bringing it back to me. "What do you want me to tell you? It's another reason I worry. You're a hundred and ten pounds of backtalk. You're bound to piss off the wrong person."

"*Jeez*, tell me how you really feel."

He gave a small laugh through his nose, and I felt like I was watching the ice thaw around his eyes. *Limp noodle totally worked.* "I just mean that if someone wanted to take you, I'd like to make it as hard as possible for them to do that."

Those words struck an abnormal cord in me, setting my heart on edge. I angled a curious look up at him, a hesitant curve to my lips.

"That's such a hero thing to say."

Reflection speckled across winter eyes. "Is that a bad thing?"

"No." I shook my head, speaking sincerely. "I'm just used to villains."

EIGHTEEN

Over the next hour, we got down to work.

Dominic showed me a handful of moves, some difficult and some not. We practiced what to do if someone grabbed me from behind like he had or what to do if your attacker was coming in from the front. My favorite was when we worked on how to break your attacker's nose, Miss Congeniality style.

A quick thrust of the heel of your palm up into their nose and they were wailing like a baby on the floor. Or so Dominic said they would be. It was such a brutal move and yet so simple.

Plus the word 'thrust' coming out of Dominic's mouth over and over again was sugar-coated sin.

By the end of that hour, I was damp with sweat and actually having fun. Dominic's mood had also significantly improved, and it felt like things were blending back to normal for us.

"I'm pretty sure you're trying to kill me," I wheezed, sprawled out on the mats.

Dominic's dazzling smile was almost too bright—too stunning—as he strolled over to where I was on the floor. "That's the exact opposite of what I'm doing. I'm trying to save you from anyone who might want to kill you."

I scoffed. "Who's gonna wanna kill me? I'm so lovable!"

The smirk that rose on his sensual mouth was damnable and devilish. "That's a word for it."

Staring up at him from the floor, I realized I'd never liked an angle between us more. Him standing over me the way he was—a little smug, a little sweaty—was potentially lethal to someone like me. It made me ache in all the places I shouldn't.

Pushing all of that to the back of my mind, I held my hand out. "Help me up."

He drew a stiff brow up at me.

"A 'please' would go a long way, Ms. Sanders."

My limb dropped back to the mats. "Are you teaching me manners or self-defense?"

"Both if we're lucky," he mused, a lazy smile riding his lips.

How come even when he was being an ass, he was funny? And sexy. And all I wanted to do was show him just how unmannered I could be and watch those eyes burn cold. I wanted to ruffle his perfectly coiffed feathers just to see what he would do, and resisting the urge was downright painful.

"God, it is never more clear to me that I have daddy issues than when I'm with you."

He went on immediate defense, face falling and eyes hardening. "Meaning?"

"Every single word you say, I wanna do the exact opposite."

Pride curled the ends of my mouth up as Dominic's fell into a frown.

"Really? I hadn't noticed."

Sarcasm. Nice touch, sir.

I perched up on my elbows. "You could really use that to your advantage, you know. Get me to do whatever you want by telling me to do the opposite."

Dominic folded his arms over his chest, widening his stance. His grim-set face was already giving me the fun sort of jitters.

"All right, Ms. Sanders. Please continue to stay on the floor, mouthing off and wasting time."

A wide grin splashed up my face. I felt fucking *giddy*. "Damn. It's kind of hot when you're mean."

Dark brows lugged together. "I'm not being mean."

"Fine, then." My grin turned wicked. "Just hot."

Lightning danced in my belly instead of my veins for once. I didn't get butterflies like normal people; I got bolts of electricity buzzing around to tell me I was happy. The feeling didn't happen a lot, and thank God since it was kind of overwhelming. I wasn't sure my body could take this dosage of electric joy very often without giving out or exploding.

Teasing Dominic was worth the high though. I'd happily overdose on this exhaustive lightning if it meant seeing him pretend not to enjoy it.

Our game was so fun when we played it right, and I was so freaking happy we were both back on the same board again.

Or—

At least I thought we were.

My giddiness stumbled and then so did my smile. Dominic wasn't saying anything, and he didn't seem like he was holding back any presumed amusement either. His jaw had cemented tight, and I could even see small pulses in his cheeks as he ground his teeth together.

My gut pulled to the back of my body thinking I jumped the gun. Had I been too quick to fall back into routine and think he was okay with it? He was smiling and joking and I just *thought*—

"Aren't you gonna say 'line'?" I asked in a rush.

I needed to hear it. I needed to hear it like I needed to remember to breathe under his crushing stare. The word in the air would burst the sudden tension that flooded the garage. It would allow me to breathe and us to move on from this moment that was beginning to taste too much like yesterday.

Like a delicacy so sweet, it would make us both sick.

Dominic didn't let up the severity fixed in his stare. "I should have."

"Then why didn't you?"

He was right. He *should* have, but he didn't, and now we were here in this place where even lying on the mats, I felt like I might fall over.

He held my gaze long and hard before the word broke through his stiff lips.

"Line."

And now it meant nothing. "Too late."

Dominic inhaled what looked like fire from the pain that rippled across his face. The sight of it spurred a ravenous curiosity within me. It poked up my spine and burrowed deep beneath my tongue, keeping a calculated grip around my vocal cords.

Dominic tried to turn away. "Let's move on."

My curiosity pulled its strings and made me say something I shouldn't have.

"What were you gonna say to me yesterday in your office?"

He flinched. Even *he* wasn't quick enough to hide the reaction. Using the floor as a distraction, he said, "I don't know what you're talking about."

But that wasn't good enough, and I was pushing for more before I even thought through the words coming out of my mouth.

"It was when we were up against the wall and you were trying to make your point about all of this self-defense bullshit, you said 'You have no idea how' and then you stopped talking."

He slid his piercing focus over to me. "I don't remember."

Then he made a mistake.

He lingered. It was only for a moment, but I saw the evidence of his lie burn beneath his eyes. And I only saw it because I was right. Dominic *was* slipping, and in his fall, I was able to see flashes of all those truths he kept hidden.

And my inquiring mind wanted *more*.

"Now, who's the liar?"

I gave him a once over, witnessing every muscle clench beneath his sweat-glistening skin as I passed it. My sweep of him finished and settled back on his stare, a war breaking out behind darkening skies.

Dominic let out a breath, both steady and struggling. "Ms. Sanders—"

"Let's make a deal," I interrupted, scooching a few inches closer to where he was standing. "If I get a leg up on you and pin you down, you tell me what you were gonna say."

His ice-like expression broke with a chuckle of arrogance. The sound drew my neck back, and I hoped in that moment that what I was about to do next would leave him sore in the morning.

"Okay. Deal."

A man's ego is destined to be his biggest downfall.

Eyes still holding his, I slid one foot between his feet and locked the other around his calf. All it took was a jerk and twist of my legs, and Dominic crashed down to the mats on his back. A groan pushed from his lungs as he hit the floor, eyes stretching wide as he tried to catch up to what happened.

Before he could, I spider monkey crawled over to him and swung a leg over his waist. Sitting proudly on top of him, I poised my fingers over his slapping heartbeat with a winning smile.

"I also saw that in Miss Congeniality. Pretty cool, huh?"

A little wrinkle formed between his brows as they dipped. "That was a cheap shot."

"Well, I'm not rich, so what did you expect?"

Dominic closed his lips, filling his chest with a slow inhale and letting it out just as carefully. The breath cleansed the emotions on his face, draining out anything revealing and left him looking cool as a cucumber beneath me.

"Well done, Ms. Sanders."

"Thanks." Sitting taller, still straddling his waist, I crossed my arms. "Now, tell me what it is I have no idea about."

He inhaled again, and this time I knew what he was doing—trying to wash away any evidence that he was in the midst of a high fall, soaring through the limbo sky we created together and trying like hell to pull his parachute.

He spoke through his exhale. "That's an extensive list."

"So educate me."

Dominic's arms were on either side of him, fingertips fighting up and back down on the mat before curling into fists. Out of the corner of my eye, I watched him draw those fists to my knees, glimpsing the bare skin.

"For one," His tone was sharp, words sharper. "You have no idea how vulnerable you are right now."

I arched an eyebrow down at him, pushing back my posture. "I feel pretty powerful."

In fact, I'd never felt more powerful before. Knowing it was Dominic beneath my thighs, his abs contracting against my core with each forceful breath he took was something beyond power. I could get drunk on it and blackout to the point of only remembering this unparalleled feeling and Dominic's name.

The position had started a pulsing between my legs, a subtle beat playing inside of me at the feel of his hard body against my mound. That pulsing cranked to a full on throbbing when knuckles grazed my thighs—purposefully.

Air choked in my throat, but Dominic didn't stop there. He took it until his hands spread flat across my thighs, the brush of rough calluses searing desire right through me. It was hot and sticky, just like the air bubbling between us as he scoured my prickling skin with masculine hands.

He was a touch tanner than me, and his hands easily covered almost all of my upper thigh with their size.

And his fingers...

Fuck, I couldn't stop looking at them. They were long and his knuckles were thick, and my mind kept dragging them down between my legs, wondering how they'd feel buried inside me. A quiet hum of need started thrumming at my center, getting louder as he let a lazy thumb curve my inner thigh in slow circles.

My breathing stumbled, desire shamelessly being the one to push it off its feet. The change over in my breathing pattern was audible, a heavy, uneven thing of proof that I was turned on.

Then my world went topsy-turvy in seconds flat.

I was on my back before I could blink. A flash of dark hair and darker eyes covered me, fitting between my legs and pinning my arms above me. Hot air packed my chest in shock, bowing my back against the mat to push myself closer to Dominic in a move I should have been ashamed of.

The withering look in his eyes held me still beneath him.

"How powerful do you feel now, Ms. Sanders?"

I had no response, only rough breathing to give away how okay I was with being powerless against him. Again, I should have been embarrassed, but I just couldn't find it in me when he was staring at me like he had every intention of destroying me.

"You know the most important thing you're taught in self-defense is to look for someone's weakness," he spoke, the warmth from his breath heating my lips.

I melted further, muscles turning to jello.

"A trick knee that will take them down. An old injury. It's usually physical, but not all the time." His grip around my arms tightened to a bruising pinch, and I stifled a moan.

Knowing flashed across Dominic's face.

"Sometimes it's something you unravel about the person that makes them easier to control. Easier to tame." My fingers were beginning to tingle from blood loss just as Dominic lessened his hold, taking his touch away completely.

He eased back just slightly. "Do you want to know what yours is?"

"I have a feeling you're gonna tell me."

Dominic hesitated for only a second, raking his eyes over my face. Forehead, chin, nose, mouth; everywhere was awarded a meeting with his loaded stare before he finally leveled it on mine. Chills sprouted before he even spoke.

"You're a dominant personality who wants the chance to be submissive."

"Excuse me?" I tried to sound upset, but it just came out all breathy instead.

"Maybe submissive is the wrong word, but if we're talking on a strictly physical level—" He paused, running a furtive glance down the slope of my neck. "You tend to bend to physical touch rather easily."

Taking after him, I moved my gaze down between us. I started at my chest that was trying to get closer to his, down to my legs that were spread down the middle for him without any real thought. I'd even hooked one around the back of his lower thigh. His hips were fixed between mine, and just a small wiggle found the bulge of a soft cock sitting right against my heat.

Desire strained every muscle in my body as I bit back a moan, using Dominic's face as a distraction from what was between my legs.

"Why do you think that is?"

Okay, even *I* heard the arousal in my voice. Dominic probably did too, but he chose to ignore it. "Because it lets you give up all control in the only way you'll allow yourself."

Just like that, my flame was pinched out.

And he didn't stop there.

"You're good at being in control and calling the shots because you have to be, not because you want to be. You take care of everyone, but no one takes care of you, and you're afraid to admit you want that. You at least want the option to give up all control, but you don't trust anyone enough to let go in any substantial ways."

I blinked up at him like he'd just backhanded me.

The word 'line' was sitting on my tongue, but I was too stunned to get it off. This was all fine and fun when it was him not so subtly admitting he was between my legs right now because he knew I'd let him do it. *That* was fun, and I wanted to go back to that before he fucked it all up and got serious.

Before he grabbed ahold of some of my faultiest wiring and yanked them loose.

"You think I *need* someone to take care of me?"

"No," he chided, glare disapproving. "You're not listening. I said you *want* to give up control. That and needing to be taken care of are profoundly different."

They didn't sound different. They sounded like insults. Judgements. He saw my sad little life and assumed I wanted out of it, a hero to swoop in and save me. He diagnosed me when all he knew of me were the ugly parts.

Then again, maybe that's all I had to offer him.

Any beauty born inside me had been boiled up in my mother's veins, and the morsels I had left were all for Charlotte. So yeah. Dominic only saw the ugly, but he was *attracted* to that ugly to whatever degree. My wrong seduced his right. My crazy charmed his sane. My defiance hypnotized his law and order.

For a man so keen on perfection, he had to hate me for it.

"Is this little analysis supposed to impress me?" I pushed myself up to my elbows, fixing my face up to his. His stare jumped a pinch wider. I could see every fleck of grayscale color composed in his eyes from this close, and if I wasn't so miffed at him, I might have wrapped my arms around his neck and held him there so I could count them all.

But I *was* miffed, and Dominic's monochrome gaze could wait. "All you did was just prove that you're up in that head of yours all the time thinking about everyone else's downfalls so you don't have to think about your own."

Instead of inhaling to erase his reactions, Dominic just stopped breathing all together. The push and pull of his breath across my face was gone, every inch of my skin cold without it. His lips had gone thin, and his husky murmur barely made it through.

"I'm well aware of my failings."

"And what are they?" I pitched myself up to my hands, sitting all the way up. This time, Dominic smartly retreated. Actually, he retreated up to his feet and backed away from me like my question was on fire.

"I think it's time for you to go."

I didn't have the quickness to hide my disbelief. I knew my jaw had slacked and my brows were halfway up my forehead. Of all the ways I pictured today going, Dominic kicking me out of his home sure as shit wasn't one of them.

"Why?" I stood too, bringing the fire closer to him. The *lightning*. "Because we're talking about you now instead of me? You can shell out your diagnosis of what brings me to my knees, but when it's your turn, the game's over?"

His strong back to me, he said, "I apologize if I went too far—"

"I don't want you to apologize to me," I interrupted, catching his hands ball up. "I want you to *answer* me."

Dominic whipped around to me. "I don't have to answer you, but you do have to leave. *Now.*"

Something inside of me caved in, hurting like a phantom pain you couldn't cure or name. The pain of it spurred me though, igniting that electricity that moved me, conducted me, *owned* me.

"That's not fair." My head was shaking and my heart was pounding, blood rushing in my ears. "You don't get to treat me like a science project and then send me on my way."

He shoved a rough hand through his hair. "I don't *want* to."

"Then don't." My voice was nearly a plea, and it wasn't until then I realized how much him throwing me out threatened to hurt me. I wouldn't allow that. "I'm not gonna let you throw me out just because you're too prideful to admit you might not be perfect. You said you had failings, and you've already pointed out some of mine, so just tell me *one* of yours. I don't even care which one it is. Just even the fucking playing field again, Dominic."

He hit me with a furious glower, eyes boiling over. "It is astounding to me how unaware you are sometimes."

I jerked back. "What the fuck is that supposed to mean?"

"It means that you need to leave before either of us says anything that might clue you into the obvious," he bit at me, teeth snapping.

"What the—" I stopped, feeling dizzy from the amount of pissed off I was. My anger crackled through me, fritzing my vision in streaks of white-hot light. "Clue me in! If I'm so fucking dumb, spell it out for me."

He sliced me over a warning look. "You're not dumb, but you are blind if you're being sincere right now."

"Sincere as it gets." My jaw clicked, offense brewing. "So open my eyes for me, Dominic."

This time, he sent both hands back into his hair, properly mussing it up for good with a rasping groan. "You're making this impossible."

"Making *what* impossible?"

"*Kat.*"

"*Dominic,*" I pressed right back.

If Dominic wanted my ugly, I'd give it to him. Attitude and all, if only just to prove that he wasn't so perfect. That was all I wanted. Our dynamic was all sorts of fucked up now, and it was his fault. He didn't have to make yesterday a big deal.

He didn't have to go and diagnose what made me weak in his opinion. Those were *his* mistakes, and I was just trying to fix this so things could go back to normal.

A low rumbling curled up Dominic's top lip—the start to his thunder.

"You make *this* impossible." He threw a gesture between the two of us. That fragile organ in my chest stuttered.

My lips struggled to form the word. "Us?"

As if there was an *us* to talk about.

"Yes, *us*." My confusion sharpened as Dominic growled out his confirmation. He began approaching, eating up the space between us in slow, predatory steps.

"*This* is my biggest failing. The one that keeps me up when I should be sleeping. The one that turns my morals inside out. The one that turns me into a complete bastard and I still can't help it."

Dark clouds were closing in around his pupils, the storm roaring with the detriment of a category five hurricane. The intensity of it was palpable, like ferocious winds whipping around us, pushing and pulling us together. There was even howling in my ears as Dominic came so close, the tips of his shoes brushed my bare toes, and I stumbled back.

He kept coming though, determined steps easing me right back up against a support beam in the middle of the garage. I wrapped my hands around my back to hold on to it. I needed something to brace me up while Dominic's confession did its best to tear me down.

I expected an explosion. I anticipated pushback from him. I was ready for a fight that would balance us out again.

I was not ready for this.

My head craned back until it met the support beam holding me up as Dominic completed the distance to me. He didn't come close enough to touch me, but I felt him like he was. I felt him all over me as if the hurricane in his eyes contained actual rain, and it was dripping down my entire body just because of him.

Every inch of me was acutely aware of him as he hung his face above mine, weathered of all restraint. "It doesn't matter what I do or how I try to ignore it.

My weakness is always there, whether it's miles away... or standing right in front of me."

Oh my God.

"What's your weakness, Dominic?" I whispered, knowing I shouldn't ask and he shouldn't tell me.

In the next second, the dark clouds evaporated. The thunder quieted. Dominic exhaled a breath that tasted like giving in felt, lifting his arms above my head to rest on the beam. The weight of whatever he was about to say slacked his muscles, slumping him forward until his forehead nearly kissed mine.

Then everything was still except his two perfect lips.

"Foul-mouthed twenty-year-olds that I can't get out of my head."

Holy fucking shit.

A *zap* of lightning struck in my stomach. An unfamiliar tightening followed, twisting up my chest and stealing my voice away.

"Those are the worst," I breathed just barely.

His heavy eyes traced my mouth. "You have no idea."

Dominic's unabashed focus on my lips spiked the almost painful sensation in my chest, and part of me wondered if I was dying. Maybe the lightning was to blame or maybe it was Dominic and his confession. Maybe the two were synonymous and we'd started a phenomenon from the moment we met.

It's said that lightning never strikes the same spot twice, but I'd been struck so many times since I met Dominic, I lost count.

And apparently he wasn't as unscathed as I thought. I wrongly assumed he started to slip just yesterday, but he'd been in a silent fall since the beginning just like me. He wasn't slipping anymore. He was crashing *hard*, because this wasn't just an attraction he was fighting like I thought.

I was wrong. Fuck, I was *so* wrong. He felt the heroin chemistry too.

He was just as drugged up as I was on our connection. I was riding in his veins like he was riding in mine, both polluting each other's desires to be everything neither of us should want.

And it had been eating him alive this whole time.

Usually confessing something made someone lighter, but Dominic had never looked more burdened as he moved his tired eyes between mine.

"You say I'm in my head all the time, but it's you," he croaked. "*You* are in my fucking head all day long."

My eyes dropped on his mouth as he cursed, watching the vulgar letters touch his teeth to his bottom lip and his tongue move with the word. *God*, I'd never wanted to suck a word off of anyone's tongue so badly. Dominic had cursed in front of me before, but never the F bomb, and I was so glad he waited until after he confessed to lay it on me.

It was an experience I couldn't hide how much I liked, drawing back a breath shaking with dirty, filthy want. Dominic watched my reaction, hooded eyes telling me he knew exactly the impact he had on me. He clenched and unclenched his jaw, developing a slow dance pattern between my eyes and my mouth.

After a few more turns, the dance came to a standstill on my lips... and never went back up.

I'd never been so aware of my mouth before Dominic decided it deserved every ounce of his attention. My strawberry chapstick lips actually started to tingle the harder I breathed and the hotter the air between us became. There came a point where all the hot air warped my sense of boundaries and I asked another question I shouldn't have.

"Are you gonna kiss me?"

Dominic held a strong, silent beat, flicking his stare back up to mine. "No."

"What if I kissed you?"

A vexing warning flashed up his face, eyes thundering. "That'd be a very bad thing to do."

"But I like doing bad things." As I said it, I arched my back against the beam to press my tits up against his solid chest. "In fact, I'm very good at doing bad things."

A threatening noise rumbled in his sternum, vibrating down my whole body. Even still, he didn't move away. "I have no doubt about that."

We stood there, breathing against each other and eyes locked. It was like we were fighting a war on opposing sides but were anticipating the same winner. I'd done plenty of bad things before, but kissing a man that wasn't mine would be the worst. Religion wasn't really my thing, but I knew it was a sin. Adultery. Thou shalt not covet thy neighbor's wife or husband or whatever.

Dominic wasn't my neighbor though, so did that exempt me from the rule?

He was my boss, and he was married, and they had a kid together, and I knew all of this but I wasn't thinking about it. I *couldn't* think about anything except the chemistry. It bubbled in my veins, fueling the need growing inside of me until it bordered on painful. It was doing its thing to my brain, poisoning it to have only one singular want.

The chemistry wanted out. It wanted a display of its brilliance that both of its victims knew would blind us from any sense, any logic, any anything that wasn't each other.

It wanted heat and sweat and moans, and it didn't care who it hurt in the process of getting them. This was a *bad* thing we were about to do, and I didn't have a problem admitting I was a bad person for wanting to do it.

"It's not just you, you know. We're an ailment to each other."

Dominic watched my lips as I spoke, each word striking across his face, intensifying his look of pain with every blow. "Sometimes I close my eyes, and I see yours. I see them even when I don't want to, and they're so *cold*."

My voice slipped, quivering as my control began to fray as Dominic's breathing ran deeper, tiny razors in each exhale. Each taste of him cut through me, warmth and icy mint filling me up in a conflicting combination.

"They're so cold, Dominic, they look like they could actually *burn*."

Those blistering eyes snapped up to mine, a look of hate scorching them nearly black. I shuddered beneath it, dipping my stare to his mouth. "And all I can think about is how badly I want to get burned."

The timbre of his voice sunk low. "I'd do more than burn you."

The promise in his words wound my hands up to his chest, fisting his shirt and dragging him close. I gasped and he grunted as our chests collided, lips one bad decision away from following suit.

"I've survived worse," I breathed.

The air between us was a pollution of heavy panting and indecent confessions. We created our own brand of oxygen to breathe that would sustain us in our limbo sky, allowing us to exist in a plane where everything we were doing was okay.

The way Dominic cupped his rough hands on either side of my neck was okay.

The intentional press of his thumb just below my chin, tilting my head back for him was okay. So was the way he palmed my throat, and how I swallowed for him so he could feel how completely I was surrendering to him.

I was proving our weaknesses right, mine for him and his for me.

There was the slightest pressure around my throat, then a growl in his—

And then his mouth covered mine.

Lightning and thunder crashed in my chest. Light and sound exploded behind my eyes in vibrant colors. Somehow, even though it didn't make sense to know, I just *knew* there had never been a more perfect storm.

A strangled noise ripped through Dominic, vibrating his anguish against my lips. It was raw in both sound and flavor, clawing at my heart to be able to feel his torment. Fear that I would deny later made me hold him tighter, sliding my arms around his neck so he didn't let go.

He didn't, but his kisses were slow and agonized. Each one felt like an experience of torture to him that he just couldn't stop. He came close once, but I pulled down on his neck and sealed my mouth over his in a kiss that made him groan. He reciprocated, bruising my lips with a kiss that said he knew what I was doing and hated me for it.

That was okay. He could hate me so long as he didn't stop kissing me.

His lips were plush as I always knew they'd be, making me want so much more than these slow, angry kisses were giving me. I wanted his taste on my tongue, his moan in my ears, his musky scent seeping through my pores and diluting my blood until I was high on him.

Greedy and impatient, I passed my tongue along the seam of his lips.

The hand sitting on my throat jerked me back, breaking our kiss.

Dominic held me by the neck to the beam behind me, watching me with pupils blown wide. His grip wasn't hard, but I was sure he could feel my pulse flying beneath his fingers, drumming my desperation into him.

My chest was heaving, my breathing wild as I did my best to beg with everything but my lips for him to come back. To kiss me, and really kiss me this time. To hold me, and not let me go until I told him to. To explode with me like we were meant to, and deal with the blowout tomorrow.

I didn't know how far this would go tonight, but I knew it couldn't end here. There was this frenzy building inside of me, and I thought I might scream if he told me to leave again. I'd lose it. I'd certainly lose my goddamn mind if he threw me out before we ever got to ride out this chemistry.

There was no telling what Dominic was thinking either, because he'd never looked at me this way before. Like he wanted to rip me apart, and then carefully put all my wounded parts back together just so he could have a go at me again. He hated me, and he wanted me. He *hated* that he wanted me because I was everything bad and he was everything good. I was reckless and he was married.

He'd just kissed a woman who wasn't his wife, and it was my fault he'd done it. It was my fault he wanted to do it again, because I was tempting him, chewing over my bottom lip in hopes of making it redder than he already had.

A bullseye target for Dominic to land his own.

Weakness was closing in around his pupils as he eyed my freshly bitten lip. His nostrils flared in defiance of it, jaw raking back and forth as he fought with fate. That's what this moment was. That fickle bitch Fate put us in the destructive path of each other, knowing the end result would be chaos.

Pure, fire-blooded chaos that would feel way too damn good to ignore.

That chaos was running through Dominic's eyes, tying the muscles in his face so tight, a snap was practically imminent. And it came in the form of three little words, two buckling eyes, and one strangled utterance.

"I give up."

And then he consumed me.

A moan struck up my throat as Dominic's mouth smoothed over mine, giving me no time at all to operate on my own. In the same second that he decided he could and *would* have me, he took me like he knew he would own me eventually and wanted to show me all the ways he knew how to play with his new toy.

Every whimper I gave was because Dominic wanted the sound. Every ragged breath I took was because he pushed his oxygen into my lungs. The ache I felt wherever he wasn't holding me was because he made me a one-touch addict.

One brush of his skin anywhere on my body, and I was already in relapse for another.

Everything about how he kissed me now was different from the first time. This wasn't slow or tortured. These were feverish, pissed off possessions of my mouth with his, and I couldn't get enough. Dominic sucked in my bottom lip like he was trying to make it swell, grabbed it between his teeth like he was hoping to taste blood.

I cried out and let him do it, holding onto him for dear fucking life as he battered my mouth with his lust-muddled hatred for me. A sting cut into my swollen lip suddenly, making me hiss and tense up. Then the delicious swipe of his tongue over the stinging soothed the pain, making me groan and melt.

That was the first taste of him, and I was famished for more.

I flicked my tongue over his full lips, wanting to kiss him back and taste him like he had tasted me. His thunder rolled in his chest as I tested him, reached out to him, asked to form a connection with him that would link us for good.

Once you flavored someone, you never forgot it. Even if you went years without kissing them, it was a sensory memory that would flare up whenever you tasted them again.

Dominic would always know mine, and I would always cherish his—

Sweet mint.

Oh *fuck*, his flavor was sweet mint. It hit with an explosion as Dominic slid his tongue along mine sooner than I anticipated.

This time, we both moaned in a serenade of satisfaction, and I sunk into him completely. My muscles were drunk on him like every other part of me, folding against his hard body and knowing he'd keep me upright.

He did, slipping a hand up the back of my head, angry fingers splicing through my hair to grab a fist full. I whimpered, his knuckles digging against my scalp as he eased my head back by my hair, moving his lips over mine in greedy swipes. Dominic swallowed my small noises, tilting my head all the way until he could deepen the kiss exactly how he wanted to. Until he could reach every corner of my mouth, stroke his tongue around mine, and feel my throaty moan resonate inside of him.

Going against my earlier argument, I felt tiny against and beneath this man. Dominic made me feel like he could throw me over his shoulder and take me to his dark chambers where he'd have his way with me, and I'd happily let him.

But, no matter how small he made me feel, my libido was still the size of a porn star's. Between my legs was as swollen as my mouth and throbbing, a dangerous pulsing that wouldn't stop without friction. Hitching my leg up to his hip, I tried my very best to climb up him, a whine singing up my throat for help.

I was maybe the neediest bitch to ever exist, but I got what I wanted.

Dominic didn't sound pleased about it, but hoisted me up to wrap my legs around his waist, ankles locking.

"Happy?" he mumbled against me.

Lips over his, I breathed, "For now."

Another growl of sorts warmed his chest, and then we were kissing again. With each kiss, we were swapping silent admissions, sharing secrets, forming newer, dirtier ones with our tongues. Dominic grabbed my ass in both hands, palming a part of me he never should have touched and squeezing it like he'd thought about doing it every day for the last six weeks.

He let out a faint moan as he groped me, and I rolled my hips against him to hear it again. Except it was *me* who made the noise next, bucking myself over the huge erection sitting in Dominic's sweatpants. An unhealthy excitement drenched my pussy in seconds, practically crying to know that he was hard for me and unable to help it.

I knew without asking that he wouldn't fuck me, but that didn't mean I couldn't make his decision not to an excruciating one.

My hips rocked over his, grinding in jerking, desperate rhythms until both of our breathing had gone ragged and turned to steam against our faces. That fucking glorious pinch of pleasure was growing between my thighs, and I knew I could get there if Dominic helped, if he put even the slightest pressure behind his grip on my ass to help me grind into him harder.

He was barely moving at all though, holding himself so tight, his muscles felt like rocks.

It was like he was afraid if he moved in even the smallest way, it would break whatever control he had left and we'd end up back on the mats, bodies joined and consequences forgotten.

"*Kat.*" He struggled to even say my name over my lips, his fingers digging into my flesh as punishment for the erotic assault I'd unleashed on us both. It didn't *work* like punishment though, encouraging the tease in me to suck back on his tongue, and pass the word "Sir" between our lips to make him fucking ache like I was.

Dominic groaned something fierce, and then we were walking.

Well, Dominic was walking, carrying me with him until the clank of metal startled the air and ran cold along my ass as he set me down. My eyes flashed open, noticing the metal table I was now sitting on only for a moment before feverish hands ran along my bare thighs and nabbed my hazy attention.

I parted our lips just long enough to gasp his name as he grabbed under my knees. My small gasp then shattered expectations, breaking into a loud cry as Dominic yanked me forward, hitting my bundle of nerves right against his stiff cock.

My head flew back, ecstasy shooting up through my spine and threatening to paralyze me in this needy state. A paw of a hand clamped over my open mouth, holding on tight as I panted beneath him.

"Too loud, Ms. Sanders," he tsked, the low pitch of his voice drenched in lust.

Fuck, every part of me was throbbing to be touched by that lust. My nipples were pebbled and wanting to be pinched, my mound was like a million electrified nerves shocked awake with one touch, and every other part of me wanted to be bitten, squeezed, or slapped.

I shook Dominic's hand from over my mouth. "Then kiss me again to shut me up."

For just a split second, Dominic Reed looked helpless.

The gleam that flashed over his eyes was out of control; something even the man whose marrow was fused with authority and discipline couldn't get a handle on.

Then it was gone, and he was drawing my mouth back to his with an undone mumble.

"You were sent to destroy me."

I nodded, locking him closer with my ankles around his back and thrusting my hands up through his impossibly thick hair. The strands were silken against my skin and I messed them up as best I could to prove his point.

I was the villain of this story, wicked in all the worst ways.

"I take full responsibility," I confessed through heat and heavy breathing. "This is my fault." Dragging him back down, I fit my lips to his again, collecting his groans as tokens to count like sheep when I was lying in bed tonight, too hyped up to sleep. I swallowed his intimate sounds, his sweet mint essence until the chemistry was sated.

Still, *I* wanted more. "I'm the fucked up one, not you."

And I went to get the more I craved, but was stopped by Dominic's hand on my shoulder. He eased me back before I could steal another greedy kiss.

Those eyes of his were hitting silver now, bright with such a refined cocktail of arousal and release. His lips were plump from mine, a bright and devilish red, and his oh-so-almost-perfect hair was in total discord from my fingers plowing their way through it.

My lust tapered back as his trademark seriousness eclipsed those silver eyes in shadow.

"You are not fucked up." This was a statement. One that didn't have a weak syllable to argue with. "We can talk about all the ways our power dynamic makes this much more my fault than yours later—"

My shoulder under his palm slumped. "We don't have to do that."

This wet, hot kiss was my fault, and he'd never convince me otherwise. Dominic fought it tooth and nail. I pushed for it using every part of me, teeth and nails included.

Ergo, my fault.

He pulled back an inhale, drowning his argument on that particular topic for now. He searched between my eyes, sincerity tracing a lucent ring around his overcast eyes.

"I didn't mean you would destroy me as a bad thing."

I sat just a little straighter, tracing a fingertip down the coarse hair angling his jawline. "Usually things that destroy are bad."

The clouds casting over his gaze got a little heavier. A little sadder.

"You're not bad, Kat."

"I am," I whispered back.

He was shaking his head before I disagreed, moving closer and offering his reply on my lips. "No." He kissed the word gone, smoothing his soft mouth over mine with a newfound affection.

I'd never tasted a more honeyed kiss before, all sweetened and cloying. It swept waves of electricity from my toes to my fingers, igniting me with warm sparks. My butterflies.

I sighed and pressed my chest to his, tracing circles in his manicured five o'clock shadow with my thumbs. Strong arms held me close, our hearts slamming over each others' in drumbeats that had never sounded so full before, so alive.

One of his hands slipped forward, guiding my chin up and waning our lips apart. My eyes fluttered open, and Dominic was already watching me... a *distinct* change over in the make up of his eyes. I blinked a few times just to make sure I was seeing them right.

For the first time since I'd known him, they weren't some degree of freezing. Not a sliver of chilly winter to be seen.

They were nothing but warm.

"Stubborn." He awarded a peck to my lips, gone before I could reciprocate.

"Impulsive." Then one on my jaw.

"Insatiable." He found the arch of my neck, lips dragging up thoughtfully before his teeth nipped playfully. I moaned, head falling back and proving his point. He was right about all three things, and I was very much a fan of wherever this game was going.

Silken hair brushed my chin as he moved his mouth's attention to the other side of my face. He started the process all over again, feathering hushed facets of my character and kisses against my neck.

He began with, "Brave."

Something in my chest started to quiver, started to *hurt*.

His next caress of lips went to my cheek. "Strong."

I forced a breath down to stab and deflate whatever was hurting, but it didn't help. It only got worse as Dominic found the shell of my ear, dripping his husky voice all over it.

"Beautiful."

He finished his gradual assessment with a peck to my nose and a shake of his head. "But not bad. Never bad."

I sat there, and then I sat there some more until a burning fizzled in my eyes, and I realized I hadn't been blinking. So I did. I blinked at him, but I didn't speak.

I didn't have words. Nope, none were in my head while I stared back into *warm* eyes. Like after charcoal that had its fire put out, relaxing back into its natural color and peaceful heat. There were no words to be found.

Only the pain.

And it was widening up my throat, taking over all my room to breathe. Dominic didn't seem to realize what was going on in my head, or *not* going on in my head. He was still gazing at me like I was all the stars and he was the moon, which splintered the pain deeper.

It became a stabbing, a full on assault to my nervous system, and my heart—*fuck*, my heart was losing its goddamn mind. It had never beat so hard or so fast, bulldozing between my ribs trying to rip free. Pinpricks sprouted beneath my skin, hot, fiery pinpricks that needled my body into a full on mania.

What the fuck was happening? Why the fuck was everything hurting?

"I—" My failed attempt at talking creaked out, lighting my brain up with embarrassment. Now Dominic knew something was wrong, cupping my cheek with concern.

"Are you all right?"

Was I all right? *Fuck* no, but why? Why wasn't I all right? I'd just had the most toe-curling, world-stopping, sensational, blow-every-other-kiss-out-of-the-water kind of make-out session with a man I'd been fantasizing about for a month and a half.

I'd never been kissed like Dominic had kissed me. He took me and he altered my fucking DNA with just a kiss. Or multiple. Whatever. It was the singular greatest kiss of my entire life, and—

Panic knifed straight through me.

Numbing cold trickled down my body next.

No. No, no, no.

Mentally, I sped through my checklist for the symptoms of one of those fatal Hollywood kisses.

During the kiss, I remembered seeing bright colors like stars. *Check*. I remembered feeling the lightning running through my veins like wildfire. *Check*. Most of all, I *didn't* remember thinking of a single thing outside of my immediate realm of Dominic the entire time.

His kisses exempted my mind of anything but him.

Check.

That kiss—that perfect, explosive, mind-blowing kiss—was everything that could kill me.

I jerked back from Dominic like he burned me. Hurt splashed over his face, and *fuck*, he still was so handsome even doused in confusion and wounded. I was panting—*no*, hyperventilating—pure fire, my eyes trapped wide on Dominic's as pain rippled through my blood.

His pain consumed my vision while mine consumed everything else, eating up the last seconds of composure before it was ripped clean out of me, and I jumped. My heart got free of its strings, bounding around my chest and lurching me off of the metal table. I stumbled on weak feet, muscles giving out like I'd never used them before.

Dominic reached out to help me—stabilize me—but I recoiled farther away.

There was no stabilizing this meltdown.

"I have to go," I muttered. Or at least, I thought I did. I wasn't so sure. I was just moving, panicking, and fucking booking it out of the garage. Pounding footsteps trailed me, but the pounding in my ears was greater. Significantly more intimidating.

"Kat," Dominic called, pushing my feet faster. "*Wait.*"

But I didn't. I was a one-track mind that was quickly losing its sanity, and I needed to get out of there before it was gone completely. I nabbed my purse off the counter, breaking into a sprint towards the front of the house.

Dominic yelled for me again, but it faded as I threw the front door open and rushed down their driveway. I was going, going, going, until I was in my car and gone. I didn't pause to look back, didn't wait to see if Dominic had followed me out and was watching me drive away from him.

I didn't do anything except scream. The inside of my car became a war zone of lacerating curses aimed at myself, and all of it done at top-notch volume. I screamed about how dense I was, how ignorant I had been to what was happening. It had been going on for weeks, and I hadn't caught it.

Well, I *did* catch it, but I misjudged it.

Fucking *chemistry* should come with a warning label.

Might Contain Feelings. Entertain At Own Risk.

Had I known, I wouldn't have risked it. I would have stayed as far away from Dominic as possible if I knew our heroin chemistry could make me sicker than I ever signed on for. I was okay being lust sick. *That* had a cure.

Feelings were unpredictable. They either went away on their own or they grew into malignant tumors all over your heart, weighing it down with sick love. Even though I'd taken every precaution to avoid it, chemistry had tricked me, and now I was sick.

My heart was sick for Dominic Reed.

NINETEEN

Monday morning, I found myself on the other side of the Reed's front door, not moving a muscle.

One of two things would happen once I walked through that door.

The first would be the obvious—a swift boot right back out. The dreaded pink slip delivery. The always good 'We're going in another direction, and that direction isn't you.'

Worst part was that I'd have no one to blame but myself. I wouldn't even have a right to be mad if Dominic fired me. I mean, I still *would* be mad and probably throw a bitch fit, but only because anger was my clutch, and I'd been known to shove it into first gear without really thinking.

Honestly, I'd been expecting a call or text message all weekend telling me not to come in today or ever again, but nada. So, here I was, squaring off with a giant door, expecting option one but hoping for option two.

Total denial.

Both of us would pretend like nothing ever happened in that garage and happily ignore each other for the rest of my employment. We wouldn't have to talk about the kiss. We wouldn't have to talk about why I ran.

We could ignore the chemistry and the stupid *feelings* that came with it, and the less attention we gave them, the quicker they would die off, and I'd be cured of them altogether.

Fingers. Fucking. Crossed.

With a shaking breath and flimsy expectations, I put on my big girl thong and pushed open the door, making my way inside. The expansive foyer and empty staircase were silent for about three seconds before—

"Ms. Kat is here!"

Maya's enthusiastic announcement of my arrival exploded the fragile silence, sending shrapnel of its wreckage straight through my chest. I tensed, instantly missing when I first started working here, and Maya was still shy around me.

Oh God. Kid, love me less.

She bounded around the corner, a flash of dark curls and bright white teeth. I tried to force a smile of my own, but it felt as lame as it probably looked. Mid-run, Maya slipped on her socks on the hardwood floors, falling to her side with flailing arms. I would have ran to her if she hadn't popped right back up like a jack in the box, giggling up a storm at herself.

Suddenly, my smile wasn't so forced.

"Hey, Kiddo."

"Ms. Kat, I made a play-doh mansion yesterday that Daddy let me keep up so I could show you when you got here today!"

"Oh..." *Well, that play-doh is hard as shit now.* "Is there a room for me in said mansion?"

She wrapped her hand around mine, dragging me into the belly of the beast where the beast himself could be waiting around any corner. "Yup! There's a living room, ballroom, and four bedrooms. One for me, you, Mommy, and Daddy."

Separate rooms for Mommy and Daddy? Ouch.

"What about bathrooms?"

She huffed, running a hand back through her fly-aways. "We can go outside."

I swallowed a laugh as she pulled me around the corner leading into the living room where it was surprisingly empty. A sigh of relief deflated my lungs and my shoulders slouched over.

Then in the exact next second, every relaxing physicality went in reverse.

"Daddy, Ms. Kat says we need bathrooms in our mansion, but there're no rooms left." She angled herself towards the kitchen directly behind me. "Can you and Ms. Kat share a room so I can make yours a bathroom?"

If I could have left my body, floated above the house and screamed until the sound barrier broke, I absolutely would have.

Kids, man.

Dominic couldn't have been much better. How uncomfortable he was with his daughter putting me and him in a bedroom together in this play-doh house reeked through his dismissive tone.

"That's fine."

Not even on his most fatigued days did I hear Dominic disregard anything Maya said. Her words were gems, and he collected them all with a smile. Well, usually.

She didn't really seem to notice though, scrunching her sweet face together while staring down at her pink and orange oblong creation. I looked down at it too, wondering with a twisting stomach what made Maya choose me as a bunk buddy with her father instead of Heather.

Kids were perceptive as hell, sure, but that would make Maya a freaking mind reader.

Eventually, she abandoned her work of art and trotted behind me. My gaze followed her around as she climbed to her knees on one of the high-rise kitchen table chairs and forked a giant, syrupy bite of pancake in her mouth. She munched happily, staring out the bayside windows at whatever caught her creative attention.

With Maya choosing to kick it with the *window* over me or Dominic, there was an acute silence left in the air. One that put a guiding finger beneath my chin and turned my head in his direction.

God, he looked good today. It actually *hurt* how handsome he was. For the amount of agonizing I'd done all weekend that earned me these puffy bags under my eyes that no amount of concealer could hide, he could at least have the courtesy to look just a little worse for wear.

I wasn't asking for much. Messy hair. A wrinkle in his shirt. Mismatched socks maybe? I could still hold out hope for that one, but the chances were sucky.

Dominic's focus was down, long fingers clasping sleeve buttons on his crisp white shirt. Swarthy brows were furrowed in fixed concentration, his mouth curved in the most exquisite frown. I couldn't believe I kissed that mouth. Even frowning, it was such a perfect mouth, lips like curved candies I wanted to suck on and get a sugar high from.

His sweet mint taste lingered on my tongue, still as potent even days later. It wouldn't let me forget what I'd done to acquire the taste and what I thought about doing again and again despite how sick it made me.

Feelings were such a strange addiction.

I was too entrapped in my staring, my mind-fuckery feelings, to be at all prepared when Dominic flashed his eyes up and caught me in his. A burst of electricity shocked my heart to skip about fifty beats in a row, stuttering my brain to a freeze. Dominic locked me into his gaze, sharing memories between us like an exchange of oxygen. Except the air we were sharing was suffocating, pouring guilt down my lungs as he showed me his memories.

Bright and vivid. Sensual and passionate. Devastating and furious.

Dominic was livid, and within only a few seconds of drowning in his eyes, I was breathless. Breathless and so fucking sad because they were back to cold.

His eyes were back to the coldest winter's night, and it was my fault.

Shame thrashed up my throat, an apology trapped in its grip and ready to toss out. Anything to smooth out the edges of that razored glare. I didn't have to get into specifics with it.

Just a quick 'I'm sorry', and the rest would be implied.

I'm sorry for pushing you to tell me your weakness. I'm sorry your weakness is me. I'm sorry I bent you until I broke you into giving in and kissing me. I'm sorry that I ran out without an explanation after you said all those nice things.

Everything I was sorry for proved what I was trying to tell Dominic back on Friday. I was *bad*. I had a lot of broken parts that had sat and withered over the years, growing more calloused and mucked over. The more those dirty parts acted in blind pursuit, the less control I had over them.

Eventually, I realized those parts were what kept me safe, and ever since then, I handed the reins over to them and let them work. And it *had* worked up until now. My bad parts had never hurt anyone good before this.

Only people who deserved it.

Dominic didn't deserve it, and with our eyes still locked, I opened my lips to tell him just that.

"I'm late for work," Dominic cut me off, snipping our connection dead.

He tore through the kitchen, grabbing everything he needed for work off the counter in a quick sweep. My gaze trailed after him, sitting wide with shock.

He ping-ponged from the counter to the island in the middle of the kitchen to palm his keys over to Maya to drop a swift kiss on her head. He avoided me completely. That, and acknowledging the fact that I totally knew he wasn't really late for work. I knew what time he had to leave in the mornings to get there on time, and we still had a few minutes to go.

Dominic ignored the lie and how bold-faced it was and kept moving until he was out of sight and out of the house. I gawked at where he just stood and followed the trail of smoke he left gunning it for the front door.

Well...

Now at least we were even.

Four hours, three peanut butter and banana sandwiches, and two games of hide and seek later, Maya and I were conked out on the couch for a dual afternoon nap.

Chores could wait.

Beauty rest was a must.

I wasn't sure how long I slept before stirring awake. The couch was warm beneath my back and my muscles felt all jello-like and relaxed. Maya's even breathing was a gentle push and pull down the dip of my cleavage. She'd fallen asleep on my right tit, and I couldn't even blame her.

Tits were comfy as fuck.

Eyelids still slacked by sleep, I rolled my head against the plush pillow that probably wasn't designed to be slept on, but looked at. My neck cracked something delicious, muscles stretching as I lulled my head to the side with fluttering eyes.

Every lazy muscle in my body seized, eyes jumping wide as I realized we weren't alone. Dominic was a strong presence sitting on the small sofa parallel to us. His long legs were set wide, elbows resting on his knees while his chin rested on his folded hands.

He watched me go through the motions of realizing he was there, trying to hold in my freak out, and settle on a shaky exhale to relax from the subdued panic. His gaze was wholly unashamed on me, his concentration tight and thoughtful.

What he was thinking, I didn't know because of the chill in them I'd brought back. It froze out any vulnerability he'd shown me on Friday, and that was probably for the best. Before Friday, an inscrutable glance from Dominic had the potential to overwhelm me. Being given his full range of expressive emotions and thoughts sent me into a freaking panic attack on Friday.

I couldn't take more than the basics from those eyes.

It was definitely past lunchtime, so I couldn't even say why he was home. His forefinger covered his top lip with how he had his hands pressed to his mouth. Slowly, he lifted his lips over the bridge of his fingers, the velvet timbre of his voice flowing out.

"You two are cute together."

A cloud of sour smoke filled my chest, or at least that's what it felt like. The smoke constricted everything, eating up every bit of oxygen in my lungs so all I could do was smile at him, and even that was weak.

Dominic's phone buzzed on the arm of the chair, his eyes rolling down to it like a ton of bricks were sitting on his eyelids. One look at the screen, and those eyes fell shut.

"Work still crazy?" I asked softly, finding my voice.

With a languid inhale that lifted his whole chest, he nodded.

"Any luck with the nurse's case?"

He slid his whole hand over his mouth this time, joints moving slowly. He took a steady beat before shaking his head. A quiet settled over us, somber and heavy.

Dominic may have been upset about our kiss or how I ran away from him this morning, but his sadness was about more than that now. I wasn't selfish enough to believe that this degree of blanketed stress was about me and our little kiss. This was a *palpable* upset, the drawn lines on his face enough to illustrate an entire despairing novel.

His stare was still lowered to his phone even though the screen had gone black. He curled his fingers back into a loose fist over his mouth, gliding a knuckle back and forth over the seam of his lips.

Dominic was so lost in thought that he dragged my mind off course too, making me lose all concept of time and awareness while I watched him. My thoughts floated in fragments all dedicated to Dominic. I wondered what he was thinking, why he was home, what was bothering him so much, if he'd dreamt about me this weekend like I dreamt about him.

I could force my brain to steer towards other topics when I was awake.

My subconscious was the treacherous bitch.

She liked to dream about him pressing me up against a wall—any wall, really. My subconscious wasn't particular, just horny—and bruising my lips with kisses so filthy sweet, it made my stomach ache. In the dream, he said all those kind words again, and this time, I would cry. There was no shame in the tears like there would have been in real life, and in Dreamland, Dominic kissed each one away until my sobs turned over to moans. Then I woke up.

Pissed off and super horny.

All my floating, angsty, silver-eyed thoughts went poof as Dominic spoke out of nowhere.

"She was the sixth woman taken in the last year." My eyes were wide and waiting on his when he brought them up to clarify. "The nurse. She's victim number six, and we only found the first one last month."

My eyebrows shot up, and I did my best to keep my enthusiasm to a whisper.

"You found someone? That's *great*." Except nothing in Dominic's expression said it was. Confusion folded with dread as my eyebrows lowered with my expectations. "Isn't it?"

His stare was half-hooded by lids too exhausted to stay upright.

"She was found in Florida, dead in a swamp on the side of a highway."

A gruesome picture painted itself to life behind my eyes before I could stop it. My heart felt punctured by his words, by the image, by such an unfair death. Saliva crawled down my throat, slow and bitter tasting.

"How did she...?"

For just a moment, his ice melted to reveal a regarding sadness.

"Overdose. Heroin."

Panic with teeth clamped down on my windpipe. It didn't let go, burying its fangs in deep until it scraped bone. A shiver drew goosebumps all over my skin, Dominic's sorrowed stare watching them grow. He knew heroin was my mother's favorite from her arrest report. His sadness was for me.

Because someday that might be my mom on the side of the road, except she would have gotten there all on her own.

"Her name was Jessica Serrano." I inhaled her name deeply, using it as a vice to ease off the panic's biting grip. It felt nice to be able to give her a name. "We initially concluded her as a runaway. She had all the signs. Problems in school and at home. Her parents waited four days before even reporting her missing because she'd run away before."

I wanted to ask him why he was telling me all of this, but I didn't want him to stop, so I kept my mouth shut. Even as his words got more grim, his eyes dimming to a muted, dreary gray.

"It wasn't until two sisters were taken on their walk to school a couple months later that we even considered Jessica might be a victim."

My heart stilled. "Two *sisters*?"

Dominic forced a slow nod. "Twins. Both 16. Jessica was 17."

Oh holy fuck, that was *young*. Anguish ate away the gray edges of Dominic's eyes, his pupils narrowing and the whites expanding as he lost himself in his head again.

"What do you think is happening to these girls?"

Dominic pulled back a breath, but didn't let it go. It held his chest full and wide, and for a second, I worried the thoughts that carried his focus away were too constricting to remind him to breathe.

His loose fist still hovering in front of his mouth wound tight, thumb pressing down until his forefinger made a *pop*. The more he tried to fight out an answer, the more his stare turned to a frenzy. One dark possibility jumped over another and another, skipping past his eyes with razored feet, each one leaving an open gash. Nightmares bled through him, smearing with every shade of gray his eyes had ever been into a mural of morbid colorings that made my heart fucking *ache*.

He shook his head once and then stopped. He still hadn't let out that breath of air either, and now it looked like he couldn't. He looked stuck. He couldn't move. Couldn't breathe. Couldn't speak past the horrors of what he thought was happening to these women.

He jumped a quick glance up at me, brows diving together as he struggled.

"It's okay." I shook my head as much as I could, fingers itching to reach out and lay on his forearm. "You don't have to say."

He didn't acknowledge with anything more than a bone crushing clench of his jaw, the backs of his cheeks pulsating. He flicked his stare down and back up to me, leaning forward to rest his elbows back on his knees.

He leveled several calming breaths, pinching the bridge of his nose.

"I apologize for unloading. It's been a difficult day."

Guilt flared a heat wave up my front, reminding me that I was a part of what made his day difficult. "It's okay. You've been there when some of my messier shit spilled out." *Thanks, Mom.* "Plus, this will all be over once you catch the guy."

He shook his head, eyes still closed. "We have almost no leads. Any time we get anything, a pattern, a witness—*anything*—it disappears. We thought we had a pattern with the ages since most of the women taken were under or around twenty, but then there was the nurse. Thirty-four years old... and we're back to zero."

Just like that, dots connected, puzzle pieces fell into place, and Dominic's outburst about me walking home by myself at night after he picked me up from that party made a lot more sense.

"Is that why you wanted me to learn self-defense?" I asked carefully.

His brows were a severe line all the way across, mouth just as flat and serious.

"With the exception of the nurse, you fit the age profile."

My heart twisted forward, backwards, and around itself, tangling into a tight knot at the dead center of my chest.

This man. This poor, thoughtful, protective, stupidly beautiful man. His hero complex was going to send me to the friggin' ER if he didn't stop. He'd had this huge burden of knowledge this whole time, the weight of each missing girl crushing him from the inside out. He wasn't able to save them, so he was trying to do what he could with me despite how difficult I made it for him. He just wanted me to be safe. *Actually* safe.

He actually cared about what happened to me.

Fuck.

Eyes locked together, my voice dipped into unfamiliar territory, all soft and beholden. "I'll be more careful."

He didn't nod or anything. Just kept his concentrated gaze on me. As the seconds piled on, those reflective shards of gray burned with a different intensity.

An acknowledgement rearing its head.

My stomach buckled, terror flaming up my throat as he looked at me like he did this morning. Intrusive. Accusing. So fucking intimate. Reminding me that he knew how my tongue tasted, how my lips felt, how I sounded when he made me moan and whimper for more of him.

More, more, more until I'd consumed too much and ran away sick.

With Maya still knocked out hard on my chest, there was no fleeing this time. She was Dominic's secret weapon, making it so I *had* to talk to him. I was pinned under her tiny body and her father's intensive stare, peeking beneath sullen eyebrows as his bass voice rolled out, quieted by a heavy heart.

"Why did you run?"

Because it was selfish to kiss you, and it was selfish to run away from you, and I'm a selfish person and don't know any other way to be.

Instead, I chickened out. "You first. You were pretty quick yourself this morning."

His eyes ducked, hidden in admission that he was a fast-footed hypocrite. He carefully held the silence, rolling his dusty pink lips together to press them a darker shade of rouge. A flash of them swollen and ravished a sinful red passed behind my eyes.

He thumbed the edge of his shaded jawline. "I didn't want to hear whatever you were going to say."

"Even if it was an apology?"

The ice in his eyes sharpened. "Especially if it was an apology."

Now *that* took me back with what was probably some ill-placed frustration. I did a bad thing and now he needed to let me apologize for the bad thing. Isn't that how this shit worked?

"So you don't want me to say sorry?"

Dominic collected my angry confusion with shrewd eyes. His jaw ticked. "No, I don't. I want to know why you ran."

Guilt dropped my stare to the floor, and not a single other emotion. Not fear for what I'd experienced during our kiss: the wildfire lightning and neon-colored stars blinding my world of anything but him. Not humiliation that I'd let myself fall down that trap of fairy-tale feelings that I knew better against.

No, if I lied to myself enough times, then all I'd remember was the guilt, and guilt I could work with.

"I just had to," I admitted, my heart pounding between each word.

He waited for more, but I was done talking. The less I talked about why I ran, the more the why would fade away until the sickness was gone completely. I just had to breathe through it.

Breathe...

Through the jitters, through the feelings for him, through the panic they caused. I just had to breathe, and ignore it was all there on an inhale and filter out everything I was ignoring on an exhale.

I called it Denial Meditation for Beginners.

Seriously, so much cheaper than therapy.

Dominic needed to take a few sessions himself so he didn't go blurting out crazy ideas like he did next.

"We need to talk about it."

I quickly countered. "Or we can pretend it didn't happen."

Dominic blinked, absorbing my proposal. That stupid organ in my chest coughed through its sickness, terrified for his reaction. Would he be mad or relieved? Finally fire me or refuse to let me off the hook so easily?

The thickest shade I'd seen yet cast over his eyes, blocking out any single thought or reaction. Visible tension struck a chord in his neck, straining beneath his golden skin. The dark gray around his pupils was sucked dry, becoming as dull as his gruff voice.

"Is that what you want?"

Truthfully? "Yes."

Breathe it in, breathe it out.

Denial. Denial. Denial.

I kept my eyes on his, no matter how anxious they made me, so he could see how sincerely I meant it. I knew with every pass of my face those dissecting eyes did, he was trying to dig up lies.

But I wasn't lying this time, and there was a strange, almost solemn flicker in his gaze as he realized it. He nodded just once, taking in a generous sweep of my face.

Like he was trying to memorize it.

"Okay," he spoke, his timbre even. Heavy but professional.

"Then it never happened."

TWENTY

I t went on for three weeks like that.

Dominic and I would greet each other in the morning and pretend everything was ordinary. We would smile like we hadn't totally lip-locked and make polite conversation like we weren't thinking about the dirty confessions we shared through moans and sighs.

He was nothing but professional in those three weeks, and I was...

Trying.

Professionalism was not a skill in my wheelhouse, and it took an absurd amount of active awareness not to make flirty quips or ogle Dominic's perfectly toned ass. I blamed that one on him, though.

He didn't *have* to work out to make it such a fine piece of ass. That was all on him.

I'd slipped into easy habits over the three weeks with an inappropriate comment or two, always by accident. My wicked tongue was quicker than my brain a lot of the time, and it had never been such a problem until now.

Dominic always reacted the same when it happened. A brusque sigh, a release of that infamous jaw tick, and then he'd pretend like I hadn't said a word at all. I felt awful each time because he always looked like he was in actual *physical* pain trying to ignore it and ignore me.

He was much more careful with our chemistry than I was.

There was only one time over the three weeks he came close to slipping.

It was last Saturday, which Heather called Date Night, and Dominic called a work function. I called it awkward as fuck, but hey, I wasn't one to turn down extra money. Plus, I got to bring Charlotte, and her and Maya played and laughed until they both passed out on the couch within the first twenty minutes of Frozen.

I was supposed to babysit until 10 pm that night. Dominic and Heather were home by 8:45.

I remembered hearing their angry voices walking up the driveway before they even got inside. Dominic hushed Heather, and she stomped upstairs like the reasonable thirty-year-old woman she was.

I tried to make a quick getaway, scooping up a sleeping Charlotte and holding her on my hip, but Dominic was there when I turned around. The way he was watching me that night wasn't with the professional lens we'd forced back in place over our relationship.

He was just so fucking sad and too exhausted to hide it.

As he signed my check that night, he asked one of those questions where the pauses in between said more than the words themselves.

"Do you like to slow dance?"

My lips parted, thinking over my answer. "I've never actually done it. No one's ever asked me." I shrugged, the tail end of my mouth curving up. "I'll try anything once, though."

Hand splayed out on the kitchen island, Dominic allowed himself a moment of freedom to rove my face with eyes unhidden. Thick slats of black lashes fluttered softly over raindrop eyes, dreary and the loneliest shade of gray. They dripped to my lips, and my heart scrambled to clot my throat, refusing me to speak and interrupt this moment he'd given himself. He'd been so good at pretending since I asked him to, it seemed cruel to take anything away from these few honest seconds.

I counted to nine in my head before he dropped the mask back in place and pushed my check over to me. "Goodnight, Ms. Sanders."

I dreamt about slow dancing that night.

About burly arms wrapped around my waist, a soft melody swaying us around a room dressed in silver, hanging crystals that I was sure only existed because of the man holding me in the dream and his eyes that resembled them.

Even though Dominic and I agreed to pretend like nothing had happened, my brain wasn't following along. It was my brain's *brilliant* idea to ignore the kiss and the sick little feelings that charged in with it, but still, every thought that wasn't distracted was about him. The only thing helping me get through this week was knowing my 21st birthday was at the end of it, and I'd be getting away from this sickness for a couple days with Layla.

She knew something was up, but I hadn't had the ovaries to tell her what an idiot I was yet. I was expecting a full-blown episode of shock that I was capable of these lovesick feelings at all, followed by a battering of curse words and slapping hands for who they were aimed at.

Developing feelings for a married man? Dumb. Developing feelings for your boss? Dumb.

Developing feelings for your married boss? And the dumbass award of the year goes to—!

Maya's 5th birthday was actually tomorrow, coming just before mine. Family was coming into town, and she was having a "party" that, from what I understood, would be mostly adults who planned on getting super boozy. Maya asked me if Charlotte could come to the party, and *of course,* I said yes.

Then came the catch-22.

The inescapable moment when she asked if Charlotte and I could spend the night before the party. The birthday princess wanted a good ol' fashioned slumber party with her favorite people, and it was painful to smile through the panic when she asked.

Dominic was standing right there when it happened, and his pensive face said he remembered I wouldn't stay at my house without Charlotte there. Rather than worry where I was and if I was safe all night, he encouraged me to stay and help with 'party prep'. Heather would be out of town until the morning of the party anyway, and Maya's squeal of excitement was so shatteringly loud, the ability to say no shattered right with it.

So that's where I was, late afternoon Thursday, elbow deep in cupcake batter with two sugar-high five-year-olds taking bets on if their stomachs turned purple like their tongues after eating half a tube of purple frosting.

"But look at my tongue!" Charlotte stuck hers out at Maya for examination. "Tongues are pink and tummies on the inside are pink, too! If my tongue is purple—"

"But I don't want a purple tummy. I like pink," Maya cut in, frowning at the idea of purple insides.

Charlotte stood straight, shoulders pushed back and proud. "Then eat more pink frosting!"

"*Or* maybe no one else needs anymore frosting today, yeah?" I cocked a strict eyebrow at both girls, smearing the purple frosting at the center of the debate over a vanilla cupcake top. "You gotta learn to pace yourselves today so you can get sick on sugar *tomorrow*. Game the system, girls."

Bright blue and chocolate brown eyes beamed the same level of excitement. Charlotte swung to Maya, clipping her lightly on the shoulder as if to say '*duh*'. Maya giggled up a storm, feet bouncing like she was trying to take off and run straight into tomorrow where she could have all the sugar she wanted.

Amusement pulled at the side of my mouth, setting the fully frosted cupcake down on the tray of two dozen. The girls' buzzing excitement carried over my skin, warm and fuzzy like a blanket. I'd have wrapped myself up in that cozy blanket for the rest of the day if it weren't for the voice of silk and thunder that carried into the room and ripped it clean off.

"That's got to be some of the worst advice I've ever heard."

My serene smile slipped as Dominic came around the corner, casual confidence floating him right into my line of sight. In one of the smarter moves I made around him, I swiped a quick finger through the pink frosting bowl on my left and shoved it in my mouth.

Anything to stop me from blurting out how fucking dreamy he looked.

His nearly perfect hair was a bit tousled, a bit darker. Almost a jet black. Had he just showered? He was wearing jeans, and I already knew without him turning around that his ass was flawless in them. The jeans were paired with a super casual baseball T-shirt, gray with red lettering. I didn't know who the team was written across his chest, but I was jealous that their faded cursive got to stretch across such well-defined pecs.

I curved my stare down to his feet, rolling my tongue over the sweet frosting on my finger. My gaze cocked, noting he was only wearing black socks with no shoes. I'd never seen Dominic Reed going shoe commando.

"You're only wearing socks?" I asked, popping my freshly sucked finger to the forefront of my mouth.

"Is that a problem?"

I jerked my head up, pinching my bottom lip between my fingernails. "No. Just different."

Dominic's mouth parted to reply when his stare fell to the pout of my lips still nipped between my nails. I released it without thinking, sucking the tender lip back between my teeth like I'd been caught doing something criminal.

The way the gray ring of his eyes darkened definitely made me feel corrupt in some type of way.

An apology leapt up my throat, but I held it behind my teeth when I remembered. He didn't want me to be sorry, though I still didn't get why. I tried to change the subject as fast as I could to get his attention on anything other than how my pink frosting mouth might taste right now.

"Also—*ouch*. It's not bad advice to save the sugar coma for tomorrow. You're just jealous you're not fun enough to think of it yourself."

I swiveled my focus back to the cupcakes, plucking a naked one out of the bunch. Dominic was in the corner of my eye as I scooped a spoonful of frosting out with my knife, layering it on the dessert. My eyebrow twitched in humor when he cocked his head.

"Are you calling me boring, Ms. Sanders?"

As if a fist was clenching my insides, all five fingers eased back as Dominic swept in, composed and waggish.

"Oh, I didn't say that." I angled towards the two five-year-olds, lowering to a whisper. "I'm thinking it, but I didn't say it."

Both girls bubbled over with laughter, loving being in on the joke. Quiet chuckles of my own knocked around my chest to join in with theirs. It was Maya whose big eyes jumped back behind me, alerting me just a half a second before I felt his heavy presence pressing against my arm.

The hairs on that arm stood to full attention, goosebumps raising them higher. The musky fresh scent of him wafted in waves beneath my nose, drowning all my senses in one go. His smell was more potent, crisper than usual and confirmed that, yup. He'd definitely just showered for the night.

In the same house as me.

Naked. Wet. Rippling muscles. Huge—

Fuck.

My breath held tight as Dominic moved, hand reaching over to the bowl on my left. He scooped out two fingers dipped in bright pink frosting, apprehension ballooning my lungs as he brought them to my face.

A giant smile cut through my gasp as he slicked his two fingers down my cheek, painting my face with a streak of pink. Both Maya and Bugs draped the room in an explosion of tinsel giggles.

"Am I boring now, Ms. Sanders?"

God, his voice was honey and sin, riding over my ear and burrowing bad ideas in my head. Bad, filthy, wicked ideas. Scorching heat flashed down the entire length of my body even as I tried to shake the ideas gone. Dominic grabbed a kitchen towel to clean his fingers with, eyeing me for a reaction.

Somehow my voice was a perfect match of breathy confidence as I swiped my fingers in the same bowl. "Joke's on you." I batted a kittenish glance Dominic's way. "This stuff makes great blush."

Maya screeched while Charlotte tittered like she wasn't at all surprised as I slathered my other cheek as pink as its mate. Surprise backlit Dominic's stare, silhouetting every speck of awe floating through it. He was gorgeous when he was looking at me like I was something that could save him, even though we both knew better.

Selfish as it was, I wanted to keep that spellbound shine in his eyes for as long as I could. So I turned back to the bowl of cotton candy pink frosting and scooped a dollop full on each hand.

"You know..."

I trailed off, pivoting to the man with suspicion twisting his brows downward.

Those downward eyebrows peeled up as I slapped both my hands on either side of his face, covering him in frosting. "It also makes *great* moisturizer."

High-pitched squeals padded the kitchen wall to wall as I rubbed my fingers along Dominic's sculpted cheeks, massaging pink into every coarse hair. Dominic had frozen, gaze steeled on mine as he watched me with zero reaction whatsoever. I trapped my lips between my teeth to keep a dopey grin from breaking my face in two.

Dominic dropped a glance to my imprisoned smile, pausing there for just a moment before his eyes rolled shut. Then, a lazy grin spread across his sealed lips.

"This is so much worse than what I did to you," he mumbled, peeling thick lashes back up to pin me with eyes built of starlight.

Incandescent and finally—*finally*—that burning warmth from three weeks ago.

My lightning stirred.

"Mhm," I hummed, passing my thumbs over the brittle hairs above his top lip to get every inch of his neat scruff. My finger hovered over his lips, painting the feeling of them across the pads of my thumbs just from memory and making my spine tingle.

Don't do it. Don't fucking do it.

My mind warred with temptation, knowing if I slathered his full mouth in sweet, artificial pink, all I'd be doing was creating a scenario where I'd want to lick it off.

Smartly, my thumb passed his lips to his chin, curving a line of pink into the stubborn dip of it. Other parts of my body weren't so smart. My back bowed like a magnet was between my ribs, drawn to his chest like its twin was hiding inside of him. I tried not to pay it any attention, how naturally I leaned into the position and how he didn't push me away or tense up against me.

His eyes only warmed.

"Daddy, you have a pink beard!"

Indeed he did. A pink beard and eyes of silver starlight gazing down at me. "This is going to take forever to wash out."

Agreement hummed up my throat as I arched back to marvel at my masterpiece, pushing a candied thumb between my lips. Dominic either forgot to hide his reaction or didn't care to as he watched my mouth suck at my finger.

"Payback is a sweet, sweet bitch." I tagged a coy wink, knowing it was completely obliterating our new boundaries.

But he started it.

"I want some blush too!"

"We can do all our makeup with icing!"

Reluctantly, I turned towards the sugary-sweet mess unfolding behind me and out of Dominic's warmth. And because I was maybe sicker than I realized, I didn't move far enough away that I couldn't still feel him pressing against my back. He didn't move either.

Maya screamed like she touched a frog as she dabbed the rise of her cheeks with frosting. Charlotte had already dimpled both cheeks with purple and pink and was reaching for the rainbow sprinkles.

"This is your fault, you know."

Yeah. Most messes were.

TWENTY-ONE

Dominic agreed to clean up the kitchen while I cleaned up the girls.

Only issue with my end of the bargain was that they were still so high on sugar that bath time became an epic fiasco that ended with more water on the bathroom floor than in the tub. Both girls were donned in cute little princess bathing suits from Maya's room, but me?

By the time Dominic walked in, my cherry-colored tank top was soaked all the way through, and I was a sopping mess with my back against the counter and the shower hose aimed and ready at the girls.

Dominic looked at me. Then to Bugs and Maya. Then back at me.

Then he walked right out.

I was afraid he was mad for .2 seconds before he came back in with arms full of fluffy towels. He called me trouble, I spritzed him with a spray of water, and then Bathtub Royale Part Two was a go.

I'd laughed so fucking hard, my abs were actually sore as I laid in the guest bedroom after putting Maya and Charlotte down for the night. They were out cold, crashing hard from the sugar and water battles.

Me though? I was totally and completely wired.

After my own shower, I didn't have anything to do except watch YouTube videos on my phone using the Reeds' WiFi. I needed something—anything—to distract myself from the fact that the man of my dreams and I were sharing a house for an entire night.

Like, *literally* the man of my dreams.

My fucking subconscious was going to give me an aneurysm it dreamt of him so much. It was to the point I was afraid to fall asleep at night, knowing he was waiting for me in Dreamland with a smile and another dose of the infection.

Maybe that's why I wasn't sleeping now. I didn't know. I was just rolling and tossing for long enough that the exercise actually worked up an appetite. Groaning, I kicked my legs out from the blanket burrito I'd made myself into and left the guest bedroom with the flavor of cupcakes growing on my tastebuds.

I'd already had like four, but one more couldn't hurt?

It was well past midnight, so it was just me and this monster of a house as I climbed down the stairs to the first floor. The dead air seemed quieter at night. Colder, too. The cotton pajama shorts and virgin-white tank top I'd brought to sleep in weren't exactly cutting it, but my nipples sure were.

Every inch of me was puckered from the temperature in the house, and I hurried my steps to the kitchen to grab a cupcake so I could zip back up into my comfy blanket burrito. My quick steps slowed though, the peel of my bare feet on hardwood coming to a stop as I saw a light still on in the living room.

My brow furrowed. I mean, not everyone had to worry about saving money on the electric bill like I did, but come on. Conserve energy to save the planet and shit, right?

Sighing, I did a drive-by cupcake pick up in the kitchen before turning on my heel into the living room—

Stopping short at the large frame of a man sprawled in his big red lounge chair, shadowed eyes fixed on me.

"Oh." *Shit.* "I didn't think you were up."

The light I'd seen was from the tall lamp over his chair, spotlighting a dim, golden hue above Dominic as he sat in otherwise darkness. My breath was chased away by the jaggedly beautiful angles the mix of shadows created on his face. His cheekbones and passionately straight nose were highlighted slants that glowed, while his darker features basked in the shade.

Gray eyes were nearly obsidian and glittering. That mouth of his was a prominent source of attention, all dusky pink and pouty. A wet shine caught the light on his lips, and a furtive glance to the glass of dark liquor hanging loosely in his left hand over the arm of the chair connected those dots.

I shifted my weight, every instinct in me screaming that this was the perfect setup for an epic disaster. Dark lighting, the house asleep except for us, and the man who was *far* better at keeping our positions platonic blurring his inhibitions.

All that left was me and my sick little heart between us.

And my cupcake.

Half-hooded eyes dropped to the dessert in my palm. "Bit of a sweet tooth, hm?"

My knees wobbled like they'd been replaced with KY jelly. The alcohol had done such unfair things to his voice, making it all rough and thick, almost like he'd just woken up.

"Yeah." I sucked back a breath, trying to walk towards his chair without reenacting a baby doe standing for the first time. "I figure I should take advantage of the fast metabolism while I can."

His dark gaze skimmed down the length of my body, slow and absorbing, as if I was put in front of him to feed his starving eyes. My fingers itched to pull at the hem of my shorts even though it wouldn't do me any good. He wasn't even trying to conceal his greedy observation of me, proving that the alcohol in his glass had done its job and staying down here was a bad, bad idea.

Bad ideas were my kryptonite, though.

Dominic's shadowed stare worked up my top, and my nipples hardened under his gaze. The backs of his cheeks pulsed dangerously, pupils searing with fire as my braless tits pebbled beneath my shirt just for him. He could see them, and there wasn't a doubt in either of our minds that they were taut for and because of *him*. The thin fabric of my tank top coasted my sensitive skin in tempered strokes with each heavy breath, and it was high time I changed the subject.

"Is that bourbon?"

Dominic blinked a hard-bitten stare up at me and then drew his focus down to his drink, lifting it up to sit on the armrest. "And coke."

I nodded, swallowing down the golf ball sized lust blocking my throat.

"Trouble sleeping?"

He made a noise in his throat that sounded like confirmation, but there was something in his cast off stare that said it might be something else. Something younger and off-limits and super fucking wicked.

I was ruining this man's life and didn't know how to stop it. I was a black hole sucking up all the good out of him, and pretending it wasn't happening was proving to be useless. Trying to force us back to before the kiss was like trying to put shattered glass back together with your bare hands. It would never be the same, and we'd both be cut up and scarred by the end.

Still, I fisted a glass shard and kept trying. Blood and scars be damned.

I sauntered between his wide-set legs, feet planted solidly on the floor. Dominic watched me, a subtle twitch to his eyebrow as I stole his drink and pulled back a sip.

Way too much spicy bourbon and not near enough soda popped across my tastebuds, sliding down my throat with a burn. I almost reared back with a grimace, but kept my facial expression in check as the alcohol warmed my chest like sweet fire.

Ah, and just like that, my muscles relaxed from the more spicy than sweet sample, and I found myself wanting more.

I pondered the flavors for a second, tilting my head from side to side.

"It's not bad. Mine woulda been better."

Mirth sparkled across those unusually dark eyes. "Did you want me to come knocking on your bedroom door, asking you to make it for me?"

Now that would have been a brilliantly awful idea. If Dominic had come knocking at my door tonight asking for a drink, there was a fatally high chance I would have invited him in for dessert too.

I kept things light and cheeky though with a cock of my hip and a smirk.

"I probably would have said yes."

Umber brows hooked upwards. "Probably?"

"Yeah. I'm off the clock, sir."

There was an actual internal gasp inside of my head, like my brain took in air as it registered the 'Sir' that just slipped my lips.

Dammit! Light and cheeky. No flirting.

Dominic didn't show a falter in his expression. Just shifted his hips in his red chair. "You wouldn't do it out of the goodness of your heart?"

Before I could fight it off, a melancholy magic swallowed up all my attempts at being light, casting them in pitch black guilt.

"We both know my heart's not all that good."

My heart was sick. It was fucking choking on the way he was staring at me like he wanted to shield me from myself. Take all my bad words and insults and smother them beneath him until they turned to a puff of smoke he could blow out of existence.

My ailing heart nearly gave out all together when long fingers wrapped around my thin wrist and tugged me down. A gasp stuck in my throat as I fell to his thigh, and he perched me on his lap.

A whole bunch of *'what the fucks'* barreled through my mind as I sat taller, spine pulling as straight as it could go at the feeling of Dominic's strong thigh beneath me, all rock solid and big. My heart fluttered like it was trying to grow wings to fly out of my chest and hover above us to be an out-of-body witness to what just happened.

Then on an even stranger note, those deft fingers sectioned out a piece of my cupcake and stole it up to his mouth and ate it. He fucking ate my cupcake. Well, a part of it, and he did it with this goddamn *gorgeous* lopsided grin that had me batting my eyes at him just to make sure he was real.

"That's thievery," I said, voice failing in volume and succeeding in giving me away.

The feel of his powerful, hard muscles sitting right against my core because *he* put me there was too much. My thin cotton shorts were no match for the almost rough brush of his sweatpants as I shifted myself against him.

I needed a distraction, pressing the cool glass of his drink to my bottom lip and sipping. Those shadowed eyes traced my tongue as it peeked out to clear up the remnants of bourbon, pointing his chin up at my mouth.

"And that's underage drinking."

Yeah, for like, two more days.

"You didn't arrest me the last time you caught me doing it."

Mischief pulled a blurry line through his stare, setting my pulse offbeat. "Are you saying you'd like me to correct that, Ms. Sanders?"

The bright metal of handcuffs flashed a blinding bolt of desire across my mind. Sweaty heat followed a pathway down the valley of my breasts, making me clench every muscle in my body. This was bad. This was bad, bad, bad. *Those* words coming from him were a drunken invitation to give up pretending and give into temptation. Give into the addiction, the sickness, the hurricane we created.

Together, we were so many catastrophic things, and the look Dominic was showing me said he wanted to get absolutely wrecked on us.

"You're a little drunk, aren't you?"

He donned a look of lazy consideration, eyelids blinking slowly. "Potentially."

I waited with expectancy for him to realize that was a risky thing to be right now. That realization never came. He only picked the glass tumbler out of my hand and brought it back to himself, downing another mouthful of liquid regret.

So I'd spell it out for him. "As the responsible one between us, that's pretty dangerous."

More amused than anything, he asked, "How so?"

Contemplation held my breath in limbo for a solid five seconds before agreeing with my blunt logic. *Honesty is the best policy.*

"Because I'm reckless and impulsive even when I'm sober, and *apparently,* you're a flirt when you're drunk."

There. I said it. I'd keep us on track, using my wheezing heart as a compass to navigate where the safest ground was for us to land.

Dominic made an irritated groan in the back of his throat. "God, flirting sounds so juvenile."

I felt my eyes bulge out. *That's* what he cared about?

"What would you rather I call it?"

The sharpened edges of his face softened under the yellow-amber glow, even though the switches on the lamplight hadn't changed one bit. It was just the electricity in the room bending to the current of what he felt, to the raw magnitude of Dominic Reed.

I knew because my lightning reacted to him the same way—ebbing and flowing and riding his soul as it entangled with mine.

Dominic settled his warm gaze on me, searching through my eyes with this quiet satisfaction, like he discovered something he liked more and more each time he looked at me. "Just call it talking. That's what it feels like with you. Like the easiest conversation I've ever had."

My heart zapped, choked, and flipped all at once.

This man would kill me.

"That's just our dumbass chemistry." I tucked a loose strand of hair back behind my ear, ducking my head so I didn't have to stare at him anymore. It was too much. Everything he made me feel was just too much.

A thumb curled under my chin, leading my head back up. "You don't seem too fond of it."

His eyes were as honest as my voice that followed, trembling and breathless.

"I'm not."

I'm terrified of it.

"Why?"

His question was a slow croon, a husky melody burrowing between my ribs. I pulled back air to respond when he cut me off with a warning. "And don't say daddy issues, because..." The curve to his mouth was slow-rising and roguish. "I'm not sure what I would do with that in this state."

My parted lips didn't stand a chance, even in this anxious atmosphere. They stretched back over my teeth and soft titters of laughter poured out of me. There was all the proof I needed that I was rubbing off on this man. My shoulders shook, Dominic's quiet rumbles joining in with mine, and together, our uninhibited laughter made the room glow.

Or at least, that's what it seemed like. As if the sound we created was so beautiful, it could be seen.

When it died out, we were left in the afterglow, a smile still spotting both our mouths. I popped off a nibble of my cupcake that was almost gone while Dominic took a drink out of his glass. There was only about a pinky width left.

I didn't want to go back to where we were before the laughter. I liked this new current we'd drifted to, so peaceful it almost felt like we'd gone back to pretending.

I even tucked my legs up to fit where Dominic's thighs were parted, getting comfortable like I probably would have a month ago if we found ourselves in this position. It probably would have made Dominic tense up back then, still fighting his fall with our chemistry.

Tonight, he ran an affectionate thumb up and down my spine.

I tried to get used to the feeling, but couldn't. How could a person get used to the feeling of thunder running up their skin? Instead, I decided on distracting myself with a burning question I'd been wondering all night.

"Have you been sleeping in the bedroom I'm in?"

I wouldn't have ever asked if it hadn't been for the wingtip shoes sitting like red handprints in the corner by the closet.

He didn't stop stroking my spine, but his razored jaw did tick. "You're avoiding my question."

"So are you."

He was quicker to cave than I ever would be, and we both knew my stubbornness could keep us here all night. So, he made it easy with the most difficult answer.

"I have."

Guilt stomped down on my chest, leaving a giant black imprint.

"Since when?"

The seriousness in his eyes was sobering, and I wasn't even the one who was tipsy.

"Three Fridays ago."

The Blame Game teamed up with Guilt this time, both playing ring-around my ribcage, changing the lyrics to, *'Ashes, ashes, it's all your fault.'*

My appetite evaporated, and I crushed what was left of the cupcake in its casing and fisted it tight. I kept my focus on Dominic so he *knew* that I knew the truth, even if he would fight me on it.

"I did that."

And of course, he fought.

"No, *I* chose to sleep in separate bedrooms."

"Did you tell her why?" I countered, knowing the answer before it was given.

His mouth pressed into a thin line. "Not yet, but when I do, it will be an overdue conversation about our marriage." The hand on my back gave a squeeze around my waist. "Not about you."

I didn't mean this selfishly, but how *couldn't* it be about me? Sure, their marriage had been rocky before, but now they were in separate bedrooms as a direct result of our kiss. Heather hadn't been anywhere in my mind that day in the garage, but she was now.

I kissed Dominic that day because I wanted to, and kissing him was the only thing that made sense in the moment. It felt like breathing to kiss him. Necessary and inevitable. Natural and sustainable. It wasn't until the sickness set in that I realized it wasn't like breathing at all.

It was drowning. Choking on air and packing your lungs full of death.

Once I made that connection, and our kiss wasn't just a one time consequence but a lingering ailment, I started thinking about Heather.

I plucked his drink from him almost out of spite. "You two just had date night though."

Date night that ended in a fight, but date night nonetheless.

Dark eyes watched me as I tipped back a swig, finishing the bourbon off. He took the empty glass from me like I was a child worth punishing and lowered it to the floor next to him. "It was an officer's going away party, and Heather has always liked to be at any of the department parties. She's very good at schmoozing. It's like a sport to her."

"Did you slow dance with her?"

The pointed edge to his stare dulled as I brought us back to a week ago. His expression relaxed, but not because he was calm. Because he was sad, and he shook his head just once.

"The last time we danced together was our wedding."

Pain split my chest in two, each ache dedicated to something different. One was for Dominic and his broken heart and the defeat sitting in his somber eyes. The second was a stupid, pitiful, *ugly* ache inspired by the thought that he only wanted me because Heather didn't want him.

That was the sickness talking, and I knew it. In fact, the sickness kept on talking right out of my mouth as I asked the dumbest question.

"Is that why you wanted to know if I liked to slow dance?"

Because your wife doesn't?

If I thought Dominic looked sad before, that was nothing against the upset shaping his face now. A wrinkled frown pursed his eyebrows together, silver ringing around his eyes.

"Heather was standing right next to me on her phone. I could have asked her to get off of it to dance, but I didn't. Instead, I spent half the night *in my head—*" he made sure to enunciate, forcing me to breathe a laugh. "Wondering about this fiery little brunette I know, and if she'd hate the music they were playing like she loves to hate things."

My lightning went *zap*.

Dominic looked back and forth between my eyes, making sure I understood him, making sure there was no second guessing going on in my mind or second choice in his.

He kept going. "I was wondering how long into the evening before she got bored and did something like steal a bottle from behind the bar and pour everyone a shot or convince the band to play something upbeat and get the whole room dancing."

Both. I would have done both.

"I was wondering what she would have worn and if it would have been something picked *specifically* to drive me up the wall." His fingers around my waist squeezed, chastising me for something I hadn't done but totally would.

I inhaled, squirming on his lap as his confession got deeper, throatier, and slowly spiraled me out of my senses.

"I wondered if she knew how to slow dance or if she'd be clumsy at it and that filthy mouth would spin out of control until I kissed it shut. I'd kiss it until she forgot what she was saying and I forgot that she was dancing all over my feet, and all I'd remember was the taste of those strawberry lips."

My whole body pulled tight, tensing up to keep his dangerous words out of my heart and head, but I felt them slip between my legs anyway, licking and encouraging me to open up to him.

My body was in such an oxymoronic state, terrified to get any sicker than I was but vying for a taste of that sweet death. My mind yelled to get out of there, run back to my bedroom where it was safe while every inch of my skin ached—literally *ached*—to touch him, kiss him, rub myself all over him.

And my heart. God, my fucking heart was too feverish to make a decision either way.

Two firm hands found my hips and moved me more center, fixing me up on my knees on the seat of the chair between his thighs. I was weak as he moved me, kneeling over him with Dominic's hands sliding up to the dips of my waist, holding me still. His eyes were shining, fucking *shining* up at me, his truth creating its own light.

"I thought about that spitfire woman all night long, and that's why I didn't ask Heather to dance."

My breathing stumbled. Actually, all of me stumbled in a full body tremble with only Dominic's sturdy hands to hold me up. Something in my chest was crying, screaming out sounds that cut like knives. They sliced up and down my front, jagged, unkind rips that hurt so fucking bad, I thought I might die.

Even breathing hurt, and so I stopped that too. I only left enough air to mumble my escape. "I should go back to my room."

Except the hands around my waist wouldn't let me. They tightened, fingers biting into flesh and making me grab onto the globes of his shoulders for support. I pinched my eyes closed through the pain so I couldn't see Dominic's concern as he spoke, but I sure heard it like it was a gunshot.

"Why do you keep trying to run from me?"

My breath rattled, a lie spilling out between its shakes. "I'm not."

There was a pause. A deadly one. Something changed over in the air around us, in the way Dominic's hands burned through my top. What had started as amiable warmth had now turned flammable, like he was hoping to burn my shirt back to threads.

"Ms. Sanders," Dominic hummed, voice as hot as his touch. "I'd have thought you'd have learned better than to lie to me by now."

My lower stomach clenched at the change in him—impassioned to controlled in just a few seconds. I squeezed my eyes tighter, filtering my breathing in through slow, uneven patterns. A rough patch—a thumb, I think—placed itself dead center over my chest where it hurt to breathe the most.

He pressed down, denting the blunt edge of his nail just above my cleavage.

"Spread your thighs."

Air rushed out of me, eyes flying open. "What?"

Dominic was waiting for me, his stunning features the darkest I'd seen them yet. He took his hand up my neck, feeling every inch of my soft skin he wanted. Dark eyes devoured every reaction I gave him, every quickening of my breath, every flutter of my pulse in my neck that his hand rode up. He consumed it all until he cupped my jaw, trapping me in a firm grip. His fingers indented in my jaw, making my neck curve against his wrist.

"Spread your thighs over my hips," he ordered, voice composed and final.

I was crumbling inside out and didn't stand a chance, deciding instead to crumble into him. My knees slid over his thighs, muscles melting against his hard body as I straddled his hips like he told me to.

A lethal rumble of hot breath fanned beside my ear.

"Good girl."

My heart *banged* against my chest as it came flush with his, inhaling another hit of the infection. I felt like crying, my back bowing into him because I simply didn't know what else to do. All I could do was feel and *let* him make me feel; take away all of my control so I didn't have to make any decisions about what was happening right now.

Dominic was doing this on purpose, pulling my strings loose so he could control them because he could probably tell I was losing it. I was coming off my axis, and he knew just how to balance me.

He ran his nose down the column of my neck. "You ran from me once. I won't let you do it again."

Scorched panic blazed across my bare skin when I realized I didn't *want* to run this time. Not if it would hurt him. I didn't want to do anything ever again to hurt him. So I nodded, limply and desperately, heart spasming as lips made of silk caressed the arch of my neck.

"Why did you run from me that day?"

My focus was loose, muddled between his question and the sensations he was running all along my prickling skin.

"I wasn't planning on it," I breathed, somewhere between a sigh and a whimper.

His hand around my jaw slipped back into my hair, fingers wrapping around strands until he had a fist full of it, but he didn't pull. Not yet.

"Did you plan anything you did that day?"

I shook my head back and forth. "Impulsive, remember?"

Nuzzling his face in my neck, he growled, "Hard to forget."

My hands on his shoulders squeezed, a moan lining up my throat as he pinched that place on the back of my neck. That place that made all my muscles slack and my power give way to him. I was nothing but heavy panting and feelings. Hot, sticky, needy feelings that centered in my pelvis that was sitting *right* over his.

The thin cotton fabric between my heat and his was too much and not enough at the same time. I could feel him beneath me, growing hard and thick inside his sweatpants.

"Keep talking, Ms. Sanders," Dominic instructed, bringing me back to him. I searched every corner of my mind for what I was saying, but my growing need had shoved it all out of the way. The feeling of his cock swelling against me was the only thing in my thoughts.

My head shook feebly. "I don't remember what I was saying."

"*Why* did you run?" A sharp gasp shot out of me, knuckles digging into my scalp as Dominic tightened his fist in my hair.

"Because I'm selfish," I rasped. The confession tumbled out so quickly, a braid of pain and pleasure pulling the words free.

"I think you have us confused." Dominic tilted my head back down to him, the black of his pupils eating up the color of his eyes with desire. "Kissing you was the most selfish thing I've ever done."

"I made you do it." I sunk closer to him, wanting his spicy bourbon breath on my lips and his heart pounding against mine. He let me, watching me from up close like I might disappear any second.

"You didn't make me do anything. I'd been thinking about what your lips tasted like for weeks." He thumbed my bottom lip as if he could taste it just by touching it. When he tried to take that thumb away, I flashed my teeth out to keep it in place.

Dominic hissed and grunted at the same time, hips flexing up as I bit down on his finger. I wasn't thinking, just moving, acting on pure instinct to keep him right where he was. Through a curtain of eyelashes, I peeked up at him as I wrapped my lips around his thumb, sucking back on it.

If punishment ever had a color, it was whatever shade of black Dominic's eyes grew to just then. I could practically hear his teeth crunching as he ground his jaw together while I swirled my tongue around his finger. I stroked it, nibbled at it, hollowed my cheeks around it until fingernails bit into the side of my jaw he was grabbing me so hard.

The blunt outline of his cock in his pants twitched against my core, trying to break through to me. I moaned around his thumb, popping it out of my mouth with a wet smack.

"You only wondered what they tasted like because I never respected our boundaries."

To prove it, I ground my hips over his, rubbing our arousals together. Two large hands slapped on either side of my hips, stopping me with fingers that bit like teeth.

"No, you didn't."

My head fell back as Dominic kept me from moving, need building at the apex of my thighs that only he could touch, that only he could make go away. Again, I was panting, my back bending so my braless tits were right in his face, right where his mouth could reach them. My nipples were so fucking tight they ached, and I knew he could see them through the fabric of my shirt, puckered and dying to be sucked on.

We were only here because of him, because he wouldn't let me go back to my room and decided he'd keep me from spiraling the only way he knew how. My head was a lost cause of fuck ups and panic that neither of us could control, but my body?

That he could control.

That he knew how to rule as if it was his God-given right.

We were stuck in our limbo sky, floating on heavy breathing and hormones as the thunder decided what to do with his lightning. Subdue her tonight so she could explode another day, or give her the release she needed so maybe she could have a peaceful night's sleep.

The thunder rumbled his chest, brewing a storm to unleash. His hands roamed lower, fingers denting one by one under the hem of my shorts. Skin to skin. I held my breath, held my thoughts, held my soul still for him.

"You were always flirting with me."

And then it all came undone as the thunder decided to give into his lightning.

"*Yes*." The word cracked out of me, pleasure spiking up my belly as Dominic pressed my hips down, grinding me over his stiff cock. I sucked back my bottom lip, chewing over it, knowing I had to be quiet even in this big house.

He did it again. "Provoking me."

"Yes," I whimpered, the pressure at my clit singing up to my mouth.

"Driving me to the edge of my fucking sanity," he groaned, squeezing my ass as hard as he could. Bruises. I would absolutely have bruises of fingerprints in the morning.

I dropped forward, mumbling my, 'Yes.' into his shoulder.

He rolled my hips against him again and again and again, his voice getting deeper and hotter and meaner.

"And now I miss it." His breath was in my ear, kissing dirty lines up my neck. I clung to him, clung to his words and the winding feeling creeping up my legs. "Every day without it has been worse than the last."

I pulled back just enough to see him, just enough to look him in the eyes. "You've been doing so good at pretending though."

"Because you asked me to."

"I did." This time, I was the one to grab his jaw, but only so I could feel him, touch him, bury my feelings for him in the coarse hair of his sculpted jawline. "I need to pretend it didn't happen."

"Why?" His voice gripped in desperation. "I need to know why."

"Because..." My words choked, strangled by the pressure coiling in my lower stomach that was *too* good. It was fire and ecstasy twisting together, getting tighter and tighter every time Dominic guided my barely covered pussy against his straining cock. He was dry fucking me to a climax so delicious, I could taste its tangy flavor building on my tongue.

My eyes screwed shut, blinding my world to anything but the electric sensations compiling at my center. A violent gasp ripped out of me, nearly *painful* pleasure spiking up my belly as Dominic buried my mound against his cock so fucking hard, I saw spurts of stars.

"I didn't say to stop talking," he reprimanded, rocking my hips in deeper, slower grooves. "Because *why*?"

"Because of how it felt." My voice was a rush. A desperate, pathetic rush of air. "Because of how kissing you felt."

A threatening, almost pleased growl vibrated in Dominic's chest. "How did it feel?"

I didn't think before I said it.

"Dangerous."

All movement stopped. The sudden stop cranked my eyes open, focusing on Dominic's face in front of me. Lust flushed his golden skin and dilated his pupils, but it was the earnest confusion carving his features that stood out the most.

"Dangerous?"

Again, not thinking, the words just spilled out.

"It was the kind of kiss that kills. That ruins lives and makes people do stupid things, and I can't be stupid. I can't lose myself." I closed my eyes, pinching them shut hard trying to hold onto the prickling, unsatisfied nerves tensing at my core. "I *won't*."

Choppy breathing filled the pause between us before he spoke, almost like he didn't expect me to say what I did.

"You're not stupid."

"Dominic," I cried as quietly as I could, jerking my hips.

A controlled exhale washed my chin, my lips, my cheeks, tasting of him. Sweet and spicy. I could feel him staring at me, digesting my confession and what to do with the trembling, begging, defective woman on his lap. My heart was slapping against my ribs, the need expanding between my thighs bordering on agony.

And just when it hit the line of dying out or becoming actual pain, the hands holding my ass squeezed. A sharp cut of air sliced up my throat, piercing the quiet room as he pressed my heat over his, not to torture answers out of me, but to make me come.

Dominic had made his decision about the woman on his lap, and he decided to make her come. He decided he'd have my orgasm and then my heart, taking both from me like his name was written on them.

I was already in such a delirious state of need that I didn't care in the moment. All I cared about was reaching that finish line and having Dominic cross it with me. I anchored myself to his shoulders, head kicking back as I shamelessly rubbed myself all over him, making a mess of my shorts and his pants. The air smelled like sticky sex, and I wasn't even embarrassed that it was coming from me.

Dominic liked it, I think, dropping his forehead to my chest to bathe me in his ragged breathing. He held me so tight, hands dragging my ass back and forth, back and forth, harder and harder over himself until I was writhing. My legs were twitching over him and unintelligible sounds were falling from my lips.

They were getting louder, and I was losing all control over them. All of my senses were drowning, condensing into one, narrowed focus between my legs.

Pulsing. Heating. Fucking crying through my panties.

A hand clamped over my mouth, rough fingers muffling my noises as they grew untamed. Dominic held his bear paw of a hand over my mouth, thrusting his hips up, rocking mine back, pushing and pushing us until I fell first.

The twisting, tightening, desperate feeling winding up my stomach finally wound too tight and snapped. *Hard.*

Moans raked up my throat, moans I didn't even realize I was making until Dominic squeezed his hand over my mouth to smother them. Tiny explosions went off over every inch of my sweaty skin, pulsating pleasure consuming my body. Dominic made a short, tormented groan himself as my body stiffened up the spine in his hold, and my orgasm made itself known.

He didn't stop our dancing hips though, keeping the friction going against my clit to milk my orgasm until tears pricked the backs of my eyes. It was too much. My body was on sensory overload, nails tearing into Dominic's shoulders and pulling low hisses from him.

I was on the verge of begging him to stop when his hand slipped up the back of my shirt, leaving my hips and flattening my chest to his. He ducked his face into the crook of my neck, arm looping around my bare waist and crushing another moan out of me.

Then his muscles were tensing, hips jerking once, then twice, and the sexiest slew of grunts and groans were buried into the hollow of my neck. I might have come all over again listening to him, feeling his shoulders draw taut beneath my palms, thighs flexing as he found his orgasm against me.

I hated that I loved that he used me to hide his noises in. Almost like he needed me. Almost like we were equals.

Gently, Dominic eased his hand from over my mouth, but instead of dropping it, he pushed it back into my hair. He cupped the back of my head, bringing my forehead to rest against his. We sat there, breathing in the postorgasmic haze of what we'd done, eyes locked together. He stroked his thumb along the back of my neck.

"What we just did was stupid." I tensed against him even though I knew it was true. He wasn't finished though. "Whatever you're feeling between us is not."

Lightning struck between my ribs, delivering another dose of molten sickness to my heart. A shiver raced up my spine, curling around every freshly sated muscle and pulling them rigid. Dominic just kept caressing my neck with his thumb, trying to smooth the tension out of my body because now he knew.

He knew why it was there.

"I think we're in trouble," I breathed.

Dominic looked back and forth between my eyes, that ring of truth making his shine.

"I've been in trouble since the moment I met you, Ms. Sanders."

TWENTY-TWO

Every muscle in my body was tight the next morning, despite the shattering orgasm Dominic gave me the night before.

I laid in the guest room bed, feeling the divots in the soft mattress where Dominic had slept the last three weeks while Heather was in their bedroom. He slept there last night considering Heather wasn't coming home until this morning, which I was dreading.

Fucking dreading.

Everything with Dominic spun out of control so fast last night, I still hadn't caught up to how it happened. One minute, I was trying to remind him of our boundaries, and the next, we were dry fucking each other in his chair, having an orgasms-and-forbidden-feelings free-for-all.

I was fairly certain he knew I was sick for him now, and he was growing ill for me too by the sound of it.

That's what falling for someone really was. You didn't fall in love with someone. You fell ill for them. The harder you fell, the more delirious your symptoms were until it was too late. Until your brain melted from the fever, you were sick to your stomach, and boiled up into a mindless zombie willing to do anything to be cured of your love.

Laying in bed, I was about halfway to brain-dead and clueless how to stop it now that it had already begun.

I groaned, flopping over and pulling myself to sit up. Today was Maya's birthday party, which meant a whole lot of people I didn't know crammed into this giant house, and I would spend the most of it trying to avoid just one.

Heather.

Crawling out of bed, I curled my toes into the rug laid out beneath the bed as I stretched my aching bones. Today was going to be long and exhausting, and I was already looking forward to the end of it.

I threw on the pair of olive green shorts and white knit tank top I packed. The shorts weren't too short, and the top was loose around the waist with only a tinge of cleavage showing. Totally appropriate for a little girl's birthday party and not flaunting the fact that I was kind of sort of having an affair with that girl's father.

God. Just the thought made my chest spasm like I was having a heart attack.

Affair.

Affair, affair, affair, affair.

Nope, no matter how many times I said it in my head, the notion of it still sounded fucking idiotic. Did it count as an affair if it only happened twice?

Did I even want it to happen again?

It wasn't even 10am, and a headache was already creeping up my neck from all the stress and lingering questions. I had one hand trying to massage it away while the other opened up the bedroom door.

I only made it a few steps into the hallway before a sight caught my feet in a trap.

Two faces. One slanted in fury and the other drooped in defeat. Angry words were being spit in hushed tones from one face into the other, and for once, I wished they'd fight at full volume so I could hear what they were saying.

If it was about me.

Dominic and Heather were standing in the frame of their bedroom door, her fists all balled up at her sides and his shoulders slumped and sad. My heart stuttered, caving into itself to see him so upset. Neither of them had noticed me yet, and maybe that's why what happened next wasn't stopped.

A gasp punctured my lungs as the slap echoed through the hallway.

Dominic's head whipped to the side, Heather's hand still raised like she was waiting to do it again. That violent hand held all of my wide-eyed focus, burning at the center of my vision like a flame held over a photo, slowly consuming the picture until all that was left was the fire.

White hot, explosive fire.

"Hey!" I yelled.

Both of their eyes snapped towards me before I even fully registered I'd spoken. The blue of Heather's glare blazed from all the way across the hall, but I barely felt it. I didn't feel anything except hate—churning, ugly, boiling *hate*.

Pinning her stare with my own, I snapped and snarled, "That's not okay."

A pathetically obvious statement, but it was true. How dare she. How fucking *dare* she. Dominic wasn't mine to protect, but I sure as fuck would if she put her hands on him like that again. My dad was the occasional abusive cunt too, and that shit didn't fly with me.

Not anymore.

If possible, Heather's glare seared even hotter, and she reached for the door, readying to slam it shut.

Before she did, I sought out the man next to her with desperate eyes. He was staring at me just the same, but his desperation was a sorry one. I had no idea what he had to be sorry for, but before I could even ask, he was gone.

The door slammed shut, and the couple was alone again.

I stood there, so tense, so tight, so ready to explode and nothing to explode at. Their closed bedroom door mocked me, rearranging its warped wood into pictures of what was going on behind it. All of it bad. All of it violent.

None of it my business.

I ran a hand back through my messy hair, fisting at it and then checking my forehead for a fever. My skin was clammy and hot, I was so overheated by furious passion. There was nothing I could do. Nothing. I was completely and utterly stuck on this side of the door.

I hated that. I hated all of this. If this fight of theirs had anything to do with me, I was pretty damn sure Heather would have ripped me a new one right here and now, but she hadn't. The fact that I was still standing without manicured claws embedded into my face said Dominic hadn't told her what we did last night.

Trying and failing to settle my heartbeat, I turned towards the bathroom, mumbling about needing a shot for breakfast.

I didn't see Dominic for another hour.

I'd been keeping the girls busy downstairs, playing with them outside in the backyard while caterers—yeah, *caterers*—set up food and beverages. For a five-year-old's birthday, Heather had ordered in Spanish and seafood inspired tapas. Every kid's favorite.

This party was clearly a hell of a lot more for Heather than it was for her daughter, and I was glad we made cupcakes last night since the only 'dessert' ordered was flan.

Fucking flan.

I was turning twenty-one in less than 48 hours, and even I didn't fuck with flan.

Maya and Charlotte had long forgotten I was outside with them, too involved in their game of witches and mermaids to remember the boring adult watching over them. The sun was on full assault today, and I moved to lean back against the shed back here. The term 'shed' should be used loosely given how nice it was for something they only used to store lawn equipment for the workers.

It had a cute little pleated roof above its doors that shielded the sun just enough to dull the burn of it edging along my bare shoulders. I sighed, hand raised to sit along my browline as I watched the girls' sun-silhouetted figures playing and the caterers prepping.

Out of the back patio door emerged another outline of a figure, this one tall and broad.

Their eyes fixed on me, somehow more brilliant than the sunshine.

Dominic came over in long strides, and I pressed my back further into the wall every step he neared. His presence felt so much bigger and imposing than it did yesterday now that he knew what was going on in my broken little head.

He reached me, towering and a breath closer than he probably should have been. My eyes went right to his cheek, the one Heather had slapped, wanting to reach out and touch it so badly, I had to hide my hands behind my back to stop myself.

Dominic clocked my fidgeting hands, wide shoulders casting a shadow over me as he turned a surveying glance back to all the party prep. He angled back, moving before I registered it was happening. He pulled me by my wrist, hiding me in the cover of his chest as he shuffled me back.

A door opened and then—

Pitch black.

My eyes stretched out as wide as they could out of instinct, but not a single sprinkle of light was found. All of my other senses prickled and heightened in the darkness. The smell of cedar wood, the tickle of dust at the tip of my nose, the heavy, even breathing of the man who pulled me in here. I stood still, listening to the air—a creak going off here, a shoe knocking into something hard there.

Then, light.

Dominic was the first and only thing I saw. He was illuminated under the glow of the single light bulb in the shed, creating a halo of sorts over him. How fitting. A halo for him, and probably a pitchfork behind my head to give me horns.

If Dominic brought me in here for a reason, he seemed to forget what it was as he gazed down at me. The shitty lighting above us couldn't even touch his beauty. It made the hard edges of his face more rugged, the sharp points sharper. His stare was dazzling even now, and I was doing my best to hold it, to not let the silence get the better of me.

Eventually though, the silence won out. It always did.

"Is this where you take all the girls?" I joked.

He gave me a soft breath of laughter, which was probably all I deserved. He took a step closer, chest brushing mine.

"Are you all right?"

My head jerked back, brows fussing together. "Me?"

I shook my head, a wash of offense or something close to it pushing my shoulders back. "Don't ask me that. I should be asking *you*."

He was ridiculous to be worried about me after what Heather did to him. I didn't need him to worry about me or be focused on me. His life was a wreck right now, and somehow, I wasn't even the messiest part of it.

"Has she done that before?"

Dominic lowered his eyes, shaking his head once. "No."

There was that sadness again, the one that overwhelmed him. It swallowed him up, taking the strength out of his shoulders and letting them sink, letting the whole world's weight break his back. I hated seeing him like this. I think I hated it more than I'd ever hated anything before, because someone did this to him.

Someone who was supposed to love him.

Stupid, deceitful, *vicious* love.

I wanted to ask what the fight was about, but it wasn't the time. My hand was on his cheek without thinking, cupping it and worrying out the imprints Heather's fingers had left. Dominic leaned into it, pressing his face into my touch. His eyes fluttered closed, a sigh that sounded relieved streaming through his nose.

"You didn't deserve that," I muttered, stroking his cheek.

A deep breath filled his chest, grazing it against mine. Eyes still closed, large hands brushed up my hips and right beneath my flowing shirt, grabbing the bare skin of my waist. Dominic pulled me in until I was almost draped over him, the calluses on his hands digging into soft flesh.

I would have gasped if the move felt at all sensual. Instead, I felt like crying.

I think he just really wanted a hug.

My head tipped back beneath his, I was right there and waiting for him when he dragged those long lashes up and pinned me with his raindrop eyes.

"Maybe I did."

Though the moment was soft and ribboned with affection, my next words came out bitter. "No one deserves to be hit by someone who says they love them."

Dominic blinked slowly at me, eyes growing serious as they jumped between mine. Storm clouds brewed, dark and threatening as he guessed the truth between my words.

Whatever. He could know this about me too. Daddy Dearest hit Mommy Dearest and then turned to the daughter who screamed at him to stop. It didn't happen a lot. Just enough that I felt very personally pissed off on Dominic's behalf.

His arms drew me in tighter, squeezing me into his chest until I was small, all wrapped up in him, and profoundly protected. Which was odd, considering no one in the universe had ever made me feel more unsafe. More unbound and prone to fits of panic.

"You're so strong," he murmured, mouth glimpsing the corner of mine.

A shiver shook me, shook me right off my hinges, and I melted.

"I'm weak."

So fucking weak. I was the water in the river, and he was everything else. The current, the rocks, the cliffs, moving me and molding me into whatever he wanted me to be for him.

This wasn't me, I kept thinking. Or trying to think. I wasn't water. I was goddamn stone. *Marble.* I was hard-edged and unbreakable, right? Except it didn't feel that way anymore. Dominic took my stone and cracked it right down the middle, smoothing out the edges with his affection and sickness.

God, I was *sick*. More than sick.

I was dying for this man.

And still, I didn't have the strength to stop it as he placed those death-delivering lips over mine, kissing me like he needed me. Like he was painting himself a remedy to his sadness with my lips. Not only did I not stop him, but I kissed him back, fisting my hands in his nice shirt and wrinkling it all up.

This kiss wasn't anything like our first and nothing like our interaction last night. Those were lust-driven, pent up releases, and this? I didn't know what brand of black magic this was. It was all passion and all us. Kat and Dominic. Lightning and Thunder.

Disaster and Fate.

Stealing the breath off of my lips, Dominic rumbled, "Feelings aren't a weakness."

Liar.

I knew better. I knew better, and yet, I was still here, *feeling* until my heart felt like it might explode. Dominic's heartbeat was healing with every second, slowing to a steady, confident rhythm, while mine was losing its goddamn mind.

It was all over the place, coughing and wheezing and waving its white flag for this all to be over.

And then it was.

Because someone opened the door.

TWENTY-THREE

There are moments in life when you know you've fucked up.

They all start the same. Your heart catches on fire, nervous sweat sprouts from everywhere and anywhere, and your mind goes completely and fantastically blank.

Like right now.

I froze, still clutching Dominic's shirt and stealing his air. He'd broken our kiss, snapping his head towards the shed door to whoever had caught us. Every muscle of his against me drew tight, his hard body lining with panic, and still, I couldn't move.

Literally I was stuck, staring at Dominic's profile and taking in every tiny tick of his reaction towards the person who caught us. The twitch in his cheek. The way his bottom lip curved to form words and then stopped. Even how the strain he had over himself loosened just a hair beneath my palms.

"Mom."

Mom?

Did he just fucking say *Mom?*

I knew, just *knew*, my eyes were the size of fucking saucers when he spoke that word.

Humiliation started at my toes and ate its way up until it had consumed me whole. Dominic's robust voice breaking into the silence shattered the full body tension cast holding me still, and I balled my hands into fists, snatching them back to myself.

His touch disappeared from my back, and then altogether, but he didn't step away to a more appropriate distance because why bother? We'd already been caught. The evidence of it was smeared all over his criminal red, puffy lips.

"Is this the new nanny you've mentioned?"

Oh *god*. My chest caved into itself, and I wanted it to follow through until it became a black hole and swallowed me up. She didn't sound mean with her subtle southern twang, but her words cut like knives, spilling fresh horror in my stomach. It churned and twisted in on itself, and the thought that I might throw up all over this floor became hard to ignore.

Dominic stood his ground next to me, locking into his usual bravado.

"Her name is Kat, and I pulled her in here."

Of *course* he had to be gallant right now and take the blame. Of course. My eyes rolled shut, and I tried to breathe, tried to find some semblance of grounding to hold on to. This was bad. This was so, so bad.

Then it got worse.

"I know. I saw," his mom said.

And the ground and breath were both snatched away from me.

My head whipped towards her, locking in on his mother for the first time. She saw us. She saw us with those stone gray eyes just like her son's, save for the fine wrinkles around the edges. They were fixed on me now, taking in the girl she caught her son having an affair with.

Affair. Affair. Affair.

Fuck, that word wouldn't leave me alone, nor would the feeling like I was dying. It was happening, right now in this shed at a kid's birthday party. My heart was ripping itself out of my chest cavity, tearing valves and shattering bones on its way out. It was going *so* fast, so fast it must have grown legs to sprint with, and right now those legs were running divots into my chest with all the effort.

Dominic's mom was staring at me like she was sizing me up, figuring me out. Almost like she was dissecting me like her son did, except all the information she had about me was that I was a whore. A homewrecking whore.

And if she saw us, then who else did? Anyone could have. Maya. *Heather*.

I didn't know I was hyperventilating until a warm hand cupped my bent elbow, directing my focus back to him and the worry scribbled into his expression. Dominic feathered a stroke of his thumb over my skin—

And my heart screamed bloody fucking murder.

I jerked back, retreating in so many paces, my back hit the wall behind me, jostling a few clatters of metal to the ground. Dominic looked both hurt and sorry at the same time, taking a careful step towards me.

"Kat—"

"I'm sorry," I blurted out.

Then I ran.

My sprinting heart took off, blowing me past Dominic and his mom, breaking out of the shed, and running up to the back patio. I crashed through the doors, practically spilling into the house which was now half full of nameless faces with prudish pouts. The sea of Prada and Gucci overwhelmed me, throwing me back like a wave, engulfing my lungs with stinging saltwater.

I didn't know where I was going, but I had to keep moving. Keep moving and keep the blood pumping so I didn't fall apart into a mess of weak limbs and guilty screams. I looked all around me at everything and nothing, stumbling forward until I stumbled right into one of those nameless faces.

The woman let off a chiding scoff, pulling her posture so far back, I thought her spine might snap in half. Blue eyes cut of ice sneered down at me by the raise of her chin. She wasn't much taller than me, just had her nose stuck so far up in the air that she felt at least a foot taller.

I knew I should have apologized, but the words weren't coming. All that did come out was a frank and impatient, "Excuse me?"

The woman batted in subtle shock, neck dressed in pearls pulling back as she gave me a once over.

Then a second over.

Then a third before she focused back on my face, glacier eyes fixating with a biting curiosity. She didn't say a damn word. Just kept sweeping her poised stare over every inch of me she could reach, like she was taking inventory of the bitch who'd just tried to run her and her dirty martini off the road.

She looked to be about in her fifties, all dolled up with makeup like she was trying to forget she wasn't still twenty. There was something very... *heavy* about her. Almost like her daggered stare could actually kill, and she wouldn't lose a wink of sleep about it.

Maybe if I wasn't in the midst of a panic attack to rival all others, I'd have stayed and talked to her and found out what her deal was, but I didn't. I just pushed around her and beelined it for the hallway bathroom.

Except it was locked. Fucking *locked*.

Someone was using it, and I was trapped out in the open. What a fucking oxymoronic thing to be. I spun in circles, seeking out anywhere to hide, anywhere to throw myself into so I could lose my mind in peace, but before I found a safe place, the consequence of fate found me first.

"Ms. Sanders."

Her voice tracked icy tendrils down my arms and legs, turning my body into a hyperaware chasm of dread. She was behind me, and the tone of her voice *dared* me to turn around. I did—somehow—on feet that had gone numb.

Heather was waiting for me, primed for my slaughter from the looks of it.

Her voice came out the lowest pitch I'd ever heard it.

"A word?"

She didn't wait for me to respond—just walked right past me and let me follow her as she veered off into the corner of the house where her office sat. I went inside first. She closed the door behind me.

Then we were alone.

There had never before in the existence of silence been a moment as quiet as this one. It was next level torture. Pins and needles dropping had nothing on this silence. Even my thoughts were too loud in here.

Heather rounded me, heels clicking in slow taunts as she brought herself around to her desk. She didn't stand behind it though. She placed herself dead center in front of it, leaving nothing between us but the silence and the dirty little secrets that screamed through it.

My pulse was in my ears now, blood rushing my head like it was trying to make me dizzy. It felt like my body chose a side in this Heather vs. Kat face off, and it sure as shit wasn't mine. I swayed on my two feet, curling my toes into my flip flops to try and grab some grounding.

What Heather said first threw it off completely.

"I've never liked you, and you're not dumb enough to not know that."

Straight to the bulleted point.

"From day one, you have been rude," Check. "Obnoxious," Check. "And disrespectful." Three for three. She was on a roll and I was on a quick downward spiral.

"You have no manners," she sneered. "Some of it can be excused by your less than civilized upbringing, but something tells me that no matter what your junkie mother did to raise you, you would have turned out to be this *leech* of a person regardless."

My temper tangoed with my anxiety, pirouetting my sanity into a tailspin.

Everything was hot. My skin prickled and my heart was aflame, given up all attempts at running and simply trying to burn itself alive to escape.

Also… Dominic told her about my mom? I couldn't place why in the chaos going on inside my head, but that felt like the deepest cut he could lay on me. That was *personal*. He knew how personal it was and how ashamed I was of that part of my backstory, but he still told her.

Heather folded her thin forearms over one another, her pale pink lips pulling back over her perfectly straight teeth. "I never wanted you in my home. I never wanted you around my husband, and now this house *reeks* of you and your filthy attitude."

Her manicured nails dented into her arms as her anger grew, and her porcelain facade cracked for just one, ugly moment.

"I knew you would be bad for Dom. I *knew* it."

My lungs heaved like I gasped, but I didn't take on any air. What the hell did that mean? Did she know?

Did she know, did she know, did she know?

My eyes jumped back and forth between hers, unable to hold my focus anywhere for more than a second. I probably looked as drugged up as I felt, overdosing on panic and willing the blackout in faster so I could be done with all of this.

I didn't want this. I *never* wanted this.

"You look so goddamn *guilty*, Ms. Sanders," she spat, taking a dominant step into me, filling up my space with her accusation. "Why might that be?"

She was fishing, right? She wouldn't be asking if she knew, and if she knew, this office's stark white walls would be decorated in my blood right now instead of diplomas and certificates Heather had collected over the years.

"I'm not." I swallowed, my throat dry and scratchy. "This conversation is just making me uncomfortable."

The rise of one of her thinly plucked eyebrows was drawn out and spiteful. "Uncomfortable? You mean like having someone in your house, around your husband, around your child that you don't want there?"

Her words made me pause, taking a beat to realize that she was right. That *was* shitty. It wasn't my fault that I was here though, and for the first time in this mess, there was something I couldn't take the blame for.

Maybe Dominic wasn't as innocent in this as I told myself.

"I understand, and that's a fair point," I said, gripping onto a slim barb of grit. "But a job was offered to me, and I took it. As you've made sure to point out, my life isn't all caviar and rich daddies, so I have to take any opportunity I can get."

Her stare narrowed. "And did you see an opportunity in my husband?"

I sucked back a steadying breath.

"No."

Not an opportunity. A downfall.

Heather uncrossed her arms, catching me off guard with her height as she crowded me in a few swift steps. My head bent back, neck stiff and my grit slipped, sinking back into the mouth of the anxiety attack. She came so close, I could see the beginnings of age in her frown lines and feel the hate she bore for me radiating out of her like shock waves.

"I've seen the way you look at him." Her affront scratched at my cheeks as if her words could make me bleed. She took her pale gaze all over my face in observing lines, mouth snagging on a low sneer. "You're way out of your league, sweetie. I could tear your *whole* world apart."

Barely standing still, I somehow held her stare as I murmured. "Is that a threat?"

The blue around her pupils flashed with promise.

"A warning, and you'll only get one."

Little did Heather know, I only needed one, and I'd already gotten it. My warning came minutes before Heather ever got to me when Dominic's mom walked in on us, and I realized it had gone too far. All of this. Me. Dominic. Us.

Our thunder and lightning had exploded, and now it was taking victims.

Me, Dominic, Heather, their marriage, Maya's future, *Charlotte*. I didn't want to lose myself for Dominic. I couldn't die for him. I had too much to live for in Charlotte. She needed me. She needed me to fight this, to inject myself with an antidote even if one didn't exist.

I wouldn't survive if I stayed here, if I kept falling sick for Dominic. We'd both let it go too far last night, and it was bound to get worse now that we weren't hiding our symptoms from each other.

My symptoms had already taken a turn for the worse, a fever breaking sweat on my hairline and shutting my organs down from the inside out. I was sure Heather could see just how badly I was already crumbling, and that's why she went in for the kill.

"You are nothing. You *come* from nothing. You have *nothing* to offer, and that's all anyone ever sees when they look at you. A poor little nothing who wants what she can't have."

Everything I could've or might've said to defend myself refused to come out. It sat in my chest, strapped down by the heavy ropes of panic. No matter what I did, the words didn't come. My cheek twitched, jaw locked, nostrils flared, and nothing.

So Heather continued.

"I don't care what Dom says." She cast a glance over me like I was literal trash in her way. "I know women like you, and I can *smell* the slut on you. You have no place in this house, and you certainly have no place in my marriage. Our business is not yours."

Then, her tone got pointed.

"How I choose to touch my husband is none of your business either."

Pointed enough to cut some of the ropes loose.

"You can't *hit* him," I pushed out, voice shaking.

The look my response inspired in Heather was breath-taking, and I already had so little air left to give. Her features slanted into something insidious, something entitled and unapologetic.

"I can do whatever the fuck I want because he is my *husband*, and you are just the help."

She drew back, taking in the hyperventilating that I was trying and failing to hide with an unimpressed grimace.

"You're a *cliché*..." she drawled, tone building to a peak. "And you're fired."

Fired.

You'd think that hearing that would have resurrected my lashing tongue or stubborn fire, but no. My stomach gave a whiplash of a reaction, searing in horror before relief quickly smothered it out. The relief is what stayed, and it's what I held onto as Heather landed her final blow.

"I want you to get that snot-nosed sister of yours and get the hell out of my house."

Tail tucked between my legs, that's exactly what I did.

I bolted as soon as she was done, tearing out of that office and not stopping until I found Charlotte. I grabbed her without words, without explanation, without even telling Maya happy birthday. I just grabbed her and ran out of there as fast as I could.

People were staring at me, but I didn't care. I barely even saw them. All I saw was the exit, and all I cared about was never coming back. Damn this job. Damn this sickness.

Damn Dominic fucking Reed.

My remission started today, and it started by never seeing that man again.

TWENTY-FOUR

T he first step of my remission lasted just shy of 24 hours.

The first call from him came in at 9:07 the next morning.

The second at 9:33.

A third and fourth both before 10 o'clock.

I ignored them all, turning my phone on silent as I made Charlotte her break-fast.

Cheerios.

So sue me, I wasn't in the mood to make a full buffet-style breakfast. I couldn't even stomach anything more than a glass of orange juice. Solid food hadn't been going down easy since yesterday.

I was right in the middle of washing out Charlotte's cereal bowl when there was a pounding at the front door. Bugs jumped, sitting on the counter next to me watching me clean. Turning off the faucet, I told her to stay where she was while drying my hands on a nearby rag.

There was a nagging feeling pulling my gut for who was behind the booming knocks, and the closer I got to the door, the more that feeling began to sizzle. Hand on the knob, I took a deep breath that did absolutely jackshit to calm my nerves and peeled the front door open.

Dominic whipped around, locking me in the path of sterling eyes that were absolutely burning.

For just a second—a stupid, sick little second—my backbone wobbled.

I pictured in that blink of a relapse falling into him and letting him catch me, curling me up in his arms and kissing me until I forgot who I was or why I couldn't have him. I spent so much of yesterday stewing about this man, and now, one look from him damn near destroyed it all.

He was the picture of agony standing there on my front steps, raking his gaze over every inch of me like he was ticking boxes in his head that each part of me was here. Worry had exasperated his expression, chiseling little divots in his forehead. Those burning eyes jumped up to me, relief crawling in from all sides as he pushed a hand back through his hair for what looked like the twentieth time this morning.

"Why haven't you been answering your phone?" he snapped, tone accusing.

Just like that, the relapse righted itself and faded back, allowing my temper the chance to do what it did best. Explode. Defend. Keep the life I'd built for myself and my sister safe.

"Because I didn't want to talk to you." I lowered my voice but kept my anger at top volume. "What the fuck are you doing here?"

Dominic bypassed my question, bringing his shadow looming over me. "I don't care if you don't want to talk to me. If I call, you *answer* your phone so I know you're all right."

My temper glitched, interrupted by the realization of why he was here and so wound up. The wind from outside blew over my cheeks as I took a beat to stare at him.

The worry, the relief, the multiple calls.

"You thought something happened to me." That someone had taken me.

Great, now *I* was the dick.

He didn't nod or say yes. The backs of his jaw just pulsed once, eyes reaching back and forth between mine. "I called when Heather told me what she did, and

I thought maybe you were sleeping for the first call. Then I kept getting your voicemail..."

He trailed off, not able to and not needing to finish what he was saying. He was worried about me, and I hated it. I hated it like he knew I loved to hate things, except this hate wasn't normal. This hate *ached* like a splinter stuck between my ribs. Every touch of his concern pushed it in deeper until the skin around it was sensitive and raw, and all I wanted was for him to stop fucking poking at it.

"I didn't want to talk to you," I said slowly, flashing my hard stare to him. "And I still don't."

Dominic's chest deflated, an apologetic look taking the place of his distress.

"I thought you left yesterday because of what happened in the shed. I didn't find out until this morning that she fired you, and—" He cut himself off, casting an irritated glower out to the side before bringing it back to me. "She shouldn't have done that, and you are most certainly not fired."

Panic swelled, filling my lungs with lightning bugs all buzzing and itching to rise to the potential of their name. I didn't want my job back. I didn't want to be around him ever, ever again.

"No, she *should* have fired me. She had every right to fire me."

Stepping outside, I pulled the door closed shut behind me so Charlotte wouldn't hear me lose my mind. My bare feet planted on the cement, catching Dominic in my glare with my shoulders pushed back and chin jutted up.

"You're *married*, Dominic. Something I think we both forget to care about, but Heather was right to fire me, and I'm glad she did."

Dominic's eyebrow twitched, face lowering. "You're glad?"

"Yes, I'm *glad*. I'm glad she fired me, and I'm glad she called me a slut, and I'm glad your mom caught us because I needed all of it to shake me out of this fucking *daze* you have me in."

Every muscle in his perfect face crystalized to marble, and he almost looked like he was in pain. A streamlined exhale ran through his nose, and he unlocked his tight jaw.

"Kat—" He swallowed my name, his voice coming out thick. "You are not... a slut."

That word. He hated that word, and Dominic didn't hate easily like me. It was a razor blade sliding down his tongue as he used it in the same sentence as my name.

"I *kind* of am." An overwhelmed breath of laughter crushed out of me, and Dominic frowned at the noise. "I kissed you, and I knew you were married. I let you dry-fuck me in the living room of the house you share with your wife whe—"

My words dried up, connecting dots casting the drought.

Horror flushed my bloodstream clean of any warmth, turning my limbs frozen and my heart into an ice brick of pumping dread.

The cameras.

Oh my god, I'd forgotten all about the cameras that night. Both Dominic and I had. We'd been so wrapped up in each other that we'd completely neglected to remember we were being recorded the whole time. Heather could have already watched it. Or she could be watching it right now.

I raised a stiff neck up to Dominic, panic sitting heavy in my eyes. I didn't even get the words out before he shifted his weight, lowering his focus to just below my chin.

"I already erased the footage on the cameras from that night."

I was still frozen by the fear of being caught as I digested the information. Dominic had been smart enough while we were being dumb to cover up our tracks. I should have felt relieved. We were safe.

Instead, I just wanted to scream until my vocal cords burst.

"See, that's shit I shouldn't have to worry about!" I ran a quick hand back through my tangled mess of hair, squeezing at the strands. "*Neither* of us should have to worry about that kind of stuff. We let it get too far. We let this get way, way, way out of control."

"That night wasn't smart, no." Dominic paused, easing a hair closer, looking as sure as the sun above him. "If you think I regret it though, the answer is no."

"Because you got off, and what guy doesn't love that?" I clapped back before I could think.

Regret tied up my muscles in a cringe. That was a cheap shot.

I couldn't keep up with what I was saying though or where it was coming from in my head. Disapproval thundered across his face as he moved a step closer.

"I think you need to take a pause and breathe."

"I *can't* breathe when I'm around you, Dominic." My back hit the door behind me as I stumbled away from him. He was right. My breathing was all over the place, ragged and panting. "At least not now. Being around you makes me feel like I'm spinning out, and I can't—" I stopped, shrugging and licking my dry lips. "I can't have that."

"You feel out of control because—"

"I don't need a dissection of *why* I feel this way." I cut him off, throwing my hands up into my hair again, stringing anxious fingers through and pulling. "I just need it to stop, and now it will, so I'm sorry if you're here to offer me my job back, but I don't want it."

His voice dipped lower as his face drew serious. "You need a job."

"I'll find another one."

Over the straight bridge of his nose, he stared down at me in a way that said he intended to trap me with whatever he would say next.

"And what about Maya?"

Ouch. I wasn't the only one who was throwing out cheap shots today. Through gritted teeth, I said, "We can schedule playdates."

He shook his head before I was done speaking, denying the idea before it formed. "That's not the same and you know it. She's attached to you. You can't just leave her."

The thought of not seeing Maya every week was as close to heartbreak as I hoped I ever got. It split my chest in two, spurring my well-loved loathing at myself because it was my fault I wouldn't see her anymore. I let things get too far with her father, and now I couldn't handle being in their life.

I fucked myself over by fucking myself to an orgasm on her father's lap. If that wasn't poetic irony, I wasn't sure what was.

"As much as I adore her, I have to think about what's best for Charlotte first." *And that means never seeing you again.*

"She'll be devastated."

So would I, but I lied with hope behind my words. "She'll be fine."

"She *needs* you." He charged closer in just a couple strides, the devastation he spoke about ringing around his irises and more blinding than the sunlight. I reared back with a shaking inhale, the back of my head kissing the door as Dominic towered so close and tall.

Staring up at him, I wasn't so sure we were talking about Maya anymore.

Determination had shadowed every hollow of his face, his breath tasting like desperation over my lips. Thick and heady. I curled my fingers against the door, wood chipping off and splintering beneath fingernails. It hurt. The pain invaded my skin, burrowing beneath layers, but Dominic's desperation hurt worse.

It burrowed all the way to the back of my heart that coughed up blood at the intrusion.

He was killing me, and I was killing him. How did he not see it?

"I can promise you," I whispered gently. Pointedly. "She's better off without me."

At that, his jaw sawed back and forth, teeth grinding as he planted both palms flat against the door on either side of my head. He caged me in, bringing himself so close, I felt every stroke of his words over my lips as if they were painting me a plea in hushed tones.

"You can't just decide that for anyone. If someone wants you in their life, they should at least have a say."

Okay, fuck this hidden message bullshit.

"You only want me because you were lonely," I said, wielding the fact like it was a sword that could cut his affection for me in half. Instead, he took that same sword and turned it back on me, piercing straight through my bleeding heart.

"You're right. I was lonely," he began, voice rumbling. "Then you came along with that loud mouth and spitfire attitude, and I have never been so aware of another person in my life." He looked between my eyes, faint happiness tilting his lips. "It's honestly distracting."

When he said it, it sounded like a good thing. Like a welcomed fall down the same rabbit hole I was willing to break every finger for, holding onto the edges so I didn't drop. He kept going, and I kept spiraling.

"We can be sitting in that silence you hate so much, and I can hear you from across the room even when your lips are shut. It's been that way since the beginning. You scream to me, and I know by how upset you get that you hear me the same way I hear you."

"Yeah, and that's a *bad* thing."

"No. That's a connection."

"That's insanity!" I exploded, my chest heaving all out of control again.

Fuck this *fucking* panic that always attacked when he was within arms length. I hated it. I hated this. I hated the spiral, the perfect storm, the sickness. If I hated it all so much, and Dominic was the impetus for it all, then maybe I hated him too.

Hate I could deal with. Hate I could swim through with my head held high above the water to somewhere that was safe. Safe was *not* with Dominic Reed.

"Whatever this is," I gestured between our chests. "I want out."

The tips of my fingers pressed at the hard ridges of his sternum, pushing him back. His heart slapped my fingers, startling my hand back and shooting shocks up my arm, almost like he'd stolen my lightning for a second.

His heart knew what I was about to say and was trying to burst through to keep me from saying it. I ignored it, leveling my stare to his and speaking low.

"I *am*... out."

A finality draped over the moment, sinking into my skin and making all my hairs stand on edge. Whether that was good or bad, I didn't know. It didn't stop me from saying what I did next.

"Go home to your wife."

Dominic pulled a hard-bitten look, arms still latched on either side of me. His nose crinkled, top lip twitching as he fought himself in that head of his over who knows what. I watched the war go back and forth in his cast off gaze, trying to steady my breathing before he brought it to me.

"Do you want to know why Heather slapped me yesterday?"

Fuck. Yes.

"Nope. It's none of my business."

His upper lip twitched yet again. "It could be if you'd stop being so difficult for five seconds," he growled, hands balling to fists beside me.

His frustration fueled mine, jabbing at my bristling temper. "Funny you say I'm the one being difficult when I've asked you to leave and yet you're *still* here."

He didn't even give me a goddamn inch. "I'm not leaving until we're done talking."

"We are done!" The bark behind my bite came out louder and harsher than I meant it to, but I didn't correct. In fact, I leaned into it, showing him all my sharp teeth. "We're done talking, we're done working together, and we're done fucking around behind everyone's back."

His handsome face pinched together like he'd eaten something sour. "Don't boil it down like that. That's not what this is."

I laughed. A real disgusting, mocking kind of laugh. "That's exactly what this was. Don't romanticize it. This was an *affair*."

The word slapped him as if it had fingers, outrage pouring through his eyes. I knew I was hurting him, pushing him to the edge of something raw, but I didn't stop. I couldn't even if I wanted to.

"Affairs aren't romantic. They're dirty and shallow and all about doing the wrong thing with the wrong person." I pressed up on my tiptoes, getting right in his face, so close I could count each shade of rage braiding together his grayscale eyes. "And we, Mr. Reed, are *wrong*."

The tip of his nose brushed mine as he lowered his head, his pretty mouth pulling back into something less than. "You're in denial."

"Or you are."

His eyes flamed. "You're scared."

"And you're married," I threw back, watching it splash over his face.

He withdrew with a clenched jaw, giving me back some of my air to breathe with, and I did. I breathed and I breathed as much clean air as I could that wasn't polluted by sweet mint or his earthy cologne to cleanse my body of him. It was working, but not enough. I still felt him everywhere on my skin and beneath, coasting in my veins and wrenching my stomach.

My head was spinning, a tornado of emotions having made it to my brain. I reached back to the handle of my front door, leaning on it for support as I said, "Go home, Dominic."

I lifted my foot, turning the knob...

Then I paused when I shouldn't have to tag on one last, sardonic bite.

"And be sure to tell your mom the whore from the shed says hi." And I fucking winked.

Why did I do that?

Regret poured in fast and heavy. I was being a bitch, and not even for the reasons I should have been because those *did* exist. There were a few reasons I could have picked to unleash on Dominic today, but none of them were finding their way to my tongue over the upset of his presence. Just him being here threw my world sideways, and I needed to leave before I fell off the edge completely.

Except thanks to my little guilt trip wink, a warm hand wound around my upper arm, stopping my escape. Dominic pulled me back, fixing me in his gaze that was really, truly sorry.

"I never should have put you in the position to be caught like that."

Fuck, those eyes were so sincere and vivid. He wasn't hiding anymore like he used to. "I wasn't thinking, and I spoke to my mom in length after you ran out."

"Yeah, and what'd you say?"

I wanted to ask him a million questions about it.

What did you tell her about me? Did you tell her that I'm kind of crazy and you kind of like it? Did you mention you talk to me about your sadness or how you wanna slow dance with me? Did you tell her our hearts are dying for each other against our will?

Instead of any of that, I asked, "Did you tell her you tripped and your tongue accidentally fell down my throat?"

Exasperation sunk a deep frown into his forehead, disappointment crushing his stoney eyes to rubble. He parted his lips to respond to my nasty question when screeching tires cut him off.

He twisted over his shoulder to my street and I looked around him to see what the commotion was. There was a black SUV sitting in the middle of the road, dead center in front of my house.

It wasn't moving.

It was big and sleek, a lot nicer than anything we had around here that I'd seen. Dominic's broad back obstructed my view of the car as he placed himself between me and the road. An annoyed puff of air pushed between my lips, and I rolled my eyes back.

Always the hero.

The SUV stayed unmoving for a while, almost like it was in a standoff with Dominic. The atmosphere tingled with this strange electricity that felt like antic- ipation but sat on my chest like dread. A bird chirped from somewhere up in the sky.

Then, dirt kicked up, silver rims spun in circles, and the car sped away. Both Dominic and I watched it go, peeling down the street and turning left before disappearing.

We were both quiet.

"Well." I clicked my tongue. "That was fucking weird." I gave my attention back to Dominic. "Can you leave now?"

Please?

He turned back around to me, his expression split down the middle by the bizarre SUV and me standing in front of him. Eventually my words pushed the SUV from his mind and he shook his head, brows pinching together.

"No. We're talking about this."

"There's nothing to talk about. You're not my boss anymore, and I'm not your side chick."

He thrust a hand up over his mouth, swiping his fingers around his shadowed jawline with a piercing gaze. "Do you really think that's what you are?"

His heavy tone caught my lashing tongue in a falter. I paused, switching my eyes between his in consideration. Did I really think that? Maybe not, but he was still married, so that's exactly what it made me. It didn't matter what I thought past the facts, and those were the facts.

"I think I'm tired of this conversation, and I'd really like you to leave."

My voice was weak, trampled by how exhausted I was from this infection. It was taking a part of me every single day it was inside me, eating away until I'd wither away from it like Mom had. I just wanted to go inside and face plant into my mattress and not wake up until it was gone.

But Dominic wouldn't let me. He kept poking and pushing me closer to the edge.

"Do you always do that?"

My stare snapped up to him and the scrutinizing angles of his face.

"Do what?" I spat.

Dominic didn't back down at my tone. He didn't even flinch at it. "Run away from anything that might push you out of your comfort zone."

Angry wind slapped in my veins, striking up a flurry of white spots in my vision like leaves. "Why are you always trying to *analyze* me? Do you get off on thinking you're better than me by pointing out all of my flaws?"

There was that goddamn disappointment again, tugging at his features. "I think you know that's not true."

"How would I know? That's all you do!" I emphasized, every muscle in my body screwed tight. "You analyze me and pick me apart so you can show me all of what makes me fucked up. Well, that's not news to me. I *know* I'm fucked up—"

"Stop saying that," he cut in sharply.

"Then stop pointing it out!" My voice bounced down the street, echoing my breaking point for all to hear. The storm inside propelled me forward, getting right up under those dark and cloudy eyes. "You did it the night of the party, you did it in your garage, and you're doing it now."

Every uneven inhale I took, my chest grazed his as I held his stare. Even when I felt like he was trying to look *through* me, down to the very soul that pined for him, I didn't look away. I let him take it all in until he saw I was right.

I didn't recognize it myself until I started rambling, but that's exactly what he did. Not just once. Not just twice, but again and again. He cracked me open and ripped out what made me tick, what made me sad, what made me less than, and prided in how easily he found them all.

How many more times would I have let him point out what was wrong with me because I was too sick in the head to realize that's what he was doing?

"That's not what I—" Dominic stopped, words falling away into a black hole of guilt at the center of his sorrowed eyes. Wow. *He stutters.*

"I never saw it like that," he spoke, voice smooth and gaze roaming my face. "That's not why I said any of it."

"Then why did you?" I bristled, sensations snapping and popping in my chest. "To put the attention on my flaws so you could forget that I'm yours? That's what you said, right? I'm your weakness? I'm your only imperfection, and I accepted that. I even *liked* that." I thrust my fingers back through my hair, lightning striking out of me in a splitting cry as I turned and bent at the waist. "*God*, how fucked up am I that I liked being your flaw?"

Dominic caught my wrist, snapping me back to face him.

"You are *not* my flaw."

"I am!" I cried in fury, letting him see all the cracks in my heart. "I am, and you're a fucking *stereotype* and you made me into one too."

That infamous thunder of his rolled in from all sides, packing around me and daring me to say another word. "Don't think I'm not aware of the cliché of our relationship, because *believe me*, I am. I wrestled with it for a very long time to come to the conclusion that no matter how we met..." His voice held, stringing me up by resolute eyes. "It wouldn't have changed anything."

That statement struck me like fucking whiplash.

My heart surged forward on a slingshot, belting out a high note of passion for what he was implying. We were inevitable. Our stars would have crossed now or years from now because our meeting was fate.

Then, ropes yanked my heart back, plunging it down, down until it shattered when it remembered that I didn't want to fall through his sky. I didn't want to soar. I wanted to be safe, and that meant keeping my feet planted firmly on the ground.

Dominic ignored what I wanted though, picking me up and sweeping me off my unstable feet with what happened next.

"What did I say your weakness was in the garage that day?"

"That what I really want is to be submissive and helpless so some big hero can come in and save me," I bit back.

His browline flattened, words leaving his lips slowly. "Your memory is selective."

A bratty comeback prepped in the back of my throat, but got choked down as Dominic stepped into me. One step, and I countered. Another, and I repeated the move. He walked me back until I'd found the front door again, shoulder blades flattening against it as he huddled me into it.

My wrist was still caught in his deft fingers when he said, "I pointed out that when I touch you..." And he did, riding both hands up my arms until he cradled my neck on both sides, calluses skimming over my skin. I froze up, breath stuck in my chest as he lorded over me.

"You always let me."

He thumbed the edge of my jaw, looming in until he'd eclipsed the sun entirely and was the only world I knew. My head fell back, exposing my throat to him.

He ran his nose along it, heated breath trailing behind. "You let me get as close to you as I want, and that's important."

Breathy and unconvincing, I replied, "It's not."

"It is, and it's important because of what I said today. You run from things that scare you out of your comfort zone." With a ragged gasp, my hands jumped up to fist his shirt as languid lips dragged against my skin. I pushed him away just to pull him back in, muscles melting beneath his hot mouth.

"I can kiss your neck and feel your body loosening, how you arch yourself to get closer to me." As if he needed to prove it, he did just that, smoothing a kiss so bittersweet against the hollow of my neck, it pulled strangled whimpers into the air.

"But then," Those bittersweet lips glimpsed the shell of my ear, rich notes ribboning around my sensibilities as he spoke. "I can also tell you that I'm out of my mind, addicted to being around you and want nothing more than to kiss you senseless every time I see you..."

The warmth of his palm moved down my neck, settling over my heart, which in seconds had malformed into a pounding, screaming, sobbing mess beneath his hand.

He laid his forehead against mine, eyes like teardrops reaching up to mine. "And your panic is tangible."

I was trying to hold it in, but wasn't idiot enough to know I wasn't doing a good job. My shoulders were shaking, the skin around my collarbone hollowing out as I fought to hold in my gasping. Dominic looked so fucking sad as he watched me swallow my anxiety, running his thumb over my heart as if he had the power to talk to it through touch.

"I didn't point any of those things out to make you think you're more flawed than I am," he started. "I did it because your body is more honest about how you feel about me than any other part of you. Your body doesn't overthink. It just trusts me."

Trust.

Now there was a word to hate. It was so much worse than slut. It was worse than any word in the dictionary, because 'trust' wasn't just a word. It was a trick.

Trust was a ruse that, no matter which way you dressed it, always—*always*—ended in disappointment. Trust meant something sturdy and certain, but the end result was always something broken. It may take days or it may take years, but trust was the least trustworthy bitch out there.

I latched onto the hate I had for that word, letting the hate fill me up, up, up until I was swamped in it. Hatred ruled my body and curled my lip back.

"My body's a whore and doesn't like to remember that you're married."

Speaking of trust...

"Or that you used me to make your wife uncomfortable on purpose."

Dominic's face fell and he eased back. "What?"

"Heather never wanted to hire me, so why did you?"

"Because you were best for the job," he replied, voice flat.

"No, no more bullshit." I shook my head, thrashing my shoulders so he'd back up. He did. Barely. "Why did you *really* hire me?"

"You *are* the best for the job."

"*And?*"

Dominic stared at me long and hard before jerking his head to the side, showing me his profile chiseled in tension. My gaze was locked on him, drilling into his face like I could drill out the guilty words that I knew were coming.

His lips thinned, a brusque exhale pushing through his nose. "You unnerved Heather, and I'm not proud to admit that I enjoyed that."

Ah, love. Marriage. Happily ever afters. What a fucking dream, ammiright?

"Was making her suspicious always a part of the plan?" I asked.

He brought his stare to me, looking so goddamn serious. "Do you really think I planned any of this?"

"I don't know. Who's to say you didn't plan on using me to make your wife jealous from the beginning."

"*I* say."

"And because your word is so fucking honorable, I should just believe you?"

His eyes zapped wide like it was obvious. "Yes, you should."

"Well, I don't!"

The outline of Dominic's body grew beastly over me, crowding from even a foot away, suffocating without ever touching me. Every line on his face was dedicated to me—loathing me, wanting me, wanting to throttle me.

"You are so goddamn *stubborn.*"

I jabbed my chin up at him. "And proud of it."

Dominic took in my prideful, spiteful declaration, his stare never waning from me. His focus was harsh and pointed, that little wrinkled frown between his eyebrows showing.

"Do you know what might happen if you stopped being on defense all the time?"

Yeah, I might turn out exactly like my mom, and you might turn out exactly like my dad, and I might ruin Charlotte's entire life.

But I couldn't say that. I'd never admit that out loud out of sheer, paranoid fear that the universe might hear and decide it'd be funny to watch me eat my words.

So I curled up the end of my mouth and shrugged. "Guess we'll never find out."

That little frown marring his forehead deepened, carving into something a bit scary. Something a lot upset.

"You're really willing to risk this just so you can keep being stubborn and scared?"

"What 'this'?" My hands flew out in wild flares. "There is no *this.*"

The gray of his eyes sharpened like a fucking knife.

"Us."

And that knife punctured through the last of my stability.

"There is no us!" I yelled, the ferocity behind my voice scraping up my throat. My hands shook, balled up at my sides as I breathed fucking fire all over Dominic; my words and temper were that hot.

Dominic ducked his face immediately, hiding his expression in the cement beneath our feet. We stood in the silence of my outburst for a few more seconds than I could stand, but I'd already exploded once and didn't know if I had anything left to do it again.

Softly, almost like he was unsure of how to say it, he asked, "Can you not shout?"

Through clenched teeth, I questioned, "Why?"

His shoulders lifted and fell in a slow move, eyes of liquid silver peeking up beneath thick slats of eyebrows.

"Because all I do is fight with Heather, and I don't want to fight with you."

And here I'd been proven wrong.

I didn't think I had anything left to spiral with, to use as kindling to another explosion, but that did it. Those words and that look inspired another detonation to rise within me, except these flames would be made of tears.

"Don't—" I stuttered, his honesty kicking me square in the chest. "Don't put that on me." I shook my head, shaking my tingling fingers out too. "That's not fair. Telling me I can't yell just because she does."

"I'm not telling you that you can't." He sighed, looking as worn as I felt. "I'm asking you not to because the idea of fighting with you makes me unbelievably sad."

The proof was in his voice, sadness coiled all around it and punching through my chest. Its sadness gripped me, crushing my lungs, my windpipe, my ribs all to dust that I choked on.

I coughed and sputtered, backing away from Dominic on feet that were crumbling too. "Don't *say* shit like that to me."

His face creased. "Why not?"

"Because I don't want it!" Every bit of breathable air clawed right out of me, leaving me gasping and tears pricking. "I don't want any of this! I just wanted a *job*, not—"

I stopped, holding my forehead in my hands and feeling the fever begin to sweat. The sickness was coming on fast and unapologetic. I dropped my hands over my chest, squeezing with all five fingers until I could feel the outline of my dying heart. It was pulsing, slapping, and maybe it was the panic or maybe it was delusion, but I swore I could feel it bleeding out.

Blood dripping down my insides and filling me up with sickly sweet death.

A blurred movement of blue jeans and a darker blue shirt came towards me.

"Kat—"

"Don't come near me." Disintegrating nerves stumbled my feet back until I hit a wall, bracing myself into it. I squeezed my eyes shut as hard as I could. "You need to go."

Please. Go now.

"*No,*" he fought.

"Yes!"

Oh god. Maybe his intentions to stay were good. Maybe they were selfish. It didn't matter to the panic why he was refusing to leave though. Nothing mattered except the pain. Nothing mattered except the needled sensation cutting through my chest and doing whatever the fuck I could to make it stop and make him go away.

"You don't want me to yell?" I sliced a glare up to him that held everything bad about myself inside of it. "Well now I'm fucking yelling! I will yell and yell and scream bloody murder until you leave, Dominic!"

He held himself steady through my onslaught, giving me every ounce of his concerned focus. "Kat, you're having a panic attack."

"Yeah, no fucking shit," I spat, turning towards my front door.

A creak in the wood behind me whipped me back around, stopping Dominic where he was with a blasting scream.

"Dominic, I don't want you!"

His unique eyes widened, touched by shock. It was the first thing I said that had affected him. The first thing I'd said that made him stop, and so I kept going and going until I'd spewed all my ugly over him no matter how much it hurt to watch his misguided idea of me crumble.

"I don't want someone who used me. I *can't* have you because you're still married. I *won't* have you because I'm not gonna be the one to break up your family. I've already fucked it up enough, and I'm done."

I was so fucking done, and maybe—*maybe*—Dominic finally was too. My cruel words had dragged his mouth to a frown, his browline strict and grim-set all the way across. And his eyes...

The chill was back where it belonged, and I was the ice queen that put it there.

"Save yourself the fucking torture of wanting me, and go back to Heather," I finished, hearing the hitch in my voice that said I was about to cry.

I didn't wait for it to happen. He knew I was breaking down. He didn't need to see it too.

So I ran, just like he said I would. I busted through my front door and slammed it shut, tears already leaking down my cheeks that hurt way, way worse than any other tears I'd cried.

For once, my tears were for someone who deserved them.

For once, I had someone in my life who deserved my sorrow, my guilt, my heartbreak. We'd both been to blame for how it started, but I was solely to blame for how it ended.

Every tear I cried was his.

They were the only part of me left that was.

TWENTY-FIVE

That night in the middle of my sulking, I got a text from Layla telling me to pack a bag.

I texted back, 'No'.

She texted back, 'Yes'.

I texted back, 'I'm sleeping'.

Ten minutes later, she texted that she was outside my house, and I officially lost the birthday battle. We'd done this tug of war on my birthday ever since we knew each other. She'd try to do something big and showy, and I'd hide under the covers until she literally pulled me out by my ankles.

I hated my birthday, but I wasn't one of those people who hated it because of the attention or the fact that society said it was 'cool' to not care about birthdays. When I was little, I loved the attention, loved the parties, loved it all.

My eighteenth birthday was when it all went down the shitter.

Layla insisted this year though, bribing me with unlimited drinks and seclusion away from all the bullshit she didn't even know I was sitting in at home. She'd planned the entire thing, even confirmed with Mrs. Sharon to watch Charlotte overnight.

And that's how I ended up here, lounging in a pool chair on my twenty-first birthday at a resort outside of town, halfway to drunk and whispering not-so-subtle objectifications about the pool bartender with Layla.

"Can you imagine how much he pulls with a face like that? Walking around, handing out extra boozy drinks and throwing out winks like he did to us?" Layla drawled, teeth still clenched around the straw of her drink, eyes peeking over the bridge of her lowered pink polka-dotted sunglasses.

"Oh, that thing was fucking deadly." I pulled back another mouthful of whatever Layla had ordered me, fruity pops of flavor sliding down my throat and adding another fuzzy layer over my brain.

"Why don't you go get yourself some birthday sex?" She jabbed her sharp chin in the bartenders direction. "I'm sure he'd be better than Daren."

Laughter made a *pfft* past my lips. "That's not setting the bar all that high above average."

"I'm so glad you broke up with him. He was such a tool."

She wasn't wrong.

"Do you remember how he basically tried to piss all around you in front of your cop boss?" she continued with a chuckle.

At the mention of Dominic, I shoved my straw in my mouth and nodded a distracted, "Mhm."

"He wouldn't stop moaning while you were gone with him. I came *this* close to shoving my ice cream in his mouth so he'd shut up about it."

"No need to throw perfectly good ice cream down a shithole."

"Yeah." There was a small splash a ways away, and I squinted through my sunglasses to see the only other person out here emerging from the turquoise water. It was an older dude—like a lot older. The kind that thought speedos were cool and my eyes needed to be melted today.

"Gross," I muttered, speaking around my straw. "Is it just me or does no one look good in speedos?"

"What about your boss?"

I gritted my teeth, swallowing hard. "Well, I haven't seen him in a speedo."

"Are you saying you wouldn't want to?"

The goddamn smirk in her voice was too much. The alcohol hadn't healed enough of what I'd inflicted upon myself yesterday to be ready to talk about him again. The freaking swimming pool could be filled with top-shelf liquor, and I wasn't sure even that would help unless I drowned in it.

I bit down on my straw until the plastic broke and shoved my drink on the small table next to me. "I'm *saying* we're done talking about him."

"What—" Layla blustered, shooting my profile a keen look. "Why?"

"Because it's my birthday, and I say so."

At full-tilt, Layla sprung up in her sunbathing chair, pushing her sunglasses back into her hair to show me her big eyes. Uh oh.

"*Fuck* your birthday. Did something happen with him?"

"*No.*"

She let out a sharp gasp. "You're lying!"

"How does everyone always know when I'm lying?" I exclaimed, sinking down in my chair and folding my arms.

"Because you're really bad at it. Like epically bad at it." Two hands wrapped at the base of my chair, pulling with Hulk-like strength until I was facing Layla and her hungry-for-gossip eyes head on. "So what happened?"

Lips parted, a strangled whimper cracked through.

What a simple question with the least simple answer. Where to start? At the first kiss? The second? Or just straight to how I was fired because his wife was totally suspicious and with every right to be because I was absolutely, idiotically sick for her husband?

"Holy shit, okay. Your face is telling me we need another drink for this." Layla shifted to standing, pulling her fingers along the underneath of her baby pink bikini bottom. "Hold the tea while I go get more alcohol."

She disappeared, and I flopped back in my chair, hiding my flushing face in my arms.

Once Layla returned with a drink stronger than the last, I launched into the story. I told her everything. I started at the heroin chemistry and worked my way to yesterday when I screamed at him and cried all because of that stupid chemistry.

Layla was quiet and surprisingly patient while I spoke, only nodding, gasping, and squeaking when she couldn't hold in her reactions. By the time I finished, my chest was all knotted up, and I was slurping at the ice in the bottom of my drink, trying to suck whatever alcohol I could out of them.

Layla hadn't actually said anything while I was talking, and now that I was finished, her mouth was parted, but no words came out. The look she was giving me, however, was talking up a fucking storm. She was just *staring* at me like she'd been caught in a freeze frame of an epiphany.

The knot inside my gut rolled around, sloshing with the alcohol in my otherwise empty stomach. What had started as a fun and tipsy kind of birthday was quickly leaning more towards something that would have my head in a toilet by noon.

"You like him," Layla stated. Fucking *stated*, not questioned. My stomach curdled. "You like, *really* like him."

Groaning, I slid my empty glass on the table. "And I don't want to talk about it."

"Because he's married?"

"Because he's married, because he's got a family, because he used me to make his bitch of a wife uncomfortable, *which* just proves that he's not this knight in shining armor like he tries to pretend to be."

"Yeah, no. That was a shitty thing to do, no doubt." She paused in a way that said more was coming, and whatever it was was something I wouldn't like. "But it sounds like he's pretty serious about liking you too."

A bitter laugh tipped over my lips. "You seem to forget that he's married just about as easily as I do."

A pause. Another splash in the pool. Then—

"But what if he wasn't?"

I cocked a real indignant brow up at her. "What do you mean?"

"Like what if he wasn't married when you met him? What if there was nothing standing in between you two?"

For some reason, I noticed the intensity of the sun more all of a sudden. Scorching a little hotter, burning a little deeper, making me sweat a little more beneath my bikini. "I don't see the point of this since he *is* married. Married as in for *life*."

"I'm *getting* to the point of it." She waved her hands in front of her, catching my arm with a slight slap. She was definitely feeling the buzz in her bones while I was feeling it in my anxious gut. "I'm *saying* that if he walked in here right now and told you he was getting a divorce, would you go for it or would you find another excuse why you couldn't be with him?"

Okay, I was not prepared for this type of emotional dissection on my birthday.

"I'd say being married isn't so much an excuse as it is adultery."

Layla deflated with a huff back down in her chair. "You're missing the point on purpose, dumbass."

Yeah. So?

Just then, my phone started to vibrate inside my purse strung over the back of the chair. Grumbling, I scrambled up to my knees on the flat part of the chair to grab it out.

When I saw the name on the screen, the alcohol conducted my reaction before the panic could.

"Oh my god, *no*," I cried out, dropping my head back to the sky.

Layla sprung up to standing in seconds. "What's wrong?"

I shoved my phone towards her. "It's him."

Dominic. The man my heart would love to die for.

"See what he wants!"

"No!"

She not-so-gently nudged my shoulder. "Maybe he wants to tell you happy birthday."

"He doesn't *know* it's my birthday."

His name flashed over my screen again and again, pulsing like my heart was in quick-timed beats all dedicated to him. Why was he calling? Didn't he hate me after what I said to him yesterday? Didn't he have a wife to attend to?

"Just pick up! Now I'm curious."

My thumb hovered over the answer button, sweat gathering along my hairline in a sticky mess that I swiped through with my other hand. *Fuck*. I didn't want to talk to him. I *couldn't* talk to him, but the rum and sugar running through my blood pressed my thumb to the screen before I could think straight.

"You just hung up!" Layla screeched.

"Oh, fuck, I didn't mean to!"

"Yeah? You *really* didn't mean to?"

I met her sarcasm with equal bite. "No! I really didn't. He made this whole point yesterday about always picking up if he called so he'd know I was all right and shit."

My best friend let out a coo. "That's so sweet."

"Shut up!" My phone lit back up in my palm, Dominic's name flashing over the screen again. "He's calling back!"

"Okay, press the *green* button this time."

I made a gaggle of unintelligible noises to mock Layla's instructions before answering. "Hello?"

The loudest pause I'd ever experienced passed between the phone line. Every muscle I had screwed up in anticipation for the impact hearing his voice would have. And then it happened, curving its base note around my obstinance and tripping it up.

"Kat," he sighed my name on a wave of relief. His voice flooded between my ears, drowning my mind in a way the alcohol could only ever hope. Plucking words to speak out of the sea he created in my head felt impossible, but I somehow managed.

"What do you want?"

He bypassed my terse question with one of his own. "Where are you?"

The thought to lie to him evaporated quickly. Why bother?

"Celebrating my birthday."

When he picked up, there had been this odd mix of urgency and alleviation; a strange tone to begin with. All of that shoved aside as he quieted his voice for me.

"Today's your birthday?"

Sucking back my bottom lip and biting down hard, I said, "Yeah."

A heavy beat. Almost a somber one.

"Really?"

My face pinched together, and I caught Layla's curious eyes. "Yeah, *really*. Do you think I'm lying about my birthday?"

"No, I—" He dropped off with a sigh, and I pictured his jaw sawing to the side and back. "You're not at home. Where are you?"

He'd been by my house?

"I'm at a hotel outside of town. Why?"

"Which hotel?"

My brows plunged together. "I don't really think that's any of your business."

"Don't do that right now," he shot back. "*Where* are you?"

I pulled the phone away from my lips, mouthing to Layla that he was asking where I was. She mouthed back that I should ask him why he wanted to know so badly.

"Why do you wanna know?" I asked, earning a thumbs up from Layla.

A clipped groan came through. "Can you please not be difficult right now? *Please?*"

I shot up with my temper, standing on two feet on the base of the pool chair. "I don't think I'm being difficult by asking why my ex boss wants to know where I am after checking my house. I'd say I'm being pretty fucking smart, actually."

Irritation growled at me through the phone, and he didn't say anything to me for a few moments. He was talking to someone else, barking out things I couldn't understand and words that got muffled.

His deep voice cut back in for a short second. "Do you have it?" Another male voice followed, and then Dominic was talking to me again.

"Kat, who are you with?"

Something about his tone set my nerves on razors, one wrong move away from splitting in half.

"Layla...?"

"Okay." Then his voice sounded closer. More honed in on me, just for me. "Take her and stay indoors. Don't talk to anyone. Don't go outside. Tell me you understand me."

I eased down in the chair, knees in my chest and curled the phone against my cheek. "Dominic, what the fuck is going on?"

"*Tell me* you understand me," he snarled back with so much power, I gasped.

"I understand," I said. Even though I didn't.

"Good." Over the line, his breathing lingered for a few seconds like he was afraid to hang up. He did, though, and I dropped my phone from my ear and met the wide stare of my best friend.

"What'd he say?"

I blinked, still digesting. "That he wants us to go inside and not talk to anyone."

Layla nodded, adjusting her polka-dot sunglasses back down on her face. "Are we doing that?"

I paused at her question, feeling my emotions as they overruled my smarts. All I felt was *pissed* that he'd called and tried to ruin the first birthday in four years that wasn't shitty. All I felt was livid that I was thinking about him and even considering doing what he said rather than enjoy this day that Layla planned.

"*Fuck* no." A rush of defiance pulsed through me and blew a smile up my cheeks. Layla met that smile, giving me an impish grin. "We're gonna order another drink, get shit-faced, and go swimming."

My natural rebellious flare had been asleep lately thanks to Dominic and the sickness, but today?

I was gonna let it fucking shine.

About an hour later, my blood was pure sugar and alcohol, and the pool had become my second home. The water was cool and perfect, smooth over my bare skin like a brush of silk. The yellow sun had taken a small dip behind a cluster of cotton white clouds, and I closed my eyes with the momentary shade, gliding on my back over the water.

Everything about this was perfect. My body was all warm and fuzzy from the kiss of the sun and constant buzz I had going on. I only thought about Dominic and his weird phone call once, and I took a quick shot to douse those thoughts back into muddled fragments.

The only thing taking away from the perfection of this moment was the pang in my stomach that whined for more food.

The world rolled with me as I spun onto my front and wobbled as I planted my feet on the cemented pool floor. "Do you think we could get any more of that fruit from Golden Locks?"

Layla sputtered, stroking her fingers through the water. "First off, the character is *Goldie* Locks, and second, I don't think Mr. Bar Boy's supposed to give us that stuff. He only did it cuz you offered to flash him."

A rum-inspired smirk peeled across my lips. "I'm pretty sure he thinks he's having a threesome with us later."

"I wouldn't be mad about it," she commented, shrugging and somehow finding a beat to groove to within the movement of the shrug. She popped her shoulders up and down, bopping her way through the water with exaggerated pursed lips like a duck.

"What music do you hear in your head right now?" I laughed.

She pointed up near her high ponytail with a fluid hand twirl. "Despacito is on full blast up in here."

She started humming the notes of the song now, shimmying towards me in the water. From drunken Layla experience, I knew once she hit the bridge of the song, the notes coming out of her mouth would turn not so quiet and not so pretty. The water around us would turn to glass just so it could shatter.

"Okay, *you* keep dancing, and I'll go see if Goldie will give us another bowl of strawberries for one tit, mkay?"

"Aw, only one?"

"Are you saying one isn't good enough?"

Layla sent a splash of water my way. "Bitch, you know you have great tits. I'm straight and I would still jizz all over them."

I barked a laugh, treading through the water over to the pool steps. I wound my fingers around the metal pole angled along the steps, lugging myself up the first step. In the back of my mind, I knew the metal was hot and I probably should let go, but all of my nerve endings were too numb and tingly to care.

I hoisted up, only for gravity to push me right back down as I lost my balance. Layla's laugh shot off behind me, and I whined aloud, going back in for a take two with the steps.

"Huzzah!" I reached the top step, throwing my arms in the air in celebration and gaining a slow clap from our blonde-haired, blue-eyed bartender. Hand to my heart, I bowed dramatically without falling over a second time, knowing he was getting a great show of the girls in this bathing suit.

Red was always my best color.

I spun back to Layla to give her a suggestive wink, except something behind the gates sectioning off the pool caught my winking eye first.

Something tall and big. Something shaking and pissed off. Something staring right at me with enough intensity to drown me on dry land.

My breath hitched.

"Oh, fuck me."

TWENTY-SIX

D ominic charged through the gates, practically breaking the thing off the hinges before I could even think how to react to him being here.

Panic? Sure. Shock? Definitely. Sarcastic outrage? Not exactly what I might have chosen to go with in a sober state of mind, but that was the reaction fast-acting through my blood as Dominic closed the distance between us, storm clouds roiling through his eyes.

"I told you to stay indoors."

His nearness pulled my shoulders back and strung my chest tight, like every vein in it was stretched to the max around my heart. My eyes jumped between his as he came within feet of me, trying to find a focused thought in my hot head.

"So, I'm not *totally* sure, but I think being fired means I don't have to take orders from you anymore," I went with.

Dominic pressed his lips together in a thin line as another man came from behind him. I vaguely remembered him being at my house the day my mom called the cops. Must have been Dominic's partner. He was a head shorter than Dominic, but still taller than me. His hair was shorter too—buzz cut, and his nose was crooked in that rugged kind of way that said he'd been in a fight or two.

Electric blue eyes—almost the same color as the pool water—observed me with a scrutiny that said he knew more about me than I knew about him. *Great.*

I tipped my chin up towards him. "You wanna tell me why you guys are here, crashing my birthday?"

A spark of surprise lit up his pupils. His mouth curved up just so at the ends. Dominic rumbled out a warning next to his partner. "Ryan is going to stay with Layla, and you and I are going to go talk."

He nabbed a hotel towel from a nearby chair and held it out to me.

"Dry off and cover up."

I frowned at the offered towel, swatting at it. "No."

"*Kat.*"

"It's Ms. Sanders to you," I bolstered, keeping my chin high.

From the pool, Layla added, "That's kinda hot."

My tongue clicked, and I swiveled towards her with a wistful tone. "It really was. He used to use it a lot. Then, this one time, after that party he—*oop!*"

All it took was one slick step in Layla's direction, and my foot came out from under me. It slid against the watered cement, and I saw a flash of bright blue sky before silver-gray took over and stopped my fall. Dominic caught my arms on either side, cupping my elbows and steadying me without coming too close.

"Oh my god." I threw my head back in laughter. "That would've hurt so fucking much."

Even though I was stable-ish, Dominic didn't let me go.

"Are you drunk?"

"You can't arrest me for it this time, boss man. I'm *legal*."

His partner cut in. "You arrested her?"

Dominic's navy blue button up stretched over his chest as he heaved a sigh. "It's a long story."

I cocked my head at his outfit. It was the first time I really took in what he was wearing. The button up, black slacks, and his wingtip shoes. My brows furrowed, and my nose scrunched. "Isn't today your day off?"

My stare trailed back up to his face for the answer, except the way Dominic was staring at me didn't answer anything. In fact, I had *more* questions—mainly, why was he looking at me like the world was ending and he was on his way to its funeral?

Before I could ask, a hand touched the small of my back, and Goldie came around my shoulder, sizing up Dominic with a polite but stiff smile.

"Hey, fellas. You two staying at the hotel with us or..." He shrugged in that casual, kind of provoking way, blue stare fixed on Dominic. "Just passing through to bother our birthday girl?"

Aw. Sweet Goldie. Nice Goldie. Dumb Goldie.

Dominic dropped his focus to Goldie's hand on my back, the gray of his eyes souring. He flickered an annoyed glare up at me, sticking his hand in his back pocket and fishing out his badge.

Eyes still locked on me, he flashed his badge in Goldie's face, and the warm touch on my back vanished. He mumbled out his apologies and retreated back to his bar cabana.

"Hey, that's a cool party trick." I yanked my arms away from him, stepping back. "I wish I could just flash a badge that would get people to leave me alone."

Dominic curled his hands into fists by his sides, casting a furtive glance behind me and to the side. He was tense. Every single muscle visible was stressed, from the veins outlining his forearms to the ones in his thick neck. He was radiating stress all over my birthday, and for *once*, I kind of actually cared that today didn't suck.

"Hey, Sir." I cocked my hip out, raising my hand. "Pretend this is a badge."

And I showed him how straight my middle finger could go.

Layla laughed wildly, high-pitched trills soaring up with the breeze. Surprisingly, Dominic's partner joined in, his cheeks twitching as muffled chuckles broke through.

Dominic's lip curled back, shooting him a look over his shoulder. "Don't encourage her."

"I'm sorry." He lifted a fist to his mouth, coughing to cover up another bout of laughter. "You did say she was funny."

Ah, so he did talk about me.

"Yeah." Dominic snapped his focus back to me, the shadow of the sun making his expression meaner. "Except for when she's being a stubborn brat."

Villainous memories blew a soft laugh through my nose because we both knew how much part of him *loved* how bratty I could be. The brat in me brought out the animal in him, and right now, his animal was breaking skin, shredding right through Dominic's good to show me all of his bad.

Number one million and one for reasons why we were wrong for each other.

"Yeah, I *am* that. I'm a brat, and you weren't invited to this party. So go."

A panic attack wasn't at the top of my wishlist for my birthday, but if he stayed, that's exactly what I would get, gift-wrapped in screams and humiliating sobs.

"Kat," He drew in close, lowering his pitch to a serious note. "I really need to talk to you."

His proximity hit me with a whiff of that sweet mint right from his lips, and the first string of my panic was plucked. Thanks to the alcohol, it misformed into rage that tingled my upper lip until it was fucking shaking.

"*No*. No, Dominic. I meant what I said yesterday. I *meant* it. If you really cared about me, then you'd high-tail it right the fuck out of here before you make me cry on my birthday."

Like that would be a first.

Hurt needled at his pupils, but his staunch determination wouldn't budge. "This is not a negotiation. Either you come with me or I take you with me."

A mocking laugh puffed out of me. "I'm not going anywhere with you."

Dominic cut his hard gaze over my head, almost like he was watching my laugh rise up in the sky before disintegrating in a wisp of particles to add to the tense air. The backs of his cheeks pulsed in angry waves, a controlled exhale releasing from his chest.

Then, he ducked.

"Dominic! What the—!"

The words and my breath all flipped upside down as a wide shoulder caught under my bare stomach, lifting me up off the ground and over his back. "Hey!"

"I gave you the option. You chose to be difficult."

I propped my hands up on his muscled back as he rummaged through my purse, fingers folding around our hotel room card. I kicked out with a ferocious cry, and his arm just beneath my ass squeezed down hard.

Turning towards the pool—and me towards the bushes—I heard him again. "Layla, what room are you guys in?"

"102."

"Layla!" I screeched, whipping back to her. "Whose side are you on?"

"I'm sorry! I'm confused and drunk!"

Another feral noise ripped up my throat as I pounded my fists on Dominic's back. It didn't phase him though, not one goddamn bit. And before I'd even put up a fight worth talking about, the pool, Layla, and my lonely drink were all getting smaller until they were gone entirely.

Who the fuck do you call when a cop was the one kidnapping you?

A door banged against the wall as Dominic busted through it to inside the hotel. If it weren't for the alcohol and anger heating my blood, the frigid air would have frozen every single droplet of pool water taking this ride on my bare skin. I was running too hot to feel it though, yelling out with fire in my lungs.

"Put me down! What did I say about manhandling?!"

He ignored me, barreling around the beige corners of the hotel, passing maroon doors with silver numbers written in metallic cursive until he got to the maroon door with *102* scribbled across it.

I released my arms holding me up on his back, flopping down on his slabs of muscles with a dramatic sigh. The robotic unlocking of the door sounded off, and Dominic pushed through it, kicking it shut behind us.

Now we were alone, pissed off, and the moderately-sized hotel room was anything but quiet with our presence. Our storm was brewing a soundtrack for our inevitable clash, vibrating the walls and electrifying the air. I thumped my fist on Dominic's lower back again—purely out of spite—and he spilled me over unceremoniously onto one of the two beds.

My back bounced against the sheets, throwing my head in a tailspin of dizzying, tiny white stars. I squeezed my eyes shut against them, holding my head in my hands.

"*Woah*. Head rush."

The white dots poked little holes through the blackout provided by my closed eyes, and slowly, I blinked and I blinked until I blinked them all away. Until the only star in front of me was one with silver eyes and a deep frown.

Dominic watched me with such a heavy intensity, not saying a goddamn word now that he had me here. Alone. On my birthday. 24 hours after I told him I didn't want him.

"What?" I snapped, slightly breathy. Still, he said nothing. Just stared at me like he'd never seen me before. "*What*, Dominic? Say something. You dragged me away from my birthday, drove all the way out here to get to me. So tell me whatever the fuck is *so* important that you had to do all of that for?"

He took back a breath that seemed painful, an ache I didn't understand bleeding in from the corner of his eyes. When he finally spoke, it was barely a murmur.

"The black SUV from yesterday."

The room got heavy, and I wasn't quite sure why. My eyes shifted from side to side, brows cinching together. "What?"

Dominic sent his gaze to the floor, periodically clenching his teeth and unlocking them seconds later. "I didn't put it together yesterday. I was too focused on our fight to remember why a black SUV felt strange to me."

"I don't get it?"

A muscle in his right cheek throbbed as he rolled his stare up to me. It was still *so* serious, and somewhere from the back of my rum-blurred mind, I recalled his tone of voice when he called earlier. Frantic. Urgent. I asked him what was wrong, and he didn't answer.

Something *was* wrong, wasn't it?

My gut started to twist.

"The victim before the nurse, Kallie Becks," he began. "She was the only one taken where someone witnessed it happen, and the only key detail they could give us was the type of vehicle she was pulled into before disappearing."

My lips parted slowly, like damp paper peeling apart. "Is this some big set up to tell me it was a minivan or a... clown car or something?" I breathed.

His thundercloud eyes softened at my attempt. My mouth dried out as he shook his head only once. I sucked back a sharp breath, suspended in time for less than a second before my gut reaction hit hard, and I was convinced it was right.

"That's probably just a coincidence."

Stare lowered to the ground, he nodded. "It could be."

Then he flickered those all-too-serious eyes up to me, delivering a blow with it right through the center of my world and my conviction. He left them both gaping and gasping with that look of his that said coincidences were for dummies, and I'd be a fool to believe this was one. That look terrified me. Enraged me. Shoved me right from denial to pissed off in the time it took to blink.

"Don't look at me like that." My temper wobbled, confused. I pushed myself up to sit on the bed. "Don't look at me like something's wrong when you don't know if it is. This could literally mean *anything*. You don't know."

"You're right. I don't."

In his voice, I could hear it. He was trying to appease me. Calm me down before I burst.

That second stage anger burned hotter, charging up my lightning through my veins, coiling it around my blood until it *was* my blood.

"If you don't know, then why would you come down here and make this huge deal out of it when it's just a *hunch*?"

Passion scorched across his face. "Because my hunch could be the difference between keeping you safe or losing you."

"I am not yours to *lose*." I hit every word on the head, nailing them into existence so Dominic understood them once and for all. For a teeny second, vulnerability cracked his expression down the middle and out poured torment.

Hurt. The very next second, he sealed it all back up behind rigid lines and frostbite eyes.

"Thank you. You made that clear yesterday, but it's not just me who would care if something happened to you."

"Oh my god, can you just stop? Please?" I begged with my hands in front of me, shaking like I was picturing shaking his throat. This was insane. Absolutely insane. "You've jumped to, like, the biggest, most *dramatic* conclusion you could based on almost nothing."

Looking about as fed up with me as I was with him, Dominic breathed back a barely contained inhale. He folded his arms over one another, and I had the most ill-timed flash of longing for one of his t-shirts instead of this long-sleeved shirt so I could watch his biceps flex. *Dammit.*

"All right. Let's go through our options of what this could be."

In frustration, I threw myself back on the bed with a growl, focusing my topsy-turvy vision on the ceiling as he listed them out.

"One, I'm completely off, and that SUV at your house has nothing to do with any of the kidnappings. Two, in the SUV were the kidnappers and they made a purposeful stop in front of your house when they saw you, they clocked you as a potential for later, and they'll be back."

I fisted the comforter beneath my fingers, strangling the soft material as my heart *thump, thump, thumped.* "And three," he continued, sounding closer than before. "They were there for you. They knew you, knew where you lived, tracked you down and got spooked when they saw me. In that scenario, they will also come back."

My eyes jumped over to him as he approached the side of the bed, hovering over me and bringing the entire rainstorm with him. It was in his eyes and in his words and in every pause in between, filling my lungs with raindrops so heavy, the weight held me down against the mattress.

I couldn't move, couldn't speak, couldn't breathe. My throat was too full of sloshing dread.

"That makes two out of the three most likely scenarios, ones that put your life at serious risk." His voice rolled deeply like the thunder he was. "You may think I'm overreacting, but when it's your life, even one percent of a chance is too much to take."

Laying there, I was feeling a lot of things, thinking a lot of things, but I couldn't quite pin any down. None of this was digesting. None of this made any sense. I had to look away from Dominic. When I saw him, I *only* saw him, and there was a shit ton else I had to get into perspective right now.

"I don't get it."

He rubbed a hand over his mouth. "I know it's a lot to take in."

"No, *no*. I mean, if any of this is true, I don't get why *me*." I heaved myself up on my elbows. "I'm not anyone. I'm not special. Why would they go through that extra effort to target me? It doesn't make sense."

It made such *little* sense, that the lack of sense actually helped bring me some relief. I breathed just a little deeper, felt a little lighter. The rainwater was draining from my lungs.

For a moment there, he really had me worried. What a fucking birthday present that would be. *'Happy Birthday! Prepare to be kidnapped!'*

Relief tingled in my chest, like fireflies buzzing around, and I pointed my attention back at Dominic now that I felt better.

A critical *something* was waiting for me on his face, and one by one, my fireflies began to fritz out and drown. That *something* wrapping around his rugged features suddenly took on a name as his gaze fell to the floor and spelled it out.

Guilt.

Dominic spit out the words so fast and so monotone, I barely understood them. "The other officers working the case seem to think you might have been targeted because you're connected to me."

I blinked. "What?"

Dominic leveled a sigh. "There are six others who have been working these cases off and on since it started. We assume the suspects know who each of us are since we've all given interviews on the cases or our names have been in the reports. None of the others have anyone in their immediate lives who fit the profile of women they've been taking. Except you."

Staring up at him, all I could think was that such a handsome face shouldn't be used to deliver such awful news. Such nasty, death-dealing words didn't belong in such a pretty mouth.

Sensation swelled in my chest as I processed them, rising up, up, up—almost feeling like a high—before crashing against ribs and nearly cracking bones. It rolled inside of me, flipping my stomach over again and again, caught in a tumbleweed of stinging nausea that grew bigger, and my mouth began to sweat.

I sat all the way up on the bed, crossing my legs and reaching my fingers through the cloud-soft comforter. My knuckles leached nearly as white as the fabric I was strangling, gripping so hard just to feel anything but the telltale pinch in my stomach.

Dominic squatted down next to the bed, laying his big hand near mine. He didn't touch me though. "What are you feeling?"

Sucking back a shaky breath, I said, "I'm debating whether I'm gonna throw up or not."

He left the side of the bed and came back a second later with a woven wood trash can, holding it in front of me. I stared at it, tracing the braided twigs as they overlapped with my eyes, going line by line until I made it down to where Dominic's right hand wrapped around it.

It was so strong and sturdy, knuckles thick and fingers long. Those were hands that were built to help. They were built to save everyone except me. His hands were crafted to specifically set me on fire. They burned so deeply whenever they touched me, they melted my brain and set my fears aflame. Now they'd dragged me to the bullseye of a deadly target.

I couldn't let him touch me. I didn't *want* him to help me.

"I don't want this." I chucked the wastebasket to the side. "I want you to tell me that this is some big fucking joke."

His head drooped, back rising with a deep sigh. "I wouldn't joke about this."

No. No, he wouldn't.

Everything went numb; the type of numb where you felt everything in your body more than you'd ever felt it before. The type of numb where you felt *too* much, and it all blurred into this overwhelming feeling of burning paralysis.

That's what it was. Everything wasn't numb.

Everything was *burning*.

My skin. My chest. My world. It was all burning to the fucking ground, and I couldn't move out of the flame. It consumed, raking red-hot talons down every inch of me, inside and out. Sweat burst into existence on my forehead, my neck, my back. My skin was rapidly turning the same crimson shade as the bikini I wore.

Smoke poured up my throat, spilling out in a voice that was already suffocating.

"So... wh—" I rasped, taking a moment to breathe. "What the fuck does that mean? Wha-w..."

Dominic stood to his full height in front of me, my head bowing back to watch him. He claimed my focus, every bit of it, looking as paramount as he did.

"I'm not letting anything happen to you. I promise."

I promise.

Those two words hit me the hardest, diving between my ribs and sinking their teeth in the core of my heart. I whimpered a pathetic kind of noise. Promises were like trust. They were made to be broken.

Angry blood poured out of the teeth marks in my betrayed, sick little heart. The blood filled me up, mixing with the flames to create a resentment so hot, I went off like a bomb set to obliterate.

"This is happening because of you," I seethed at him. "Because you just *needed* to hire me to fuck with your wife."

On his face, surprise made the quick change to affronted in seconds flat. "That's not very fair. You have no idea how responsible I feel already."

I cut over a narrowed glare. "Do you want points for feeling bad?"

"I want you to be *safe*."

"Kinda already fucked that up, didn't you?"

We held each other's furious stares for enough time that I dropped my face into my palms and screamed. "*Fuck!*"

My fingers slid up my heated face until they met damp hair, threading through and pulling. At first, the pull was moderate. Then a little harder. Then hard enough to feel that bite of pain that distracted from everything else going on, and all I felt was the burn in my scalp.

Eventually, I let go and panted into the crook of my knees. *Fuck* this fucking birthday.

"Is Charlotte safe?" I huffed.

"They don't take kids."

I sliced a cutting glower up to him. "Well, they didn't make fucking house calls before me either, so make sure my fucking sister is safe."

Dominic pondered only a moment before nodding. "I will. I'll send a patrol car out there to station for the night. Ryan and I are staying here to watch over you until tomorrow."

My head ripped up, eyes rounding.

"You're *staying*?"

"I know you'd rather me not, but this surpasses how you feel about me or don't." He hit that last word particularly hard. Hard enough to tell me I'd been successful yesterday in getting my message across. I *didn't* want to want him, and I bet I could get good at weaning my heart off of him if I had any practice at it.

That would mean he'd have to stop showing up anywhere I was within 24 hours of me swearing him off, trying to win me over or save my life. It was stupid bullshit like that that made my heart wheeze and wither.

"No," I said, shaking my head fast. "No, get someone else."

His reply was flat and infuriating. "I don't trust anyone else."

"And I don't trust you!" I shot up to my feet on the bed, wanting physical leverage over him if it was all that I could have. He had everything else. He held it all on a spike, teetering it this way and that and one misstep away from gutting my world straight through.

"You don't have to trust me," he gruffed, eyes like silver bullets. "You just have to stay where I can see you and let me do my job."

Staring down at him, horror jackknifed up my throat as I felt it begin.

No, no, no, no.

Heart palpitations—yeah, I fucking looked up what it was called—launched off in my chest. They went from non-existent to unbearable in mere seconds. The feeling was merciless, and I wanted to scream that this was happening *again*. I slapped my hand over my heart, trying to claw at my heart to make it stop. Even if it stopped beating altogether, it was better than this.

I'd rather die from a heart not feeling at all than a heart feeling too much.

The manic thrumming crawled up to my head, swamping it in too much. Too much of everything. Too much feeling. Too much fucking life skating around my mind with blades of flames instead of wheels. My head went round and round with the skates, spinning and burning until my face felt like it might actually erupt.

"Kat." Having been witness to now *three* of my panic attacks, Dominic came forward, ready to play hero. "Try to breathe through it."

His tone was an apology for bringing me to the point yet again, but I didn't want his apology. I just wanted it to stop.

"I *can't*." The searing fire beneath my skin was drying out all of my oxygen to a puff. My lungs contracted around nothing, eyes watering.

"Yes, you can."

Dominic pushed closer, coming right up beneath me, eyes bright with confidence that I could do this; I *could* fight the panic and win. Except I couldn't. His confidence in me was misplaced just like his affection.

"No, I *can't*, Dominic!" My feet dipped into the mattress until my back hit the wall with the headboard. "This—!" I choked down a gasp that tasted raw, like death. "Oh, god, *this* is what happens when I'm around you."

"And I won't force you to be around me after we clear that you're safe. You'll just have to survive until this is over, and then you won't have to see me again."

"That could take weeks or *months*."

My heart would give into the sickness by then, the issue of his marriage be damned.

"Then hope we catch these suspects soon. The sooner we catch them, the sooner this never has to happen again." This being the panic. The panic that attacked whenever we talked about us.

The way he spoke, he was pushing through smothered pain of his own, driving out the words he didn't want to say but forced himself to mean. He sounded like he was bargaining with me, trading my sanity for his infected heart. It had to hurt him to say those words.

It had to hurt worse knowing it was what I wanted.

"Can you just stop? *Please*?"

"Stop what?" He floated closer, concern and the want to do whatever it was I asked him brightening his stunning eyes. It was that selfless look that broke the lock holding back my thrashing temper and let it fucking rage.

"*This*. All of this! *You*. Stop acting so fucking nice when I don't want it! After yesterday, after all of that, you still ride in here like Prince Charming to save me. You made me into a damsel in distress, and I was already helpless enough around you to begin with. Now *this*? Are you fucking shitting me?"

"Kat—"

"How would Heather feel right now if she knew you were here, huh?"

"It doesn't matter how she would feel," he spoke carefully, lowering the tilt of his face. "I truly don't care how she would feel either."

I blanched, eyebrows skyrocketing into my hairline. "Did you seriously just say that? That you don't care how your *wife* feels about you being here?"

"Yes. I did. My being here isn't exactly of her concern."

Dominic edged closer to the bed, stalking in with slow movements and hands ready and waiting at his sides. I didn't even realize until then that I was dangerously close to the lip of the bed, my indignation wobbling me back and forth over the line of stable and falling face first on the floor.

The four or five drinks I had before probably weren't helping.

"Well, it should be!" I declared, a rush of adrenaline spiking in my veins. The feeling came on so fast and hard, you could have fooled me into believing I'd taken a hit of it. My blood was saturated with it, moving through my veins with more purpose than ever before, and I could *feel* it circulating through me.

I could feel goddamn everything.

"How is this happening? How is *any* of this happening?" I gripped at my damp hair again, tugging on the roots. "This is shit from *movies*, not real life. In real life, people don't-don't—"

"Kat, *breathe*."

"Is this, like, payback for trying to enjoy my birthday for once?" My toes found the edge of the bed as I leaned towards Dominic for answers. "Or karma for kissing you?"

"Be careful—"

"I need to know what the fuck I did to deserve this!" I yelled, but it fell out of me like a sob instead. The sob hit the air and crashed, detonating into a billion tiny shards with all I was afraid of smeared on their pointed edges.

I was afraid. I was so fucking afraid, my fears winding around my bones until they were the flesh creating me. My shoulders rose and fell as harsh breaths flooded through me on a relentless loop. I was locked on Dominic, one more hint of bad news away from imploding and splattering the hotel walls in fruity rum and all my crazy.

I hadn't even realized my hands were shaking until Dominic carefully folded his around them. Crescent indents from where my nails had been smiled up at me before Dominic smoothed them over. His gentle touch wracked my body in a shiver, both audible and physical.

"You didn't do anything," he began, voice resonating the deepest bass notes. "And no, this is not karma for what happened between us."

Air rattled up my chest, and I focused every ounce of frazzled energy I had on Dominic below me—on the timbre of his voice, and how it was so low, I could feel it vibrate through the air. It was its own energy, humming over my bare skin and trying to smooth down my erratic edges.

Soft tips of fingers traced the line patterns on my palms, and occasionally, the rough brush of his well-worked calluses scraped as well. Each touch delivered tiny shock waves and felt like heaven trying to sedate my personal hell.

"These are bad people, and they do bad things to people who don't deserve it, and I won't let them touch a goddamn hair on your head." Dominic angled his head up, eyes burning diamonds of sure-fire determination.

This man. This fucking man with his perfect words and perfect heart and perfect touch. I hated it. I hated *him* and how much I wanted him despite everything. He made me into a hypocrite of myself, and the sickness gave absolutely zero fucks about it.

The sickness didn't care that he was gazing up at me in a way he never should have. He had no business looking at me like I was his sun, bathing him in warmth. Especially after everything I said to him yesterday. I tore him apart, and I did so purposefully. I *hurt* him intentionally, and here he still was, rubbing the back of my hands like they were his hands to hold.

He curled his long fingers over mine to close my hands into loose fists. His thumbs ran over the thinnest part of my wrists, curving the underneath of my palms where it was most sensitive, pulling another shiver up my spine.

Dominic painted invisible art work over my skin, and I watched helplessly as he turned my sun-kissed body to a canvas to lay his hidden messages. The blunt edge of his thumbnail drew rotations of the infinity sign over my veins, and together, we watched them glow bluer for him than they'd ever been before.

Blue like the ocean. Blue like the ocean you swam through if you chose to love. Blue like the ocean that would crash and drown you in that stupid love.

Then, something not so blue caught my eye. Something out of place rather.

Something not there entirely.

My breath stuck in place. My heart followed.

"Where's your wedding ring?"

His gentle designs over my wrist slowed to a stop. The moment was so still, tied up on a string so delicate, breathing too hard might make it snap.

"I took it off."

Still staring at his big hands wrapped around mine, I asked, "Why?"

Cold swept my fingers as Dominic took his hands back to himself, leaving them dangling at his sides. Without them as a distraction, there was nothing giving me an excuse not to look at him. So I did, daring to stare back into eyes so profound, I wasn't at all convinced that they weren't their own worlds with stars of constellations making up their beauty.

"I tried to tell you why yesterday."

I thought back to yesterday, and I thought hard. He tried to tell me? All I remembered was screaming and crying. So much crying. I cut him with my words of knives and sent him away, bleeding out.

Yesterday felt like a tornado that we both walked away from, but neither of us survived. Thinking about it, remembering what was said in my current anxiety-high, intoxicated state of mind felt like trying to thread a needle with a frayed string. I kept trying though. I kept thinking and thinking until I pushed the thread through, pulling the string of words with it.

"Why did Heather slap you?"

My voice was soft, my question softer. There was nothing soft about my heartbeat though. It was pounding in my ears, crashing against my ribs, and loud enough that I was afraid I wouldn't hear what he said.

Then he said it, and I was afraid because I *did* hear it.

"Because I asked her for a divorce that morning."

My mind blanked. It became a vast gray landscape of nothing but those words. They cropped up like weeds, reaching their spindly roots out until they'd taken over. The soil they sprouted from made it easy for them to grow, saturated by guilt and watered with shame.

"The morning after we—"

"We'd been separated for almost a month before that," he cut in. "That's why I've been staying in the guest bedroom."

Awe parted my mouth, eyes searching through his for more answers.

"Why didn't you tell me?"

"You asked me to pretend like the night in the garage didn't happen. I didn't want to pressure you into feeling like anything had to change between us if you didn't want it to."

I didn't mean to, but shock literally pushed a loud puff of air out of my lungs. I didn't know what to think or say or feel. My tongue touched the back of my teeth to try and form words, but nothing came out.

Dominic waited patiently for me to find the words, and when I couldn't, he let his take their place. "I wasn't planning on asking her until that night, but she cornered me, and I didn't want to lie to her anymore than I already am."

With the mention of lying—of how much he'd already had to do it because of *us*—I found my voice to whisper, "I don't want you to get a divorce because of me."

His gaze became soft, delicate like satin.

"I'm not."

He drug his hands up his work slacks, stuffing them in their pockets. "Kat, my marriage has been over for a long time. Years. It started before Maya was born and got worse after. I fought for a few of those years to make it work, and then I kept fighting a little after that. I'd stopped fighting before you ever came along and accepted that my marriage would be an unhappy one."

His voice lowered with his stare. "I've never liked the idea of divorce. It felt so much like giving up."

I believed him. Fuck me, but I believed him.

I believed that sadness drenching his tone too. He really wanted his marriage to work, even if it broke his back trying to hold it together. He'd broken so many parts of himself for their relationship, and I saw them all now like he never let me see them before.

His heart was scarred from too many breaks, too many times. His spirit had been beaten down to a bitter thing, calloused and cold. His shoulders were worn and bruised from carrying the brunt of the failing marriage for years, and I wanted to scream how that's all love ever amounted to: broken hearts and broken souls.

I couldn't though. Not right now. Not when all his broken pieces were creating such painfully beautiful fragments that, all combined, crafted this breathtaking mural of a man.

I didn't think about what I was doing. Just moved with the flow of my heart as I reached out to touch him. My fingertips danced in hesitation over his shoulder, my thumb hovering along the line of his jaw.

Slowly, I gave into the pull of his skin to mine and cradled his cheek in my palm.

An immediate, reactionary sigh poured out of him. His eyes shut for a moment, feeling me and allowing me to erase some of his pain. I'd never done that for anyone before. I'd always *been* the pain.

Never its cure.

Languidly, he peeled those dark lashes back up and showed me his eyes that had been doused by starlight. Glowing and warm from just a touch. *My* touch.

"You're not the reason I asked for a divorce, Kat, but you were my wake up call," he emphasized. "I knew fairly early on that you could do me in. I tried to ignore it or fight it because I was *so* certain that, one taste of you, and I'd be done. All the fighting, all the hours spent wondering how I could fix it, all nine years of marriage wouldn't matter anymore because you would destroy me..." His perfect mouth curved up on the side. "In the best way possible."

'I didn't mean you'd destroy me as a bad thing.'

His words. He said that the first time we kissed. I argued I was bad, and he insisted I wasn't. He knew then. He knew kissing me would be the end of his marriage, and he did it anyway. He'd always known I would be his ruination if he let himself get too close, and he wasn't afraid of it—of *me*. He wanted it.

He wanted me to destroy him so I could build him anew.

My mind overwhelmed and reeling, Dominic kept leading us closer to the precipice as he slid his hands around my waist and held me.

Adoration softened his features as he gazed up at me.

I'd never been looked at like that before.

"I get this feeling sometimes that I've been waiting for you for a long time." He squeezed me tight. "I missed you before I ever even knew you."

Thunder clapped inside my chest, placed there by him. His thunder rolled around, clouds of it tangling with my lightning and encouraging it to not strike, but just *be*. The thunder wanted the lightning's submission so it could keep it safe, envelop it, do what thunder did best and chase away all that made it scared.

Never had I ever thought of giving myself to someone like I was right now. It was a crazy thought. A sick need. I'd never wanted so badly to fall and detonate and forget about the consequences.

Then again, I'd never met anyone like Dominic Reed who promised I could fall through his sky and he would catch me.

Like he did that day in the park.

His hands were still firm on the dips of my waist, and I didn't think, not for one sensible second, or else I would have thought myself back to safety and kept my feet on the ground.

Instead—

"One, *two*."

And I jumped.

I was airborne, feet launched off the mattress, heart jumping with me up and up. I held my breath like I was jumping feet first into that goddamn ocean, pinching my eyes closed as I braced for the stinging onslaught.

Hands tightened around my slim waist, and my entire body became suspended in mid-air, vice grips above my hips letting me soar.

Testing my eyes, they fluttered open, looked down... and there he was.

Smiling up at me in that speech-rendering kind of way, lopsided and dazzling.

"Always," he heartened. "I'll always catch you."

The sound that came out of me next was somewhere between a sigh and a sob, and before he could say anything else, I threw myself off our cliff and sunk my mouth down to his.

Warm lips pressed against mine, and I realized just how cold I was without him. I clung closer to him, slipping my arms around his neck so I could steal his warmth and the breath right off his soft lips. Dominic groaned something almost pained, running his hands up my back to hold me better, to fit my body against his like the interlocking puzzle pieces they were.

This kiss was sweet. Sweeter than milk and honey. Sweeter than sugar. It tripped my brain, inebriating it more than all the drinks I'd consumed, and I became addicted to the high. Maybe I had an addictive personality. Maybe that was something else I got from my mother. The chances were looking more likely as I got greedy, locking my fingers through his hair and anchoring myself to him like I had every intention of sucking his soul straight out and replacing it with mine.

Dominic even tried to stop me.

"Kat," he mumbled against me, but I kissed my name off of his lips and stole it back. I didn't want to stop. If I stopped, then I'd have to think about the aftermath of this kiss when I just wanted to keep soaring. I wanted to keep tasting him and touching him and colliding with him like devastation wasn't inevitable.

I teased my tongue along the seam of his soft lips, my teeth following behind as I nibbled at the bottom one, earning myself a primal grunt in response. Satisfaction spread from cheek to cheek, a wily thing that disappeared as Dominic kissed it gone, forgetting he was trying to stop me seconds ago and stealing the flavor of me for himself with his hungry tongue.

Moans ripped up my throat as he deepened our kiss, my fingers untangling from his hair and dropping to the buttons on his shirt. I plucked them open one by one, locking my ankles behind his back.

"Bed," I muttered against his lips, tugging at his shirt.

His response was a throaty groan and a shameless squeeze of my ass in his big hands. We were falling back on the bed the very next second, him between my legs and my fingers tearing his shirt down his well-built arms. Dominic helped rip it off at the end, not ever breaking our lips to do it. Heavy breathing quilted the hotel room as we groped and violated every line set in front of us from day one.

I pawed at his undershirt, wanting to feel his bare skin on mine so badly, I would even risk praying for it. I would beg one god for the chance to fuck another. Thankfully, God didn't have to get involved because Dominic listened to my needy tugs, pulling our kiss apart long enough to peel his undershirt off.

Holy fuck.

I paused, eyes stretching wide in my head as I realized I'd never seen Dominic shirtless before now. I was kicking myself for not stripping him of his shirt any time I was ever within arms reach, because *wow*.

That home gym did *not* go to waste.

"You're like a fucking Ken doll," I breathed, flattening my hand over his bare stomach. Each hard ab contracted beneath my fingers as he laughed, and my mouth watered enough to drown me.

My nails traced in light strokes between every sculpted ridge and defined plane of muscle, and Dominic let me. He let me get to know his body, memorize every line and bulge of his golden skin until one bulge in particular caught my eye.

"Well..." With a smirk, my hand traveled down the thin trail of dark hair that disappeared under the band of his pants and grabbed onto the bulge tenting them. "Except for this."

Dominic hissed through his teeth as I fisted his cock through his pants, squeezing just so. "I don't think any of my Ken dolls had this growing up."

Dominic slumped to his elbows over top of me, leaving just enough space so my hand could stay where it was between us. His forehead crinkled as his brows dove together, uneven breaths pushing and pulling out of him as I stroked my hand up.

"Kat," he warned, a low growl.

I repeated the movement and arched an eyebrow. "Sir?"

Eyes of burning lust flashed up to me, striking a match between my legs that made my core sweat with arousal. He was so fucking hot. My fingers could barely touch around his cock, and I couldn't wait any longer to feel him without the barrier of his pants.

Stares fixed together, I brought my hand up to the buckle of his belt.

Only to have his hand move it away.

I pouted up at him, a real award-winning pout, and tried again. This time, he wrapped his hand around mine and pinned it next to my head.

"What gives?" I whined, really leaning into the pouting thing.

He reprimanded me with a slanted look. "I'm not having sex with you."

"Ever?"

Every single inch of his oh-so-serious face cracked as Dominic let out a bark of laughter, throwing his head back. He came back down with a smile in his eyes.

"No, not never. Just not now. You've been drinking, and I'm still married."

"So you can give me an orgasm while you're still married but can't have sex with me?" I tipped an impish smile up at him, catching the absurdity of his standards roll across his eyes.

"I know. I'm not going to pretend it makes sense, but it's the last rule I have standing with you. I broke all the rest."

"Breaking rules is so much *fun* though," I said, grinding my hips up. His erection pressed into my pelvis, the feeling soaking my swim bottoms and tearing moans from both of us. A rough hand clasped around my hip bone, trapping my tormenting pelvis to the bed.

"We're waiting," he stressed, granite stare leaving no room for argument.

A scoff that was mostly playful raked up my chest, and my head lolled to the side.

"Fine."

I acted annoyed, but really, I understood. I even kind of appreciated it, though I'd never admit that out loud. My reputation would be at stake if I even hinted that I liked the idea of him wanting to wait until it was right rather than dive into my pants the second he's able.

No. I could never, ever admit such a corny thing out loud.

Dominic cast an eyebrow up, his smile pulling amused and lopsided.

"Thank you."

I hummed in response, rolling my eyes and making him chuckle. He lifted a strand of my damp hair from my forehead thoughtfully, moving it back with the rest. The move was so simple, and he did it so absentmindedly, it slowed time to a pause for me.

This man was so unique; I wondered if he was even a man at all. Maybe he really was part god. It would explain his behavior today and every other day that

I'd known him. He didn't act like any other man I'd ever met. He didn't act like the world existed only to revolve around him.

He *especially* proved that to be true today.

"And thank you," I whispered. "For coming here even though I was a bitch yesterday."

A crease of sadness folded across his face. "You weren't—"

"I was," I cut in, touching my fingertips to his bare chest. "I know I was. I was trying to hurt you to make you leave and..." I steadied myself, swallowing down gobs of oxygen. "You didn't deserve that. When I'm wrong, I say I'm wrong, and that was... *wrong*."

Uncomfortable tingles poked at my chest, and I found my fingers working distractions into the sheets beneath us. I sucked back my bottom lip, chewing it over as the awkward moment lingered.

"I shouldn't have kept pushing you either." *True.*

I was still way more wrong than he was. He wasn't the one who wielded words and feelings against him because hurting him was the only way I knew. What I felt for him was an attack on everything I'd built my life on, and lashing out was all I knew how to do to keep the world I'd constructed for Charlotte and I safe from people who would hurt us.

"Do you want to talk about the panic attacks?" His gentle question breathed down on me, weaved of deep notes and no judgement.

"No. No..." My fingers resumed fiddling with the comforter below, not looking anywhere at him. "I'd actually really like to pretend they don't exist and kidnappers aren't after me and that I'm not totally fucked in the head."

I breathed a laugh to push away how pitiable I was, but it got absorbed into the silence. A lump fused to life in my throat when I stopped being a little bitch long enough to meet his gaze.

It was so fucking beautiful, pearly rays streaking through like the sun piercing storm clouds. His bright affection quite literally stole my volume away to no more than a murmur.

"Make that my birthday wish. Pretend with me. Just for today."

Dominic gazed down at me, his devotion never dulling in intensity. A faint curve twisted to life at the ends of his full lips. A grateful breath expanded in my lungs when he placed those lips on mine, gifting me a slow, tender kiss.

He pulled back, drawing my soul right to the surface to follow him.

"Happy Birthday, Ms. Sanders."

TWENTY-SEVEN

I t took a few more kisses, a lot more not-so-innocent touching, and a promise of free food before Dominic and I left the hotel room.

We met back with Layla and Ryan—Dominic's partner—at the pool, and all four of us went to lunch at one of the hotel restaurants. I wanted to go to this fancy Mexican place right down the street from the resort, but Dominic put his foot down and said it wasn't safe.

Did I really think that *if* these kidnappers were after me—big if—that they'd followed us an hour out of town to snatch me up on my birthday?

No. Not really. As far as I was concerned, with Dominic and Ryan here and being nowhere near our town, we were safe.

Unfortunately, Ryan had filled Layla in on the situation while Dominic and I were gone, and she freaking took Dominic's side in the restaurant debate. Whatever. Free food was free food, and Dominic had already said I could get whatever I wanted for my birthday.

Cut to three margaritas, two baskets of cheese fries, and one red velvet cupcake *with* a candle to blow out later.

Layla had some drinks with me, and even Ryan ordered a beer. The only one who didn't participate was Dominic, who sat in stiff enjoyment for most of the meal, one eye on me and the other watching for any threats.

That continued when we took the party to the game hall, and Layla and I kicked their asses in ping pong and pool. Twice. Ryan was having a way better time than his counterpart, shooting sly glances Layla's way that she shamelessly reveled in.

"'I'm totally fucking him tonight,'" she'd whispered to me when we were chalking our cue sticks. I chuckled and muttered back, *"'Do it. Someone should get laid on my birthday.'"*

That's about where we were in the night.

Layla and I were back in our hotel room, and she was getting dressed with the hopes of being undressed soon after. I was laying on the bed Dominic and I made out on hours earlier, inhaling the elemental scent of him and sighing.

"Are you *sure* it's okay if I go out?" Layla asked. Again.

"For the thousandth time, yes." I rolled over onto my stomach, propping my head up on the heel of my palms. "Just because I'm not getting any tonight doesn't mean you can't."

"Okay, okay! I just feel bad."

"Well, don't. Ryan's cute. Plus, he had a hard-on for you the entire time we were playing pool."

"Well, I *was* shoving my ass in the direction of his crotch as often as I saw an opening."

I snickered, remembering Ryan's face as the evening progressed. When I said he had a hard-on the entire time, I meant it literally. The dude kept shifting his stance and hiding his crotch behind the pool table, cheeks flushed red. He had this boyish charm and panty-dropping grin that complemented Layla's wild streak and big brown doe eyes perfectly.

They'd only met today, and already, they were more of an item than Dominic and I.

He and I had been keeping a respectable distance since our heated tryst earlier. He was too busy being on guard, and I was too worried about what Ryan did or didn't know about us to make a move. We'd done a lot of dancing around each other, and my dancing feet were fucking tired.

Layla nodded her head towards the hotel door.

"Is he still outside standing guard?"

She meant Dominic. He and Ryan were taking turns standing outside our door through the night. Right now was Dominic's shift, and Ryan was back in the room they'd booked for the night.

"He should be. I doubt Mr. Rulebook would stray."

"Hey." Layla was giving me a glare that reminded me of her mother when I slid a sulking look her way. "Don't be mad because he's taking this seriously. He cares about you. Get used to it."

"It's hard," I grumbled, smothering my face into the mattress.

The bed dipped next to me, cool fingers shifting my hair from above my ear, tucking it back and behind. Groaning, I twisted my neck to lay my cheek against the covers, peeking a squinting eye up at my best friend.

"I know. You're used to shitty people. 'Cept for me, 'cause I'm fucking awesome." She flipped a lock of dark hair over her shoulder, and I sputtered a laugh. "I know he's not what you're used to, and that's exactly why you deserve someone like him, Kit Kat."

My mouth peeled to the side. "Someone married?"

She flicked my ear, and I hissed out a laugh.

"Someone who will take care of you."

"I don't need anyone to take care of me," I said, muffling my voice into the bedding.

"I know you don't *need* it, but wouldn't it be nice?"

No. Because then I might get used to it. Then I might begin to need it. Then he might leave, and I might not remember how to live without it, and Charlotte would suffer.

"*Hey.*" Another flick to my ear. "Stop overthinking."

"Ow!" Grabbing my ear, I scrambled back on the bed until my feet were back on the floor. "Don't you have someone to go fuck so you can leave my ears alone?"

She popped up, fixing her little black dress back in place. "I do. And you..." She bent over to her suitcase, rummaging through before yanking something loose and tossing it my way.

"You're gonna wear that and finish your birthday right."

Kneading the silken bathing material between my fingers, I sighed and shook my head. "He won't have sex with me until he's divorced. I told you that."

"I know, but that doesn't mean you can't still have fun with him." She shoved on a pair of four or five inch golden heels, readying to go. "I *know* you're not trying to tell me you two weren't the reason your bed looked like it'd been through a thorough romp when we got back here."

Guilty.

Layla walked up, now a good half a head taller than me. She blinked her gold smeared eyelids, fixing me with a stare that kept my lips shut. "Your birthday isn't over yet. Spend the last of it looking like a queen with that knight in shining armor standing outside our door."

So, she got that vibe from him too, huh?

Exhaling, I dropped my eyes to the bathing suit and gripped it tight.

Stupid birthdays. Stupid expectations from everyone that today had to be special. Even stupider that I kind of wanted it to be special. I kind of wanted exactly what Layla described, and I hated myself for it.

I hated myself because I was going to do it. *Fuck me*, but I was going to end today exactly how I wanted to, despite how dumb it might be come tomorrow morning when Dominic and I were done pretending.

Layla, sensing my decision, gave a supportive squeeze around my arm before disappearing out the door with her phone and room key in hand. I heard her greet Dominic, his ocean-deep voice addressing her back before the door fell shut.

With anticipation in my belly, I strode into the bathroom, the thin piece of fabric in hand and wiggled my way into it. *Wiggled* being quite a fitting description given how it was Layla's, and her tits were a good two sizes smaller than mine, and squeezing the girls into this plunging one piece was a bit of a workout.

I managed though, tying midnight black strings around the back of my neck to fix the suit in place. Smoothing my palms down the soft material, I jerked my head up to take in the finished product.

I watched my jaw drop in the mirror.

"Holy shit. I'd fuck me."

The front of the suit left little to the imagination, dipping a deep V to just above my belly button. It clung around my slight waist, leading up and up to the swell of my tits that were brazenly visible. They looked like soft mounds of pure white snow strapped beneath the strict black lines of the little one piece. I ruffled my fingers through my thick waves of hair, zhuzhing it up, and pinched my fingers over my cheeks.

People did that in movies, right?

A swipe of strawberry balm over my lips and a satisfied wink in the mirror, and I turned for the door, electricity buzzing in my stomach. I didn't let myself stop once I made it to the thick-wooded maroon door. No stopping to second guess, no stopping to give myself a pep talk, because I knew I'd pep talk myself right outta this.

For tonight, we were still playing pretend, and my favorite birthday present was standing on the other side of this door.

Fingers on the knob, I twisted it open and stepped out.

Dominic was standing against the wall next to the door, stance wide set and arms crossed. My eyes were on his face as one of his thick eyebrows kicked up, head angling down in my direction. His stare touched mine for only a second. Then it was gone, raking down the trap of bare legs and well-placed curves I'd set for him.

He ate me all up, devoured the sight of me with unblushing dedication. I cocked an audacious hip out, and his eyes followed it, jaw pinching tight and pupils blowing wider, making him look just a bit wild. A bit predatory.

"Fancy a midnight swim?" I hummed, leaning against the doorframe.

A slow inhale filled out his chest, eyes of burning charcoal never lifting above my chin. His lips parted, but it took a few seconds before any words came out. And when they did, they were rough as grinding rocks.

"That's not playing fair."

Excitement welled in my stomach, and I innocently crossed my ankles over one another.

"I have no idea what you mean."

Slowly, that dark embered gaze rose to me. A pleased-as-punch grin quivered my cheeks, and I locked my lips together to hold it in place.

He was *mad*. Not mad mad, but the kind of mad that was fun to poke at and see what happened next. The kind that said he knew the game I was playing, and he wasn't amused.

He spoke through lips barely parted. "Go back inside your room."

"I wanna go swimming."

"The pool is closed."

"And?"

The side of his mouth twitched despite him keeping his voice even and lecturing. "That usually means something to most people."

"Yeah. Boring people."

He argued. "Law-abiding people."

I hummed, dropping a glance down his front, a heavy smirk dragging across my lips. "Those are the worst offenders of all."

Flickering my gaze back up, I found Dominic caught in a war of wills with himself, and my playful smirk parted in sorrow. He'd been so worried all day despite promising me he'd pretend everything was okay until tomorrow. I wasn't sure he'd taken a full breath since he'd gotten here. He was all shallow breathing and laser-eyed focus around every corner.

Now, our chemistry had polluted the air between us, poisoning his strict principled compass and making it spin out.

He was clearly struggling for what to do.

So much of him wanted to lock me back in the room where it was safe and no one but him could get me. So much of him wanted to play along and forget about the danger so we could be *us* for a bit. Once we left this hotel tomorrow and went back home, nothing would be as easy as it was at this very moment.

I pushed myself off the doorframe, closing in on him. "Dominic, my birthday's almost over. Tomorrow, everything goes back to normal." Wives, kidnappers, the panic. The whole twisted shebang. "Are you really gonna make me spend the last few minutes of my birthday alone?"

"Guilt trips aren't fair when your safety is at risk."

The hard-lined muscles in Dominic's stomach tensed as I pressed myself to him, coming right up beneath him with whispered words and fluttering eyelids. "I'm very clearly not playing fair."

"No," he rumbled, eyes flaming hot. "You're clearly not."

Tilting up on my tiptoes, I brushed strawberry flavored lips against his, pulling his hot breath into my lungs.

"Be a little bad with me, Mr. Reed," I murmured. "It's the only rule I'll ask you to break tonight."

Punishing hands came to rest on my hips, squeezing them tight like he meant to push me away, but instead he drew me in. Regret slashed a line down his handsome face. "I'm supposed to be watching over you. Not going for late night swims."

"But you will be watching over me." I slid my arms around his trim waist, fusing us into one beating, breathing heart. "You'll be with me the whole time. Plus, since it's closed, no one should even be around for you to worry about."

Still, he didn't look convinced.

"Or we could go back in the room and hang out?" I suggested.

Dominic cut the room next to us a dark look. "I'm not going in there with you."

My head tipped back beneath his like I was star-gazing in his eyes, and I pouted. It was kind of my thing today. "Why not?"

He lowered his fixated attention to my mouth—to the swollen bottom lip I'd pushed out just for him—and swallowed hard.

"Because I'm positive I would break our only rule if I did."

Immediate flashes of his naked body and mine, tangled together in crisp white sheets, skipped behind my eyes. I saw my mouth parted in a moan, sweat clinging to his forehead, our bodies joined in a tantalizing rhythm of slapping hips. Tingles that felt both hot and cold zipped down my spine, pooling between my legs in such an obvious way. I shifted my legs, squeezing my thighs, and held onto Dominic tighter.

Oh I was so fucked—except literally.

Even the implication that he wanted to have sex with me got me wetter than any swimming could.

"Do you like the outfit?" I asked, pressing all my ten fingers into his strong back, nails waiting in ready to strike.

He felt them, eyes going hooded. "I hate it."

"You don't hate anything," I breathed heavily.

"I hate that I can't rip it off of you."

My breathing tripped over itself, core clenching. More images of us in positions that would make nuns fall to their knees and pray piled through my head. Lust mingled in the air, braiding with our chemistry and knotting Dominic and I together like our souls were trying to fuck as much as every other part of us.

My back arched me against him, a tether in my chest linked right to his heart. His eager hands dug deeper into my waist, holding me closer and branding his touch beneath my skin, his thunder riding my veins. I sheathed my nails into his back just to watch sparks fly over his gray sky eyes and feel that growl of warning vibrate up his sternum.

This was turning too hot too quickly, and somewhere in our desire-addled brains, we knew we had to stop until those papers were signed.

"So..." I swallowed down my lust, wetting my parched throat. "Pool?"

Dominic pulled back a deep breath, sliding his palms up to my bare back. "I don't have any swim shorts."

"You have gym shorts. I saw you buy them earlier at the gift shop."

He tipped a small smile. "To sleep in."

"So sleep naked."

That small smile drew all lazy and charmed, his hold on me going softer and sweeter than moments ago. He stroked tempered lines across my back, the tenderness in his touch fanning up to his eyes and warming them.

He was deciding what to do with me. His little lightning who wanted to celebrate her birthday all wrapped up in the thunder until the sun decided to shine, and we'd have to go back into hiding.

We couldn't very well keep standing outside this door, torturing ourselves to see just how close we could come to tearing each other's clothes off without actually doing it. We had to do something, and a decision solidified across his rugged face that had a smile turning up my cheeks.

He sighed.

"You get 30 minutes."

TWENTY-EIGHT

"See? I told you. No one out here."

Dominic held the pool gate open for me to walk through, tossing watchful glances up and down the walkway. "All that does is remind me we shouldn't be out here either."

"Would you relax?" I saddled up next to one of the pool chairs, kicking off my flip flops. "They even left the gate unlocked. They're basically inviting people in."

Dominic cut me a hard look over his shoulder.

"Your reasoning is impressive."

I beamed, pushing my posture straight. "Thank you."

His eyes rolled shut, a slight tug on his full mouth. He let the gate close behind him, easing it shut so it didn't make a sound. I puffed a laugh, shrugging off the sleeping shorts Dominic made me put on for the walk down here.

He strode over, glints from the gently lapping pool water casting white streaks over his shadowed face as he watched me kick out of the shorts. I loved that he didn't hide the way he was staring at me, soaking up every inch of me with eyes so intense, they burned brighter than any star above us.

He didn't have to hide his hunger, his want, his infatuation with my body.

Tonight, it was all his, and he knew it.

Silver eyes traveled up to mine, the backs of his jaw pulsing once.

I pointed my chin in his direction, speaking low. "You next."

Fixed on me, Dominic began removing his shoes—his godforsaken wingtip shoes because that's all he had. Next went his undershirt, riding over smooth slabs of muscle up and up until he pulled it over his head, gaze still trapped on me.

His already dark hair appeared darker against the night, nearly onyx as it struggled to stay in place and perfect. He folded his shirt neatly, laying it on a chair next to him. The way the ropes of muscles moved as he did was fucking mesmerizing, especially in the dancing light from the pool.

"What are you thinking?"

The gruff of his voice zapped my focus back to his face, a flash of heat running down the length of me. I swallowed, clearing my throat.

"That we should get in the water."

"Why's that?"

"Because if I don't, I might actually combust," I admitted, tonguing the corner of my mouth.

His sharp eyes tracked the movement, smoldering dangerously. He nodded, and I hightailed it to the steps leading into the pool, not waiting a moment longer before sinking into it. Every fire-hot patch of skin sizzled and steamed, cooling off as I drowned myself up to the shoulders in the cool water.

My neck loosened, a sigh leaving my lips as I closed my eyes. Gentle licks of water brushed against my shoulders as Dominic entered the pool behind me, silent and an undeniable presence. In my heart of hearts, I believed the water moved for him unlike it did for anyone else. I believed the breeze rolled in softly to match his calm, and even the moon shone brighter and bigger to give him the perfect spotlight.

I rose up and turned around to face him, water sloshing over my waist. He was waiting for me, beautiful in a way I couldn't describe. Beautiful in a way that didn't have words. His beauty struck thought from my brain and air from my lungs, leaving me exposed and unable to tell him just how much I liked that he was here.

Unable to string the letters together to tell him how much that terrified me.

Somehow, he seemed to know.

"Come here."

I was moving before he finished the sentence, cutting through the water up to him. I threw my arms around his neck and pulled my legs up around his waist like I was climbing him. A quiet laugh caught between the wind and splashing water, peeking an easy smile on his lips. Warm hands cupped beneath my thighs, helping secure me in place as I wrapped myself around him, molding our wet bodies together in every place possible.

Dominic was smiling in every way a person could. "Hi."

"Hi," I breathed back.

Lapping water filled the silence as he scanned across my face.

"How was your birthday?"

Despite the potential kidnappers? "Considering I usually try to skip out on my birthday entirely, I'd say this one wasn't so bad."

Dominic's thick brows pinched. "You don't like birthdays?"

"I like birthdays. Just not mine."

"Any reason?"

You could say so.

Usually, I would tell a lie because I didn't like talking about it. It was a shitty day that started off a shitty year that produced a shitty life. That day was at the center of everything fucked up with me. With Dominic though, lying had never gotten me anywhere and maybe... maybe I didn't hate the idea of telling him.

Maybe I wanted him to know because I knew he'd care.

Dominic gave an affectionate squeeze around my waist and pushed the truth right out.

"My eighteenth birthday is when my dad walked out on us."

I held my breath. Over his face, I waited and watched the outrage take hold, stringing through his thickly shaped brows and seeping into the divots of his quickly souring stare. Even his skin beneath mine scorched hotter, boiling the water around us.

"In his defense, I think he forgot it was my birthday, and he left at like, three in the morning the day of, so..." I trailed off, feeling awkward and naked, never a good combination of things to be.

Dominic hadn't said a word, instead taking on that favored expression of his that made his thoughts hieroglyphic.

"You're kinda wondering what you got yourself into, aren't you?" I asked, pushing out a weak laugh.

The pathetic noise seemed to jostle him out of his own head. He blinked, taking his stare up to my forehead, moving it down and around my entire face in a sweeping caress. Eventually, he centered back on my eyes, wearing a sadness woven just for me.

"No. I just don't know how anyone could leave you."

My heart or the lightning—or both—*zapped*.

"It's pretty easy." I curved my fingers over some flyaways tickling my ear. "Once you get to know me."

"I know you pretty well, and I don't want to leave you."

I smiled a sad smile. "Give it time."

Everyone left everyone eventually, one way or another.

My dad left on my birthday. My mom disappeared into herself shortly after. My grandparents already dead at that point, there was no one left to leave. It was just me and Charlotte. Aside from the exception of Layla, I was a person people left. It was something about me. The ugly in me made them do it, I guess.

Lucky people were loved in spite of their ugliness.

No one wanted to stick around me long enough to love me in spite of mine.

That was okay, though. I didn't need them to love me. I only needed my baby sister, and that's why Dominic Reed was such a complication.

Especially when he said things like, "Time is one thing I'm sure will only make me more addicted to you, Ms. Sanders."

My lips stretched to a closed smile, and I looked down between us.

"It's funny that you use the word 'addicted'."

"Why?"

"Because that's what I call what we have in my head. I call it our Heroin Chemistry."

The silence that followed stretched out like a ripple.

"That sounds intense."

I flashed my eyes up, catching him with unflinching focus. "Because it is. Isn't it?"

Almost like he didn't want to, he nodded—a rigid thing of uneasy acknowledgement. I was glad to see he was unsettled by it, or at least by the potency of its name.

"Is that why you panic around me?" he asked, voice soft like the water. "Because of this heroin chemistry?"

A fist clenched in my chest, gripping all my air tight.

"You said we wouldn't talk about it on my birthday."

Out of the pool, Dominic raised his arm. His eyes fell to the black watch fit around his wrist, bright blue numbers lighting it up, and he showed it to me.

"Your birthday ended twelve minutes ago."

My mouth fell open at it, an indignant grumble spilling out. "Stupid technicality."

Dominic's hand dipped back below the surface, grabbing around my upper thigh. Then, we were moving, walking back through the water to the edge of the pool. I let him move me where he wanted me, lifting me up and setting me on the pool's lip, my butt and legs still in the water and Dominic still between them.

He'd given me physical leverage over him, my head slightly above his and him staring up at me, the high slant of his cheeks donning shiny droplets and his eyes looking like rain. Sorrowed and serious, gloom swelling his pupils.

"When we leave here tomorrow, I'll be around you to protect you. It could be weeks, it could be longer. How are you going to feel having me around that much?"

"Depends. Can we go at each other like two teens who just discovered 3rd base?"

While the edge of his mouth curled up, it didn't reach his eyes.

"I'm serious." My kittenish smile fell, drowning in the water below. "Tell me what happens tomorrow when we're done pretending nothing's wrong."

A shaking breath packed my lungs, and I dropped his intense stare.

Come tomorrow morning, the clock was up on this act that I'd been playing more than him. All he had to do was pretend I wasn't in danger—which he failed—and not talk about my panic—which he failed.

I was *way* more willing to play the part of careless and willfully ignorant. Sign me up for that all day long. Ignoring whatever danger Dominic thought I was in was easy peasy. Ignoring that how I felt about him crumbled my entire foundation was the real trick, but I was loving pretending.

I loved kissing him when I felt like it. I loved holding him and him holding me without fear of being caught. I loved pretending like, for just a day, I was allowed to drown in him, and it was okay if I never came back up for air.

For today, the sickness hadn't been deadly. It had been like flying.

Now, Dominic was clipping my wings and letting me crash back down to reality.

The truth rammed around my ribcage, letting me experience the pain of it from the inside before I let it out. Guilt, even though I didn't have a reason to be guilty, muted my voice to a murmur.

"The only thing that's changed since yesterday is your marriage ending."

Wind rustled bushes and swayed trees around us, whistling a soft note for the pause between us to ride along. Dominic ended it, breaking the softness with his hard-edged voice.

"You still don't want me?"

My teeth clenched at his words, grinding as I turned my head away. Steam could have come out of my nose I was suddenly so hot and so angry. I hated that he was bringing that up. I hated that I said it. I hated that by the timbre of his voice, he knew it wasn't really true.

So much hate and nowhere for it to go.

"Kat, look at me."

"What?" I snapped, a one word dagger. He searched back and forth between my slitted eyes.

"Why did you get so upset just now?"

My lip curled back. "Because you're bringing up things I don't want to talk about."

"Why not?"

"Because I'm childish and immature and *petty*."

He didn't buy it for a second. "You and I both know that's not true or why."

"Then why did you ask me?"

"Because I wanted you to say it."

"Say *what*?"

He hesitated for only one second, and that silent second only built the anticipation higher. Made it and me breakable.

"You're scared of your feelings for me," he stated boldly.

And I was right. It did break me.

Panic felt like a balloon expanding inside of me, fast and squishing between every organ. It was *more* than uncomfortable, *more* than intrusive, and I shifted myself where I was sitting as if I was about to bolt. The only thing keeping me there was how Dominic had started rubbing his hands up and down the tops of my thighs in purposeful, steady movements.

He was smoothing down the razored edges of my panic one stroke at a time, a firm look in his eyes saying he knew what he was doing. He was pushing me and pacifying me at the same time, dropping me in the middle of the ocean but keeping my head above water so I could breathe and talk and survive with him.

"You like me, and you don't want to. You care about me, and you don't want to. You think about me as much as I think about you, and you wished you didn't."

An audible breath rattled up my chest. My stomach cramped and I grabbed at where it hurt, fisting my skin like I could tear it off and pull out what hurt.

Our eyes still locked, Dominic cupped a hand over mine, carefully easing my fingers back and away, replacing my hand with his, flattening it over my stomach. He pressed, but not hard. Just enough to put some pressure behind the heat he was delivering with his touch, relieving some of the ache like he was slowly burning it out of me.

"The only thing I don't know is why you're so afraid of it all."

"Didn't you hear the story?" I rasped. "Daddy issues."

The gray of his irises turned thoughtful. Weighty.

"Do you think I'll leave you?"

Yes, but that wasn't it. He'd leave me, and he'd take my heart with him and away from Charlotte who needed it more than either of us. She already had a heartless mother. I couldn't hollow out my chest and become another zombie parent to her.

"I think you'll ruin me like I ruined you." I held his eye, stomach fluttering as I told him, "Except I don't want to be ruined."

I was already damaged goods.

Plenty damaged and plenty brittle, despite the hardened face I put on. A strike from Dominic would do me in for good. He had *that* much power in his potential to love me.

For the first time since he set me up on the pool ledge, he looked away. His focus centered on my chin instead, spots of somber consideration fading in and out over his face. Muscles in my hand twitched to reach out and touch him, run my fingers through his thick hair and stroke the stubbled line of his jaw.

I kept my hand where it was.

"So what do you want from us?" he questioned after a moment, setting his attention back on me.

Truthfully?

I wanted to be selfish with him. I wanted to kiss him whenever I wanted. I wanted to always be touching him in any small or big way I could. I wanted to always be there when he laughed because it was such a fucking blessed sound, and I loved watching his dimples sink into existence.

I wanted to soar with him and *be* with him like there was nothing to be afraid of.

That was my truth that I'd never admit out loud because my reality was deafening in comparison. My sick heart wanted those things, but my brain knew I couldn't have them. I had every potential inside of me to be weak like my mother, and it was wrong to let Dominic think it was a weakness I'd ever give into.

"I don't wanna lead you on and get your expectations high." Or up at all.

His face fell, but only slightly.

"What if we go slow?" he countered, treating me so carefully.

I pushed a pathetic laugh. "Well, you're still married so I think we'd have to."

At that, something eased over his expression, molding it indecipherably. He took his stare out to the water, breathing deeply and evenly. I stayed still, studying his strong profile as I felt his hand over my stomach lose tension, and then I lost it completely when he took it to the side of me, resting it on the ledge.

I'd never felt colder than I did in that empty spot where his hand no longer was.

With his gaze still cast off, he started talking.

"Ryan interrogated me on the way here about you. I think it was half him trying to keep me from spiraling out, half him wanting gossip. He's—" Dominic paused in thought, the end of his mouth twitching up as he shot me an arched glance. "Layla's going to have her hands full is all I'll say."

I breathed a soft laugh, and so did he. He kept his gaze to the side, watching the water like I caught him watching me so many times before—quietly considering and lost in his own head of intricate thoughts.

"But I... wasn't hiding my worry over you well, and I knew that," he continued. "So he had questions, and I told him about the divorce and that you were special to me."

Special to me.

Those words warmed my chest like a match lit right beneath my heart. That same flame caught my heart on fire and consumed it in the mouth of the flame, foreshadowing the disappearance of my heart altogether to this man.

"He asked me what was going on between us, and I didn't have an answer."

Finally, he turned those heavy-hitting eyes back to me, serving me a blow that put the first crack in my resolve tonight.

"I don't have any interest pretending I don't want to see where this can go with you. Any thought that I could stopped existing the moment I realized you were in danger, and I couldn't breathe again until I saw you. The thought of anyone taking you away from me hurts enough to know that this isn't fleeting and that I want you in my life."

His words said he wanted me in his life.

The way he was staring at me said he *needed* me in it.

My brain went all topsy-turvy and my heart started squeezing, suffocating on all the sickness. "You're just getting out of a marriage. Shouldn't you want to pump the breaks a little before flinging yourself into anything stupid?"

And we both knew this would be stupid. He was older and a father. I was younger and broken in more ways than one. Knowing him might have put my life in real danger and knowing me turned his upside down in less than three months.

He didn't seem to care.

"Like I said, we can go slow."

My cheeks barely moved as I breathed a laugh, confounded and overwhelmed. "This doesn't sound like you're giving me much of a choice."

Dominic thought that over for a minute, the ends of his eyes turning up.

"You're right. I'm not. I'm forcing you to date me and give this a shot."

He looked rather proud of himself. Proud and smug and sexy as fuck.

Why did he have to be *so* hot?

"Somehow I don't think dating should be at the top of either of our lists right now."

A peculiar glint developed in his eyes, gathering slowly as his hands moved next to me. They came back to my thighs, sliding deliberately up to grab my hips.

"Maybe not," he agreed. A low, throaty agreement.

Excited air hitched in my throat, realizing that curious glint in him was a mischievous one as he gripped my body, dragging me back down into the pool until my legs crossed behind his back. The wet heat of our bodies met beneath the water, desire pulsing one goddamn *blinding* flash between us as he rumbled against my lips.

"But I don't want to wait to have you, Ms. Sanders."

Then he claimed me like we both knew he could.

He took ownership of my mouth with a kiss so hot, the water threatened to evaporate around us. I melted—muscles, defenses, resolve, all of it. It all melted into him until I was as pliant as the water, moving and whimpering and moaning whenever he told me to.

Dominic overpowered everything about me until I was basic instinct and nothing else, clawing at his back to get closer. He pressed all of me into the pool wall, my back grazing against the cement as he folded me against it with his powerful body.

An untamed moan tore up my chest as greedy hands gripped the underneath of my thighs, his thumbs coasting near the strap of black fabric between my legs.

I bucked against him, wanting more than I knew he'd give me.

This was sexual manipulation at its finest, knowing I lost all my sensibilities whenever he touched me, and also knowing he wouldn't take it farther than this kiss.

"Maybe—" I tried to speak, but he kissed over it, pouring all of himself into that kiss until I was drowning. God, it was like being crashed in waves over and over and over, barely able to catch my breath before being sunk under again.

I broke away, throwing my head back, gasping for air and trying to save myself.

"Maybe we do no strings attached," I panted, his lips latching onto the arch of my neck. He growled into me, the noise reverberating all the way down between my legs, my core clenching.

"We can go into this with no expectations or labels or anything."

I gasped a sharp cry, his teeth sinking in above my collarbone and making my pussy fucking weep. I clung to him, knowing his bite was a discipline for the suggestion, but it was the only way I'd agree to this.

If I set his hopes low now, the crash would be easier later on when I let them down.

If we kept it strictly physical and agreed to something casual, maybe I could survive him. I'd be playing with something deadly and addictive, but if we shook hands on keeping this light and fun, I could bow out before it ever became anything else.

We were going to be around each other a lot until this whole kidnapping thing blew over, and we'd already proven we couldn't keep our hands to ourselves.

Now that he was getting a divorce, why not have a little fun until the papers were signed?

Then we could fuck each other to our hearts content and part ways not having to wonder what we were missing. We'd know, and we'd get our fill of each other and move on.

Dominic pulled himself away from my neck, fixing me with eyes both speculative and intense.

"If I agree, will that help you not panic around me?"

I nodded.

He searched my face, taking notes in his head that I had no privilege to. I hated how he could do that, turn the light to his thoughts on and off whenever he wanted.

"All right." The backs of his jaw pulsed once. He nodded stiffly. "For now."

For now was all that would ever matter.

I grinned, pulling him back down to seal our dirty deal with a kiss. Dominic had just deepened it when a voice called out awkwardly.

A voice that did *not* belong to either of us.

"Hey, you two?"

Dominic ripped our lips apart, a scathing crimson finding the rise of his cheeks as his eyes jumped to the new guy behind us.

"The pool is closed so..." The voice trailed off, and I sputtered a laugh. Grabbing the back of Dominic's head, I hid his face in the crook of my neck with a roll of my eyes and turned my face to our cockblock party ruiner.

"We'll get out. Thanks." And I waved the tall, lanky janitor away, his shoulders slouching and cheeks pinked as he went.

Laughter still bubbling in my chest, I twisted back to Dominic, the flaming humiliation contained beneath his skin enough to turn the pool into a hot tub. I nudged him out of hiding with my shoulder. A streamlined exhale blew through his nose as he raised his head up, expression flat and grim.

"This is why people shouldn't break rules," he grumbled.

I threw my head back, the echo of amusement carrying off into the night. My stare found his, the tips of my fingers pushing back a rogue strand of his dark hair so it looked perfect like he would want.

With a smile on my face, I mused, "That was adorable."

He groaned, pulling me in tight. There was just the faintest curve to his mouth.

"Something tells me you'll be the death of me, Ms. Sanders."

I sighed a happy sigh, ghosting my lips over his.

"And what a sweet death it will be."

TWENTY-NINE

So far, age twenty-one could piss off.

And not just because I may or may not have been targeted by murderous criminals.

But because I got a motherfucking cold from night swimming.

Go figure.

I was a lousy sick person, too. Pathetic as they came. I'd been holed up in mine and Charlotte's bedroom since I got back from the hotel two days ago. That's where I was now, showered in crumpled up toilet paper wads and with my face stuffed against my lumpy pillow trying not to die.

My head felt like it was about to explode from all the sinus pressure and snot.

A couple knocks thumped from the bedroom door, followed by its whining groan as it opened.

"Katty?"

Face still smashed into my pillow, I muffled, "Hey, Bugs."

"Um, your friend is here."

"Which one?"

"The one that looks like a mean prince."

My heavy head perked up at her flippant tone and choice of words. *Dominic?*

Wait—

"Did you answer the front door?" I asked in a rush, pushing myself up to fix my sister with a scolding glower. "Charlotte, you—"

"No, Mommy did."

Her answer cut me off and shut me up. I blinked, a cough tingling at the back of my throat from talking. "She's awake?"

She nodded brightly, twisting her toes into the carpet. "Mhm. She made breakfast too."

"She did?"

This time, the cough surpassed a tickle, and I turned my face into the bend of my elbow, hacking up half a lung and scoring my throat raw. Groaning something pitiable, I sifted my hand through the toasty bed sheets until my fingers found the shape of my phone.

Flipping it over, the screen lit up with the time and missed notifications.

My eyes jumped wide. "It's almost 12:30!" Cue another coughing fit before, "Oh my God, Bugs. I'm so sorry. You should have woken me up."

"You were sleeping," she said like it was obvious. "Mommy stayed with me and put on Finding Nemo, but then she fell asleep on the couch before the part with Squirt. She woke up when your friend got here."

Shit! Dominic.

Thoughts about my mother's abnormal behavior dashed to the back of my mind. Her acting like a real mom was probably just a sober fluke, anyhow.

"Yeah. Uh, I'll be right there."

Charlotte beamed and skipped out, leaving me wallowing as I drove my legs to kick out from the warm sheets and find stable ground. Every move I made, there was a pathetic noise to accompany it. A whine, a grunt, a mangled curse. They all tracked my journey to the bathroom where I somehow managed to brush my teeth without gagging more than once.

Lazily, I threw my tangled hair into a careless bun and shuffled out to the living room where Dominic was waiting, tall and breathtaking and completely out of place in this ugly little house.

The saddest noise creaked out of me when I saw him, suddenly flushed hot with embarrassment that I was sick at all and that he had to see me like this. My emotions always sat closer under my skin whenever I was sick, and it made for a lot of uncharacteristic displays.

I snatched a blanket from the couch and wrapped it around my shoulders, sulking up to him. "Are you here to babysit me today?"

We hadn't seen each other since yesterday morning. He and Ryan had to go back to the station and do... whatever detectives do, and I spent the day in bed with some no-name officers stationed outside our house.

Dominic nodded, a lazy smile contorting his mouth as he completed the distance between us. "Not feeling any better?"

I groaned in response, and his large hand found my forehead. My shoulders slumped and eyes rolled as he checked my temperature, but there was also this stupid little nagging twitch tugging at my lips that I couldn't get rid of.

He drew his hand back. "You don't have a fever, so that's good."

"Thanks, *Dad*."

He angled his face down, stern gray peeking beneath dark eyebrows.

"That will not become a thing."

Usually, I probably would have challenged him or teased that he might like the kink too much to admit it, but today?

I sneezed instead.

Charlotte ran up out of nowhere, holding a roll of toilet paper out to me.

"Here you go, Katty."

I sniffled, accepting her offering. "Thanks, Bugs."

"Toilet paper?" I met Dominic's arched brow while ripping off a few sheets.

"Yeah. Tissues are a rich person's game."

The hook in his eyebrow deepened, and I blew my nose into the rough paper. Below us, Charlotte pointed to something I hadn't noticed yet.

"What's in that bag?"

Through slitted eyes, I finished wiping my nose and glanced down to see what she was referring to. Slung around Dominic's forearm was a white plastic bag with something heavy at the bottom.

He lifted his arm up, a crooked smile widening across his face.

"Soup."

A slow, unwanted simper spread up my cheeks, and I sunk my teeth into my chapped bottom lip to keep it from taking over. He brought me soup. *Soup.*

What a stupidly cliché, totally unnecessary, thoughtful thing to do.

I plucked the bag from his hand, still trying not to smile.

"Cheeky bastard."

His grin broadened before I had a chance to turn away, and the sight of it crawled beneath my highly-sensitive skin and burrowed a warmth there that lingered like smoke.

"What kind of soup?" I asked to distract from the tingly feeling.

"The only kind to feed someone who's sick."

"Chicken noodle?"

He came around me as I set myself up at the kitchen counter, sliding onto a stool. "You sounded like you could use some on the phone last night."

Yeah, get that. He *called* me. Dominic called me on his drive home from work and we talked—well, he talked—and I tried not to blow his ear out with all my coughing.

He wanted to update me on my 'situation'. Which, the update was that there *was* no update. It was still all theorizing and him being overly cautious, but we talked until I fell asleep with him on the phone. His sonorous voice was the last thing I heard before drifting off into a sick-induced sleep—in more ways than one—just like in one of those god-awful teen romances.

I even woke up around midnight to see I had a text from him.

'Sweet dreams, Ms. Sanders.'

My freaking lightning did all sorts of flips and shit when I read it.

I shifted the blanket around my shoulders so I could still wear it and eat, and Dominic helped get the container of soup out of the bag while Charlotte grabbed me a spoon. It was strange being waited on instead of the reverse, but I was too stuffed up to care.

Steam billowed up and out of the container of soup as Dominic uncapped the top, heating my face and wrapping around my sore bones. The smell, oh *god*, the smell was heavenly. I didn't waste a single second before dipping my spoon in the homey dish and piling a mouthful of broth and goodness into my mouth.

A moan that would have embarrassed most women shredded up my thankful throat. It was the perfect temperature, savory flavors sliding down and soothing the ache in my throat that had been there all night.

Dominic hummed in amusement, his chest brushing my back.

"I take it you're pleased?"

Without removing my attention from the soup, I answered. "If this soup had a dick, you'd be in trouble."

Airy chuckles flowed through him, his chest shaking against me as he laughed. I poured another spoonful of soup back, moaning again.

"I thought you might. Maya calls this my sicken chicken soup. It's cured every cold it's been up against."

"Wait." My spoon paused mid-air. "You made this?"

He simply nodded.

I was sure I was looking at him like he wasn't real, like he'd been sent to me just to prove how unrealistic a man had to be to snag my attention.

"You catch bad guys, look like you walked out of a GQ magazine, and now you cook?"

Most men might have transitioned to looking pompous after my compliment spew. Dominic, however, grew more content than anything. His stare warmed, and my heart did that awful flipping, tingly thing again. It was sicker than I was.

We needed a subject change.

"On top of all that," I cleared my throat, readying another sip of soup. "From what I've felt, you have a huge—"

A bearpaw hand slipped over my mouth, shutting me down. I tipped my head back to him, just *feeling* my stare sparkling with all that mirth he loved to punish.

His was sparkling too, glinting with all sorts of adoring stars I wished would blind me so I wouldn't have to know they were there.

I wasn't anyone who deserved *adoring*.

His voice dropped to an alluring murmur. "Feeling better, I see."

I hummed in agreement, letting him feel my smirk as it rose beneath his palm. And you know what? I actually really was feeling better. It was going to take a hell of a lot of lying to myself later on to convince myself it was because of the soup.

Stupid cold making me stupider than normal.

"So, who's watching Maya today?" I asked, swallowing more soup.

"My mom agreed to stay in town until we find someone else."

Then, I did that thing where I started talking before I thought about what I was saying.

"She send any well wishes to the whore from the shed?"

A smugly pleased grin was beginning to rise up my cheeks, but one disapproving glower from Dominic cut it dead.

I ducked my head back towards the soup. "Sorry."

He set a hand on the back of my stool, his body heat burning hotter. "You have an unnatural ability to insult yourself."

"I was joking." Sort of. "I just—"

Out of nowhere, a coughing fit plagued my body. The spoon I was holding plunked back into the soup; my hand slapped to my chest to try and stabilize the choking and the pain. Dominic rubbed circles on my back, and I twisted into him, my other hand finding his stark gray shirt and grabbing onto the soft fibers for dear life.

"Oh God, I'm dying," I wheezed, tears forming in the corners of my eyes from all the effort.

I rested the top of my head to his chest, feeling every deep note resonate through as he spoke. "Don't you think that's a tad dramatic?"

I tried and failed to give a good thwack to his chest, hand crumpling and fingers latching onto him for support again.

"You can't be mean to me when I'm sick."

A smile tinted his voice. "I brought you soup."

"Yeah, and…" I arched my head back all the way so his handsome face and pursed mouth hovered inches away, and all thoughts went fuzzy and fragmented.

Instead, I croaked pathetically. "I'm too sick to think of a good comeback."

His pillowy lips twitched. "Then shut up and eat your soup."

I inhaled to reply… and then crumbled back into his chest.

"Okay."

See? Total anomaly of a person.

Dominic continued rubbing my back in soothing strokes as I put back a few more spoonfuls of soup. Charlotte had busied herself somewhere behind us, and for just a couple precious moments, all was still.

Not quiet, but still.

Big difference.

Then, a weed I hadn't seen more than a few glimpses of over the last month reared her head.

"Aren't you her boss?"

I swallowed my mouthful of soup, this bite curdling sour as I turned to my mother. There she was, standing not so tall and thinner than I'd ever seen. Her skin was ghostly pale though, so veiled I could see every noxious vein glowing beneath her flesh. The bags beneath her eyes had sunk deep, hollowing out enough that they molded her face into something truly eerie.

She looked wrecked, like a gust from my weak and haggard lungs would break her in half. Even in her worst highs, she'd never looked this bad, and I tried not to wonder what'd changed.

"Was. He *was* my boss. Life update, I got fired."

I turned back to my soup.

"Because you were sleeping with your boss?"

Annoyance scraped up my throat, and I twisted to face her again, wielding my spoon like a knife.

"No, Kathy. I wasn't fired for sleeping with him," I said pointedly. "We haven't made it past second base yet."

Dominic squeezed the space between my neck and shoulder, not hard enough that it hurt, but enough that I understood it was a reprimanding move. I pitched him a look and flicked my eyes around in a furtive roll, wishing I could disappear and drown in my soup.

The floorboards whined as Kathy took a bare-footed step towards us, her arms crossed and hands cupped beneath her elbows. Her weary stare was tacked on Dominic.

"You're a cop, right?"

Detective.

But he didn't correct her.

"Yes ma'am."

"Why are there so many of you..." She flitted her bony fingers towards the front door. "Hanging around here yesterday and today?"

Dominic shot me a sharp look. "You didn't tell her?"

I shrugged. "Why would I?"

"Tell me what?" Kathy interjected. She even tried to sound concerned.

Cute.

A weighted exhale dragged out of Dominic, and I couldn't tell if he was about to scold me or launch into the tale of what was going on. Thankfully, before he could do either, his phone rang.

He dropped a vexed look to it, jaw clenching. He gave my mom a polite glance. "Excuse me."

Moving to the door, he jerked it open and put himself on the other side of it. The sound of stress and police jargon muffled through the chipping wood. It was the only sound besides Charlotte playing behind us to cover the uncomfortable minute.

Purposefully, I clinked my spoon on the counter to add my own soundtrack to the air. One clink. Two clinks. A rustle of what was probably drawing paper from Charlotte.

My mother's voice broke over the clinking and rustling.

"Are you in trouble?"

My muscles all froze, fused tight by the fraudulent worry she was trying to play off. I realized I'd stopped breathing too when a scratch itched up my throat, reminding me I wasn't healthy enough to hold my breath today.

Forcing air back through, I ducked my head and threw her a pity glance.

"Just keep worrying about yourself, and I'll worry about me."

Out of the corner of my eye, I saw her pointed shoulders cave in. There was this thing in the air that almost—*almost*—tasted like regret, but my taste buds were too clogged by disdain to tell for sure.

The front door jammed open again, Dominic wedging through. His phone was clutched tight in his hand, hard stare set on the floor.

The tension he brought back with him strung my posture a little straighter. It parted my dry lips as I sucked down even drier air. All the soup I'd consumed swirled uncomfortably around my stomach.

That wasn't a happy look.

"Did something happen?" My voice cracked, and I cleared it of the weakness to pretend it wasn't there.

Dusty pink lips broke apart, a stagnant beat holding his tongue in place. Then, "We got a notification that someone tried to pull your school records."

"What?" My confusion screamed, eyes pinching. "That's a weird thing to do, right?"

Dominic's footsteps washed the sound of rich leather across our poor floors. He came as close to me as he was before, the air around him thick enough to be a choking hazard.

"They pulled surveillance from your high school, and who it was introduces a new threat."

"Why? Who was it?"

He shook his head. "You wouldn't know his name. He's big on the streets and in organized crime units in the area. We've only ever been able to bust him once for drug possession, but he's been named in theft cases, drug trafficking, a few unsolved homicides. We've just never had enough to charge him on those."

A chill ran up my spine, and I tensed every muscle I had not to let it show.

"What does he want with me?"

Dominic passed his gaze over my face, heartache fanning up his own as if he'd already lost me. Quietly, he admitted, "I don't know."

"What's his name?"

Dominic glanced over my head at my mother who just *had* to butt into this private moment. He squared back his shoulders as if he'd forgotten she was there too.

"Tommy Lynch."

A pause.

"I know Tommy."

I whipped around to her so fast, my head spun as if those three words ripped my entire world off its axis. Dominic stabled his hands on my shoulders, his strength keeping me from doubling over.

Breathing hard, I pinned my narrowed glare to my mom. "Excuse me?"

The ferocity in my tone rippled preliminary lightning across the small house.

"You know him personally?" Dominic asked behind me.

Slowly, she nodded.

"How *exactly* do you know him, Kathy?"

She pinched two fingers around her bottom lip, pulling at the dead skin. Her eyes went beady and nervous, skipping from me to Dominic. Eventually, she swallowed thickly and spoke.

"He pushes the new product and collects any overdue payments."

On wobbling feet, I tried to stand and move towards her. Fades of neon red pulsed in and out around my vision as I narrowed my focus on her.

"Did you do something to him? Do you owe him money?"

"*No*, no." She dared a step closer. "He was the one here last month that I-I paid."

She was stupid. She *had* to be stupid to think telling me that would make me feel better.

Instead, ice trickled through my veins, stealing my volume and my blind confidence that none of this was serious.

"He's been to our house?"

In my grave tone, she seemed to realize the huge fucking problem glaring us in the face. Her coffee eyes watered, turned muddled and red-rimmed. She shook her head, whispered noises falling from her pale lips.

"I don't know what he could want with you."

I ignored her, spinning back to Dominic with more life in my body than the last forty-eight hours. He was already waiting for me.

"What are the chances that this is also a coincidence?"

I could trick myself into believing the SUV was a coincidence. Nothing more than bad timing, but this? Breaking into my house last month was deliberate. The connection to my mom was undeniable. Pulling my school records was sketchy as fuck. Dominic was right before. I'd be a fool to believe in coincidences more than I believed in miracles or prayer.

His bright-with-worry eyes burned into mine.

"You can't stay here."

My gut pulled itself in and out, a fist of anxiety tugging it this way and that. I thought I might actually be sick.

"Where am I supposed to go?"

"Katty's leaving?" Charlotte's innocent voice broke through the madness, and my heart squeezed, finding her curious face in the living room.

"Uh, Maybe. You're coming with me though, Bugs." I landed an inarguable look on Dominic. "She comes with me wherever I go."

He nodded, not even questioning it. "Can you stay with Layla?"

"She left with her parents today to go visit her grandparents for a few days." *Think. Think. Think.* Fuck, it was hard to think when my head was already so full of this cold and now this. Everything was spinning.

"What about a hotel?"

His eyebrows flatlined on his forehead. "Where anyone can have access to you? No."

"Okay, well I don't know where else I can stay," I argued, frazzled and sure that a fever was coming on fast. My palm slid up to my forehead, cradling it as sweat began to slide down my back. I dumped the blanket off my shoulders, suddenly too hot and scratchy.

Dominic watched me, the strict lines of his face angling harsher, and his jaw raked to the side. I panted, nothing making sense, and every nonsensical bit of me concentrated on Dominic as an idea cemented his hard-bitten stare to stone.

An idea that made my face fall. An idea that was asking for more trouble than my entire life was worth.

Oh no. Oh no, no, no, no.

The cut of his gaze bladed through me.

"Pack your bags."

THIRTY

The sun had begun to set by the time I pulled up to the Reed's residence, Charlotte and a few bags for us both packed into the backseat.

The sky was this faded watercolor portrait of oranges, pinks, and purples, breaking a crimson red at the very dip of the horizon. The air outside was feather light and cooling with the sinking sun. Everything about the picture of this moment was so much more soothing than the bullshit going on inside of it.

Dominic had left only a half hour before us to try and smooth the worst of it over with Heather before Charlotte and I got there. Mom had been crying when we left. Not sobbing, but a constant trickle of tears down her blotchy face that I guessed were supposed to spell out how sorry she was.

We were in this mess because of her. Her ugly life bled over into mine and now threatened the very existence of it. She still couldn't reason *why* Tommy Lynch had taken an interest in me, but did admit—through even more tears—that she had mentioned me a few times to him when she was high or as small talk.

She used me as water cooler material, and now I was fucked.

Dominic seemed convinced that this Tommy guy was at the center of these kidnappings, and had taken a special interest in me like no other victim because of something my mom did. Except, no matter how long or how hard he grilled her, she couldn't figure out what she'd done.

Whatever it was was probably information lost in the poisoned stream of her veins. In the end, it didn't really matter. My life was apparently in danger all the same.

I texted Dominic to tell him I was there and then turned to Bugs in the backseat. "You excited to spend a few days with Maya?"

She nodded, her sprouting ponytail boinging on top of her head. "Yeah, but I still don't know why Mommy couldn't come too."

"Well, Bugs, she had to stay and watch the house. Someone's gotta keep it standing while we're here having all the fun."

And neither Dominic or I were putting that woman anywhere near Maya.

My sister squished her mouth to the side, staring out the window. "I guess." Then she turned her face back to me. "Do you think we can have cupcakes again?"

Soft laughter broke through, and I was so fucking glad in that moment for her innocence and ignorance. My smile ran deep, all the way to my bones and blood that pumped for her.

"I'll see what we can do."

From inside the house, a sudden, jarring crash shattered my smile.

Both Charlotte and I snapped our heads towards the loud noise. My chest tightened, worry firing to life as my thoughts bounced from Dominic to sweet Maya, and before I could think, my driver's side door was cracked open.

"Stay here and lock the door," I threw back to Charlotte.

I pushed out into the open air, legs carrying me up the driveway to the stone-faced house with visions of violence flashing behind my eyes. I already knew Heather wasn't afraid to use her hands to fight with, and the echo of that crash splintered through my one-track brain, pushing me faster and madder towards those imposing front doors.

Dominic was a big man. A strong man. He didn't need me to defend him, but I'd fucking stomp all over her porcelain face if she hurt him because he was trying to help me.

I sniffled as I reached the door, head still clogged and nose too stuffed up to smell the ripe stench of money that polluted this street, but I knew it was there.

The breeze flirted with the waves of unbrushed hair framing my face, bringing with it angry voices.

I paused in my quick steps, pressing my ear to the thick door, surprised when the voices came through clear.

Dominic's was the first I heard.

"You were supposed to be leaving for a work trip these next couple days anyway," he argued, his grip on his exasperation surprisingly steady. "Telling you was more of a courtesy than a necessity."

"So you were planning on sneaking her and her sister in here while I was gone?" Heather spat. "How *noble* of you, Dom."

"I think the fact that I'm telling you negates the idea that I planned to sneak them in."

"Why would you ever bring them here in the first place? Why would you think I'd ever be okay with having *her* here?"

I could picture Dominic so perfectly, sighing and his strict jaw tensing.

"I didn't think you'd be okay with it, but I hoped you'd have some compassion for the situation."

"Compassion for what? Her mom being a drug addict or karma biting her in the ass?"

The callousness of her words struck me back from the door like an actual shove. I brought my hand to my chest as if I could feel all five fingered indents from the shove, stinging my fevered skin and bubbling my temper to the surface.

There was a lull in the fight, and a bird chirped somewhere in the background. I hissed, swatting blindly at its sky to tell it to shut up so I could hear what came next.

I leaned my face towards the door again, my blood rushing too loudly in my ears.

"I don't know what happened to you, or if you were always like this and I somehow missed it." God, he sounded *so* disappointed. Defeated, even. "Despite your feelings about Ms. Sanders, think about how devastated Maya would be if anything happened to her. You remember how she was when Shelly stopped showing up."

It was almost weird to hear him use my name so professionally, but it was smart. Definitely smart.

"That doesn't give you a free pass to bring her into my home!"

"*Our* home, Heather," Dominic clipped. "It's still our home until we sign the papers, and I can bring anyone I want into it."

A screech of epic proportions ripped through house and home.

"What the *fuck* do I have to do to get her out of our lives? I fire her, and you run after her. I tell you to stay away from her, and you decide to move her into our *home.*"

"What did you expect me to do, Heather?" he pressed, his tether on his anger fraying. "Really? What did you expect me to do when I found out *Tommy Lynch* was after her?"

There was a deafening pause, and then a muffled, bitter reply.

"Not this."

Her reply hit me harder than I expected it to. My chest felt bruised from it. I knew she hated me. I got that. I accepted that. She had every reason to even if she didn't know all the reasons. It wasn't her hating me that was such an oxygen-snatching gut punch.

It was how *much* she hated me.

Her hate was visceral, a palpable thing with claws and teeth that ate through the thick wood of the door and chomped down on me.

She really sounded like she'd sleep better at night if Tommy got me and took me away. Maybe she even *hoped* it happened. I didn't blame her for wanting me gone, but couldn't I blame her for the extreme she was willing to go to to let it happen?

I understood hate. I *loved* to hate. Hate was my coat of armor, and I wore it proudly.

Hate wasn't my weapon though. It was my protection. Heather was using hers like a gun aimed right at my head, and she could pull the trigger and end me anytime she felt like it.

And she *did* feel like it.

A low-pitched rumble resonated through the door, and I pressed me and my sore chest back up against it to listen.

"It shouldn't be for more than a few days," Dominic said.

Hearing him again, my heart withered just a bit. He'd detached all of his beautiful emotions from his broad voice. Sure those emotions could be fucking terrifying to a person unequipped to deal with them like me, but I didn't like his voice without them either.

It was like a garden without any flowers.

"We're putting a restraining order on Tommy, and we'll tail him until he comes too close to her. Then we can at least begin to build a case against him."

That was news to me. It sounded like a good plan though.

"Well," Heather's shoes clicked, her tone as pointed as the heel of the stilettos she invariably wore. "If you thought I'd be leaving so you two could be alone, you'd be mistaken. I'll be staying as long as she is."

"That's fine. There's no reason to, but I understand if you want to."

Ah, there's the lying he talked about. You could tell he hated it. The words even sounded different coming from him, like they'd been rolled around in mud first.

I wondered if Heather could hear it too.

"Each time you tell me there's nothing to worry about, your words get weaker," she fumed with slow-forming venom. "Because you keep choosing her over me *every* time you have the chance."

"I'm not choosing her over you." *Liar.* "I'm choosing her safety over your contempt for her."

A loaded beat lingered, and in it, I felt the devastation of what came next as if the grief that drove his words flowed through me the same as it lived in Dominic.

"And I chose you in our marriage, Heather. I chose you plenty of times, and it didn't matter. I'm divorcing you so I don't have to choose you anymore."

Ouch.

Even I felt the sting of that, prickling across my skin like fire ants set loose. Those words weren't even for me, but they were a fresh reminder of how toxic love could become once it had gone stale, and that even men like Dominic could succumb to its villainy.

There was no response from Heather after that.

Distinct footsteps carried towards me, and I backed up into the shadowed coverage of the garage and out of view of the front door camera.

The heavy door opened with a loud click, and I shot a quick glance to Charlotte to see her staring at me through the backseat window, head tilted and innocent eyes on me. Seconds later, an imposing shadow fell over me, and I looked up into sterling eyes.

The silhouette of his broad shoulders sunk an inch or so, and I knew he was pissed I was out of the car and in the open. Like an idiot.

"I heard a crash," I said pathetically.

In the fading sunlight, the tick of his jaw looked even more fearsome. "She threw a vase."

"Is Maya—"

"My mom took her out for a drive." His even-toned voice delivered a breath of relief I didn't realize I needed. I let it out, the rhythm of it shaking.

"That's good."

I trailed off, a tightness burdening in my chest that had nothing to do with my cold.

Everything was so fucked up, and it had happened so quickly. Dominic and I slipped the night before Maya's birthday, and we'd been falling ever since. A kiss used to be our biggest worry, then it was the growing sickness, and now it was my life and his future.

I always said that we'd be catastrophic, and here was the proof of it.

I locked my eyes on him, wanting to close the distance between us but not daring.

"This is such a bad idea."

He stuffed his hands in his pockets. "We don't have much of a choice right now."

"She sounds really suspicious."

He leveled his stare to the driveway, his Adam's apple moving beneath his skin that glowed like amber beneath the sunset.

"She is, but she doesn't have any proof." He flashed his serious eyes up to me, quieting his pitch. "We can't give her any either. I could lose Maya in the divorce if she had proof that I cheated on her."

My lips parted to take that in, inhaling the severity of what we'd gotten ourselves into. Sometimes I forgot it was cheating. Sometimes I forgot how bad of a person I really was. Even with them separated, the reminder that if we were caught, it could rip Maya out of his world forced me to remember that it was still wrong.

It was wrong to touch him and kiss him like he was mine. He wasn't, and I wasn't his either.

"This is a lot," I breathed.

He held a silent beat, back jaw pulsing. "I know."

We held each other's gaze, the streaks of scarlet pink and burnt orange from the sky painting his face the color of warmth; the color that happiness should be. However, burning at the center of all that happy warmth was unimaginable sorrow—two laden pits of it.

He knew before I said it what we had to do.

"Maybe..." I breathed, preparing myself and the words. "Maybe we should cool it?"

Dominic dove his stare to the ground the second the words were out. His shoulders went rigid.

"Maybe," he agreed, voice thick.

I felt the same thickness widening up my throat, no matter how hard I tried to swallow it back. That tightness in my chest was pushing it up, forcing me to feel every single ache of it.

Aching morphed to pain—real, unbearable *pain*—when Dominic brought his eyes back to me and showed me how much he was suffering.

It exploded almost in slow motion inside of me, trickling fire and poison through my organs, between my ribs, filling my stomach until I was inflamed with the pain. It felt like actual death.

Something was dying, that's for sure. Somewhere in the sickest parts of my heart, a tiny whisper came that said it was our souls. They were being ripped apart, shredding back to single cells and screaming as they went. They had been nuzzling, intertwining, composing together a symphony that drowned out the world when they were in the same room.

They shouldn't have meshed so well, but they did, and in their defiance of right and wrong, they had been possessed by the potential for greatness.

They wanted it. They had a *taste* of it, and now it was gone.

Our dialogue might have left room for something later on, but the way we were staring at each other felt like a goodbye. Our timing was shitty, but it was now, and who knew if there would ever be a later.

Actually, I knew.

I knew there would never be a later. We'd agreed to light and fun, nothing serious and nothing permanent, but this hurt *felt* permanent. It felt serious. It felt like all the strings I'd agreed to keep unattached between us had wrapped around my heart and were strangling it to death.

My poor, sick little heart wouldn't survive this again, and the little girl sitting, watching this goodbye unfold in the car wouldn't either if I let it happen.

"So..."

And then my throat closed up.

Wow. I couldn't say it. I actually couldn't fucking say it.

Dominic knew though. He knew and every muscle visible in his body rippled against the solemn nod he jerked out.

So that was that.

We were going back to basics. Back to ignoring the burn of heroin chemistry in our veins. Back to lingering looks and hiding them from harsh blue eyes that would be watching us around every corner we went.

Dominic had this tension in his body and blaze to his eyes that said it was taking all his strength not to reach out to me. He'd hidden his hands in his pockets when he first got out here, and now it made sense why.

He was struggling not to grab me and wrap me up in his big chest. He wanted to hide me in the shadow of his body so he could kiss me goodbye and goodnight.

I wanted that too. So fucking badly. I wanted him to smother me in bittersweet kisses until all the pain went away.

Instead, Dominic turned his feet towards my car.

"I'll help you get your bags."

And so it had ended. And so it began.

THIRTY-ONE

I didn't sleep well that night. Shocker.

Though Charlotte stayed in Maya's room last time we were here, I swindled her into bunking with me at least for the first night. With everything going on, I liked having her close and knowing she was safe and with me.

Even if that meant being kicked during the night about a dozen times.

Even if I hadn't been battered by a five-year-old all night, I still wouldn't have gotten a good night's sleep. I heard every noise in this huge house as if it was on blast, and my haywire mind couldn't stop wondering if it was Heather sneaking into the room to smother me or Tommy sneaking into the room to steal me.

Heather had stayed out of sight after we got here last night, and I hid away in Maya's room with Charlotte most of the time until bedtime anyway. I had a sneaking suspicion Heather probably wouldn't choose to spend her spare time hanging out with her daughter, and I would be safe in there.

And what do you know? I was right.

Dominic stayed away for the most part too, only coming in towards the end to tell Maya it was time to wash up and brush her teeth for bed. I helped with all of that and put her to sleep so Dominic didn't have to see me again, and I didn't have to see him.

Yesterday was hard, and this morning would be even harder for us.

That's why I hid in the spare room as long as I did, tossing and turning in a lonely bed since Charlotte had gotten up about an hour ago. I stayed buried beneath mountains of soft sheets, pretending I could burrow there and no one would ever find me.

Technically, it wasn't any*one* that found me and finally dragged me out of bed, but a smell.

Bacon.

It carried all the way up the stairs, down the hallway, and shoved its savory smell right up my nose, making my mouth water and stomach grumble.

Groaning, I kicked my bare feet out from under the cozy covers and laid them on the floor. I didn't bother changing before I went down, still rocking my plaid pajama shorts and gray tank top.

Throwing on a bra and some concealer, I made the descent.

My steps were weary as I padded down the staircase, muffled voices trailing up from the kitchen and turning my empty stomach over with bubbles of nerves. A velvet bass voice rose above two smaller ones, sliding over my skin and pulling goosebumps to the surface.

God, he sounded sexy in the mornings.

Sexy and perfect and not at all mine.

Pulling back a calming breath, I allowed the smell of frying bacon to guide me the rest of the way down the stairs until I made it to the kitchen. My feet got stuck in the entryway, refusing to move any further and risk disrupting the picturesque scene before me.

Both Charlotte and Maya were at the kitchen table, smiling and giggling as they half ate, half played with their pancakes—chocolate chip ones from the look of it. The sun was streaming in behind them both from the bay window, silhouetting their smiles and bliss. Dominic was standing at the stove, spatula in one hand and a frying pan gripped in the other.

His focus went back and forth between the girls and the food. He wasn't facing me, but I could envision a lopsided crease on his full lips as he savored the simplicity of the moment.

Too bad my entrance on the scene shattered it all.

"Katty, you're awake!"

I tried not to cringe too openly at Charlotte's loud announcement but felt the reaction clamp up the muscles in my shoulders anyway. I gave a wave and a mumble, purposefully not meeting Dominic's stare as he twisted around to me.

"How are you feeling?" he asked.

"Uh…" I checked in with every part of my body and concluded that everything except my heart felt better. The cold was gone. The real sickness, however, remained and it fucking hurt.

"Much better," I replied anyway.

I specifically did *not* look at Dominic as I told the lie.

"Daddy made chocolate chip pancakes!" Maya squealed. "He wasn't going to put chocolate in them, but Charlotte made him."

I arched a brow at my sister, sitting looking innocent at the table. "*Made* him?"

"She used that famous Sanders charm."

This time, Dominic used a voice I couldn't ignore. Its low, dulcet notes pulled my head to him like one of his elegant fingers guiding beneath my chin.

He was looking at me over his shoulder, eyes glinting beneath curved brows. In a rarity, it was *me* who clenched my jaw, biting back all my comments on how attractive he looked and if he could please stop it.

We were supposed to be cooling it, not setting me on fire first thing in the morning.

Thankfully, Maya pulled my attention.

"Are you hungry, Ms. Kat?"

"She's always hungry," Charlotte answered for me.

My neck jerked back with her offhanded comment, blinking at her. "Thanks, Bugs."

Deep, soft laughter came from Dominic who'd turned back to the stove. He was in a surprisingly good mood this morning given how yesterday went. I passed behind him, eyeing his strong back and fisting both hands so I didn't give him a teasing slap for his laughter.

That, or flat out grab his ass.

He was wearing those gray sweatpants again, and they were hanging dangerously low on his hips.

I was going to burn every one of his sweatpants before I left here. I swore it.

"One time, she ate so much, um, what was it?" Charlotte turned to me, eyes wide and searching for help on a story that I had no clue where it was heading. Then those eyes brightened. "Oh! It was nachos. She ate so many nachos that she said she felt like a whale, and I laughed at her, and she squirted me with a water bottle and said it was her blowhole!"

Maya pulled a face. "That's weird."

"That's comedy," I countered, brow hooking upwards.

She shook her head, shelving a wild curl behind her ear. "I don't think it's funny."

I sunk down in a chair at the end of the kitchen table, jabbing my chin towards her. "Want me to squirt you with a water bottle later and see if you laugh?"

Initially, her sweet face crinkled, and she started to shake her head. Then, slowly, light found her sapphire blue eyes, and she grinned a toothy grin, nodding fast. "Yes."

Laughter sputtered free, and I kicked one of my feet up to rest on the lip of the chair adjacent to me.

"We'll see."

"I'd say we had more than enough water play the last time you were here, Ms. Sanders." Dominic stepped up to the table, placing an overflowing plate of crispy, juicy bacon at the center. The smell of it was enough to make me salivate and ignore the multiple inappropriate comments piling through my brain about just how *wet* I was last time I was here.

Leaning up, I snatched a piece and brought it to my lips. "There's always a killjoy." Then I snapped off a bite between my teeth.

"Daddy's a killjoy!" Maya shouted, going in for a piece herself.

My shoulders shook as I munched on the bacon, my lips twisting up on both ends. Dominic hovered at the table, sliding me an arched glance.

"Thank you for that."

I snapped off another bite. "No problem."

Our gazes lingered longer than they should have, eyes smiling and hearts suffocating. It took *actual* effort to break the connection, and that stupid bruise in my chest hurt worse when it was over.

I swallowed the rest of the bacon, throat a little drier, heart a little sicker.

Then Maya asked a question that made me cough it all back up.

"Daddy, did Ms. Kat give you an orgasm?"

Saliva-coated bacon bits spewed back up my throat, my eyes bulging out of my brain as I choked to what I hoped was death. Dominic wasn't any better.

"Wh-what did you—*what*?" I'd never seen this man stammer before. Aside from his mouth, the rest of him had gone rigid, jagged as rock. Color rushed to his cheeks, flushing them a shade of red I'd only ever seen on tomatoes.

I smacked my chest again and again to get the choking to stop, and Maya's eyes flew between us both, growing wide with fright as she took in our distressed states.

"Ms. Kat said it!" she defended herself, throwing me right under the bus. "She said you needed a drink and an orgasm the first time she was here! She said it!"

Oh my god. Fuck me.

She was right. I *did* say that, and here it was, biting me in the ass nearly three months later. Why did kids have to remember every little freaking thing?

All of my choking, coughing, and wheezing stopped in the same second Dominic flashed his outrage towards me. It all stopped, because my breathing malfunctioned and fizzled out on the spot. The flames in his eyes snuffed out any oxygen left in me, and I actually wondered if a glare could burn someone to ashes.

In the background of me being burned alive by a stare, Maya continued.

"I think she said it 'cuz you were sad a lot, but you always smile more when Ms. Kat is around, so I thought—" She huffed, and both Dominic and I swiveled our attention back to her. "I just said it because you looked happy, Daddy."

As if the atmosphere had been a howling windstorm of outrage and humiliation, it all pulled to a quiet with those words.

Everything slowed. Everything softened. All eyes were on Dominic, and his were on his daughter. It had to hurt, knowing she knew he'd been sad for so long. I was sure he thought he hid it well, but kids were perceptive as hell.

Then he twisted back to me, and I held my breath the entire time he stared at me.

A slight frown was knit into his forehead, outlining the intensive thoughts overlapping in his head—that ever-dissecting mind of his. He scanned my face down to my lips, and I didn't move a freaking muscle. He worked his way back up, and I watched with a tightening heart as his handsome face carved itself in every shade of adoration.

He shouldn't have looked at me like that. He *couldn't*.

But my stupid fucking face didn't get the memo and broke with this sheepish grin anyway. I ducked my head, rolling my traitorous lips between my teeth and scrunching up my nose. *Dammit.*

"Am I in trouble?" Maya's tiny voice brought Dominic back to her. He smiled softly and shook his head.

"No, Munchkin." He grabbed her face between his fingers, tilting her head up at him. "Just don't say that word again, okay?"

She nodded, and he rubbed his thumb over the corner of her mouth, cleaning a spot of syrup off. He popped that thumb back behind his lips, sucking off the syrup, and Maya dove back into the half a pancake she had left.

About three seconds passed before—

"*Orgasm.*"

"Charlotte!" I scolded, trying so hard to keep the laugh out of my voice.

A deep sigh heaved from Dominic as he sat in the chair next to me, folding a hand around his waiting coffee mug. "She's definitely your sister."

Got that right.

Dominic lifted his mug to his lips, and I realized my foot was still resting on the lip of his chair's seat and close to touching his thigh. I went to jerk it away.

His hand not around his mug stopped me.

It was a subtle thing—a light grasp around the base of my ankle, hidden by the tabletop. Dominic wasn't reacting in any way that would let anyone know he was touching me. He kept sipping his coffee, watching the girls as they ate breakfast while passing a stroke of his thumb up my ankle.

Then he did it again.

My lightning tracked down to where he touched, sizzling and warming my skin against him. He wedged my toes beneath his thigh on the chair indiscreetly, keeping my foot where it was. The physical contact was slight—not even inappropriate—but I felt it everywhere.

Like he was holding my withering heart in his hands, and nothing had ever felt so overwhelming and underwhelming all at once.

My fingers trembled visibly as I reached out to grab another piece of bacon.

"What is it anyway?" Charlotte asked after a lull.

Dominic arched an eyebrow over the rim of his mug. "What's what?"

"The word we can't say."

Dominic faltered. Like, super duper malfunctioned. His mouth popped open and nothing came out. He clearly was *not* ready for a conversation about orgasms with two five-year-olds before ten o'clock in the morning.

"It's like a party." All eyes at the table shifted to me.

Maya tilted her head, cheeks puffed out as she chewed a mouthful of pancake. Dominic's mouth quivered, lifting to an upturned crescent, his gray eyes spirited. Okay, he *had* to stop looking at me like that.

My sister's stare narrowed in suspicion.

"What kinda party?"

I broke my bacon in half, keeping my voice cool. "An adult party."

Her chocolate brown eyes slid between Dominic and I. Her intensity was impressive, and her next question was a fucking riot.

"And you two had the party together?"

I had to bite my bottom lip *really* hard to keep from laughing out loud. Dominic's face was goddamn priceless. His smile fell behind his mug, and he ripped his stare to the center of the table to not look at any of us. Even without eye contact, I could still see faint smile lines fading in and out of existence next to his eyes.

He was trying just as hard as I was not to bust a gut.

How in the hell *this* was the beginning outline for our stay here proved just how prone to catastrophe Dominic and I were. Our chemistry was determined to wreck us even less than a day after we agreed to go back to ignoring it. We were clearly doing a *very* shitty job given how easily we both bent to its addiction this morning, and I wondered if we had any hope at all of surviving it.

Like I had a death wish, I kept teasing it.

"We partied together once," I replied. "It was *great.*"

His hand around my ankle squeezed tightly, breaking the seal on my laughter right open. That tension looming in my chest all morning evaporated as my amusement set free, soaring up to the ceiling and draping the kitchen in my surrender. The chemistry was fucking masterful, and a reckless part of me wondered if, as long as we weren't really touching or alone in the same room, maybe moments like these were okay?

Dominic swallowed his laughter down with his coffee, but the diamond glint to his eyes was undeniable. He was a willing victim to it too this morning.

"How old do we have to be before we can have the party?" Maya perked up.

Dominic took this one. "At least fifty."

I rolled my eyes back, finishing off the last half of bacon and dusting my hands of the greasy remains. Dominic picked up a handful of the breakfast meat and put it on his plate, producing an orange and cutting it in half and then into meticulous fourths.

He placed one on Maya's plate, offered one to Charlotte which she accepted, and then turned to me with the second to last one, not bothering to ask before setting it on my plate. I cocked my head at the fruit.

"You didn't ask me if I wanted one."

"I did not."

"What if I didn't?"

"That's too bad."

"Why do I *have* to eat the orange?"

"Because you're recovering from being sick."

I scoffed with a light smile. "I feel fine."

"You might not if you don't eat the orange," he replied, focused on peeling the fruit's rind. That same smile teasing my lips was in his resonant voice, and I pushed myself back with a dramatic hand over my heart.

"Is that a threat, Mr. Reed?"

Eyes of liquid silver flashed up to me, stretching my smile even wider. I couldn't help it. I couldn't fucking help it when he was looking at me in that roguish way of his, that way that said he wanted to steal me away to a dark closet and make me take back all my misbehaving words that he not-so-secretly loved.

I saw the ideas of what he would do with me play across his stare, and how those ideas dilated his pupils and made him a bit predatory, a bit untamed.

He parted his lips, drawing the anticipation out before slowly grinding his order out at the lowest register imaginable.

"Eat your orange, Ms. Sanders."

At the corner of the kitchen table sat a napkin holder. White, frilly napkins bookended the thing, but in the middle was a section of pens with Reed Real Estate printed on the sides. I snatched both pen and paper, scribbling down a quick note before sliding it in Dominic's direction on the table.

Stop flirting with me, it read.

A twitch danced on his mouth as he read it, and a flash of throwing myself at him to kiss it right off zipped across my brain. He plucked the pen I was using out of my hand, a grin across his mouth as close to boyish as Dominic Reed had ever come.

Carefully, he set the pen down and passed the napkin back.

How can I when you look so beautiful this morning?

A smile so big and fat, it actually *hurt*, peeled across my face.

Oh, we were so screwed.

Then, as if to prove just that, a door I'd never even noticed opened up behind me, and a fresh voice floated in.

"Morning, Crew!"

My hand holding the note fisted shut, crumpling the napkin and its forbidden words.

Dominic clocked the action and laid his eyes on mine that had blown wide and were drying out in my head.

I'd completely forgotten about her.

"Gramma, there's chocolate pancakes!" Maya beamed as the woman I'd only met once before rounded my chair, kissing her son and granddaughter both on the cheek. Oh my god. I'd been so worried about running into Heather that it completely slipped my mind to be worried about running into his mom.

The older woman swept curls from Maya's forehead, smiling sweetly. "That sounds absolutely delicious, Pumpkin."

I ripped my foot from beneath Dominic's thigh so fast I hit my knee on the edge of the table. He flinched as I hissed and inched his hand towards me, holding it out as if to offer help or support or whatever. I jerked away from him, the legs of my chair scraping across the wood floor.

"Is everything all right?"

Panic was stretching my eyes open, and I knew it was, but I looked up to her anyway. His mother was waiting for me with raised eyebrows and worrying eyes the *exact* shade as her son's.

"Yeah, I just..." Stealing my hand with the note beneath the table to hide it, I scooted from my chair until I was standing, all eyes on me as I came up with an excuse.

"I just forgot to brush my teeth. So, I gotta go do that."

I didn't wait for any responses or questions or anything. I just beelined it back upstairs, practically throwing myself in the guest room.

Oh god. Both my palms flattened against the door as if his mother was chasing me and about to break it down. Actually, the napkin I'd passed with Dominic was stuck beneath one of my hands, burning my skin, and I rushed over to my overnight bag and stuffed it to the very bottom.

Hiding the evidence and all.

Fuck. Dominic and I agreeing to go back to basics had actually been a really stupid thing to do. Colossally stupid. Basics for us *still meant* flirting. We'd done that before we kissed, and it had only become relentless after.

Remembering back to how it was with Dominic before we'd admitted and given into the addiction, I remembered how stupid being around him made me. I broke all the rules then, and I was doing it now when a *lot* more than a job was on the line.

I stayed in the room for another ten or so minutes, pacing and breathing and reminding myself what was at stake here. We had our first test this morning, and we failed.

Big fat F.

Next time we were around each other in this house, we would be cool, collected, and keep our fuckable parts in our pants.

Centering myself as much as humanly possible for someone as off their rocker as me, I marched up to the bedroom door and opened it with the determination to face my downstairs audience again.

Except, one of my audience members was waiting right behind my door.

"Shit!"

I smacked my hand over my gasped curse, my other hand fisting where my heart was and holding onto it with all I had. Dominic's mother jumped back a step, her hands coming up next to her head as her eyes shot wide.

"Oh, I didn't mean to scare you, hon." She put a hand to her ample chest, her mouth pulling down with humor. "I guess that's what would happen when I stand outside your door like this, wouldn't it?"

She tittered a jovial laugh and I joined in, because what the fuck else was I supposed to do?

The last time I saw this woman, I was lip-locked with her son who was still totally married at the time. *Still* was totally married, and now I was crashing with him and his soon-to-be ex-wife like it was a normal thing to do.

"It's okay." I forced another laugh. "Nothing like a good jump scare to wake you up."

She did that whole sweet frown thing again, still kind of laughing and nodded. "I guess that's true, isn't it?"

I nodded back and pushed another chortle because I still had no idea what the hell was happening. I was a puppet with all my strings strung up high, being worked by a hand that had zero communication with my brain or mouth.

The situational laughter slowly died out, leaving a lonely and awkward as hell pause.

"It's Kat, right?"

Oh shit. Here we go.

"Yeah. You're—" *Dominic's mom.*

Except she cut me off by saying, "Meredith. We weren't properly introduced last time."

She angled herself a little closer, lowering her twangy voice like it was a fun secret between the two of us; the fact that she caught me with her son's tongue down my throat at his daughter's birthday party.

An uncomfortable note strangled between my lips, another awkward chuckle following. "Yeah, that was probably my fault."

"Oh, no. I—" She thinned her peach colored lips, a sharp sigh leaving her nose. His mom looked at me, the fine wrinkles embedded in her fair skin deepening around her eyes. "I'm sorry if I made you uncomfortable that day or now, even."

My lips parted in readied defense...

And then snapped shut.

What?

Those navigating puppet strings pulling me this way and that all dropped loose, whoever was orchestrating this interaction not even knowing how the hell to respond to that. I was on my own, free-falling, opening and closing my mouth like a freaking idiot.

My eyebrows pinched together, and I cocked my head at her, still not saying a goddamn thing. A slightly humored curiosity sketched an outline on her delicate features.

"You look confused."

Yeah, no shit, I wanted to say, but refrained long enough to think out my words.

"I am. I just—" *Say words. Say words, dammit.* "I didn't expect you to apologize given what you, uh, walked in on."

"Oh, well." She smiled down at the floor. *Smiled.* My confusion and wariness regarding this woman deepened. "I talked with my son for quite a long time after you left. I never would have expected to find him like that. He's not..." A flustered look came over her, and she shook her head as if shaking the truth right out of it. "He's not that type."

Until he met me.

She didn't say the words, but I heard them.

He wasn't the type to cheat until I came along and ruined all his good. I already knew that though. I *lived* that knowledge. I didn't need it spelled out for me by his mother that I'd tainted her precious little boy.

"He's loyal and he's dedicated, and he and Heather got married very young," she said all at once, her tone oddly level. Almost like she'd said this all before. "He was convinced it was true love, and once that boy is convinced of something, there's no deterring him."

Mhm. I'm familiar.

She flattened her lips together again, and I got flashes of her son doing the same thing several, several times during our conversations. The resemblance was probably more in his father, but I could see bits of Dominic in her too. Little ways she moved her eyebrows, her mouth—though surrounded by tiny wrinkles now—had the same shape as his, and of course, their eyes.

The color and intensity in them both were unparalleled by any other

Every single one of her slightly familiar features loosened, a solemn sadness blanketing her expression. She kept her attention to the floor, nodding her head just barely.

"It's been really hard as a mother watching their marriage break and him break with it."

All of my moxie slacked.

The tension in my mouth did too, and it fell to an open frown. I blinked at her and her brutal honesty. This hadn't been where I'd expected this conversation to go.

"After I found you two in that shed, he told me it wasn't what it looked like, and then he told me about asking for a divorce."

Oh shit. Okay. So she knew *everything*.

My gut loaded up in preparation to be stabbed at, gutted through, ripped apart for being the downfall to her son's marriage. This had to be it. The blow she came up here to deliver. My abs locked together, readying for the assault.

His mom—Meredith—brought her pointed gaze up to me. "I imagine most parents when they hear their child is getting a divorce feel sadness or anger. You wanna know what I felt?"

"What?" I asked, on edge.

Meredith's expression softened. "Relief."

My reaction was as obvious as Dominic's good looks and perfect ass. My eyebrows cranked high and my lips peeled apart yet again.

Okay, what?

She absorbed my clearly taken aback response, breathing a soft laugh. Her eyes were nothing but warm, and all that warmth was aimed right at me. I shifted against it, the heat sticking to my skin and slicking between joints and bones.

"My son deserves the world and the greatest love in it, and that unfortunately was never Heather," she admitted, shaking her head of flaxen hair.

Out of instinct, I flickered a vigilant glance behind her shoulder. She was speaking so candidly; it shocked and terrified me. Heather could be lurking around any corner listening in on her mother-in-law spill the truth.

Instead of hushing or stopping, she kept on. "When I found you two, I asked him what the heck he was thinking shacking up with his daughter's nanny. Like I said, that's not him. He wouldn't do that because he was bored or... because he liked the way you looked or whatnot. Which, you're very lovely by the way."

"Thanks," I breathed, feeling lightheaded all of a sudden.

"And he said...." She held her tongue to smile a real *genuine* smile right up at me. "He said he wasn't doing it because you were beautiful or because he knew he wasn't happy in his marriage. He said it was because you were the most incredible woman he'd ever met, and he didn't know how he'd lived so long without you."

Air escaped my lungs and inflated my head.

My feeling lightheaded was now more of a dizzying sensation, my vision and hearing both sort of fading in and fading out to blurs.

I was in that same ocean Dominic helped me float in back at the hotel. The same one that I avoided all my life, but Dominic made it so I could breathe with him there, holding my head above water. His mom found me in that same dangerous ocean, except she didn't give me a life raft to hang onto.

She shoved my head right below the cusp of salt-stained water.

"You look a little shell-shocked, hon."

My eyes were already burning. "A bit," I replied, throat and tone dry.

"You know," Meredith closed the distance between us finally, dropping to a whisper. "My room isn't very far from the kitchen, Kat."

Oh, holy fuck me.

I sucked down just enough breathable air to ask, "So you heard...?"

She nodded, a knowing smile quirking up her cheeks. "The orgasm question is what initially caught my ear."

"Oh, *lord*." My whole body slumped into the doorframe, head knocking against it.

Good. I needed the throbbing to keep me awake and processing.

She shook in mild laughter, a smile brightening her whole face as she worked to catch my eye. "You're very funny, and you're very good with those girls... and I could hear it in my son's voice that he is absolutely smitten with you."

And there my head went again, plunging beneath the surface break.

"I don't judge anyone on how they fall in love. My husband and I met at my first job. He was my *manager*," she divulged like the hottest gossip in town.

I barely heard it over the roiling, rushing water filling my ears, lungs, drowning my world.

Fall in love. Fall in love. Fall in—

The sickness choked.

My heart vacuumed into itself as it tried to breathe, suffocating on its own skin and veins. My chest felt like it was caving in, taking ribs, organs, and oxygen with it. The sickness had never *ever* been so powerful, so enlivened and thriving at his mother's words.

Dominic and I *weren't* falling in love. Did Dominic give her that impression? Because he knew better. He knew that wasn't where our story was headed. We were passing chapters in each other's lives, but our endings were nowhere near each other.

We had *chemistry*. We didn't have love.

However, the sickness preened at the very mention of us falling into it, sinking its polished talons in my heart and latching on.

"I'm just happy he's found someone like you and I wanted to clear the air between us in case it was all *weird* from the shed."

She pushed another hearty bout of laughter. This woman liked to laugh a lot. I didn't try to match her this time. I couldn't even try. Once she finished, she settled her kind eyes on me. Her fingers reached out and touched my wrist, a conflicting sensation of cold and soft.

"I'm really looking forward to getting to know you, Kat."

I nodded, forcing out a wispy response. "You too."

She was one hundred percent unaware of the sanity spiral she'd just nudged me into, simply squeezing my wrist in her too soft hand before taking a step back.

"All right. Well, I only had two pancakes and I think I'm about to go get two more." Another. Fucking. Chuckle. "I'll see you down there, hon."

She left, and I watched her go.

I watched her instead of following her because I couldn't. I couldn't move a damn muscle. Everything—every nerve, every fiber, every molecule had gone numb.

This was all wrong.

Yes, I knew the potential for love existed between Dominic and I, but *because* I knew the danger was there, I would get out before it got me. *That* had been the plan. Well, I'd actually had like five different versions of a plan by now, but falling in love was never one of them.

I knew that, and I made sure Dominic knew that. Though, if his mom got the idea from him that a chance at falling into stupid love still existed between us...

Then I needed a new plan.

THIRTY-TWO

"So, are you working for them again or what?"

I turned to Layla on the bench, squinting against the sun blinding me to anything but her silhouette of dark hair and button nose. "Nah. Dominic offered, but his mom is around a lot to help with Maya, so he'd basically be paying me to watch my own sister."

"Is Mrs. Sharon still on bed rest?"

"Yeah, it's only been two days of it, and she was already going stir crazy on the phone last night when I checked in."

I plucked a leaf from one of the park's fatter bushes next to us, folding it in halves until I'd folded it to pieces. Chucking it to the side, I cast a look back over to the swings, catching Maya and Charlotte in a 'who can kick higher' competition.

Each push of their little legs, they soared higher into the sky until their squeals of laughter could reach the clouds. A soft smile turned up my cheeks, but it fell when I looked past the girls and throng of kale green bushes and spotted the silver Explorer parked behind it all.

I knew Dominic was in there with Ryan, watching me and probably talking about me and all his frustrations with me these past few days. This was a setup they'd arranged to see if we could lure Tommy out and within five hundred feet of me so they could arrest him.

So far, we'd been here for thirty minutes and nothing.

"How was your grandparents'?" I asked, removing my focus from the Explorer.

She huffed and adjusted her heart-shaped sunglasses on her face. "Fine. Boring. Glad to be back even if we're being used as bait."

"Yeah, Dominic wasn't thrilled about the idea, but it's the only move they've got right now."

"Oh, is your Prince Charming worried about you?" Her pouty lips and dramatic tone were mocking. Both struck the wrong cord in me.

"Can we not go there today?"

I pointed my daggered glare at her, holding her wide-eyed reaction for all of two seconds before moving my focus back to the girls. Layla *of course* didn't let my snapping comment go unacknowledged.

"Um, excuse me." A hand slapped over my thigh, forcing my attention back on her and all the greedy intrigue threaded through her thickly shaped eyebrows. "Did something change since the hotel? You said you two basically agreed to be almost fuck buddies until the divorce."

"That was before I had to pack up and shack up."

I slumped my forehead into the palm of my hand, groaning and wanting to rip out this heart of mine that had been on fire for days. The fear of the sickness—the fear of dying from it—had been a relentless burn since the conversation with Dominic's mom.

Fuck. I didn't think I wanted to talk about any of this. I'd kept it all in for three days now, packed up and ignoring it was there, but with Layla sitting right there, it all came spilling out as if it'd been waiting on the tip of my tongue all day.

"We agreed to press stop on everything at the beginning of the week, which was *fine.*" Except it wasn't. How battered my chest felt proved it wasn't fine, and I was in trouble. "But we're both dumbasses and that lasted all of one night. The next morning we were flirting and laughing and he was holding my ankle—"

"Your ankle?"

"Yeah, because it was all he *could* hold without anyone seeing."

Because holding me in any way was wrong. We were wrong. Every single torrid bit of us. "We barely lasted twelve hours without falling back into it, and we were sleeping for like nine of those."

Layla's face had grown alert, and I knew why. I knew my voice and mannerisms were getting a bit agitated, a bit manic. Emotions I'd kept locked down for three days now were rallying inside of me, readying to charge and fill my mouth with all their dirty little truths.

"It's just so... easy and *stupid*." Exasperation swept my arm wide as I backhanded Layla's arm. "Oh, and his mom heard it all."

She grabbed her arm, rubbing it. "His mom who walked in on you two?"

"Yup, and she *loves* me."

That got the expected reaction. Eyes bugging, jaw dropping. "What?"

"I know! She just keeps *complimenting* me and trying to make inside jokes with me like we're the best of friends," I exclaimed, heavy breathing working my lungs. "She cornered me the first morning we were there to tell me how happy she was to meet me and how she was *so* glad Dominic found me."

"Okay, I'm confused."

"Thank you!" My hands flew into the air, her already large eyes flying wider as my energy peaked. Compacted adrenaline tingled in my chest as I huffed, "Me too."

So fucking confused.

"No, no." She set her delicate fingers on my leg again. "Kat, I'm confused why you're saying all of this like it's a bad thing."

I blanched at my best friend, taken aback. How did she not understand?

The corner of my mouth cracked up, and I looked away from her out to the playground. Wind rolled the leaves and blades of grass in the park, flickering them all in waves that rustled and whispered. The breeze hit my face next, fanning its fall breath over my heated cheeks and trying to cool me off.

It didn't work.

"You didn't hear everything she said to me." I laughed; a real bitter sound. "She said that Dominic and I were falling in *love*."

I spit the word out there like it was the nastiest thing I'd ever tasted. I still felt it on my tongue even after it left. It was a lingering ghost, a nightmare that wouldn't fade away. I pressed my hand around my throat, rubbing the sides where the word had touched and feeling my fingers twitch with the desire to squeeze.

The girls both jumped off of their swings, Maya sticking her landing and Charlotte taking a small tumble but popping right back up with a squeal. They raced to the slides, climbing up ladders to reach the jungle gym's landing.

Layla hadn't said anything yet, but I could feel the force of her stare pushing against the side of my face. Half out of spite, half out of zero self-control, I snapped back to her, my sharp tongue ready to fight.

"What?" I hissed.

She didn't flinch at my tone. In fact, I didn't think anything could crack the granite exterior she'd molded around herself as she looked at me. She was so serious, more than I'd ever seen her.

Her question was carefully spoken though. "Are you?"

My response was not so much careful as it was swift and pissed off.

"*No.*"

I jerked away from her again, distracting myself by watching the girls instead of thinking about her question. A question that never should have come out of her mouth. First his mom, and now Layla? Just how many people were going to attack me with something that wasn't true while emboldening the sickness?

It was already worse than it'd ever been these last few days. Stronger.

I didn't need anyone else feeding it and nourishing it with the crazy notion that it just might win.

Next to me on the bench, Layla shifted closer. Her vanilla scent overtook the fresh air and her hand came to my back, her nails running lines up and down.

"Kit Kat. You're freaking out."

Not paying her a glance, I mumbled. "I'm fine."

"You're picking at your lips."

My fingers froze mid pull. Dammit, she was right. Damn near growling, I fisted my hand and shoved it into the crook of my arm where my mother's nasty habits couldn't reach me.

"What has he had to say about it?" she asked gently.

"I don't know," I replied like a child. Like a peevish, bratty child. Immaturity was not a good color on me.

"How don't you know? You've been living in the same house for four days now."

I folded my arms over my chest, crossing my legs too. "Because I've been staying away from him like we agreed."

"Has he tried texting you?"

"Yeah." I half scoffed, half laughed. "And how much do you wanna bet his wife checks his text history?"

It had been a miserable last three days in that house. My options of people to run into was like a freaking Sophie's Choice. There *were* no ideal candidates. I was either dealing with Heather hovering over my shoulder, throwing me icy looks and jabbing comments under her breath, or Meredith showering me in kindness that I didn't fucking get or deserve.

As for Dominic...

Running from him, hiding from him, and ignoring him had been the worst of all.

Any room we found ourselves in together, I made myself scarce as soon as I was able. We hadn't exchanged more than a few sentences over the three days, but it wasn't for lack of trying on his part. He was always trying to catch my eye across the room, find reasons to talk to me, or send me messages asking to meet.

I only replied when I needed to, and it was mostly to tell him to delete our text history in case Heather went through it. Which—it was Heather. Chances were pretty up there that she snooped through his phone.

Dominic could tell something was wrong. It was in the way he looked at me and the near desperation he'd stoop to during our occasional text conversations.

Each time he begged to see me, I felt worse. Each time I denied him, I felt like dying.

But that feeling of death was just more proof that what I was doing was right.

"Kat."

All the hair on my arms stood at the way Layla said my name. The air prickled with intensity at the same time it turned to dust on my tongue. I stopped breathing right as she spoke.

"It's okay if you love him."

Panic erupted so fast, it left me breathless.

I wasn't even sure how I got my next words out with such force and malice. "I don't, and we're not talking about this."

Layla pushed a sigh, and her hand vanished from my back. It appeared around my knee next, forcing me to twist towards her. Her Hulk-like strength plucked my surprise like it always did, yanking me around on the bench so she could level me with seriousness as piercing as the sun above her.

"Listen, I know why you're scared to be that vulnerable with someone or to care about someone like that, but... I don't think you have much of a choice."

Insult narrowed my eyes to slits. "Excuse me?"

"I don't think you have a choice." Something akin to astonishment lit behind her eyes. She tried to ease the blow gently. "I- I think it's done."

My upper lip curled back, and I fucking dared her to say it. "Meaning?"

She waited for one *profound* beat.

Everything in the world stopped to hear it.

Everything in my world imploded when she ended it.

"I think you already love him," she stated. Yes, *stated*. "Or you're at least falling for him."

It was at that exact moment that I learned you could feel so much that you felt nothing. Back in the hotel room with Dominic, I remembered feeling so much that everything inside of me burned, and I thought that was the worst.

Except I was wrong. This was the worst. This immediate explosion of every horrible, anxious, searing, blood-curdling feeling I'd ever felt hitting at the exact same time that it created a pain so intense, so unbearable, so unsurvivable, my body just quit.

It went from one extreme to the next so fast, my *soul* had whiplash.

I was left working on autopilot, saying and doing the things Kat Sanders would normally say when faced with the reality of love.

"You can't be serious."

Denial.

"I am." She nodded, sending a cross glance down my front. "I think that's why you're so snippy right now. You know it's true too."

"I don't know it's true," I spat but could hear tired syllables in my fight. I jutted my shoulders back, trying to force the venom. "I don't even know him really. I've known him, for what, three months? Do you really think that's enough time to fall in love with someone?"

"I don't think time has anything to do with it."

And again, she sounded so *certain*. I looked at my best friend like I'd never seen her before. Like she'd never seen me and had no idea the person or scarred heart she was dealing with.

"Okay fine," I conceded in spite instead of earnest. "Fine, let's play by your rules and say it is enough time to lose yourself that completely to another person. Even if three months *was* enough time, I wouldn't know *how* to love someone like that. Loving my sister and you are different. That's an easy kind of love, but there's nothing easy about romantic love. It's brutal and impossible to describe, and if I can't describe it, then I highly doubt I've fallen into it."

"You don't have to define love to experience it," she pushed back. "Love isn't a definition. It's a feeling. It's what *you're* feeling."

"The fuck it is," I countered, wrenching myself off the bench. My feet stumbled, but I managed to keep myself standing if purely by adrenaline alone. A gust of wind whipped at my hair just as I whipped to face Layla, sending power through its breeze.

"I mean it very seriously when I say that I have never and *will* never fall in love, and you're starting to piss me off accusing me of being that stupid."

"Fine. Get pissed off." She ushered her hand out to me flippantly, throwing an arm over the back of the bench. "I don't care."

I ripped my mouth apart, tongue ready to spar when she cut me off. "And it's not stupid. Your parents gave you a really shitty example of love, but that's not how all love stories go, Kat. Some people get that end-all be-all, happily ever after."

"Yeah, well those people don't have a sister to look after who depends on them to be *sane* and *present*."

She scoffed a laugh, sending it high into the air. "You talk about love like it's this mind-eating disease."

"It *is*."

"It's *not*."

She let her head fall back with another soft laugh, blinking up at the wispy clouds brush-stroking a blue sky. Her lashes were so lush, they looked like onyx butterflies flapping over her eyes from where I was standing. I'd always been kind of jealous of them.

A ponderous sigh brought her gaze back to me, a glint of inspiration dotting both eyes. "I know I've never been in love either, but unlike yours, my parents gave me a pretty stellar example of it. Love can be amazing if it's with the right person."

I sunk my stare to the earth, digging my toes into soft ground and watching the grass break around my black sneaker. The right person, huh?

"Well..." My teeth nabbed onto the inside of my cheek, chewing my voice away to a mumble. "All the signs in the universe point to Dominic not being the right person."

Our timing was all off. I was being hunted by someone my mom pissed off, and he would be in legal battles and shit for who knows how long. Our goals didn't align either. He wanted commitment, and I wanted nothing to do with a serious relationship.

Tan ankle boots met my shoes in the grass. A hand cupped my elbow, Layla's touch guiding my stare back up to her.

"You don't even believe that when you say it."

My lips parted to argue... but nothing came out.

I grit my teeth against the nothingness, grinding them hard enough they could have chiseled down to dust. This wasn't right. *He* wasn't right. Everything pointed to us being wrong for each other except my heart, but it was disillusioned by the sickness, and I couldn't trust it.

Dominic and I weren't falling in love, and we weren't right for each other.

I'd repeat that mantra again and again until it was ingrained in the grooves of my brain and as true as anything else I'd told myself. For now, I couldn't deny her accusations with enough gusto, so I'd run from them instead.

"I don't wanna talk about this anymore."

Layla inhaled a hefty breath through her nose, staring at me tightly as she pinched her mouth to the side. She let the breath out by saying, "Fine. We can drop it for now. Just—"

Her fingers dented into my arm, holding my focus and overwhelming my heart.

"You deserve some good in your life, babe. You actually deserve *a lot* of good in it. Don't run from it when it's right in front of you."

THIRTY-THREE

I didn't listen to Layla.

The next day, I kept running. I ran right into the weekend without talking to Dominic more than I had to and planned to run right out of the house as soon as Heather got home Saturday night.

6 o'clock hit, the front door *swooshed* open, and the click of heels echoed up the stairs.

I'd already set Maya and Charlotte up with a movie, and Meredith had agreed to keep an eye on them for the night when Heather neglected to. With me, Dominic, and his mother around, I hadn't seen Heather so much as look in Maya's direction now that she wasn't being forced to.

In the guest bedroom, I jumped up and down on one foot, trying to work the heel of my foot into my sneaker. I didn't exactly pack any going out clothes, but I'd been able to makeshift an outfit for tonight that worked.

My black sneakers, pitch black jeans with rips on both thighs, and a blood red tank top that cut off right at my belly button. I was gonna use it for sleeping, but desperate times call for desperate means.

And I was *completely* desperate to get out of this house.

Sneakers on, I padded over to the mirror and swiped a red tinted gloss over the curves of my lips. I'd braided my hair after showering last night and had let it set all day so my natural waves were primed in true fashion tonight.

I felt bad about lying to Layla that I'd been cleared to go out by Dominic, but not bad enough not to do it.

We wouldn't do anything crazy. A few drinks. A few bars. A few hours of blowing off some steam. Dominic wasn't supposed to get home until around 11pm tonight anyway. I'd be home and tucked into bed by then, and he'd be none the wiser.

Plus, the mace he'd given me was sitting pretty in the back pocket of my jeans just in case.

See? I was being smart about being stupid.

Readying to leave, I gave Charlotte a kiss on the cheek goodnight—and Maya one too when she pouted—and raced down the stairs, phone and I.D. in hand.

My speedy steps were nearing the bottom when they slowed and then stopped altogether, my gut gripping into a tight, uncomfortable ball as I saw her.

Watching me descend into an evening of rule-breaking and lies was the bitch in Prada heels.

"Going out, Ms. Sanders?"

Her voice had become like nails on a fucking chalkboard, clenching all my muscles as I stiffly finished the walk to the bottom of the stairs. Heather tracked my movements with eyes like a serpent, slitted and calculating and likely with fantasies of my demise playing behind them.

I planted myself flat-footed in front of her, standing my ground and tipping up my chin.

"You gonna tell on me?"

There was no reason she shouldn't. It would probably earn her some points with Dominic, and she was seriously lacking on those. If there was even the slightest opportunity for this woman to throw me to the wolves, I was dead sure she'd take it and make sure she stuck around to watch the feast.

Which is why I was so surprised when she shook her head and purred, "No. You should go out."

—*and get hit by a bus.*

Her subtext wasn't exactly subtle but whatever.

There was about a fifty-fifty chance she was lying, but at this point, I really didn't care. I had to get out of here for just one night. I needed to feel like *me* again, and I couldn't exactly do that with soon-to-be ex wives hanging around or mothers who were already planning my future out with their son.

"Thanks," I said.

Neither of us went to move.

Layla was waiting outside to pick me up, but I could spare a few important seconds to remind and *prove* to this woman that I wasn't afraid of her. Last time we sparred wasn't fair, because she had all the advantage and all I had was a panic attack.

This time, I held her gaze, and I held it fearlessly. Even as she drew herself a devilish grin. Even as she refused to blink.

Her goddamn perfectly plucked eyebrows raised an inch on her smooth forehead. The ice blue of her eyes glinted.

"Be careful."

AKA: I still mean get run over by a bus.

"Thanks for your concern." And I grinned right back at her, throwing in an unintentional wink that hit her square in her rich bitch face before I left out the front door.

Layla's car was parked down by the mailbox, base thumping her windows and shaking her doors. My grin turned up with excitement, feet traveling down the driveway with an added pep. I ripped the passenger door open on her silver SUV—I called it her *mom* car—and plunked right down next to her.

Tonight, she'd gone all purple from head to pointed toe. Even purple glitter eyeshadow swept her eyelids, and I almost laughed at how opposing we were tonight. She looked like she was about to go to a rave, and I looked like the chick at parties that you couldn't tell if they were homeless or a hooker.

She wriggled her eyebrows at me. "Ready?"

"So fucking ready."

Three hours, two bars, and one round of shots later, I was finally feeling like myself again.

Layla and I stuck to the outskirts of downtown, keeping close enough to the car that our walk back wouldn't be excruciating, especially for Layla in the skyhigh heels she'd chosen to wear.

Everything was going great. The bar we'd landed at wasn't packed, and the music didn't totally suck either. Everything about the evening was fun and careless, and the buzz I had going was one of those miraculous ones you only achieved once in a blue moon.

Then my phone rang, and that happy buzz made a U-turn into a headache real fast.

Dominic's name lit up the screen, and I clicked it off and shoved my phone in my back pocket. Then, a slightly sober thought needled through that made me pull it back out and send a quick text that said, *'I'm fine.'*

His response was immediate.

'Kat, go back to the house. Please.'

Annoyance kicked back my head with a groan, and Layla flashed me a curious side-eye at the bar while she waited for our drinks. I brushed her off, diving my nose back into my phone.

'Am I in any immediate danger?'

'If you're out without supervision, yes.'

"Sounds like you're assuming, sir," I mumbled to myself, blinking slowly at the screen.

"Everything okay?"

My head popped back up as Layla met me at the end of the bar, smiling a thank you as she handed me my gin and whatever. I couldn't decide what I wanted other than gin, so I had Layla surprise me.

"Yeah, it's fine." I slid my phone back into my jeans. "So, whatcha get me?"

"Something called a Gin Gimlet? I don't know, the bartender suggested it."

Humming in interest, I plucked the glass from her hand, condensation already slicking down the sides as I brought the straw between my teeth. Sweet notes and a splash of lime flooded my tastebuds, and I perked back, pleasantly surprised.

"You are the only twenty-one-year-old that I know who likes gin," she mused.

I shrugged, nursing the drink. "I think it's more nostalgia than anything. My grandparents both liked gin a lot and would always bring their own bottle over whenever they came."

"Ah, what every granddaughter wants. *Alcohol*."

"It wasn't so bad. They'd always let me try some."

"And how old were you?"

I took a deep breath, filling my head with smoke-tinged oxygen to fuel the answers. "The first time I ever drank with them or the first time they gave me gin?"

Layla smacked her plum painted lips. "How old were you the first time you had *any* alcohol?"

"Eleven."

Her doe eyes bulged, and I chuckled a dark laugh. "Yeah, I know. Dad wanted a drinking buddy though."

"That's so fucked up."

"If it helps, he always cut me off after one drink."

"It doesn't."

"Well, I tried."

This time, it was Layla's phone that chimed with a message, and her face lit up in a dopey grin.

Elbows on the table, I leaned closer with a smirk. "That wouldn't happen to be Ryan, would it?"

They hadn't seen each other since the hotel; I knew that much. Well, I knew *that* and about every lurid detail of their encounter the night Dominic and I were in the pool. From the stories Layla told, they'd had a *very* good time. Oh, and Ryan was apparently a screamer.

Her purple-lidded eyes rolled as she tried to hide her excitement, teeth clamping down on her bottom lip before the force of her smile ripped it free. She nodded, flipping her phone over so the screen was facing the bar top.

"He's such a dork."

I wondered if he was with Dominic right now. "Is he working tonight?"

"No, he got off about an hour ago."

A little bubble of relief popped inside my stomach. "He tryin' to get you to ditch me and go hang out with him?"

"I don't know. I didn't read it. I'm out with *you*."

Air puffed between my lips as I blew a raspberry, tossing my stare behind her to where the sign for the restrooms glowed.

"All right." I sucked down a mouthful of my drink, licking the residue pebbles off my lips. "How about I go pee and give you a few minutes to blow his mind and blow his load, and then when I get back, we'll do another shot?"

"*Another?*"

"Yeah, *another*. I've had a shitty week."

Tack that onto a few shitty years, and I think I deserved another shot, thank you very much.

Layla held her hands up in surrender, and then used them both to snatch up her phone, a greedy enthusiasm vibrating around her. I rounded her with a stupid smile, glad she'd found someone who put some shine behind her eyes.

The bar's bathroom wasn't as tragic as I pictured it would be. Tonight was the first time I'd ever *legally* been in a bar. I hadn't really thought about it until the night was already in motion. It didn't feel like a big deal since I'd been in bars with my parents when I was younger and just sat in the corner while they got hammered. Those ones were always hole-in-the-walls that smelled like piss and depravity.

This place was much nicer, and I did my business and washed my hands, taking a few extra moments to fix up my waves of hair. I waited around for another aimless minute or two to make sure Layla had enough time with Ryan before kicking the bathroom door open and stepping out.

"Woah!"

I stumbled back, nearly slipping and falling on my ass if it hadn't been for the arms reaching out to stabilize me.

"Sorry! I didn't mean to scare you!"

Slapping my hand over my thrumming heart, I hit Layla with a confused glower. "Jesus *Christ*. Thank fuck I already peed. What're you doing?"

"Oh—" For a split second, she looked totally and completely frazzled. Her eyes zapped wide, mouth hanging open while no words came out. I cocked her a questioning hook of my brow, and it seemed to break her out of whatever weird brain fritz she was in. "I was coming to get you! My friend just texted about this house party that's apparently pretty chill. We *have* to go."

"Uh," Her wide gaze dropped to my bottom lip as I pulled a frown. "What friend?"

"Some new guy we hired at work. You'd definitely like him because Marty *hates* him."

Now that brought a laugh as I pictured Marty's round face all burnt with rage. I made him wear that tomato look countless times over my years there. His ears always got the reddest.

Still, I was having a good time here and really wanted that next shot.

"Can we rain check?"

"No, come on," she whined. "I swear it'll be fun!"

"We're having fun here, aren't we?"

She rolled her eyes and scoffed, slinging her arm through mine to slowly drag me away from the bathroom and towards the exit. "Yes, and we will have even *more* fun at this party. Plus—"

A hardly shameless glance was thrown my way over her shoulder. "I kinda already told him we were coming."

"And what if I said no?"

She stopped just shy of running over this couple waiting for the drinks, pinning me with a no bullshit look. "It's a party with free booze. You're not saying no."

Touché.

After that, I let myself be pulled through the scattered crowd, some grinding their hips to the music and others blowing plumes of smoke towards the already hazy ceiling. The force she was dragging me with boiled my brain in confusion, and a small voice was chirping at me to stop her and ask why going to this party was suddenly so important.

I ignored that voice and got in my best friend's car anyway, letting her drive us off into the night.

We only drove for about ten minutes before pulling into a complex as average as any other suburban neighborhood that existed. Layla parked the car on the street in front of what I *guessed* was our party house?

Nothing about it exactly screamed rager to me.

It was a one story beige home, a wrought-iron gate over the front door, and one lonely car in the driveway. Stepping out into the street, the sound of party music was seriously lacking too.

"Lay, are you sure this is it?"

She pitched me a nod over the roof of the car as she got out too, sizing up the house with glittering eyes. Had she never been here before? "It's not supposed to be anything huge, but we might also be some of the first people here."

"Oh *great*."

My perfect buzz was already on its way out. I was gonna need to fix that fast if I was about to be stuck in a house with strangers. Layla came up behind me, and I caught her shooting strange looks up and down the street as we walked up the paved driveway.

Her bizarre behavior finally cemented my steps in place, pulling her to a stop with me.

"Are you okay?"

She batted down at me, expanding her stare. "Yeah! Definitely. It's just cold out here."

I paused, feeling the air hover over my bare arms and chest, the chill slight and damp. "It's like 65 degrees out."

"That's basically freezing."

"Oh my god," I laughed, letting her pick up our trek to the quiet house.

"If we walk in there and this is some weird orgy thing, you have to promise to stick with me the whole time, okay? You're not leaving me alone to be fucked by some rando you work with."

She barked out a laugh, wrapping her arm through mine again. "If we were ever in an orgy together, you are the last person I would bail on. Unless, like, Chris Hemsworth walked into the room for some reason."

"I give you full permission to leave me if you have the chance to fuck either of the Hemsworth brothers."

We blew through our soft chuckles as we made it up to the rod-iron gate over the door. Layla peeled the black gate back, rasping her knuckles on the white door that had seen better days. We waited not even three seconds before the door yanked open—

And my jaw dropped open too.

"Ryan?"

He was standing there in jeans and one of those old ass 'Vote for Pedro' shirts. He didn't seem surprised to see me like I was sure I did to him. My eyebrows slammed together, and I swiveled towards Layla to ask her why the fuck we were at Ryan's house.

Her entire face cracked, guilt seeping through.

"I'm sorry! I didn't like lying to you."

My lips formed around the beginning of the word 'what' when I steered my head back in Ryan's direction. He pressed his mouth together, driving his head towards the floor as he stepped to the side.

The muscles in my ready-to-spew mouth laxed all tension.

Dread gut-punched through me. Every ounce of alcohol I'd consumed tonight vanished from my blood, leaving me stone-cold sober and wishing the exact opposite.

Standing inside the house towards the back, his hands flattened against a bar counter and head hanging low, almost at a ninety degree angle with his body, was Dominic. Even from here, I could make out every harsh angle of his imposing frame that was cut with tension.

Aw shit.

I was in *very* big trouble.

THIRTY-FOUR

The room was so fucking quiet.

Layla and I were still stationed on the other side of the front door. No one was moving. Everything about the moment was very... stuck. Dominic still hadn't looked up at me, and I warred with myself if I really wanted him to or not.

His gunmetal eyes would undoubtedly be bulleted, and I knew before asking that my skin wasn't thick enough to withstand the blow right now. One heart-rendering look from him, and I'd be reminded of those *awful* accusations Layla and his mother put on me.

I'd wobble and sway, thinking about the love they claimed I had for him, and fall to my knees and beg for it not to be true.

A not-so-gentle hand pushed into the small of my back, urging me inside.

Layla slammed the door shut once we were both in. The noise of distraction wheeled me around to my best friend, questions and accusations prepped hot in the back of my throat.

Before I could get any out, fast words started pouring out of her like a faucet with no stopping point.

"You can't be mad at me! Yes, I tricked you to get you here, but you lied first when you told me that Dominic said it was okay to go out tonight. That ended up being why Ryan was texting me, to see if I was with you and if I could get you here because it wasn't safe for you to be out." She huffed when she was finished, leveling me with a stare that trampled my heart in the first stampede of guilt for the night.

I was just gonna go ahead and assume that by the end of the night, I'd be guilt trip roadkill.

Even though I *felt* sorry, the words weren't coming out. They were trapped behind teeth locked together by my stubborn temper. It was churning the longer I stood there holding eye contact with her, knowing I'd be on defense for the rest of the night.

I was trapped, literally *trapped,* in a house with the man I've been avoiding all week, and I knew he'd want me to explain myself and I couldn't. I couldn't explain what people thought was happening between us, because speaking the words just might make them true.

"I wasn't *completely* stupid." My fingers dug around in my back pocket. "I brought mace," I defended, showing it to her.

"That was smart," Ryan commented from the side.

Grateful enthusiasm snapped my stare to him. "Thank you!"

Layla sliced a fearful glare over to Ryan, and he went stiff. I could practically hear him changing from my side to hers. *Wuss.*

Moving her focus back to me, Layla took a small step in, lowering her voice to just between us.

"If you did all this just so you could get away from him for a night, that's next level commitment issues, babe."

I rolled my eyes to the side, staring at the wall instead of her. Dominic wasn't the *only* reason I'd gone out tonight. Though, she also wasn't wrong either. Calling what I had commitment issues was the same as calling a volcanic eruption a campfire.

"Kat." My sharp gaze cut back to her. "You have to talk to him."

If possible, my teeth clamped down harder. I felt my cheeks pulse out like Dominic's always did, and my vision of Layla became obscured by how deep my eyebrows sunk over my eyes in defiance of her. It had taken all my effort, all my strength this week *not* to talk to him.

Now, I didn't see how I had a choice.

"You can use the back room if you want," Ryan spoke up, talking back towards Dominic.

An impatient beat and then—

"Thank you."

My heart ricocheted at the hollow sound of Dominic's voice. Had I done that? Had I stripped the color straight out of his voice and made it this monotone vibration of meaningless letters? The ache spreading through my bones said that I had.

It was my fault, and my walls built themselves taller and wrapped themselves in barbed-wire, readying for the onslaught of blame that I just *knew* was coming. Everyone in the room was mad at me. I'd disappointed everyone in it tonight by being reckless and impulsive.

At least I was keeping myself on brand.

Heavy footfall echoed across the tiled floor of Ryan's home. The footsteps were familiar and fading farther. Confusion powered my actions as I jerked around to see the last of Dominic's back disappear down a hallway.

He didn't even wait for me.

I stared after him with a hurt I had no right to feel burning in my chest. I thought it might be my lightning, and that even *it* was mad at me. I'd chased away our thunder and gotten exactly what I wanted.

As I walked the same path Dominic went, rounding Ryan's smallish living room and heading down the hall, I thought about what a brutal storm this was about to be. His thunder would clap and my lightning would strike, and neither of us would come out unscathed.

Maybe if I was lucky, the collision would be so devastating, it would destroy whatever was left of our limbo sky, and we'd have no choice but to part ways.

Open doors and rooms flanked on either side of me as I trekked down the narrow hall. Ryan's place wasn't big, but there were an odd amount of places to be in it. I counted one bathroom, one bedroom, and a junk room slash office before I made it to the end of the hallway where the door was cracked just so.

Dim light spilled through, and I didn't stop for one second to rethink how I wanted to approach this. I didn't *want* to think. I just wanted yelling and bad blood spilt between us, splattering a line down the middle that neither of us would cross ever again.

I pushed right through the door, finding another tiny bedroom with a bed in the middle and packing boxes with all sorts of shit spilling out lined up against the far wall. Dominic was standing a few feet away, but I didn't risk eye contact. Nope. My stubborn temper twisted me back around fast, closing the door behind me to at least try to pad our inevitable clash.

I breathed a brusque sigh, pushing it out like I was preparing for battle. The air in the room already alluded to the severity this fight would go to, brittle and buzzing with explosive potential.

There was movement behind me, and I snapped around, my defenses sharp and ready to maim.

Instead, warmth and the fresh fragrance of earth enveloped me.

I froze.

Dominic wrapped me up completely, folding me into his hard chest and holding on tight. Even for how warm he was, chills racked my body, springing goosebumps up across my skin like daisies and his touch was the sun. The weight of his head rested on top of mine, a deep exhale tickling my hair.

My arms were trapped at my sides, my forehead pressed against his sternum as I whispered, "What are you doing?"

More hairs tickled on the top of my head as he spoke against it.

"Holding you."

My lips formed around another W question that I couldn't get out. Why? *Why* was he holding me instead of tearing me down and ripping me apart? He was furious at me. He had to be. I'd directly disobeyed him.

He had every right to spit in my face and tell me I was more trouble than I was worth.

Instead, he ran one of his hands up the length of my spine, stroking his affection into me. I shuddered, and so did my defenses. Those walls I'd built so high and ready for the worst Dominic could deliver were breaking down block by block. Each sweetened caress up my back wore down another and then another.

I felt them going, scrambling mentally to rebuild them as they sunk lower.

My heart slapped as I panicked to reinforce what I was losing and at how *fast* it was happening. I'd been so prepared for the storm—a fucking hurricane—and all I was getting were raindrops down my back, slowly disintegrating my walls like paper.

My hands clamped to fists as I struggled to hold onto it, shaking at my sides. Whether Dominic sensed the fight or not, everything he did next worked against it. His long fingers split through my hair at the nape of my neck, bringing my shaking fists above the waistband of his work slacks, pinching his white shirt between my angry knuckles.

I wanted to push him away with my grip.

Instead, I pulled his waist closer with a strangled whimper.

My back bent to him, that tether in my chest arching me closer than I wanted to be. Dominic hooked me in tighter, anchoring my body to his like he knew I needed him to float, but all I wanted was to drown.

Not drown in love's ocean, and not drown in him, but drown in denial that it didn't take less than sixty seconds alone in a room with him for me to lose.

A week of avoiding. Three months of trying to survive the sickness. A lifetime of trying to be better than my mom.

All of those wasted seconds of fighting faded into insignificance when Dominic held me.

Everything I was holding onto snapped inside of me, and I collapsed against him.

My weak limbs molded against his planes of muscles, trying to fuse myself to him if possible. I burrowed myself into his chest, entirely shameless now, and let Dominic make me feel as small and protected as he liked to.

Dominic was happy to hold me, happy to touch all of me so no one else could touch any of me. My head tucked into his chest and moved with his steady breathing, and I felt my lungs try to match his so we were mated in every way conceivable.

The small bedroom was nothing more than unison breathing for several moments.

Then, softly, "Do you feel better?"

I didn't think before I nodded, because I didn't have to think to know it was true.

His work shirt was getting all wrinkled between my fingers as I rolled it into my palm, but he didn't seem to mind. Messing up his nice shirts was something I did often, and the least consequential thing I ruined in his life.

As softly as he'd asked me, I asked back, "How did you know I felt better?"

A beat. "Because I do too."

My ear tingled as his voice rumbled against it, full-bodied and painted back to normal. There was a screeching in the back of my head, a voice screaming about how horrible and dangerous it was that all either of us needed was to hold the other, and all was right again. It was yelling to let go and run away before the sickness got any worse, and I heard it.

I was just too fucking tired after this week to do anything about it.

Giving in after being so tightly wound for battle felt *so* good. It felt like coming home and falling into bed after weeks without rest. I needed to recharge on him as much as he needed to with me.

Without realizing it, Dominic and I slowly began to rock back and forth together.

Side to side.

Unhurried and rhythmic.

It went on for a few more sways before I had to ask.

"Are we slow dancing?"

A smile curved against the top of my head. "Sort of."

I knew we were both thinking of the same night in his living room, the night where we both learned for the first time that we were more than addicted to each other. All because I asked him about slow dancing.

Now that I'd called it out, it felt cheesy. I couldn't bring myself to stop though.

"Is it as good as you imagined?"

"Better."

I pulled back, looking at him for the first time tonight. He was gorgeous. "Liar."

He didn't correct me. All he did was show me that adoring tug of his lips that was aimed at me. I wanted to kiss that tug, those lips, every carved angle of his beautiful face. We hadn't been this close in almost a week, and my tongue was anxious to savor that sweet mint of his.

If holding each other made us feel this recovered, then kissing would make us invincible.

Our slow dance came to a still, but the atmosphere kept buzzing around us. Or maybe I was just hearing the buzzing coming from inside of me. My electric current of excitement hummed beneath my skin, tingling all my nerve endings with the prospect of his soft lips on mine.

He didn't kiss me though. Not yet, anyway. Instead, those eyes of melted metal tracked up and down my face, a thoughtfulness fanning up his features.

"You've been avoiding me."

Ah. This conversation. "I know."

He waited for me to say more, and I kept my mouth sealed shut.

"Are you planning to tell me why?"

Because people keep telling me I'm falling in love with you.

Rather than confess the insanity of the real reason, I tried to charm my way out of it. "Can't you just believe that I turned over a new leaf and was abiding by house rules?"

"I'm 99% certain that hell hasn't frozen over yet, so no."

Joy dented my cheeks in an uncontrollable smile. This man was turning into such a smartass.

Wonder whose fault that was.

He smiled at me smiling, and it was the sickest I'd ever felt. I was so lost in it, so weak and mindless for him. Right now, I should have been running. I should have pushed him away. I should have continued ignoring him and making bad choices like I did tonight to avoid the truth stalking me around every corner.

"Are you gonna yell at me for going out?" I asked him, folding his gray-striped tie between my index and middle finger.

Dominic filled his lungs with our air—our own brand of limbo sky oxygen—and moved a hand to my jaw, tracing the line of it with his thumb.

"I wanted to when my mom told me you'd gone out after I called to check in. I wanted to find you and yell at you until you were scared to ever leave the house again." A sharpness found his cheekbones as his thumb found the plump pout of my bottom lip. He eyed it, voice digging deep. "I wanted to bruise this mouth with a kiss when I found you and make you feel guilty for how worried I was."

A breath rattled up my throat, washing my desire across his thumb for him to do just that. He could batter my mouth in punishment, paint it black and blue with his lips, and I'd beg for more.

His grazing thumb coasted over to my cheek, petting me like he couldn't help it. "But I realized that wasn't fair, and that I couldn't really blame you for acting out."

My stare refocused on his. "You couldn't?"

He shook his head, his storm cloud eyes heavy with guilt.

"Your entire life has been uprooted and put in danger, half because of me, half because of your mom. You're stuck in a house with a married man that you're involved with and his wife, and I know she doesn't make it easy. I've asked you to keep secrets and act a particular way around me in the house, and I've also made that very hard asking for your attention as often as I have."

Woah.

"That's..." His raindrop eyes washed words from my brain and shocked my electric current. The zap stunned my mind blank and overcharged my heart. "That's really understanding."

That little frown worried itself between his eyebrows. "You seem so surprised."

"Most people don't look past themselves." I had enough proof of that to last me five lifetimes. "Especially when they're angry. Except you, I guess."

I dropped my attention down, knitting my own brows together and mumbling, "Since you seem to break every standard I've pretty much ever known."

I distracted myself with his tie, flipping the tip of it up and down. Dominic's abs contracted against where we were pressed together as he breathed a soft laugh.

"I would love to take that as a compliment, but I don't think your standards were set very high."

Brutal honesty craned my head back up. "What, and yours were set on broken women who come to work for you?"

A look of displeasure etched along his expression, darkening it. His thumb curved beneath my chin, digging into the groove and arching my head back and below his thundering face. "We have to work on that."

"On what?" I whispered.

"How you see yourself." The gray of his eyes smoked as he swept them across my face, collecting every breath I gave him like sustenance. "I wish you saw what I see when I look at you."

The idea of how he likely saw me popped my lips open, and I shook my head. "I don't wanna know what you see when you look at me."

"Because you're scared of the answer?"

I blinked, a subtle cinch pulling at the side of my mouth.

"Am I getting that predictable?"

His amusement wasn't nearly as subtle, stretching from cheek to cheek. "Not predictable, Ms. Sanders. Never predictable."

Right, because who could have ever predicted the woman who bitched and moaned about love so much would go so silent in the face of it.

The fact of it was staring right down at me with those eyes that overwhelmed me from day one. I remembered how restless Dominic's gaze made me feel from the second we met. I remembered it prickling this bizarre sensation on the back of my neck like he was trying to dig beneath my spine with his steel-cut eyes, and I never could have understood why then. There wasn't an entity powerful enough in this world that could have made me believe fate was real, and that I'd just met it on a doorstep twenty minutes down the road.

Fate wasn't the hero of our story though. It was the villain, if anything.

It put us in each other's path just to let us ruin ourselves on each other, knowing perfectly well our story didn't have a happy ending.

"This is never gonna work," I whispered up at him, watching his face harden.

All this struggle, all this worry and emotion, and it would all be for nothing more than memories.

His voice wrestled through tight teeth. "Why do you believe that?"

"We want different things."

Dominic crowded me right up against a wall, eyes burning. "We want each other."

My head tipped back to the wall, Dominic's hand still a loose grip around my throat. Flames flickered in his pupils, a fire of determination to have me and to love me. My skin flushed beneath it, a fever invading faster than I had time to control the delirious spew it inspired to come out of my mouth.

"I don't get why you want me," I admitted with earnest force. "I seriously don't. I'm so much more work than I'm worth. I'm difficult and I'm stubborn and I'm fucked up. You're, you know, *good*. You're *so* good, and I've done nothing but fight you. I don't know why you're so adamant to keep fighting me back except because you wanna save me. Your hero complex probably got a hard on when we met and you realized how messed up my life was."

I scoffed a laugh that tried to bring my head down, but Dominic's grip refused the movement. He forced my head back up and my eyes back on him.

"Would you like me to list the reasons I want you?"

"*No*." God, *fuck* no.

I honestly couldn't think of anything worse.

"I will," he pressed, almost like a threat. He was threatening me with all the things he liked about me. "I'll start at the way you roll your lips together when you're struggling not to say what's really on your mind, and I'll work my way to your strawberry chapstick and tell you how I'm honestly becoming addicted to it. I'll list every reason big and small until I get to your heart, and I'll tell you how beautiful it is and how inspiring I find it."

"Shut up," I breathed—*begged*.

"No." His denial was quick and bullish. It made me snatch my hands from his tie, cowering back into myself and the wall, away from all his determined affection.

Without breaking his severe eye contact, Dominic caught my hands and brought them back up. He placed them on his chest, holding his over mine and refusing to let me go in any sense of the phrase.

"I won't stop telling you why or how much I want you until you get it. This last week without talking to you or getting one of your sly smirks from across the room or not being able to grab your hand when you walked by was hell."

He laced our fingers together against his chest, intertwining us so thoroughly, I felt it in my soul. My soul that burned for his. His burned in his eyes. "Having you in my life isn't just a want, Kat. It's a need. An unbearable need."

Unbearable.

My chest caved forward as much as it could with an outrageous huff. A humorless, single laugh with zero substance behind it. My stare danced back and forth over his, searching for the string of sanity that appeared to be missing.

"What happened to cooling it?" I reminded him.

Slowly, he lowered his face towards mine. I might have stopped breathing entirely when he came so close, his nose nudged mine, and his breath kissed my lips in confession.

"I'm a weak man when it comes to you, Ms. Sanders."

"I thought you said feelings weren't a weakness?" I murmured back, losing my will to the proximity of his lips.

Instead of being upset that I'd caught him in a word trap, he smiled. "So you do listen."

"When it benefits me."

The grooves in his cheeks deepened, threats of his dimples showing. "You're right." He nodded, easing closer. "I did say that. Except being weak for you isn't a weakness. It's a privilege."

Fuck me in half.

Did he rehearse these speeches at home or something?

My lightning loved those sweetly spoken words. They were candy-coated kryptonite. Electricity danced and hummed in my chest until my heart was vibrating, electrocuted with happiness and making a warm home for the sickness to stay.

Dominic's heart thumped beneath my hands, and I wondered about his sickness. Was it as bad as mine? Was it worse? Was he as scared to die from it as I was?

I sucked back a shuddering breath, squeezing his hands in mine and dropping my gaze to the collar of his shirt. It was safer there. It wasn't as terrifying looking at finely woven white threads as I admitted what he already knew.

"You scare me."

My voice came out small, smaller than it had ever been.

His thumbs passed a gentle stroke over my knuckles. "I know I do."

He'd told me as much back at the hotel. He knew I was terrified of just how big my feelings for him were. I'd just never said the words out loud or come as close to giving in as I was now.

Confessing had strung up my muscles so tight, a headache started to crawl up the back of my neck. How Catholics did this however many times a week they wanted, I'd never know.

I kept going though, pushing the words out with strain. "I don't know how to do this. A relationship. I—People keep thinking I do. Your mom and Layla," I sighed, unlocking a hand from his to slide up my face.

"My mom?" Dominic's tone dropped with confusion. "What did she say?"

Oh fuck. "I don't wanna say."

Somehow, Dominic got taller over me, looming until he was the ceiling, the sky, the everything above me. His eyes were the stars, glinting and burning.

"I need you to."

My mouth dropped open, and it wasn't fair the fucking *beauty* he was using to overwhelm the answer out of me. He was a goddamn masterpiece of striking persuasion, and I had to look away before I blurted out anything else tonight.

Material shuffled in the quiet room, and a hand appeared on the back of my neck. My awareness prickled, wayward fingers starting slow circles over my tensed muscles. A hushed exhale escaped my throat, eyes falling shut as Dominic worked his fingers along my neck, massaging and loosening me up.

Aw fuck. I knew what he was doing.

I also knew that when his thumb and index finger made it to that special spot at the nape of my neck, I couldn't stop him. He pinched the skin there with purpose, and my head dropped with a sigh, submitting like he knew I would.

"Dominic..." His name crawled up my throat, scratching deliciously as he turned my whole body to something malleable against him. His intentions weren't sneaky and his tactics weren't saintly, especially when he put his mouth on the slope of my neck and painted my skin in dirty kisses.

I gasped for him, striking my fingers up his shirt and dragging him in. Dominic let a groan resonate from his chest, getting lost in his own game before remembering why he'd started playing.

"Tell me what she said, Kat."

He grazed his teeth up my neck without biting down, dragging out the anticipation. Need for the erotic pain spiked up from my core, words somehow falling out of my brain.

"She said something about us. Something stupid."

"Stupid?"

"Mhm. *Really* stupid."

Hot breath washed over my ear, honeyed lips and a husky voice coming next. "Is what she said the reason why you've been avoiding me?"

Teeth nipped and nibbled my earlobe, chewing out my next answer. "There might be some correlation."

Dominic hummed against me, a deep and sensual noise, and I pressed my tits to his chest so I could feel the vibration go all the way down my body. I arched up on my tiptoes to reach him from a better height, curling my arms around his neck to drag his lips closer.

I wanted his kiss tattooed on my skin, teeth drawing out the reds, purples, and blues from beneath while his tongue sealed the art in place.

His hand not dominating the back of my neck tightened around my waist, arm crushing me into his frame of hard-lined muscle. Dominic squeezed all the rational air right out of me, leaving me to gulp down the hazy, lust-muddled oxygen we'd created as he moved his hot mouth across my jawline.

Slow, sweltering kisses tracked closer to my lips, and I panted heavily, mouth parted and waiting for his. Except, right at the corner of my lips, his paused, and he reined back a couple inches.

"Do you think I'm stupid for having feelings for you?" Dominic asked seriously—so seriously it doused all the heat in the room.

My brain jumbled in confusion for where he'd pulled that question from until I remembered again our night in the living room. I told him exactly how dangerous it felt to kiss him. How his kiss could kill, and I couldn't be stupid enough to let it get me.

So I nodded, and I didn't hold back.

"Yeah, I do. You've experienced firsthand how shitty falling in love with someone can turn out. I don't know why you'd ever put yourself through that again. Especially with Maya."

"What does Maya have to do with it?"

I paused, astounded. "*Everything*. Do you not think about her before you make stupid decisions?"

"Falling in love is not a decision you make with your head," he damn near scolded, eyes ringed with silver fire. "And yes, I think about her. I think about her happiness and who makes her happy. Who puts her first and takes care of her."

His words were *so* pointed, I knew he had really thought about it, and the conclusion he'd come to stunned my tongue still because it wasn't even one I could argue with.

Compared to Heather, it wasn't even a question of who cared for Maya more. She smiled and laughed with me. She cried and worried her little face into a pout with Heather.

Dominic watched me carefully as I put the pieces together that he'd already fit in place. He'd thought so far ahead, I could see the future he'd mapped out in his head designing like constellations in his stare. I saw all of our smiles—mine, his, and Maya's—beaming and bright with our whole happy hearts crafting their brilliance.

Dominic drew himself back until his arms were almost straight and braced his hands on either side of my head against the wall, giving me space to breathe, to think.

"Are you afraid to be with me because of Charlotte?"

The nail he hit on the head punctured right through my heart. The intrusion rippled an earthquake of pain down my chest; it felt like I swallowed rocks. All the rough edges lodged in my throat, saw-toothed points cutting into flesh and bleeding my voice out to a whisper.

"I can't get so lost in you that I forget about her."

Dominic canted his head a hair's breadth at me.

The leveled gravity over his expression lifted as he moved his eyes between mine. The slats of dark lashes he'd been blessed with fluttered over his luminous stare, black wings batting over gray skies. A curve found the corner of his full mouth too.

He cast his head to the side with a curt breath through his nose at the exact moment I felt my eyebrows plummet in confusion. He brought his attention back to me, ashen eyes warm like the air after an afternoon storm.

"I can't believe you have trouble understanding why I want you."

An unanticipated adoration came to life beneath his stare, highlighting along the strict hills of his face and carving my misunderstanding deeper. Dominic swept his wildly enamored gaze all over my face, his palm cupping my cheek.

"That's the best reason to be wary of a relationship with me," he admired, thumb stroking a line across my cheekbone. "It's also not possible."

I flitted back at his statement and the confidence he delivered it with.

How did he know?

That adoration lording over his expression stayed put as he brought his other hand to mirror its mate, cupping both sides of my face.

"You obviously don't have enough faith in yourself and your ability to be the most obstinate woman I've ever met."

Again, my brows tangled in agitation and defiance. Dominic seemed even more worshipping as he smoothed his thumbs over my scrunched browline, working out my distress and smiling faintly.

"There is no way you would ever let Charlotte come second to me."

Ah. I saw where he was coming from now. Except, he was forgetting about one key, game-changing factor that *always* accompanied the insanity of love.

"When you break my heart or I break yours," I jutted my chin up at him. "What about then?"

I didn't miss the infamous tick of his jaw as he heard 'when'. Heartbreak was inevitable though, and so was the delirium that came with it.

"Even if something like that happened," he began, forcing the words. "You're far too stubborn to let me affect how you take care of your sister. In fact, I think you'd up your caretaking just to spite me if that were the case."

I blinked, lowering my gaze to his strong chin.

I hadn't thought of it that way.

If I could choose only one certainty about my personality, and it *wasn't* my disdain for love, it would be my stubborn ability. Plenty of people I'd met, even growing up, said that my stubborn streak was my biggest downfall, but I always emphatically disagreed.

It kept me in my lane. It kept me safe. It inflamed my ability to deny until denial was my new truth, and I was fucking *proud* of that fact. I could bend my whole world to the outline I wanted it to fit, down to the most infinitesimal details if it made me feel better.

Which meant, *yes*. Dominic was right. *Of-fucking-course* I would be too stubborn to let a broken heart—to let love—interrupt Charlotte's life. Even if I was crippled by it, my tenacity would keep me upright in front of Charlotte if purely to spite Dominic for breaking my heart.

"You're cute when you realize I'm right."

His smug tone brought my gaze up, a losing battle with a smile waging on my lips.

"Shut up."

He chuckled, and the sound was somehow sweeter than ever before. It sounded new and fresh, like a million possibilities rolling through the beats of his laughter. The strangest feeling percolated in my ribcage, and I didn't know what to name it.

It didn't feel as severe as the lightning or as scary as the sickness.

It was its own unique, foreign feeling, lighter than anything I'd experienced before. It filled me with helium, lifting me up, up, up until I felt like I could soar and never come down.

Dominic had the softest look on his hard-lined face, the contrast a thing of perfect beauty. "You have no idea how incredible you are, do you?"

Familiarity prickled in the back of my mind, and my new, light as air feeling floated the words right out of my mouth.

"Your mom also said you thought that."

Dominic's mouth relaxed back to something serious as I brought us back to that topic. I might have done it on purpose too. The gray of his irises smoldered with intimacy, carrying back and forth from my lips to my eyes.

"What else did she say?"

I steadied myself with a measured breath. The words were there, sitting in my special feather-light sensation and ready to jump off. With my stubbornness to protect me, I felt like I could do it. I could say it.

And then I did.

"That she thinks we're falling in love."

And I'll be damned. He didn't look the least bit surprised.

"Does that make you want to run from me?"

The steady timbre of his voice alone had my toes itching to bolt, but I stayed in place and nodded beneath him. Just because I could admit it out loud and wield my tenacity like a shield didn't mean I wasn't still terrified. The nightmare of a broken heart and what it would turn me into still held firm in my gut.

Dominic leaned down, ghosting his satin-soft lips against mine.

"Do you want me to kiss you until you forget about it for the night?"

My mouth parted against his, our lips brushing like teasing puzzle pieces one move from locking in place. Inside, I had the terror, the sickness, and now this new weightless feeling, and it was all so much. Chaos was unfolding within me, and Dominic knew how to make it all stop.

So I reached up to fist the collar of his shirt, desire resounding through my voice.

"I want you to do more than kiss me."

THIRTY-FIVE

E very time I kissed Dominic, it was a new experience.

It was an elemental culmination. Sometimes he set me on fire. Sometimes he completely drowned me. Sometimes he swept me off my feet, his kiss like the wind ungrounding me from reality.

This kiss...

This was all of it. My body was engulfed in flames, my head was submerged under love's ocean, my heart had taken flight, and all of it while being wrapped in the smell of fresh earth.

The moan I released against Dominic's mouth was helpless and stained with his name. Even if there were no syllables to the sound to form his name, it belonged to him all the same. *Everything* about me belonged to him in this tiny back room.

Dominic swallowed the noise, his hand sliding to the back of my head and grabbing a fist full of hair. He didn't pull, even though I wanted him to. He just eased my head back so he could deepen the kiss and touch every corner of my mouth to completely devour me.

I surrendered willingly—as if I had a choice thanks to that bitch Fate—letting his tongue dominate, our teeth clash, and him fill himself with as much of my essence as he wanted.

My limbs were pretty much jelly, but I reached for the knot of his tie, yanking at it with blind determination. A whine crawled up my throat.

"I don't know how to fucking work ties."

I gave the silken material another tug when Dominic wrenched his mouth from mine.

"We're not getting undressed, Kat."

I wasn't looking at him as he spoke, instead captivated by his lips that were smeared a passionate red, fuller from my own. His words ran lines through my head, dirty, blurred lines that twisted the end of my mouth up and crossed my arms over the bottom of my shirt.

I ripped my shirt up over my head, tossing it to the side, standing now in the dim light of the bedroom clad in my red lace bra, jeans, and sneakers.

"You were saying?"

The shadows of the room played tricks on Dominic's good looks, scanting them harsher and darker as his eyes dropped to the swell of my tits. Lust burned a ring around his pupils, his jawline doing that thing it always did when I pissed him off.

A bass note started low in his throat, humming dangerously as he gripped my bare waist in his hands. I gasped, startled, as he dragged me forward until my hips pressed to his, the outline of his cock straining between us.

"You..." His head shook slowly, gaze never leaving my breasts. "Have so much *trouble* following rules."

"Yeah," I huffed. "And you love it."

Hungry eyes flashed up, a predatory glint shading the colors of his stare. "Do you know why I love it?"

"Because you get to punish me when I'm bad?"

Approval flared across his face, and well-worked hands trailed down my waist to the band of my jeans. If possible, his voice was hotter than his stare. "That's correct, Ms. Sanders."

Holding my eye, Dominic popped the button on my jeans open. He kept my gaze as he guided the zipper down *so* fucking slow, orchestrating a tension around us that felt like sweat on skin. He finished with my zipper and hooked his thumbs into the waist of my jeans, beginning the agonizing process all over again.

The rough material slid down my legs at a pace that had a scream of frustration edging in my throat. I watched him as he undressed me, his focus unparalleled as he revealed inch after inch of my naked skin. It was like he was teasing himself with the sight of me as much as he was teasing me by taking his goddamn time.

He slipped my shoes off, socks too, kneeling in front of me to help me step out of my jeans one leg at a time.

When he was done, I was bare of everything but my bra and underwear, a black cotton thong squeezed between my thighs. On his knees in front of me, Dominic saw nothing else but that tiny black thong, his smokey eyes laser focused.

"This is cute," he mused deeply, brushing his thumbs over the sides of the garment.

"It would look cuter on the floor."

His stare reached up to me from below, and I was definitely aware of his hand sliding behind my thigh. He lifted my left leg off the floor, setting it over his shoulder. My inner thigh was *right* next to his face—his dusky pink lips. The image of him kneeling between my legs alone was enough to rattle my hormones into hyperdrive.

"You need to learn patience, Ms. Sanders."

"And I think you need to put your face about three inches forward, Mr. Reed," I replied, panting even though nothing had happened yet. He'd barely touched me, but it didn't matter. I could *feel* how wet I was for him slicking between my heat, the ache to be touched pulsing louder with each second.

Dominic moved his dark gaze to what was right in front of him, taking in my barely covered pussy with exquisite attention. All the sensitive muscles down there clenched around nothing with his eyes on me, and if I was a different person, I might have been embarrassed that he could probably scent how turned on I was.

It wouldn't have mattered anyway. Not with what he did next.

"Right here?" Dominic asked, and I fucking gasped like I was having a heart attack. He nosed the front of my panties, inhaling my arousal and talking with his mouth against me. "Is this where you want me?"

My hands clenched the air for something to grasp onto so I didn't fall over and die. "Oh, fuck. *Yes.*"

"Quiet," he gruffed, burying the order inside of me. I held onto my next squeak as best I could as he kissed me over my underwear, lips moving, tongue flattening against me and stroking my covered clit. The wet heat of his mouth blended with how soaked the front of my panties were, the garment becoming a mess of mine and Dominic's unfurling desire for one another.

Electric heat spiked up to my head as he ran the tip of his tongue around my clit through my underwear, up and down, back and forth, driving me to a quick lust-addled insanity.

His breath washed hot over my core as he growled into me. "I can taste you through the fabric."

I didn't catch it through the sticky thick atmosphere, but I must have agreed out loud about how wet I was because Dominic pulled back. He hit me with a scorching glower, his fingers denting punishment into the skin of my thigh.

"I said *quiet*, Ms. Sanders."

He lifted himself to his feet in front of me, a tower of seduction and power, and even my best attempt at following his rules tonight obliterated.

"I don't give a fuck about being quiet."

And then I launched myself at him.

We fell to the mattress behind Dominic, a pile of limbs and need with me on top. Our mouths were magnets, finding each other's immediately, sighs and moans polluting the air. Dominic's hands dropped to my ass and he grabbed it, and I mean *really* grabbed it.

We both cried out for different reasons—me for the bruising grip and marks I loved knowing he would leave buried beneath my ivory skin, and him for the feel of me. The completely unadulterated feel of my ass in his hands and the knowledge that right now, that part of me and the rest of it was all his.

From everything I knew about Dominic so far, he wasn't a possessive man, but he was a devoted man. What he was devoted to, he cherished and worshiped and got deep satisfaction from knowing his devotion was mutual.

This explosion of passion was our mutual acceptance of what neither of us could stop between us. He'd been there long before I had, waiting for me to catch up so we could climb up our limbo sky and reach every potential written in the stars for us.

Dominic kissed me harder knowing I was finally accepting the possibilities of us, and I let him so his lips could erase the panic that came along with acceptance. All I wanted to focus on were the sensations building at the apex of my thighs, and the steel erection sitting right beneath me that would make those sensations ignite.

Tiny mewls dripped from my tongue to Dominic's as I ground my hips over his, rocking and building us both up. In a quick motion, our positions flipped, and I found myself beneath Dominic and all his heavy breathing.

"I'm not having sex with you."

His sharp denial meant nothing because I didn't believe him. Not one bit.

"Really? Because your cock says differently. It's hard for me and says you wanna fuck me," I breathed heavily, pushing my hips up.

I'd never *ever* felt more hollow before, more empty without him inside of me. Dominic's eyes slammed shut as I rubbed myself all over his work pants, riding his thickness from beneath him until his resilience slipped.

My head threw back, pushing into the mattress as Dominic thrust his hips forward, grinding himself into me. Then, he did it again and again and again. The room became a chasm of animalistic grunts and breathy moans as Dominic dry fucked me hard and deliberately, losing all sense of self and becoming nothing but his desire and passion.

The bed rocked beneath us, sizzling heat pouring between my legs as Dominic scraped his teeth down the hollow of my neck, his bristled jaw a heavenly burn across my sensitive skin.

"Do you like that you do this to me?" he growled in my ear. "Do you like making me break my own rules?"

I nodded a yes, going weak beneath him as he ran hot, open-mouthed kisses across my collarbone, covering my body in his taste, his scent, his craving for me. His mouth left lava wherever it touched, trailing down my neck, tongue cutting a pathway between my breasts and skipping my peaked, aching nipples.

I whined and he ignored me, working his hungry lips down my bare stomach to cover every inch of me in his delirious affection. He was tasting all of me, licking every bead of building sweat from my skin like he'd been starving his entire life without me.

His wet tongue circled the space *just* above the band of my underwear, sending a tremor through my body. That tremor broke into something audible as Dominic swept his tongue underneath the strap, and my pussy fucking wept at the feeling.

"Dominic," I cried, struggling beneath his torture. He didn't say a word in response. Just left me panting and needy as he hooked his fingers around my thong and dragged it down my legs and off my body.

A heavy tension pulsated in the air as Dominic knelt back on his haunches and took me in. Somehow, his silver eyes shined and eclipsed themselves at the same time. He was spellbound, and I spread my legs wider to show him what was his for the night.

A look of hunger—of filthy, primal need—carved his features into jagged-edged marble. He swallowed so hard, I saw his Adam's apple move in the dusky lighting of the room.

"Roll over," he ordered, tone low and controlled.

My brows tugged down. "What?"

With a flare of his nostrils, Dominic didn't wait to repeat himself. My knees knocked together as he folded my legs shut, his hands locking around my hips next, and the world flipped yet again.

My front was flush with the bed for less than a second before Dominic tugged my hips back and up, sitting my ass right against his crotch. Every muscle in my

ALEXANDRIA LEE

core fluttered at the new position, his cock right against my ass and his big hands holding on either side.

I perked up on my hands, an excited curl arching my lips. "Well, I didn't—"

A shriek ripped through my lips with zero warning, much like the hand that slapped across my ass.

Shock swallowed up my head, and I jerked around still on all fours to Dominic. "Did you just *spank* me?"

Dominic smoothed his hand over my freshly punished cheek, dark eyes on it instead of me. "I did. I've told you to be quiet twice now, and you haven't listened. In fact, you tried to break every rule I set in place."

"But—"

Another smack to my ass came just as swiftly and suddenly as the first.

This time, my head tossed back with a moan, back arching into the pleasant sting as Dominic again softened the blow with a tender caress of his palm. Oh *God*. I pushed back into him, so past the point of turned on that I could feel my arousal soaking down my inner thighs.

Dominic squeezed my naked flesh, fingers pressing a reminder into me. "Speak again, Ms. Sanders, and this ends here."

A tight breath jammed up my throat, quieting any further words.

Dominic waited for one, two, three silent seconds.

"Good girl."

My fingers twisted into the simple blue comforter beneath us, anticipation ballooning my lungs as he shifted behind me. My awareness was at 150% not being able to see him, just feel the brush of his pants over my thighs and hear his steady breathing quilt the room.

My curiosity won out after too long without words, and I craned my head back to him. I did it just in time to see him loosen the tie around his neck and pull it from around his head. Cool gray eyes met mine, a curve so small on his mouth, it was barely there at all.

"You have a tendency to touch things you shouldn't."

Wonder dropped my focus to the innocent tie he held in his hands.

"Sit back, Ms. Sanders."

I did as he said, turning my head back around and sitting up to my knees. It brought my back right to him and his sweet mint breath right next to my ear.

"Arms back," he murmured.

Before I could even think not to, I brought my arms behind my back and crossed them at the wrists. Dominic awarded a press of his lips behind my ear, telling me I'd done good.

Silken fabric coiled my wrists, binding them together before a knot was cinched tight by professional fingers. Unabated breathing dried out my mouth, the combination of curiosity and excitement doing strange things to my stomach.

Warm lips feathered up the back of my neck. "Do you trust me?"

Every bit of my wild panting stilled.

My tongue touched the roof of my parched mouth to say 'no' in instinct, but I mentally and physically stopped myself. I blinked and didn't say anything instead, waiting for Dominic to let me off the hook and tell me I didn't have to answer.

Nerves rolled my stomach into itself when that didn't happen.

He wanted an answer.

A sound of unintelligible nothingness strangled out of me, and Dominic laid another kiss against my neck, soft and sweet. I slammed my eyes shut to hold on to the feeling of it, the warmth that fused through my blood, the crackling of electricity that buzzed in my bones because it was *him* kissing me.

It was the thunder kissing his lightning, and it was the best feeling in the entire damn world.

Did it mean I trusted him though?

I didn't want it to mean that. I didn't want to believe that I might be idiotic enough or weak enough to not only potentially fall in love with Dominic, but to also trust him.

Trust *wasn't* trustworthy. Love *wasn't* loving.

They were both diseases. Lies. Oxymorons within themselves.

But maybe it was already too late for me.

"I might be dumb enough," I whispered back, the realization turning my voice to smoke.

A hand appeared on the back of my neck, driving my head to turn to the side. Waiting for me there was a man of unearthly beauty and unspeakable devotion illuminating his gaze aimed right at me, at my lips.

"That's not dumb," he assured. "That's not dumb at all."

And he covered my mouth in a kiss.

A moan struck up my throat that had nothing to do with the way Dominic's lips moved with mine or the taste of him on my tongue. It was because of the fucking *ache* that splintered dead center in my chest the moment he kissed me.

It was a pain that didn't quite hurt but consumed me entirely. It wrapped around bones, embedded itself in my cells and molecules, transfused my blood and dug into my flesh. It didn't stop until my whole body was infused with the ache, and tears pricked the backs of my eyes for a reason I couldn't name.

Dominic kissed the oxygen right out of my lungs, leaving me a breathless mess as he lowered me back to the bed on my stomach. His lips worshiped my shoulders, my back, my confined arms, every touch of skin he could as he made his way back behind me.

"I intend to stick to my word. I won't sleep with you until I sign divorce papers."

Disappointment blew a raspberry through my lips, and I buried my forehead against the mattress. The hollow throbbing in my lower stomach pinched in need, making me squirm.

Why the fuck did he take my pants off then?

"As you pointed out at the hotel however, the rules aren't very consistent." My attention tracked back to one of his hands sliding over my waist, squeezing my hip bone, curling over my backside.

"And if I've made you come before... I don't see why I can't do it again."

A gasp sliced the air, my spine going rigid as Dominic traced one of his long fingers down my drenched center.

"*Christ*," he cursed under his breath, dipping the tip of his finger inside. "Are you always this wet for me?"

"What do you think, sir?" I sighed, the sound turning to a moan as he squeezed my hip *hard*.

"I think you should go back to being quiet."

"Why?" I pinched my eyes shut as he teased his finger down to the knuckle. "Because you like it too much when I call you sir? You like being the boss?"

A faint cry shredded out of me as Dominic added a second finger, stretching me out and making me bury my face back into the covers. He worked them in and out, sliding *so* fucking slowly, I knew he was doing it on purpose.

The burn he was building inside of me was stoking just as gradually, feeling like actual flames taking over second by second. It hurt so fucking good. I wanted more, pushing back against him, trying to force his fingers deeper, stretching my bound hands back blindly to try and reach him.

I needed to touch him. I needed him to touch me more. More, more, more.

Except all I got from my efforts was punished.

"*No*," I whined, wriggling on the bed as he retracted his second finger and went back to his single-fingered assault.

"What did I say about patience?" Dominic's deep voice was inflated with arrogance, floating through the room and slapping me with madness.

"I don't *have* any." I groaned something fierce into the bed, muffling my voice. "I would have just done it myself if you were gonna be this mean."

"And why do you think your hands are tied?"

Another scratching moan ripped up my throat. Dominic didn't mind it. He didn't mind any of my frustrated noises or jerking movements. He just kept up his slow-building torture, letting me whine and struggle for more.

"Do you remember back when you said that *cake* was better than an orgasm, Ms. Sanders?"

My eyes had pressed shut before that, but fluttered open at the memory. I twisted my face to lie on my cheek, cutting a sharp look back at Dominic's large frame.

"Yes?"

"Do you remember what I said in response?"

"That... no cake should be better than an orgasm."

His finger slipped out of me completely, and I would have protested if I hadn't felt his touch on my wrists next, unwinding his tie with easy precision. My shoulders caved back to a normal position, and Dominic guided me onto my back.

He was right over me, his thick hair in complete disarray and his pink lips kissed a dirty red. Thunder clouds rolled across his eyes, commanding and dark as he played his fingers between my legs. Up and down, teasing my clit, never quite slipping inside.

Dominic watched my breath hitch, my eyes flare, my every reaction to his slow torture that had come as close to actual pain as pleasure ever could. I was so fucking needy, so drunk on it, I thought I might actually produce tears.

"I never forgot you said that," he started, hot breath teasing my lips. "Even on the days I tried my hardest to forget about it or you, I couldn't."

I sucked back a cut of air, my focus narrowed on Dominic above me as he skimmed two fingers down where I wanted them. His mouth hovered just over mine, murmuring his intentions over my parted lips.

"And I've wanted to do this every single day since."

My head kicked back with a wide gasp. Dominic sank his fingers to the hilt inside of me at the very same time his thumb pressed to my clit. He worked them in tandem, driving his fingers in and out while his thumb popped tiny whimpers off my lips with each stroke over my bud.

Dominic buried his head in my neck too, silk soft hair nuzzling underneath my chin as he mouthed my flesh, sucking and whispering filthy encouragement against it.

"I—*fuck*," I cried, clawing at the bedcover and then his back as he curved his fingers up inside of me, hitting a spot that literally blinded my vision. I went up on my toes on the bed, holding my breath as he did it again.

A hum of approval resonated his chest, a smile in his dark voice.

"There it is."

My legs actually started to shake in uncontrollable convulses each time he hit *that* place inside of me. It was too much. The sensations fusing together in my stomach were too much, and I began to tell Dominic just that.

"I-I can't. I—*fuck*, Dominic, I—"

"Yes you can," he promised, no room for question in his tone.

I shook my head against the pillow anyway, squeezing my eyes closed as the most intimidating orgasm closed in faster than anything I'd experienced. I tried to move away from it, tried to jerk my hips back to where the winding, pinching feeling wasn't so overwhelming, but Dominic didn't let me. He kept me plastered to the bed, reminding me over and over to stay put.

I cried against him, sinking my teeth into his shoulder to chew out my moans and whimpers. Maybe all of Dominic's torture, the slow teasing had been for this—to deliver me this shattering climax—but I didn't think I'd survive it if it hit.

In fact, I was pretty much sure I'd die before getting there.

The searing sensations were swallowing me up fast, coiling tighter as Dominic ran his thumb in fast circles over me, his other fingers never stopping even once. Heady oxygen compacted within me, filling my head up with dizzying, hot air as the feeling growing between my legs got tighter and bigger.

Dominic's carnal voice found my ear. "Show me how you come, Kat. I want to see it." He sped his pumping fingers inside of me. "*Feel* it."

The filthy command, proficient fingers, and the man composing it all set a match to the kindling inside my core. The last thing I remembered before the climax hit was gasping Dominic's name, and his mouth sealing over mine.

Heat exploded through me, flushing down my thighs and up my chest. Dominic groaned through our kiss as my walls clenched his fingers in pulses of pleasure that were never ending. My vision glitched in flashes of white even behind shut eyes, but I couldn't control it and I didn't care.

Dominic muffled each squeak and groan that tried to break through my lips, kissing me and shushing me gently as my body continued to quake in sparks of ecstasy. The pleasure was unbelievable—otherworldly—and Dominic proved himself once and for all to really be a god.

It took several moments and several whispered affections from Dominic until I came down from the high. Every muscle in my body went limp at the same time, a sweat breaking out on my forehead.

Dominic pulled back only so far, allowing me air to breathe and a point to concentrate on in his smiling eyes. He swiped his hand not still between my legs over my damp hairline, bringing it down to thumb my parted lips.

"Still think cake is better?"

His confident half-grin held my entire focus as I struggled for words.

"I think," I huffed, catching my breath. "I want both."

Dominic's chuckle was deep and rich, the sound helping to soothe my live-wire nerves.

"You want to have your cake and eat it too?"

"That saying doesn't make any sense."

He rolled his eyes back, a still very present grin tugging up the corner of his mouth. "You don't have to admit I'm right." He moved his fingers still inside of me, making my legs tremble and breath wobble. "I have all the proof I need."

My still too sensitive muscles jerked away from his hand, and I cut him a dopey smile.

"Fuck you."

"Later. I promise."

That brought my laugh out of hiding, making it paint the walls a color of happiness I didn't know existed before now. Maybe I was still high from the orgasm or maybe it was something else, but the world looked different all of a sudden.

Every shade was brighter. Every color was more refined, like someone had switched the lens on my kaleidoscope vision, and I was seeing it all for the first time.

Even so, with the new pop of red coming from a shirt spilling out of one of the moving boxes, or the stark, almost blinding white of the four walls around us, or the dramatic glint of gold showing off on the door knob across the room...

My favorite color in the whole room was still gray.

Dominic and I both washed up in a bathroom down the hall before meeting Ryan back out in the living room. Layla was missing, and Ryan's lame ass shirt was on inside out.

He met my eyeline as we emerged from the hallway, and I smirked at him. He had a terrible poker face.

"Where's Layla?" I asked.

He nodded over his shoulder to the front door. "She stepped outside to smoke."

Surprise jumped my eyebrows up. "You're okay with her smoking?"

His light brown brows furrowed, electric blue eyes muddling with confusion. "Yeah, I—" He paused, realization dawning. "Did she not mean smoking cigarettes?"

"Nah, she hates those. Weed. She likes weed."

His mouth dropped into an O, and I couldn't help but laugh.

"She always smokes after sex."

"We—"

"Your shirt's on inside out, man," Dominic helped from behind me.

Embarrassment tinted Ryan's cheeks, and he shot a glance down at his shirt. He sighed, leaning back to get comfortable. "Well, you guys were gone for a while."

And if he hadn't been fucking Layla during it, he absolutely would have heard why we were gone so long. Dominic did his best to keep me quiet, but we both knew the neighbors next door probably heard me.

Heading for the door, I offered, "I'll go grab her real quick."

A hand snaked around my wrist, tugging me back around and to a stop. My neck stretched back to accommodate for Dominic's height and nearness.

"Let Ryan go get her."

My eyes kicked back in a playful roll. "I'm fine. It's literally just outside."

Hesitance etched lines in his forehead as he stared down at me. His jawline cemented, and he dominated a step closer. "If you're not back in three minutes, I'm coming to get you. And bring your pepper spray."

"Sir, yes, sir," I replied, tossing him a wink.

I snagged the pepper spray laying on the countertop of the peekaboo kitchen window, fitting it in my back pocket as I left the house. The breeze hit my bare arms, and I wrapped my hands around my elbows to hike down the long driveway where Layla sat at the very end of it.

Damn, she was right. It *was* getting cold.

Layla's midnight hair glowed almost as purple as her outfit against the night. She turned to me as I walked down to her, a white trail of smoke blowing between her dark lips. She pumped her suggestive eyebrows up at me as I popped a squat on the hard cement next to her.

"Your talk go well?"

"It ended in an orgasm, and I'm pretty sure the promise of cake?" I laughed.

"*Yow*, that's definitely a good talk." Layla snapped her fingers a few times, eyelids drooping to half slits. She always snapped and made weird noises when she was high.

"And you brought out Hello Kitty." I pointed my chin at the cartoon cat themed bowl in her hand. She always carried it in her purse for moments like these. "You and Ryan made good use of the downtime."

She rubbed the back of her hand under her nose, a lazy smile pulling across her cheeks. "He asked me on a date. Like a proper date."

"Was this before or after you boned him?"

"Before. So you know he meant it."

A noise of approval vibrated up my throat as I watched her mocha eyes go all dreamy as she blew out another puff, probably finding contours of Ryan's face in the smoke. She seemed really happy.

And as I studied her and her love struck face, that light as air, foreign feeling materialized between my ribs again, except this time, I realized the name for it.

Hope.

I was deliriously hopeful for a chance at that same brand of happiness.

I was... sick for it.

Except maybe being sick didn't mean death like I always thought. Maybe it meant a different kind of death. The kind of death that brought new life, new chances, and new hope.

I fucking hated maybe's, but *maybe* I had to die from the sickness to be reborn into a life where a happily ever after existed for me.

Maybe falling sick for Dominic Reed wasn't the worst thing in the world.

Then, just as I was dreaming about the potential existence of Prince Charmings and fairy-tale happiness, *it* happened.

The SUV came out of nowhere.

Its black exterior was well cloaked by nighttime, and neither Layla nor I saw it come up until it was already there. An alarm bell so loud, I didn't even hear if I actually yelled out or not, shot off between my ears as my head craned back at the onetime familiar car.

No fucking way...

"Layla," I breathed, voice frigid in panic. "*Run.*"

The backdoor to the SUV jammed wide open, and a man in all black spilled out, looking like he could snap me in two and not even blink. I wrenched Layla up off the ground by her arm, mouth dropping open to scream for Dominic when unfamiliar arms swooped in on either side of me.

One clamped over my mouth. One locked around my waist and yanked me up off the ground.

Terror ignited fast, a wildfire pouring through my veins as I thrashed like a trapped fucking animal and reached out for Layla. Her glassy eyes were as wide as

I'd ever seen them, but she lunged for me too, grappling at my flailing hands and tugging back hard.

Pain popped through my shoulder, but I didn't care. I didn't even feel it past the dread chewing at my stomach as Layla played tug of war with my life. My life that I was *just* starting to want to live for instead of just survive for.

The man grunted behind me as I fought back, his smell of sweat and bad breath shoving up my nose and making me squirm harder. He was too close. Way too fucking close, he—

He was *just* close enough.

Fight or flight adrenaline charged through me as I remembered back to my training with Dominic long enough to remember to aim for the nose, but not enough to remember how much it was going to hurt.

With a muffled cry, I slammed my head back into a hard face.

Agony exploded in my skull, spidering around my entire face and digging its claws in behind my eyes until tears sprung loose.

The other thing that came loose, however, was me.

Layla and I fell into a heap on the road, asphalt hitting back at us and cutting slits in my palms. Groans of pain, both ours and the man's, permeated the battleground, and I was still blinking stars out of my eyes when I started blindly patting around my back pocket.

I had it. I knew I had it...

My searching fingers found and clamped hard around the bulge of the pepper spray, and I grunted in victory.

"Layla, *go*."

My momentary surge of victory vanished fast when a hand fisted in my hair from behind. My fumbling fingers dropped our only weapon, and a cry ripped out of my mouth as I was yanked to my feet by my hair and jerked around fast.

"You fucking *bitch*."

My eyes rounded by shock as the man hissed and I saw what I'd done to him, a red, bloody mess splattered on an already ugly mug. In fact, my eyes couldn't even stretch any wider in a second dose of surprise as his fist came at my face.

I went down hard, harder than I'd ever hit anything in my life.

Layla might have screamed. I didn't know. There was too much ringing stuffed between my ears to tell for sure. Oh, and the pain. That was fucking brutal. It hung heavy on every part of my body; I couldn't even open my eyes over the severity of it.

My entire head was cracking from the inside out. Or at least that's what it felt like.

Someone or something touched my arm, and there was more noise. More fighting, but all I could see was a dizzy nothing, and all I could hear was the violent ringing.

Until one voice broke through it all.

"Kat!"

Layla's cry penetrated the dense air submerging my fuzzy head. It split the cement bricks hanging over my eyelids, retching them open in time to blink up from the ground and see my best friend.

In time to see her being pulled into the SUV in my place.

"*No*," I breathed, voice completely mangled.

The man covered her mouth with his hand milliseconds after she cried out, her eyes projecting in panic. The man turned his head over his shoulder to someone in the front seat.

"Go! Go now!"

"She's not the right one," someone shouted, another man.

"She'll do!"

Ferocity boiled in me, heating my blood and glitching my already blurry vision a red as deadly as the blood oozing from the man's face. He was reaching for the door, yanking Layla back as she kicked it open.

"You're not *taking* her," I seethed, pushing myself up on arms that quivered and legs that wobbled. The movement of standing spun my head viciously, sloshing my brain like I had ten shots of alcohol directly injected into my blood.

I fell back to the ground without ever making it upright, weak elbows failing to catch my fall. My cheek smacked the cement, blinding pain stabbing to the core of my head.

My entire body cringed against the scalding shock of pain, a whimper falling between my lips. The pathetic sound hit the asphalt and bounced back a realization of the only weapon I had left.

Breathing heavily, I forced myself onto my back, sucking back a lung full of desperation and screamed up at the black sky. The sound shredded through me, through the night, through the happily ever after I was dumb enough to hope for.

Dominic had to hear that. He *had* to hear-

"Kat!" Layla's terror gripped my muscles as I snapped back over to see her, to get to her.

Get up. Get up. Get up!

"Layla, wait," I huffed as if she had a choice. As if her being taken right now was her choice and not because I'd fought back and she was probably too stoned to.

Our eyes found each other at the last second, a blistering desperation passing between us like a shooting fucking star in this hopeless night. I tried to stand again, reaching out to her from the ground, and she reached back out to me from inside the backseat of the SUV.

And then the door slammed shut, and she was gone.

Layla was gone.

End of Book One

Seducing Danger: Book Two

BOOK TWO IN THE <u>COMPLETE</u> STAR-CROSSED TRILOGY
<u>Read on Amazon and Kindle Unlimited NOW</u>

I was the one stupid enough to hope for a happily ever after.

It was my fault she was gone.

It was my fault for being dumb and being hopeful and being in love. I knew better, and I didn't listen to my own warning bells.

I'd been too deafened by Dominic Reed's love, and now others were paying the price.

People I loved were in danger—my life was in danger—and we still didn't know why. We still didn't know who was doing this or what they wanted.   Other than me.

Me. A nobody. A girl broken from the inside out. A girl with a lightning temper and death wish determination.

It was that determination that took me one step too far. I flung myself off the edge, depending one last time on hope to help me fly, and instead, I crashed hard into a nightmare world nothing in my twenty-one years could have prepared me for.

Not the horrors. Not the twisted family ties. Certainly not the bad boy with the heart of poems.

My death-wish determination had taken me to the very edge of hell, and the devil just might be the person I least expected.

Stalk The Author

Thank you so much for reading Kat and Dom's first book! That ending is cruel, I know.

Need to vent about it? Join my reader group, Alexandria's Addicts. https://www.facebook.com/groups/1155988098182494

Want access to me and all my writing shenanigans? Follow me on Instagram: https://instagram.com/author_alexandrialee

And, if you're really hardcore and like free books, giveaways, and early access to excerpts, join my Newsletter: https://mailchi.mp/d47a710b9325/author-alexandria-lee-books

Also By Alexandria

Want more forbidden, steamy angst?

Dancing with Sin

Alice Monreo is a good person who is about to do a bad thing, and that thing is fall in love with her older sister's fiancé.

There's Venom in Her Kiss (Perfect Poison Trilogy Book 1)

Enemies to lovers, Boss's Daughter, Roadtrip Dark Romance

Printed in the USA
CPSIA information can be obtained
at www.ICGtesting.com
LVHW011046150524
780224LV00018B/974